"I WANT TO M
TO YOU, RAC

Tommy Lee's voice was gravelly, intense. "I want to do all the things we were too ignorant to know how to do back then."

His head blotted out the moon, and his lips were summerwarm as they opened over hers. The wrist beneath her knees slipped away, and Rachel was drifting down until her toes settled on the bottom of the pool and she found herself standing waist deep in water, fully dressed, kissing Tommy Lee Gentry.

His hands lifted to skim the straps from her shoulders, drawing the flimsy dress to her waist. Then his mouth possessed her breasts one by one, and her head fell back, eyelids closing. He dipped lower, and the shocking sensation of heat and cold sent renewed shivers through her limbs as the water lapped near his lips. She drove her fingers through his hair and clasped his head tightly against her stomach.

"Oh, Tommy Lee . . . it was inevitable, wasn't it?"

LaVyrle Spencer
The Hellion

Harlequin Books

TORONTO • NEW YORK • LONDON
AMSTERDAM • PARIS • SYDNEY • HAMBURG
STOCKHOLM • ATHENS • TOKYO • MILAN

Published September 1984

First printing July 1984

ISBN 0-373-70130-6

Printed in Canada

To
Charles and Aline Spencer
whom I love so dearly

CHAPTER ONE

IT WAS WELL KNOWN around Russellville, Alabama, that Tommy Lee Gentry drove like a rebellious seventeen-year-old, drank like a parolee fresh out and whored like a lumberjack at the first spring thaw. He owned a four-wheel-drive Blazer for his hunting trips, a sixteen-foot runabout for his fishing trips, and a white Cadillac El Dorado to impress the town in general. He was rarely seen driving any of them without an open beer or an on-the-rocks glass in his hand, more often than not with one arm around some carmine-lipped floozy from up Muscle Shoals way, his left hand dangling limply over the steering wheel and a burning cigarette clamped between his strong white teeth.

And all this in a county that was dry and strongly Southern Baptist.

He'll kill himself one day, they all said, and one of his whores right along with him!

On that mellow February afternoon, Tommy Lee was living up to the town's expectations of him, all except for the tinted blonde he was currently seeing. After the news he'd just heard, he had some thinking to do, and he couldn't do it with Bitsy under his arm.

The El Dorado rolled beneath him like a woman just short of climax, and without removing his glowering brown eyes from the road he reached across the front seat, found another can of beer and popped its top. As he tipped it up, his shaded glasses caught the reflection of pine trees whizzing past at the side of the road he knew by rote. He scarcely looked as if he were aware of the wheel beneath his hand, or the tires spinning beneath the heavy automobile.

From his office on Jackson Avenue to his house on Cedar Creek Lake it was precisely 9.8 miles, and he knew every one of them as intimately as he knew a woman's body. Unconsciously he avoided the rough spots, driving on the left when it suited him, straddling the center line for stretches of a half mile or more at a time to avoid the ruts and ridges that put rattles into his status symbol. Blindly he reached into his breast pocket, withdrew a pack of cigarettes, tipped one out and lipped it straight from the wrapper. Lifting his hips, he found the lighter in his trouser pocket and squinted above its flame before drawing deep, then taking another pull of beer.

Rachel. Staring at the white center streaks as the car chewed them up, he remembered her face. *Rachel*.

She's a widow now.

He could make this lousy run in nine minutes

flat, and had done it on occasion in eight and a half. Today, by God, he'd do it in eight. The pines looked as if they were poured now, one into the next. Beneath his hand he felt a slight tremor in the wheel, but stared fixedly, guiding the car with a single index finger—cold yet from the beer—while taking another draw on the cigarette. He glanced at the speedometer. The damn thing had a high of only eighty-five, and the needle quivered between the two digits. He took a sharp right curve with a heavy braking and the long complaint of rubber squealing on tar. Ahead twisted a second curve. He tested his mettle by negotiating it with the beer can cutting off half his vision. On the straightaway again he smiled. *Good job, Tommy Lee, you still got it, boy.* When he hit a sharp left and gave up blacktop for gravel he lost her in a skid, braking sharply and swearing under his breath. But his heart didn't even lurch. Why the hell should it lurch? If a man had really lived, he didn't have to be scared of dying.

And Tommy Lee had really lived.

The car came out of the skid as he cranked sharply on the wheel, ignoring the fact that his driving idiosyncrasies made no sense at all— avoiding jars on the tar, then beating the hell out of the car on these gravel washboards. He reached the turnoff into his place, depressed the button for the power window and tossed the dead soldier into the underbrush. Thirty seconds later when he careened to a halt in his circular driveway, he nearly stood the car on its hood ornament.

He laughed aloud, raising his face at a sharp angle. Then he fell silent, staring out the windshield at his front door. *Rachel Talmadge*. His thumbs hooked loosely over the top of the steering wheel, and as he rested his forehead on them his eyes sank closed. *Hollis*, he reminded himself. *Her name is Rachel Hollis now, and you'd best remember it, boy.*

He left the key in the ignition and walked unsteadily toward the house. Nobody within a radius of a hundred miles would steal Tommy Lee's cars, not the way he drove them.

His front door was unlocked. If anybody wanted anything, let them come in and take it. Hell, if it came down to that, all they'd have to do was ask, and Tommy Lee would deliver it!

His bloodshot eyes traveled across the shadowed room—richness everywhere, enough for three wives and some left to spare, he thought. If there was one thing Tommy Lee knew how to do it was live. And if there were two things he knew how to do it was to live rich. Making money was child's play. Always had been.

His house showed it. He'd hired an architect from Memphis to design the contemporary structure that fell just short of being futuristic. Outside it was wrapped diagonally in rough-sawn cedar, and its steeply canting roof sections were shingled in cedar shakes. It appeared as an asymmetrical study in geometrics, a staggered cluster of unexpectedly pleasing sections reaching high, then higher, then higher still toward the Alabama sky from between the pines and broadleaves of the surrounding wooded shoreline. A railed catwalk stretched from the driveway to the double front doors, which were glossy black and windowless. Above them a single outsized hexagonal window looked out over the landward side of the property.

Crazy boy, half the town had said when they'd seen the house going up five years ago, after his *third* divorce. Crazy boy, buildin' a house with no windows that looks like three Cracker Jack boxes got caught in a paper cutter.

But the crazy boy now took three loose-kneed bounds up into the living room of a house that had more windows than most. All the windows, however, faced the lake or were tucked coyly amid the junctures of wall and stair to give unexpected splashes of light that surprised when come upon by the first-time visitor.

There wasn't a curtain in the place. Instead, the endless windows were clothed with blue sky and plants potted in glazed earthenware tubs of browns and blues. But the plants looked lifeless and drooping, many with curled, brown leaves that showed how the landlord watered them: with an occasional ice-cube dumped from a cocktail glass.

Tommy Lee stopped beside a sickly looking shoulder-high schefflera and stared through a sheet of glass at a lake that wasn't there. *Damn*, he thought, *I wish it would hurry and rise.* Pushing back his leather sports coat, he threaded his hands in his pockets and stared out disconsolately.

If I could get in my boat and open it up, I could drive her *out of my mind.*

But the Bear Creek Water Control System and the Tennessee Valley Authority controlled the flooding of the 900-square-mile Bear Creek Watershed System on which Tommy Lee lived, so Cedar Creek Lake wasn't really a lake at all but the backwash of man's whims, controlled by a series of four dams and reservoirs. And right now, man's whims dictated that Tommy Lee look out over nothing but lake bottom exposed to the sunset sky, a flat, muddy expanse of sticks, stones and logs with nothing but a damp spring-fed creek running up the middle of what would be the deepest channel of the lake in mid-summer.

Turning from the depressing sight, Tommy Lee faced another that did little to cheer him. The waning sun spilled across plush navy-blue carpeting, revealing a three-week collection of lint and ashes. It exposed glass-topped tables, which should have been lustrous but were filmed with dust and blighted by rings from sweating glasses, long dried. Twenty-dollar ashtrays whose blue-and-brown ceramic artistry had been carefully chosen by an interior decorator were buried beneath a stale collection of dead butts. Clothes were strewn along the back of a sprawling sand-hued conversation pit, which faced a limestone fireplace.

Tommy Lee stood, staring, for a full minute. Then he swiped up a yellow cotton-knit shirt, whipping it off the back of the davenport. Damn them! Damn them all! He sliced the air with the shirt as if driving a golf ball, then his hand fell still and his chin dropped disconsolately to his chest. He rubbed his eyes, opened them and mechanically dropped the shirt onto the floor.

Hungry. That's what he was. Should've had a steak in town, but food had been the last thing on his mind after hearing the news.

He leaned against the back of the davenport and pulled off his loafers, then padded in stocking feet around the fireplace to a deep, narrow kitchen. At the lake end of the room a table and chairs of chrome and cane sat in the embrasure of corner windows. The tabletop was dusty and held a motley assortment of articles: several days' mail, a jar of instant coffee, a cup holding pitch-black dregs, a fingernail clipper and, oddly out of context, a spool of thread. On the opposite side of the room the counter tops were bare of all but an electric blender, a coffee maker and a sea of dirty glasses.

Tommy Lee draped an elbow over the open refrigerator door, tugging at his tie while studying a can of tomato juice with thickened red showing at the triangular tears in its top. He contemplated it for long minutes, trying to remember when he'd opened it. Sighing, he reached, swirled the contents, took a mouthful, then lunged to the sink to spit it out. He backhanded his mouth, turned on the water full force, and searched for a clean glass. Finding none, he lowered his mouth to the running stream, rinsed, and spit again. Turning, he found the refrigerator door still open, slapped it shut so hard the appliance rocked, then stared at it.

"Goddamn," he whispered, still staring, disassociated again from all around him. In time he moved back to the living room, where his stockinged feet halted at the yellow shirt he'd dropped earlier. He studied it until it became a blurred puddle, and the silence roared around his ears. The sun was warm on his back as he dropped his chin to his chest, slipped his fingers beneath his glasses to press his eye sockets. Suddenly he snapped backward and roared at the ceiling, *"Where is everybody!"*

But, of course, nobody was expected. Only Tommy Lee. And he was home.

THE FUNERAL WAS HELD on a flawless golden day, the Alabama sky a clear blue bowl overhead. Tommy Lee Gentry was the last to arrive at Franklin Memory Gardens, pulling the white Cadillac up behind the long line of vehicles then quietly slipping into the outer fringe of mourners circling the grave.

He picked out Rachel immediately, studying her back as she clung to her daddy's arm while from all around came the sound of soft weeping.

Rachel. My Rachel. I'm still here . . . waiting.

It had been twenty-four years since he'd been this close to her. He'd been a boy then, green and seventeen, and though he was no boy now, even at forty-one being in her presence made him feel one again, uncertain and vulnerable.

After all these years, all these mistakes, the sensation swept back with unkind intensity.

A pain lanced his heart as he studied her; she had grown so thin. But there were appealing changes, too, ones he'd intrinsically sensed happening through the years, living in the same town as they did. She had acquired style, a thin-boned chic that had perhaps looked healthy until the last half year had turned it nearly emaciated. Even so, the pearl-gray fabric of her designer dress draped upon her shoulders with a look of understated elegance few could manage, given that thinness. Unlike his own, her hair had gained a reprieve from grayness. It was still as rich as black-belt loam, and equally as dark. She wore it shorter now, but with an elegant flair that spoke of costly professional attention. Watching her, Tommy Lee felt the old familiar ache in his heart.

RACHEL HOLLIS STARED at a spray of white roses bound by an enormous satin bow with gilt letters on its streamers. Beneath the bouquet, the polished bronze of the coffin caught the afternoon sun and sent it scintillating along a gleaming crease in the metal, like a white laser. A lone mockingbird perched on a nearby headstone, running through its repertoire. A soft breeze, flavored with camellia, caught a streamer and sent it tapping against the coffin cover: Beloved Son and Husband.

But Rachel shut it all out, all the draining ordeal of the past two years, clinging to her daddy's arm until some faint movement of his elbow brought her back to the present. The service was over. Hands squeezed hers, cheeks were pressed to hers, murmurous condolences were offered, and finally the mourners drifted toward their cars. Everett's steadying hand turned her toward the waiting black limousine.

Suddenly his fingers tightened on her elbow as he demanded in a vehement undertone, "What's *he* doing here?"

Rachel lifted mournful eyes and for the first time saw the man standing some fifteen feet away. Her feet became rooted and her heart seemed to come alive.

Tommy Lee. Oh God, Tommy Lee, you came.

She felt herself blanch, and she became slightly light-headed. Her father's thumb dug into her elbow, ordering her to turn and leave, but her body remained riveted, eyes drawn to the man who studied her from such a short distance away. After twenty-four years of avoiding each other at every possible turn, there he was. Deliberately.

Like characters in a ballet they stood poised, gazes fixed, seeing nothing beyond each other.

She could make out his eyes only partially. He

now wore glasses, the rimless type with only a strip of gold winking across his eyebrows. The shaded brown lenses hid his upper eyelids and left only enough pupil visible to intrigue. Beneath a rich brown leather sports coat the oyster-colored collar of an expensive shirt had been drawn up tightly by a raw-silk tie.

"Rachel, come," her father commanded sternly. "We have to go." He may as well have ordered a stone carving to move. Rachel's body had gone stiff, captivated by Tommy Lee as he slowly, deliberately crossed the space between them. She held her breath and felt her heart knocking out a warning.

He didn't stop until he was so close she had to raise her chin to meet his gaze.

"Hello, Rachel." His voice was deeper, gruffer than she remembered, and his eyes held a sadness reaching far beyond sympathy. She didn't realize she had pulled away from her father until Tommy Lee captured her icy hand in both of his, squeezing slowly, slowly, but too tightly for the handclasp to be merely consoling. She felt a tremor in his fingers, became aware of how much thicker they were, how much fuller his palms. They were a man's hands now, and it struck Rachel that in the ensuing years he'd grown perhaps two inches taller.

But there were other changes, too. He had grown heavy. Even his stylishly tailored sports coat couldn't quite conceal the extra weight at his midsection, and his constricting collar pressed a bulge of skin upward, revealing the fact that his neck had lost much of its firmness. There were deep grooves running from his handsome nose to his well-remembered lips, and lines of dissipation about his eyes. His coloring was not the healthy brown of their youth but tinged with a telltale undertone of pink. Apparently all they said about him was true.

"Hello, Tommy Lee," she answered at last, trying to keep her voice steady.

Of course they'd seen each other many times over the passing years. It was unavoidable in a town the size of Russellville. But never this close. Always, one of them had crossed the street or become politely engaged in conversation with some passerby when the other approached.

But now their eyes clung... for longer than was prudent. Suddenly Tommy Lee became aware of Everett Talmadge's scowl and dropped Rachel's hand reluctantly.

"Sir," he greeted with a curt nod.

"Gentry," Talmadge acknowledged coldly. The animosity between them was palpable and made Tommy Lee take a single step back. Still, he could not resist returning his attention to Rachel for a moment longer.

"I hope you don't mind that I came, Rachel. I heard the news and wanted to offer my condolences personally."

"Of course I don't mind. We...." She glanced

guardedly at her father and amended, "I'm so glad you did. Thank you, Tommy Lee." The name sounded ill-suited now that the boy had become a man, yet the years had schooled her till she could think of him by no other.

"I didn't know Owen personally, but everyone around town says he was a wonderful man. I'm sorry. If there's anything I can do. . . ."

The tears brightened in Rachel's deep-brown eyes, making them gleam and appear larger, childlike in their threat of full-scale weeping. He reached for her hand again. "Rachel, I shouldn't have come," he said hoarsely.

She felt her control slipping and her heart thrusting heavily in her breast. A blink brought the tears pooling as she rose on tiptoe to press her cheek briefly to his. "No. . .no, I'm glad you did. Thank you, Tommy Lee." Then she spun around, linked her arm through her father's and strode hastily toward the waiting black limousine.

Her scent seemed to linger at his jaw as his eyes followed the car along a row of bare forsythias, around a bend, until it was obscured by a line of gnarled cedars. He sighed, hung his head and stared at the toe of one shiny Italian loafer, then removed his glasses and wearily rubbed his eyes. But her face remained, revived.

What good are regrets? Almost angrily he replaced his glasses, reached for his cigarettes and lit up with the unconscious motions of the seasoned smoker.

kingbird was still singing. The click of
was the only other sound in the deserted
he smell of roses became cloying, and
flared, drawing in a diaphanous line of
gray to obliterate the floral scent. Absently he
studied the silver-spindled branches of a nearby
crepe-myrtle bush. Its leafless limbs appeared
pearlescent, like the color of Rachel's mourning
dress. Drawing on the cigarette, he turned back
toward the coffin of her husband.

Owen Hollis. What had her life been like with
him? Had she been happy? Had he been good to
her? What had she suffered during Hollis's bout
with cancer? Why had they never had children?
And, above all, had she ever told her husband
about Tommy Lee Gentry?

He swung toward the only other stone in the
Talmadge plot: Eulice, Rachel's mother, dead
four years now. He hooked a shoe on the polished
curve of marble, braced an elbow on his knee and
squinted as the smoke drifted up, unheeded. *Why
did you do it, Eulice? You and that husband of
yours. . . and my own mother and father?*

He took one last deep drag, but the taste of the cigarette had grown acrid, so he withdrew it from his
lips and with a fillip sent it spiraling through the air.

*I never should have come here today. What the
hell good did it do?* He dragged his foot from the
tombstone, slipped his hands into his trouser
pockets and turned sadly toward the car.

Nothing is changed. Nothing.

RACHEL HAD BEEN RUNNING on sheer will power for days now, months—for two years, actually, ever since Owen had learned he had cancer. Though she'd kept herself from breaking down during the graveside ceremony, she was perilously near it as the black limousine pulled up before the house on Cotako Street where she'd grown up.

Stepping from the car, she raised her eyes to the familiar beige limestone on the double-gabled structure. The entry and portico were fronted by a deep overhang behind wide limestone arches that supported the arm of the house holding her upstairs bedroom. The diamond-shaped framework of the small casement windows matched the diamond pattern of the dark shingles. Her mother's narcissus still bloomed gaily out front, and the azalea and holly bushes were carefully tended, though by a gardener these days. The same English ivy climbed the side chimney. The same cedars flanked the north side of the house. And the same sweetgum tree dropped its spiked artillery on the high-pitched roof and sent it rolling earthward. How many times had she and Tommy Lee, barefoot, stepped on those sweetgum balls and gone howling to one of their mothers in pain? Either mother. Whichever one happened to be nearby. In those days it hadn't mattered—the families were so close.

Unable to resist, Rachel glanced next door, but the view of the Gentry house was almost completely obscured by the high boxwood hedge that had been allowed to grow along the property line, un-trimmed, for twenty-four years now.

Tommy Lee. But he wasn't there. He hadn't set foot on the place for years. As if he'd been watching, Everett took her elbow to guide her up the sidewalk, discouraging her from dwelling on the past.

Inside the funeral party was gathered. Voices hummed and the scent of expensive cigars drifted above that of fresh-brewed coffee. The faces were those of people Rachel had known all her life: the town's elite. Half were close to her age, the other half closer to her father's.

When she'd weathered what seemed like hours of well-meant condolences until she felt she could stand no more, she slipped upstairs to her old bedroom. It was tucked beneath the gables, its ceiling following the roof peaks, creating a pair of cozy niches. The walls were papered with the same pink daisies she'd chosen at age thirteen. Her hand trailed over the flowers as she recalled that she had brought Tommy Lee up here to show him, the minute the paper was hung. That was in the days when they'd felt free to spend brief, innocent minutes in each other's bedroom, where they'd often played as toddlers.

The bed was a girl's, a four-poster with a canopy of airy white eyelet to match the tiered spread and the tiebacks at the recessed windows. Though the room was cleared of mementos, the fixtures remained as they'd been years ago, dredging up memories of the days when her mother was alive and everybody on both sides of the boxwood hedge was happy.

At the south window Rachel held back the folds of white eyelet, studying the house where Gaines and Lily Gentry still lived. It was brought clearly to view from this high vantage point several feet above the hedge.

The histories of the Talmadges and the Gentrys went back even farther than Rachel's memory allowed. But what she couldn't remember was kept alive in old photo albums her father could never quite bring himself to throw away.

The two couples had settled into these houses as young, up-and-coming pillars of the community. The men had played golf, the women tennis, and together they'd made up a foursome at bridge. Then, in the same year, both Lily and Eulice had become pregnant. They'd compared their discomforts and hopes, and, together with their husbands, the names they'd chosen even before their babies were born.

Rachel and Tommy Lee came into the world only two months apart. Side by side they'd had their diapers changed, been plunked into the same playpen while their mothers drank coffee, and into the same backyard splash pool—naked— while their mothers sipped iced tea and talked about their children's future. When one of the youngsters inadvertently hurt the other with a careless toss of a toy, the mothers taught them to kiss and make it better, and sat back to watch their offspring's rotund bodies grow healthy and vigorous.

At six, Rachel and Tommy Lee had toddled bravely, hand in hand, up Cotako Street Hill to begin first grade at College Avenue Elementary. In second grade they'd lost their front teeth simultaneously, and in third, Tommy Lee had broken his arm falling out of the pecan tree that intervened between the two houses while trying to string a tin-can telephone between his bedroom window and Rachel's.

Both dark, brown-eyed beauties, blessed with good health and sunny dispositions, Tommy Lee and Rachel had grown up knowing the pride of their parents' eyes each time they achieved the next plateau of maturity, and sensing their parents' approval as they ran off together to whatever pursuit called them at any given age.

The memories struck Rachel like an assault—so many of them.

Her eyes dropped to the hedge. From above, it was clearly visible where the single boxwood had been left unplanted to create a walk-through between the two yards. Not even twenty-four years had disguised its original intent; it seemed to be waiting for one of them to breach it and cross again into the neighboring yard.

She'd been reminiscing for long minutes, her head leaning against the window frame when Callie Mae found her there.

"Miss Rachel?"

At the sound of the familiar voice, Rachel turned to find wide arms waiting to gather her in and tears glittering in the kind eyes.

"Callie Mae." The black woman was shaped like a wrecking ball, her skin the color of sorghum syrup, and she smelled of the kitchen, as she always had. "Oh, Callie Mae." For a moment the two women comforted each other, then Callie Mae drew back, holding Rachel's arms tightly in her broad hands.

"What you doin' up here, hidin' away?"

Rachel sniffed and ran a hand beneath her eyes. "Exactly that, hiding away."

"Your daddy lookin' for you."

"I just needed to come up here for a while. To think."

Callie Mae's eyes roved to the window briefly. "'Bout Mister Owen?"

Rachel turned aside guiltily. "Yes. Among other things."

"I seen you standin' there lookin' across the yards. Can about imagine what *other things*." But there was no note of scolding in the older woman's voice. Instead it was reflective and sad. "Don't seem right they don't come and pay their respects on a day like this. But then it's the second time somebody died in this family and they was too stubborn to do what they knew was right."

"It's not only them. It's daddy, too."

"Yes. Stubborn fools."

For a moment Rachel tried to repress the words, but in the end could not hold them back.

"Tommy Lee came to the cemetery today."

Callie Mae silently rolled her eyes, folded her hands and said, "Halleluia." Then she caught Rachel's chin with one imperious finger, forcing it up while she noted, "So *that's* why you're cryin'."

Callie Mae had been the Talmadges' maid when Rachel and Tommy Lee were growing up, and in the years since Eulice's death had divided that duty between Rachel's and Everett's houses. There were no secrets kept from Callie Mae.

"Partly."

Again Rachel was wrapped in a motherly hug. "Well, you go ahead, get it all out o' your system. You just cry it out, then you'll feel better. And when you're done, you come down to the kitchen." She backed away and smiled down at the woman she would always look upon as a girl no matter how adult and refined she'd become. "Got your favorite down there, cream-cheese pound cake."

That at last brought a wan smile to Rachel's face. Food was Callie Mae's panacea for all the troubles in this world.

"Not today, Callie Mae. I just don't think I could hold anything down."

"Hmph! You nothin' but skin and bones, Miss Rachel. It's time you started eatin' right again." She turned toward the door with a sigh. "Well, time I got back down there."

When she was gone, Rachel listened to the sound of voices from below. Lord, she was so tired. If she waited a few more minutes, maybe the last of them would leave.

She crossed to the bed, tested the mattress with five fingertips and fell across the white eyelet spread with an arm thrown above her head. She closed her eyes and for a moment was fourteen again, a blushing fourteen, lying in bed quaking with disbelief because Tommy Lee Gentry had just kissed her in the break of the boxwood hedge. For the first time—*really* kissed her. Then his eyes had widened with wonder and he'd walked backward to his side of the yard while she'd stood staring, amazed, for several heart-thumping seconds before spinning to her own yard and racing, as if a ghost were chasing her, up the stairs to this room, to this bed, to flop on her back and stare at the white canopy in the moonlight and feel herself begin to change from girl to woman.

Rachel rolled to her back, eyes closed, soul shot with guilt for dredging up dreams of Tommy Lee within hours after burying her husband. Where were the memories of Owen? Did nineteen years of happy marriage count for nothing? She thought of their childless house, and emptiness clawed upward through her body. If only there were children—someone to comfort her now, to help her through the days ahead. Instead, Rachel faced the dismal prospect of returning to the empty house alone.

"Oh, here you are, Rachel."

At the sound of Everett's voice, Rachel coiled off the bed as if caught perpetrating an indecent act upon it.

"Daddy...I'm sorry. I must have drifted off."

"Marshall was looking for you."

"Oh. I'll go down in a minute. I just needed to get away."

Everett's eyes slowly circled the room. "Finding you here in your room this way.... It brings back memories of when you were a girl and your mother was alive." Absently he wandered to the south window, drew back the curtain and gazed at the view beyond. "Times were so happy then." As if suddenly realizing what he'd been staring at, he dropped the curtain. "I wonder if I'll ever stop missing her."

You could have friends, she thought. Two more than you've got. Two who meant so much to both of you at one time. She glanced at the tip of the Gentry house beyond her father's shoulder, then at his back. It was slightly stooped now—funny, she'd never noticed it before. But then, the weight of guilt rests heavily; it was bound to weigh him down in time.

But he was still her father, and in spite of everything she loved him. At times when she remembered, when she thought of all she'd missed, she found it possible to hate him. But he was human, had needs, perhaps even regrets, though these he never revealed.

Very quietly she asked, "Do you ever see them?"

His shoulders stiffened. "Drop it, Rachel." But his stern tone only forced her on.

"I've heard that Tommy Lee doesn't talk to them anymore."

"I wouldn't know. And it's none of my business."

You made it your business twenty-four years ago, daddy, she thought. But aloud she only observed in the quietest of voices, "I was looking at the hedge you and Gaines Gentry planted all those years ago. You can still see the break where—"

"Rachel!" he barked, swinging around. "I fail to understand how you can be preoccupied with thoughts like that on a day when you've just buried Owen."

She flushed, standing before him with fingers clasping and unclasping against her stomach. Guilt came creeping over her, and she upbraided herself for speaking of the Gentrys today of all days. She studied Everett's face, noting how gray and shaken he was. "I'm sorry, daddy. Owen's death has been terrible for you, hasn't it?" It was an odd question from a widow, but they both knew her and Owen's relationship had been staid, comfortable at best, and the past six months had been hell for her. His death had come as somewhat of a relief, so Rachel had her guilt, too.

"I had such plans for him," Everett sighed, prowling the room, avoiding his daughter's eyes.

"I know you did." Owen had been his hope, the son he'd never had, his right hand in business. But Everett's shoulders lifted in a fortifying sigh, and he turned again to his daughter.

"I guess we'd better go back down. I left the Hollises there, visiting with Marshall."

"Yes, I guess we'd better." But she wondered how she'd tolerate any more of Pearl Hollis's noisy weeping, or Frank Hollis's dolorous looks, which seemed to say, if only he'd had children.

But children, like boxwood hedges, were never mentioned; both were taboo subjects in this house.

Downstairs Marshall True was waiting, gallant and accommodating as always. "Rachel, dear, I was worried about you." He came forward quickly, reaching for her hands. She gripped his fingers, relying upon him once again for emotional support, while Marshall's kind gray eyes rested upon hers reassuringly. "Whenever you're ready I'll take you home."

An hour later, as the two of them rode toward Rachel's house in Marshall's car, she slumped back against the seat with a sigh. His understanding eyes moved to her, then back to the street. "I know the feeling well. I remember when Joan died, how difficult it was to dream up responses to all the well-meaning phrases friends came up with."

Rachel closed her eyes. "Am I ungrateful, Marshall? I don't mean to be."

"No, dear, I don't think so. Just tired. Tired of it all, and glad it's over."

She rolled her head to look at him and asked quietly, "Am I really allowed to be glad it's over?"

"You shouldn't have to ask that question of me, of all people."

She smiled wanly, remembering how Marshall had seen them through the worst of it, cheering Owen through the depressions, bolstering Rachel's courage when bleakness threatened to beat her down, remaining steadfast until the end, just as they had done for him when his wife had died four years ago.

"But I feel so guilty because I...I'm relieved he's gone."

"That's natural, when the death has been lingering."

Was there another person in the world who always knew the precise thing to say, at the precise time it was needed, the way he did?

"Thank you, Marshall. I simply don't know what I'd have done without you."

He pulled up in Rachel's driveway and reached for her hand. "Well, perhaps we're even then. You and Owen were the only ones who saved me from breaking down after Joan was gone. And I intend to hang around and do the same for you." As if to illustrate, he turned off the car and solicitously came around to open her door. "Now, what's this I hear about you taking a trip?"

"Oh, so daddy told you."

"Yes. St. Thomas, he said. I think it's a wise idea." They went in the front door of a house that could only be described as gracious. Rachel led the way through a slate-floored entry, which came alight beneath a brass and crystal chandelier, then she switched on a lamp in a living room decorated in ice-blue and touches of apricot. A quilted floral sofa was fronted by a pair of bun-footed Victorian chairs, the grouping centered around a marble-topped table holding five blue candles on five gold candlesticks of staggered heights, a pair of brass giraffes and a brandy snifter filled with potpourri. Every piece of furniture in the room looked as if it had just been purchased that day. The regal tie-backs on the windows were hung so perfectly they might have been advertisements for an interior decorator. The carpeting was so lush their foot-steps left imprints upon its ice-blue nap.

And the house smelled delicious. Rachel not only lavished it with crystal snifters of potpourri, but left tiny open cedar boxes of crushed rose petals on end tables, hung pomander balls in her closets, tucked stems of herbs into gold cricket boxes in the bathrooms and hid delicate organdy sachet pillows of Flora Danica fragrance amid her personal garments in the bureau drawers.

That lavish touch was repeated in the careful selection of each item in each room. It was the home of a woman accustomed to luxury.

Marshall studied Rachel as she stood in the middle of the painfully neat living room, rubbing her arms.

"You know, Rachel, you don't have to worry about money. The check from Owen's life-insurance policy should be here by the time you get back."

Marshall was an insurance broker, and he had seen to protecting both Rachel and Owen with adequate coverage years ago. Also, he was that kind of man—careful, a long-range planner, one who did things at their appointed time and kept life's business affairs in impeccable order. He would, he had assured both her and Owen before Owen died, keep an eye on Rachel's affairs and be there to advise whenever she felt she needed him. Having made the promise, he was certain to keep it.

"I'll drop by now and then to make sure things are working okay—the pool cleaner and the air conditioner. You know how things have a way of breaking down when you're gone," he offered. That was Marshall, all right. He kept everything of his own in sterling condition, from his clothing to his grass, and it was often joked about in their social circle that when and if he sold his property, he'd come back to reprimand anyone who dared let it fall into disrepair.

Rachel fondly placed her hands on his fore-arms. "You don't have to worry about me, Marshall. I can take care of myself."

"I know you can. But I promised Owen."

"But the furnace won't break down, and the pool will keep filtering, and...and...." Suddenly Rachel was immensely glad to have Marshall there, a living, breathing entity who knew how dreadful it would have been for her to face the empty house alone at this moment.

She bit her lower lip to keep it from trembling, but tears spilled, nonetheless. "Oh, Marshall...oh God...." Her chest felt crushed as he took her into his arms, gently, consolingly. "Oh, thank you for coming home with me. I didn't know how I was going to face it alone."

"You don't have to thank me. You know that." His voice was gruff against her hair. "I loved him, too."

"I'll...I'll be all right in a minute."

"Take it from me, dear, you won't be. Not in a minute, or a week, or even a month. But whenever you need somebody, all you have to do is call, and I'll be right here."

Before he left, Marshall walked through the house to make sure everything was safe and sound. Watching his tall form walk away, she thought, whatever *would* I do without him? He was as steady as Gibralter, as dependable as taxes, and as sensible as rain. Owen had said before he died, "You know, Rachel, you can rely upon Marshall for anything."

She had wondered at the time if Owen was hinting that he himself might choose Marshall for her...if and when. But Marshall wasn't that kind.

Not steady-as-you-go, polite, socially adept Marshall. He was simply the kindest man she knew, and one with whom she'd shared the most devastating of human experiences not once, but twice.

But when he was gone, she still faced the desolation of going to bed alone. The house seemed eerie, especially the bedroom she and Owen had shared. When she'd donned her nightgown, she crept instead to one of the guest bedrooms across the hall, lying stiffly upon the strange-feeling mattress in the dark—unmoving, for a long time. Rachel had been propelled from one necessity to the next for so long, putting off the awesome need to cry. But there was little else she could have done, with no children to take over the burdens. It was the thought of children that did it at last. The dam cracked, then buckled, and when her tears came, they struck with the force of a tidal wave. She gripped the sheets, twisting in despair, sobbing pitifully into the dark. The racking sound of those sobs, coming back to her own ears, only made her cry the harder.

She cried for all the pain Owen had suffered, and for her own powerlessness to help him. She cried for the dream-filled girl she'd once been, and the disillusioned woman she now was. She cried because for two decades she'd been married to a man with whom she'd had a comfortably staid marriage when what she'd wanted was occasional tumult. She cried because in one split second she had looked up at a man's face across a quiet graveyard, and that tumult had sprung within her when it was her husband who should have caused it to surface all these years. She cried because it seemed a sin to admit such a thing to herself on the very night of his funeral.

And when her body was aching with loss and desolation, she cried for Owen's child, which she'd never conceived.

And for Tommy Lee's child, which she had.

CHAPTER TWO

ON THE FOURTH MORNING following the funeral, Tommy Lee found little to smile about. He awakened sprawled on the davenport, still wearing a tweed sports coat, trousers and tie, a foul taste in his mouth, and a head beating like a voodoo drum. Gingerly he rolled over, sat up, and nursed his tender head.

Upstairs things were a little better. The sun was already up behind the dogwoods and cedars and came cascading into his east bedroom and bath, bringing the sounds of spring birds from the trees.

Naked, he brushed his teeth, then straightened to study his reflection in the generous mirror above the vanity. His conclusion was the same as ever. *You got to lose some weight, boy. You got to slow down with the women and spend a little time on healthier activities.*

But somehow he never did. Somehow the beer was always too cold to refuse, and the women too warm. Life had its compensations.

But out of the blue came the thought of Rachel, svelte and graceful, not an ebony hair out of place, smelling sweet, still beautiful. What would she think if she saw him this way?

Angrily he spit, drew a mouthful of water and tilted his head back while rinsing, spit again, but avoided looking in the mirror while he tossed his wet toothbrush onto the vanity top and flicked on the radio. From its speaker, WWWR announced it had been serving Franklin County and Northwest Alabama since 1949, then a strong female voice musically advised Tommy Lee to "Blame It On Love." The hiss of the shower cut her off in mid word.

For three days he'd resisted the urge to drive past Rachel's store, but when he arrived in town later that morning he gave in, passing his own office and continuing north along Jackson Avenue, the main drag of town, until he came abreast of a small dress shop on the left. Above the door hung a crisp sign bearing a distinctive stylized lily and the word "Panache." He recalled when she'd first opened the place, ten years ago, that he'd looked up the word to find it meant "dashing elegance." At the time he'd been amused. Russellville, Alabama—population 10,000—seemed ill-chosen as a town to be availed of dashing elegance. Nonetheless, she'd brought a touch of it here. Above and beyond this, Rachel was an astute businesswoman. The store had succeeded, then thrived.

Poised, well dressed, genteel, she'd set a fine example for the ladies of the town. By now, every woman in Russellville knew who Rachel Hollis was. She was the pretty one, the soft-spoken one, the one in the Evan Picone suits and the Vidal Sassoon nail polish, the one who gave something from her store to every fund raiser, attended the First Baptist Church on Jackson Avenue, drove a sedate four-door sedan, had her hair done regularly in Florence, and lived in an elegant home on the east edge of town. She was the wife of that nice young man who worked at the bank with Rachel's daddy. She was Everett Talmadge's daughter.

As Tommy Lee drove past Panache, he saw Verda McElroy approach the front door and open up for the day. For a moment he thought she'd turn and see the white Cadillac cruising past, and he breathed a sigh of relief when Verda brushed inside and closed the door without turning around. He drove two blocks farther, swung over to Washington and returned to his own office at the south end of Jackson.

He drew up before a small brick building with white shutters, the home of T.L.G Enterprises, Ltd. Tommy Lee really didn't need an office; he could easily have run his business affairs out of his home. But renting the building got him out of the empty house and gave him somewhere to go during the day. It also provided a place for Liz Scroggins to answer the phone and carry on the secretarial duties he required.

Liz was thirty-five and divorced, and one of the few women who'd ever sent out signals Tommy Lee had ignored. Oh, she'd never sent them overtly, probably never even realized she'd sent them at all, for Liz was a perfect lady. She was a looker, all right, but too damn good a worker to risk losing at the end of a messy affair. So Tommy Lee always got his poon tangin' someplace else.

He gave her a smile as he sauntered in and stopped before her desk. Though he drove like a wild man, he never appeared to be in a hurry when on foot.

"Well, good mornin', Liz."

"Mornin', Mr. Gentry."

"Don't you look like a li'l azalea blossom today." His eyes scanned her neat pink dress and he saw her blush.

"You say that every morning, I swear."

He laughed, unaware of the inborn Southern charm he exuded as he idled before her desk. "Well then, it must be true." He did, in fact, admire the way Liz dressed, never in slacks, her golden hair always freshly fluffed and curled, her makeup conscientiously applied. There were times when he thought it was a shame she was his secretary. "I'm expecting some quotes from Hensley in the mail today. Let me know when they come in."

She nodded and leafed through three written messages, handing them across the desk, one at a time. "Muldecott called from the Florence Bank. A Mr. Trudeau called from Sheffield Engineering." Liz kept her eyes carefully downcast as she slipped the last message across to him. "And your daughter called and asked to have you call her as soon as you got in."

As he took the yellow slip of paper, Tommy Lee's eyebrows drew into a frown. "Thank you, Liz." Already he was moving toward his private office. The door was rarely closed between the two rooms, and he left it open now as he picked up the phone and dialed Muscle Shoals.

"Hiya, baby, it's daddy."

"Ohhh, daddy, you'll never guess what's come up. Marianne Wills is having this pool party and I've been invited, but mother refuses to let me go because there are gonna be boys there, too. She says I'm too young, but everybody I know is going, daddy, and they're all fourteen, the same as me. Will you talk to her and get her to change her mind?"

"Baby, you know your mother won't change her mind because of anything I say."

"Pleeease, daddy?"

Tommy Lee rocked forward in his chair and wearily rubbed his forehead. "Beth, if I take your side it'll only make things worse. You and your mother will just have to fight it out."

"That's all we ever *do* is fight!"

"I know, I know...."

There followed a brief silence, then Beth's voice again, softer, more pleading. "Daddy, I hate it here. Why can't I come and live with you?"

"We've been over that a hundred times before."

"But, daddy, she—"

"Your mother won't allow it, Beth, you know that."

Beth's voice suddenly turned accusing. "You don't want me. You don't want me any more than she does!"

Pain knifed through Tommy Lee's heart. "That's not true, Beth. You know I'd have you with me in a minute if I could." He knew Beth was manipulating him again, but the pain was real, nevertheless. As he always did, he sought an antidote. "Listen, honey, just in case she breaks down and lets you go to the party after all, how would you like a brand-new bathing suit?"

"Really, daddy?" By the quick brightness in his daughter's voice it was apparent to Tommy Lee that he was only adding to her problem in trying to buy her off, but he felt helpless, and the offer of a new suit eased his guilt. "There'll be a nice crisp fifty-dollar bill in the mail tomorrow. Now, will you try to make peace with your mother, and don't buck every decision she makes?"

"I'll try, daddy, but she's—"

"She's doing the best she can, baby. Try to remember that."

Why did I defend Nancy, he wondered after he'd hung up. *She's a nagging bitch and Beth has done well to live with her for this long.*

Liz appeared in his doorway, leaned one arm against it and studied him with a sympathetic expression on her face. "You know you shouldn't send her the fifty dollars again, don't you?"

He turned from the window, his smileless face masking a thousand hidden emotions. "I know. Don't nag me, Liz."

"If I don't, who will? My ex-husband pulls that on me, and for days after the boys visit him, I'm the bad guy around home. Nothing I can do or say is right. The boys keep saying, but daddy does this, and daddy lets us do that. Sometimes I want to tell them, if you want to go live with your father, *go*."

He sighed. "Maybe I wish that's what Nancy would say."

"Do you?" she asked quietly. A man with your life-style—her expression seemed to say—what would you do with a fourteen-year-old daughter?

"That house is so big and so damn empty it echoes."

She assessed him silently for several seconds before adding softly, "When you're in it alone."

Surprisingly enough, Tommy Lee had the grace to blush. His relationship with Liz was unlike any he shared with any other woman. They were aware of each other's availability, and a fine sexual tension hummed between them at moments like this. Yet they both understood that if it ever snapped, she'd lose the best job she'd ever had—and the friendship of a man whose life-style she should abhor, but for whom she instead felt a great deal of pity, because she could see beyond the ceaseless chasing to the loneliness it masked.

Liz pulled away from the door frame. "You wanted me to remind you that you were going to meet at eleven this morning with the people from the city about the zoning regulations on that apartment complex." The tension eased and they became merely boss and employee again.

"Thanks, Liz."

He watched her pink dress disappear around the corner and wondered what he lacked that he couldn't marry some nice woman like her and settle down companionably and work toward building a home with some permanent love in it, and think about approaching old age. Wasn't one woman enough for him?

His eyes swayed back to the window. Across the street and half a block away he could see the corner of the First State Bank of Russellville, the one Rachel's daddy ran, the one Tommy Lee shunned in favor of taking his business to the town of Florence, twenty-three miles away. He lit a cigarette without even realizing he was doing it, then sat mulling.

Staring at the bank, he thought, *One woman* would *have been enough for me. But only one.*

ON HIS WAY to the eleven o'clock meeting at the City Hall, Tommy Lee slowed the Cadillac to a crawl as he passed Panache, but nobody was about. When he emerged from the meeting with the assurance that the zoning restrictions had been lifted and the plans for the new apartment complex could go forward undeterred, he paused at the curb beside his car to light a cigarette and glance southward along the street. From here he could see the sign above the door of her store. A woman came out. Tommy Lee squinted, but from this distance couldn't tell if it was she or not. He sprinted around the car, hurriedly backed out and made an illegal U-turn in the middle of Jackson Avenue, keeping his eyes riveted on the figure walking along the sidewalk ahead of him. He slowed as he pulled abreast, but even before he passed the woman, he realized it wasn't Rachel.

You damn fool, Gentry, you're acting the age of your own daughter! But the disappointment left him feeling deflated.

Back at the office, when he'd exchanged necessary messages with Liz, he went inside, flung the building-code regulations on his desk, then moved to the window behind it.

Again he studied the bank, a burning cigarette hooked in the curve of a finger, forgotten. The smoke curled up and he took a deep drag while his eyes remained fixed on the building a half block away. Then he anchored the cigarette between his teeth, crossed to the door and closed it.

Liz looked up in surprise, frowned, but decided it was none of her business.

Tommy Lee reached for a ballpoint pen and wrote the telephone number on a yellow legal pad—he knew it by heart. He stared at it through the smoke that drifted up past his nostrils. His heart seemed to have dropped into his guts. His palms were sweaty and his spine hurt. After a full minute, he thrust the pen onto the desktop and wilted back into his chair, trying to calm his breathing. *Come on, Gentry, what're you scared of? How many women have you called in your life? How many have refused you?*

He reached for the phone, but instead his hand veered to the pen. He grabbed it and wrote the number again. Twelve times he wrote it...in the same spot...until it was pressed into eight sheets of the tablet.

The cigarette had burned low and he stubbed it out absently, reached for the phone and actually picked up the receiver this time. But after five seconds he slammed it down without dialing, then ran four shaky fingers through his gray-black hair. Lord a'mighty, he hadn't faced anything this nerve-racking in years.

He grabbed the phone and punched out the numbers too quickly to give himself a chance to change his mind.

"Good afternoon, Panache."

Damn it, why couldn't *she* have answered!

"Is Ra— Is Mrs. Hollis there?"

"I'm sorry, she's not. Can I help you?"

"No thank you, I'll try again later."

He slammed the phone down as if it had bitten him. Then he sat with his face in his palms, shaking so hard his elbows rattled against the desktop. He dropped his forearms flat against the blotter, head drooped, while he sucked in huge gulps of air. Then his palms pressed his cheeks again and eight fingertips dug into his eyes beneath his glasses. *You're insane, Gentry. Plum nuts. What the hell would you have said if she'd answered?*

But after two hours he felt less crazy and decided to give it another try. He went through the same ritual again, only this time he made sure he had a cigarette lit when he dialed, to steady himself.

"Good afternoon, Panache."

Godammit, doesn't Verda ever go home? "Is Mrs. Hollis there?"

"No, I'm sorry. I don't expect her in today. Is there anything I can do?"

"No, thank you. I'll call again tomorrow."

"Can I tell her—"

Tommy Lee slammed down the receiver in frustration. *No, you can't tell her anything! Just get the hell home so she'll have to answer her own damn phones!*

When Tommy Lee lurched from his chair and flung the door open, Liz's head snapped up. But he only stormed past, throwing over his shoulder, "I won't be in till morning." A moment later tires squealed outside, and she shook her head.

Tommy Lee Gentry was a land developer. He knew every acre of every section of land within a radius of fifty miles around Russellville. He'd owned the land on which Owen Hollis had built his house, had subdivided it into lots, contracted for the installation of improvements, then resold the lots to the builder who'd eventually put up the brick house where Rachel and Owen had lived. It was on the eastern edge of town in a hilly, wooded area called Village Square Addition, but there was nothing square about it. The streets curved and curled around the natural undulations of the land, making it highly desirable property lacking the cubist severity of perpendicular neighborhoods.

Hollis had done right by her, if the house was any indication. It was a rambling U-shaped thing of peach-colored brick, hugging a swimming pool in its two outstretched arms. It had a hip roof that deeply overhung arched fanlight windows trimmed with eave-to-earth wedgewood-blue shutters. At the base of each window an azalea bush formed a precisely carved mound, while between them the warm brick walls sported espaliered Virginia creepers, trained into faultless Belgian fence designs by a weekly gardener. At each corner and beside the center door, Chinese holly bushes stood guard while the shaded yard bore lush magnolias and live oaks, with not a fallen leaf to be seen anywhere. On either side of the house a high box-cut podocarpus hedge blocked out the sight of the backyard, overlapping at one point to create a hidden entrance, like that around a tennis court.

Tommy Lee knew the exact summer they'd had the pool put in. He'd been up at City Hall looking through some files when he'd come upon their application for a pool permit. As he approached the house now, he wondered if she might possibly have taken the day off and what she'd say if he simply presented himself at her door unannounced.

But in the end, he chickened out. *Use your head, Gentry. She's only been a widow for a week.*

He drove on by, made a U-turn in a circle at the

end of her street, then left the area with a long lingering study of her house on his way out.

Once on the main road again, he angrily loosened his tie. *Damn.* He'd had such good intentions of trying to make it through one night without any liquor. But he needed a drink worse than ever. Stinkin' dry Baptist county! He'd have to make the run up to Colbert County to buy his booze tonight.

He bought enough to get him through the weekend without having to make the trip again. Then he stopped and ate a fat filet mignon with all the trimmings, and hit the road again armed with an after-dinner drink in a plastic glass. He passed his office by rote, checking it cursorily before heading home. He timed his run, tossed out the empty glass just before the last turn, as usual, and pulled up before his black front doors showing a record time of eight minutes.

He gave a roaring rebel yell to celebrate.

But a minute later, when he entered the house, his jubilant mood vanished. The place was just as silent as ever, and just as disorderly. Even more so, for there had been more garments added to the collections strewn across the davenport. *I should clean it up. But for who?*

Instead, he mixed himself a double Manhattan in the hopes that he'd get good and loose so that when he picked up the phone and dialed her number it wouldn't shake him in the least.

But his hand still trembled. His palm still

sweated. And after seventeen rings it dawned on him that Rachel wasn't home.

Nor was she at Panache the next day when he called, or any of the days following that. But finally Verda McElroy disclosed that she'd gone to St. Thomas for two weeks, putting Tommy Lee out of his misery temporarily.

RACHEL'S FATHER HAD BEEN WAITING at the Golden Triangle Airport, but even with him beside her, the house seemed eerie when she walked into it.

"Should I make us some tea?" she asked hopefully.

"It keeps me awake. I'd better not."

"Anything else?"

"Nothing. I'll carry your bags into the back, but it's late. I'm afraid I can't stay."

When he was gone, Rachel wandered listlessly from room to room, realizing that the trip to St. Thomas had only been a respite that delayed her acceptance of Owen's irreversible absence. Standing in the doorway of their bedroom, she chafed her arms, shivering. Her nostrils narrowed. The room still seemed to smell of sickness. Perhaps it was only an illusion, but Owen had spent so much of his last months here and had slipped into death right there on the bed in the middle of the night while she lay beside him.

Again she shivered. Then she was besieged by guilt for dwelling more upon the unpleasant memories created in this room than upon the pleasant.

When the phone rang, she jumped and pressed a hand to her heart, then stared at the instrument on the bedside table. It rang again and she hurried to answer it, sure it must be Marshall.

"Hello."

But the low, masculine voice was not Marshall's. "Hello, Rachel."

"Hello," she repeated, hoping for a clue from his inflection.

"How are you?" Still she couldn't identify the caller and had a sudden wary prickling along her spine—might it be one of those obscene callers who prey upon new widows?

"Who is this?" she asked icily.

"It's Tommy Lee."

For a second she wished it had been only an obscene call. Her free hand wrapped around the mouth piece and she sank back onto the edge of the bed, her throat suddenly tight and dry.

"Tommy Lee...I..." *I what? I went away to mourn my husband and thought more of you than I did of him?* "I certainly wasn't expecting it to be you."

"Oh? Who were you expecting?"

"I...nobody." After a breathless pause, she repeated, "Nobody."

"You've been gone."

"Yes, to St. Thomas."

"And how was St. Thomas?"

Her voice was falsely bright. "Oh, lovely. Lovely! March is their dryest month. No rain, and highs in the eighties.'' But once the weather report was finished she fell silent, that silence greeted by a matching one from the other end of the line. The strain grew between them until Rachel felt it in the center of her shoulder blades. When her voice came again it was low and subdued. ''I didn't expect to see you at the funeral.''

Again there followed a long pause, as if he was measuring his reply. When it came, it was as tightly controlled as hers. ''I didn't expect to be there.''

''You shouldn't have come, Tommy Lee.''

''I know that now.''

''I don't mean to sound ungrateful.'' She swallowed, eyes closed, both hands gripping the phone. ''It *did* mean a lot to me to see you there.''

A full fifteen seconds of silence followed, then, ''Rachel, I want to talk to you.'' His voice sounded tightly controlled, and she could hear his raspy breathing now.

''I'm here.''

''No, not on the phone. I want to see you.''

The very idea brought fresh pain to Rachel, laced with a hint of panic. ''What good would it do?''

''I don't know. I....'' He sighed deeply. ''Don't you think it's time?''

She hugged her ribs tightly with one hand, bending forward slightly. ''Tommy Lee, listen to me. It would be a mistake. What's done is done and there's no use reviving old regrets. We're different now. You...I don't....'' But she was stammering, voicing hollow words, unable to reason very well. "Please, Tommy Lee, don't call me anymore. I have enough to deal with as it is right now.'' She hadn't realized tears had been welling in her eyes until they slipped over and darkened two spots on her skirt. Staring at them, she wasn't sure if they were for Owen or Tommy Lee.

"Rachel, I'm sorry.'' He sounded as if his lips were touching the mouthpiece of the phone. "Look, I didn't mean to upset you. I just called to see how you're doing and let you know I've been thinking about you...and....''

"Tommy Lee, I...I have to go now.''

They listened to each other breathe for endless seconds.

"Sure,'' he said at last, but it came out so softly she could scarcely hear the word.

"Goodbye, Tommy Lee.'' She waited, but he neither said goodbye nor hung up. Finally she replaced the receiver with utmost care, as if not to disturb it again. Huddled on the edge of the bed, she hugged herself harder, squeezing her eyes closed, rocking forward and backward, seeking to blot out the loneliness that always stemmed from thoughts of what could have been. She saw Tommy Lee again, as he'd looked at the cemetery. Older, so much older, just as she was. She fought against recalling the facts about him she'd gleaned over the years, the events of his life that had aged

him, those that had brought him happiness,
wealth, sadness, hope.

*You've got to stop thinking about him. Think
of anything else... anything at all. The bedroom!
If the bedroom is difficult for you to face, have
it redecorated. Think of colors, textures, furniture... anything but Tommy Lee Gentry.*

But in the end, as she slunk off to sleep in a
guest bedroom again, the memory of his face and
his voice on the phone was her lullaby.

IT WAS BUSY at Panache the following day. Spring
had arrived and the seasonal fashion change
brought a flurry of shoppers. Verda had managed
beautifully while Rachel was gone. Sales had been
good. New stock had come in. Rachel was tagging
a shipment of swim wear when Verda remembered, "Oh! Some man kept calling for you while
you were gone."

Rachel's head snapped up. "Who?"

"I don't know. He wouldn't give his name, but
I'd recognize his voice if he called again."

A premonition of dread struck Rachel. Could it
have been Tommy Lee? The last thing she needed
was to have Verda aware that he had called. With
his reputation, eyebrows would raise in no time.

"Did he say what he wanted?"

"No, just kept saying he'd call back, and I
finally told him you'd gone to St. Thomas and
would be back today."

So he'd known when she'd get back. That's why

his phone call had come immediately upon her return. That meant last night's call hadn't been impetuous, as she'd hoped. But she'd made it clear she didn't want to see him or talk to him again. Surely Tommy Lee wouldn't force the issue.

He didn't. For two weeks.

But on the third, after suffering sleepless nights and haunted days, he knew he could put it off no longer—he had to see her.

He left the office at the end of a balmy spring day and made the run home in the usual nine minutes, bounded into the house and began stripping off his jacket before he hit the stairs to the living room. If it were Bitsy he was planning to see tonight he'd be whistling. But as it was, he found his mouth dry, so he washed a glass from the kitchen sink and mixed himself a martini to carry with him upstairs to the bathroom.

In the shower he thought of Rachel, becoming conscious once again of the twenty-five pounds he should lose. When he'd finished shaving, he paused in the act of patting after-shave on the slack skin about his jaws, scowling into the mirror. Brushing his hair, he wished he'd used something to cover the gray, but it was too late now. He recalled the ducktail he'd worn all those years ago when he and Rachel were teenagers. And she'd worn a long black pony tail, and sometimes a high-placed doughnut circled by a ring of tiny flowers to match her blouse or skirt. Lord, she'd come a long way since then. Her stylishness alone made Tommy Lee quaver. So when he dressed, he chose carefully: an expensive pair of trousers in oatmeal-beige; a coordinating belt with a shining gold buckle; a blue-on-blue woven dress shirt; and a summer slubbed-silk sports coat the color of a coconut shell. He debated about a tie, decided against it and, as he slipped his billfold into his back pocket and studied his reflection in the full-length mirror, decided this was the best he could do. But when he drained the last of his martini and clapped the glass on the dresser, his hand was shaking. He was scared to death.

Rachel's house looked closed up and foreboding as he pulled the Cadillac up to the curb and glanced at the arched windows. Yes, it was a beautiful house, he thought, continuing to study it as he slowly got out and slammed the car door. The click of his hard heels on the concrete walk sang out like rifle shots. The front door was windowless, painted wedgewood blue to match the shutters. Facing it, he quailed again, but adjusted his shirt collar, drew a deep breath and pressed the doorbell. Inside it chimed softly while he waited, his heart clamoring and a thousand insecurities making his stomach jump. Unconsciously he ran a hand over the crown of his head, then half turned toward the street, hoping to appear nonchalant.

But at the first click of the latch, he swung back eagerly. The door opened and all the rehearsed greetings fled his mind. The hundreds of yester-days came back with a nostalgic tug—how many times had he appeared at her door, both invited and uninvited.

She was more beautiful now than she'd been at seventeen, and it struck him like a blow, made him stand speechlessly far too long, taking her in.

She wore a pair of soft-lavender tapered trousers with tiny-heeled shoes to match. Her lilac silk blouse had long sleeves and buttoned up the front to a classic open collar that revealed the tips of her collarbone and a fine gold chain holding a gilded giraffe suspended at the hollow of her throat. At her waist was a thin gold belt that made no pretense of holding up her slacks, but only accentuated the flatness of her stomach and the delicacy of her hipbones. She paused with one palm on the edge of the door, the other on the jamb, her sleeves softly draping, brown eyes startled, yet somber.

When he could breathe again, he said, "Hello, Rachel."

She sucked in a surprised breath while her face took on a look of utter vulnerability. He wondered if she always wore soft rose-colored lipstick when she was home alone at night.

"Hello, Tommy Lee," she said at last. Her voice was quiet in the evening shadows and held a tinge of nervousness. She stood unmoving, guarding the entry to her house, while the smell of it drifted out to him—floral and tangy and woodsy all at once. Or maybe the smell came from her—he couldn't tell.

"Could I come in?"

Her expression grew troubled while she deliberated. Her glance flickered to his white Cadillac at the curb and he could read her hesitancy quite clearly—suppose someone she knew saw the car there? Still, he held his ground, waiting. At last, almost wearily, she let her hand slip from the edge of the door and stepped back.

"For a minute."

He moved inside then turned to watch a graceful hand with long painted fingernails—the same shade she wore on her lips—press the door closed while her head dipped forward as if she were arming herself to turn around and face him. The back of her short black hair seemed to spring into natural waves that no amount of professional attention could quite subdue. When she turned to face him she'd slipped her hands into her trouser pockets and had drawn her shoulders high, emphasizing the thinness of her frame as the blouse draped more dramatically, scarcely rounding over the vague swell of her tiny breasts. For a moment, as their eyes met, neither of them knew what to say, but finally Rachel, with her exquisite sense of correctness, invited, "Would you like to come in and sit down?"

She led the way into the elegant living room whose fanlight windows he'd viewed many times from outside. The room's pastel colors were as tasteful and proper as those of Rachel's clothing and skin. The lamps were lit, and she waved him toward a quilted sofa, then took a seat on a small chair directly facing him, a marble-topped table between them. She crossed her knees, curved her hands over the front edge of the chair seat and leaned forward, again with her shoulders drawn up in that off-putting way.

She wasn't going to make this easy for him.

So, all right, he'd play it her way.

"It's been a long time since I was in a Talmadge house."

"My name is Hollis now."

"Yes, I seem to remember that at regular intervals."

"I asked you not to come."

"I tried not to, but it just didn't work. I had to see you."

"Why?"

"To satisfy a long curiosity."

"About what?"

His eyes dropped to the pair of rich brass giraffes on the table between them. "About how life has treated you." His glance continued idly about the room, and when it came back to her his voice softened. "About how he treated you."

"As you can see, both life and he treated me just fine." She settled back in her chair, letting a hand fall casually on the far side of her crossed knees, wrist up.

No, she wasn't going to make this easy for him. But suddenly he realized she was just as scared as he; in spite of the loose-flung wrist, the nonchalant pose, she was undeniably tense. And she meant to keep him contained in this showplace of a living room that looked as if not one hour's worth of *living* had ever been done in it.

"Yes, so I see. You seem to have everything." He glanced left, then right. "Except an ashtray."

He enjoyed making her move. When she did, he could watch her covertly. As she walked the length of the room toward the dining room beyond, he noted again her thinness, but it was classy, not brittle. He'd never before known a woman with lavender shoes. On Bitsy they would have looked like a whore's shoes. He watched them as Rachel opened an étagère, withdrew an ashtray, then softly closed the glass door. Returning, she placed the heavy crystal piece on the table, resumed her seat, then watched as he reached inside his sports coat and drew out a pack of cigarettes. When he unexpectedly looked up at her, she dropped her eyes to the toe of her shoes, only to see his hand appear, extending the red and white package with one cigarette half-cocked.

She met his eyes nervously. "No thank you, I quit years ago."

"Ah, I should have guessed."

He lipped the cigarette straight from the pack—a memory from the past—and she saw that his mouth had not changed at all. The evidence of aging that had marked the rest of his face had not reached as far as his lips. They were crisply etched, generous, as beguiling as ever. When he suddenly stood, her heart leapt. But he only fished for a lighter in his trouser pocket, then bent his frame to the edge of the sofa again while she watched him light up. He scowled as the smoke lifted, then threw back his head on a heavy exhalation as he slipped the lighter into his breast pocket. At last the ritual was through, and he rested with his hands pressed butt to butt between widespread knees, the cigarette seemingly forgotten in his fingers. He studied her until it took great effort for Rachel to keep from begging him not to.

"So, Rachel, where do we start?"

His question startled her, though she tried hard not to let it show.

"I think you know the answer to that as well as I do. We don't start."

"Then maybe I should have asked, where do we end?"

"We ended years ago, Tommy Lee. I really don't know why you've come here."

He glanced around. "I wanted to see your house from the inside for once. It's a beautiful house, what I can see of it. Owen must have worked out fine with your daddy."

A faint blush heated her chin and cheeks. "Yes, he did. He worked his way up to vice-president at the bank."

"Yes, I know," he said softly.

"Yes, I suppose you do. There's probably very little we don't know about each other."

"There's no such thing as a secret in a town this size, that's for sure."

She shot him a sharp glance, but he was studying his cigarette, and when he raised his gaze she hurriedly dropped hers. "I understand you live out on the lake now."

"Yes, ma'am," he drawled with a touch of irony. "Got a big house out there." He chuckled quietly. "Folks called me crazy when I built it, but now they drive by in their boats and stare at it, and I think a few of them actually like it."

She couldn't help smiling for a moment, but she knew all the other things they said about him, too.

"Do you enjoy being...unconventional?"

"Unconventional?" He glanced up with a crooked, sad smile. "Why, I'm as conventional as the next one. What you're meaning to ask is if I enjoy being the hell raiser they say I am, isn't it, Rachel?"

"You said it, Tommy Lee. I didn't."

He seemed to consider the question a long time, all the while studying her closely. When he answered, he sounded resigned. "No, I don't enjoy it much. But it kills time."

Rachel bristled. "Is that what you consider three marriages and three divorces—killing time?"

He flicked his ashes into the crystal ashtray and answered as if to himself, "Well, it was killing anyway. But then we all can't be lucky like you and end up with a marriage made in heaven now, can we?"

"You've grown cynical over the years."

"Hell, yes. Wouldn't you if you tried three times

and failed?'' She glanced aside as if appalled by his admission. ''Does it bother you, Rachel, the fact that I've been married all those times? Is that why you're so tense?''

Her eyes snapped angrily. ''I'm tense because I've just been through two grueling years watching my husband die of cancer. It would make anybody tense.'' She jumped to her feet and he followed, catching her elbow above the marble-topped table.

''Rachel, honey, I'm sorry.''

She carefully withdrew her arm. ''I'm not your Rachel-honey anymore, and I begin to see what it is people object to about you, Tommy Lee. You had no business coming here like this so soon after Owen's death, and especially after I asked you not to.''

Their eyes clashed for long seconds, then she turned her back and walked to one of the arched windows, where she stood staring out at the fading twilight. He leaned down, studying her back while he stubbed out his cigarette. Then he crossed to stand behind her. He caught her scent again, the Rachel-scent, the lingering of fine, costly powder caught in her clothing and on her skin, and it created a maelstrom in his senses.

''I didn't come here to upset you, Rachel. Not at all. But my life is in a hell of a mess and I don't think it's going to get straightened out until I can talk to you about what happened.'' He touched her shoulder, making sure he didn't touch too hard. ''Rachel, turn around. I've been thinking of this day for . . . for years. And now you turn away. Please, Rachel."

She dropped her chin, sighed, then turned very slowly, allowing him to look at her at close range while similarly studying him. They were strangers, yet they knew each other well. Their past was best forgotten, yet it never would be. Time should have kindly seen to it that they no longer appealed to each other, yet they did.

"Jesus, you're more beautiful than ever. Did you know that?"

One of them had to be sensible. She carefully hid the pleasure brought about by his words and replied, "I'm forty-one years old, and I'm told constantly that I'm too thin. And the last two years, the last six months in particular, have put road maps on my face. It's not Rachel Hollis you think is beautiful, but Rachel Talmadge, the girl I stopped being twenty-four years ago. She's the one you came here to find."

"No. I didn't come here looking for her, only to talk about her and find out where she went and why. And why I never heard from her afterward."

Her eyelids closed and he saw the flawless violet makeup tremble on her lids while he battled the urge to draw her into his arms, hold her close and comfort her. And himself. But if he touched her, he knew she'd flee. Her deep-brown eyes opened again and she asked quaveringly, "Why, Tommy Lee? Why now?"

"Because I couldn't wait another year. I've wasted too many already."

"But Owen—"

"Owen is gone. That's why I came."

She made a move as if to turn away, but he blocked her with his shoulder. "Rachel, I'm sorry if my timing is bad. I'm sorry if I haven't given you the proper time to mourn him, but I've put this off until I can't anymore. I'm forty-one, too, Rachel. Please understand."

She was afraid she was beginning to understand all too well. What he seemed to be saying was too shattering to contemplate this soon after Owen's death. He shouldn't even be here in her house, with his distinctive car parked out front where anyone and everyone could see it. Nor should he be broaching the subject that had remained carefully repressed since they were seventeen years old.

"I want to know what happened to you, Rachel."

She met his eyes squarely and challenged, "Ask your parents, Tommy Lee. They were in it with daddy and mama."

"I asked them years ago, but they would never tell me anything. Then after just so long, I stopped asking altogether. It's been years since I've talked to them."

"I know that, too." Impulsively she reached to touch his arm, understanding fully what the estrangement must have cost all of them. "When will you decide you've made them suffer enough?"

"Never!" he spit out, and spun away, for her nearness brought too intense an ache. "Just like they've made me suffer all these years. I guess I'm not as...as magnanimous as you are, Rachel. I can't forgive them and be their loving son again, like you forgave your parents."

The bitter feelings she'd had the day of the funeral, while gazing out the bedroom window, came back again, rife and fresh. It was rare that she let them take precedent, but they did now, and when they'd lodged like a thorn in her heart, she asked, "Do you think there are times when I don't feel bitter? When I don't blame them yet? There are times when I have to guard myself against...against hating them for what they did to us." Once the truth was spoken, Rachel realized how heavy its burden had been all these years. She'd never said it aloud before, but then, there was nobody but Tommy Lee to whom she could have.

He turned, and as their eyes met and held, it struck them both that they'd suffered many of the same things over the years, in spite of the different roads their lives had taken.

"You, Rachel?" he asked, as if unable to believe it of her. She nodded, dropping her eyes to the fingers laced over her stomach. "But you and your daddy have always stood by each other. You seem so close."

"On the surface. But there are undercurrents."

Once again Tommy Lee felt a compelling urge

to touch her. Instead, he backed away a step.
"This room makes me uncomfortable, Rachel.
Could we sit at your kitchen table or somewhere
else?"

She hadn't expected him to stay that long. Still,
looking up at him now, wondering many things
about the man whose eyes she could only half
make out behind the glasses, she realized that talking about everything—at last—was something
they both owed each other.

CHAPTER THREE

SHE LED THE WAY through a pair of white louvred café doors into a shining kitchen decorated in white with splashes of geranium red. The room comprised one arm of the house and had a wall of sliding glass doors that overlooked the pool. Unlike Tommy Lee's kitchen, this one hadn't a thing out of place. The white countertops and appliances gleamed. The polished vinyl floor shone. The walls were cheerfully splattered with that same geranium color, which was repeated in a set of pots hanging on a wall beside the stove and a teakettle sitting on one burner.

Rachel touched a wall switch and a tulip-shaped lamp of white wicker came alight above a small white pedestal table flanked by a pair of bentwood ice-cream chairs situated smack in front of the windows.

"Sit down, Tommy Lee. Can I get you something to drink?"

"Yes, whatever you're having."

She moved to the refrigerator, and he to stand before the wide expanse of glass. In the shadows he could make out the brick-walled backyard, the stretch of pool reflecting a newly risen moon, and an assortment of tables and chaise lounges. The house curled around to his right, ensconsing the pool with repeated lengths of glass wall on what he guessed to be a family room, leading at a right angle off the kitchen, and the bedroom wing, straight across the water. The entire view was nothing short of sumptuous.

"You really meant it when you said he'd been good to you. This is even nicer than I always imagined it to be."

The butcher knife paused over the lime Rachel was slicing. "Than you imagined?"

He glanced over his shoulder. "I used to own this land, you know. I was the original developer who subdivided it, had the improvements put in, then sold the lots. Cauley built this house, didn't he?"

"Yes, he did."

"And I saw your application for a pool permit when I was up at City Hall that spring you put it in. I always wondered what it looked like back here behind that hedge."

Rachel felt disquieted to realize Tommy Lee had kept such close track of the personal plateaus in her life with Owen.

"You've driven past often?"

She felt his eyes measuring her, though she couldn't see beyond the top half of the brown lenses. His voice was subdued as he answered, "You've never been far from my mind, Rachel."

They stared at each other for a pulsating moment, then he added, "Not even when I was married."

Flustered, she turned to reach into an upper cabinet for two thick amber glasses. From an ice dispenser on the refrigerator door came the clunk and chink of cubes falling into the tumblers. His eyes followed each movement of her slim back, the shift of her silk blouse and the pull of the lavender trousers across her spine as she reached, bent, opened a chilled bottle of carbonated water, dropped lime wedges into the glasses and filled them.

She turned with the sparkling drinks in her hands and said composedly, "Let's sit down."

Despite her outward calm, Rachel knew a sudden reluctance to approach him. A dangerous flutter of physical awareness now hummed in her stomach. How silly. They were not at all the same people. She was thin and gaunt, and he was graying and too heavy, and beneath the unkind light she saw again the lines of dissipation that reiterated the truth about his life-style.

He took the iced drink from her hand, and without removing his eyes from her, pulled out her chair, waited for her to sit, then took the chair across from her. She felt his eyes intensely lingering and dropped her own to the white Formica tabletop, where a poppy-red mat held a thriving green sprengeri plant in a toadstool planter. But even without looking she knew he studied her unwaveringly, and it set her midsection trembling.

Between them the old compelling gravity tugged and seemed to draw her to him against her will.

After a full minute's silence he asked, very quietly, "So...where did you go, Rachel?"

Her eyes, dark and wide, lifted to his, but they focused on her own reflection in his glasses.

"They sent me to a private school in Michigan."

"In *Michigan*?"

"Yes."

"They were going to make damn sure I couldn't find you, weren't they?" He took a perfunctory sip from his glass, grimaced, and set it aside.

"They talked it over, all four of them, and decided to tell everyone here the truth—that I'd gone off to finish high school in an exclusive high-priced private school up north. No excuses. No questions. Given my daddy's bank account, nobody thought a thing of it."

"Michigan," he ruminated, staring at his glass. "How often I wondered." The room was utterly silent. Rachel waited, suspended in dread anticipation for the question she knew would come next. He lifted his eyes to hers, and his voice held an audible tremor as he asked softly, "And did you have the baby there?"

She wanted to tear her eyes away from his, but could not. How many years had she forced herself never to imagine this moment happening? Now it was here, and her emotions exploded with a force for which she wasn't prepared.

"Yes," she whispered.

He swallowed. His lips opened, but no sound came out. After several seconds he finally managed, in a strangled voice, the question that had haunted him through three marriages and the driven time since. "What was it?"

"A girl," came the nearly inaudible answer.

He jerked his glasses off, and they hung over the table edge from his lifeless fingers while he rubbed his eyes as if to stroke away the pain. He sucked in a great gulp of air. His shoulders heaved once, then sagged again. The room was as silent as they had been to each other over the intervening years.

The old hurt rushed back, sharpened by nostalgia.

He opened his eyes, stared at her delicate hand resting upon the tabletop. His heavy hand moved the few inches to hers and enclosed it loosely while he watched his thumb rubbing across her knuckles. It was not at all the way he'd imagined touching her again, if he ever got the chance.

Rachel's fingers tightened. "Oh, Tommy Lee, they said you'd be told. They shouldn't have kept it from you."

He continued staring at their hands. She still wore her wedding ring on her left hand, while his held a gold florentine band with a cluster of seven large diamonds. With his thumb he drew circles around her engagement diamond, and went on tiredly. "They did. My daddy called me into his office at the lumberyard one day that spring and said you'd had the baby and that it was a girl. But somehow I always wanted to hear it from you."

Rachel's heart softened, as did her voice. "She was born April nineteenth."

Their eyes met and held. Their child's birthday would fall very shortly. Neither Rachel nor Tommy Lee could help wondering what that day would be like if they were man and wife and she their acknowledged daughter.

"You never wrote," he mourned.

"Yes, I did. Many times. A couple I sent, but most I just threw away. I knew they wouldn't let you find out where I was. They were very powerful, you know. Once they got us to agree that adoption was the only solution, they simply—" she shrugged sadly "—took over."

"I've asked myself a thousand times why we went along with it."

"We were weaned knowing that college was meant to be part of our lives. Given their age and experience, it was easy for them to make us see the sense in what they said. We were so...immature, malleable. What could we do against all that superior reasoning they gave us?"

"And so they sent you to Michigan."

"Yes."

"I've never been there. What's it like?"

What is hell like, she thought, gazing at him. To a seventeen year old, torn away from the boy she loves, hell can be Michigan. But of course she dared not answer that way.

"It's cold," she replied quietly, "and very lonely."

The skin about his eyes seemed drawn and pale. "I was lonely, too. I used to dream that I'd be walking down the street some day and there you'd be, just like always."

They were still holding hands, and she couldn't find the inner resources to pull away.

"They kept me there until you were safely tucked away at Auburn. I got my high-school diploma in Michigan that July, then entered the University of Alabama."

"You went to Alabama, I went to Auburn, just like they'd always planned for us." His sad smile was aimed at the ring with which he continued to toy. She dropped her eyes to it and laughed once, a sad little sound.

"Their alma maters."

His pained eyes moved to hers. "While the baby went on to new parents."

She lifted her eyes and nodded silently.

"Do you know who got her? What kind of people they are?"

Oh God, she thought, *can I go through all this again? Must we dredge up old regrets and form new recriminations for what can never be changed?* But he waited, and he deserved to know the little she'd been told.

"They're both Baptist, and college graduates.

They had one other adopted daughter three years older, and they live somewhere in the Flint area."

"That's all? That's all you know?"

"Yes. They didn't tell you much in those days."

"Not even her name?"

For the first time self-consciousness struck Rachel. She withdrew her hand and picked up her glass, lifting it to her lips. "Oh, Tommy Lee, what does it matter now?"

With one finger he pushed down on the rim of her glass, preventing her from taking a drink. "It matters, Rachel. It matters."

She didn't want to tell him. She didn't want him to place ulterior meanings on a decision made years ago by a mixed-up girl scarcely past adolescence. But, again, he had a right to know.

She lowered her glass, drew a deep breath and admitted, "They let me name her."

"And?"

Even before she answered, she felt a full-body flush, but there was no escaping the truth. "I named her Beth."

His shoulders recoiled against the back of the chair as if he'd taken a load of buckshot, and his shocked face blanched. "Oh, Jesus," he whispered, and jerked from his seat to stand with both palms flat against the glass door as if doing vertical push-ups. "Rachel, I need something a little stronger right now than lime water. Have you got anything else in the house?"

The proof of his habits came as a disappointment, but she supposed this catharsis was adequate reason for needing a drink. She rose from her chair and found her knees shaky as she moved into the family room.

"We never kept much around the house, but there are a couple of bottles Owen had, somewhere in here."

As her voice trailed away, Tommy Lee pressed against the glass, then, realizing what he was doing, snapped back and stared at his own palmprints on the spotless surface. He turned to follow Rachel, scarcely noticing the plush sofas and built-in shelves of the room she had entered. He was trying to blot out the picture of her on a delivery table, giving birth to their daughter then naming her Beth.

Rachel was squatting before a low set of doors on the far wall. She reached into the cupboard, withdrew a bottle, read its label and reiterated, "I'm afraid we don't have much of a selection."

His voice sounded just behind her shoulder. "Anything you've got. That's fine."

"It's Scotch."

"It'll do, Rachel. I'm not fussy."

"I don't know anything about mixing drinks." From over her shoulder the bottle was taken out of her hands.

"I do." She swung around and stood watching as he returned to the kitchen, obviously in a hurry. When she reentered the room he was pouring the lime water down the drain. Then he replaced it with clear Scotch, added no more than a splash of tap water, stirred it with his finger, and swung to face her, leaning his hips against the edge of the sink while taking a long drink. Lowering the glass, he noted, "You disapprove."

She turned her back on him and said tightly, "Who am I to approve or disapprove your life-style?"

"Still, you do," he reaffirmed. Her shoulders were stiff and she stared at the sliding glass door as if studying something in the dark pool. "I need-ed it to get through this. . . this emotional wringer, okay?" He crossed his ankles and draped his emp-ty hand over the cabinet edge in a calculatedly casual pose, though his legs trembled. "Why did you name her Beth?" he asked, so quietly that shivers ran up Rachel's neck.

They were both vividly remembering the many nights they'd lain in each other's arms in a dark parked car, sexually sated, planning their future and the names of their children. Beth. Their first daughter would be Beth, they had agreed. As she remembered it now, Rachel's skin tingled.

In the glass doors he saw her full reflection. Her arms were now tightly crossed over her ribs.

When Rachel's answer came, her voice was far from steady. "I. . . we. . . I was seventeen, and still in love with you, and I know it was a foolish thing to do, but it seemed a way to bind us to her, even though we had to give her away."

He took another long pull and considered at

length before admitting hoarsely, "I have another daughter named Beth."

"Yes, I know." Against the fallen night he saw her image with eyes tightly closed, mouth gaping as if fighting for breath.

His brows lowered. "You know, Rachel?"

"The announcements of all your children's births were in the *Franklin County Times*. You have a nineteen year old son named Michael and a seventeen year old named Doyle, and a fourteen-year-old daughter named. . . named Beth."

A sharp stab of exhilaration lifted his ribs. "So I'm not the only one who kept tabs."

She ignored his remark and stood as before, tightly wrapped in trembling arms.

"Rachel. . . ." He'd resisted touching her as long as he could. He crossed the room and laid a palm on her shoulder, but she flinched away. Rebuffed, he dropped the hand. "Turn around and look at me."

"No. This is difficult enough as it is." She didn't want him to see her face when she asked the next question, even though they both knew the answer, both remembered those sweet shared secrets in a dark car. Her voice was scarcely more than a whisper as she asked, "Why did you name your daughter Beth?"

He touched her again, and this time she obeyed his silent command, turning very slowly, her arms still locked across her ribs. He stood close, but dropped his hand from her. "Do you want the truth or do you want a lie?" he asked.

"I wouldn't have asked if I didn't want the truth."

His glasses still lay on the table, and she could see his eyes clearly now, the pale webbing at the corners, drawn lines angling away from his lower lids. But the irises and lashes were the same clear dark brown of the Tommy Lee she'd known and loved back then. With his eyes fixed on hers, he answered, "Because I was twenty-seven years old and still in love with you."

She felt the shock waves undulate through her body and she turned safely away, dropping tiredly to her chair once again. "Oh, Tommy Lee, how can you say such a thing?"

"So you'd rather have had the lie."

"But you were married to somebody else." It made her feel guilty in some obscure way.

He laughed ruefully. "Yes, one of the three."

"You say that as if you didn't love any of them."

"There were times when I thought I did." Suddenly he wilted, ran a hand through his hair and breathed, "Hell, I don't know." He reached into his breast pocket, came up with a cigarette and lighter, and dipped his head as the two joined. When the cigarette was burning, Tommy Lee mixed a fresh drink without asking Rachel's permission, disappeared into the living room and returned with the crystal ashtray, then took up his post with hips and hands strung against the edge of the counter.

When her eyes again confronted him, there was a hint of censure about her puckered brows. "Tommy Lee, how can you be so...so blithe about it? You conceived children with two different women. How could you do that if you weren't sure you loved them?"

He took a long, thoughtful drag, then a long, thoughtful drink. "Who knows why children are conceived?" he asked ruminatively, then admitted, "I can't really say there ever was much discussion about whether or not Rosamond and I should have had the two boys. What else do you do when you've graduated from college? You find some girl to marry and settle down with, and babies just naturally follow."

"You mean you...you never wanted them?" She sounded shocked.

"Maybe just that we never *should* have wanted them. Roz and I..." He studied his smoking cigarette with a faraway expression in his eyes. "We got married for all the wrong reasons. Maybe subconsciously we thought that having the boys would pull us together. But it didn't. It was a poor excuse, and the boys are the ones who paid for it." He studied his crossed ankles as he ended quietly, "They're both sorry."

"Sorry?"

He looked up. "Rebellious, troublemakers, in and out of scrapes with school, the law, you name it. Not exactly all-American boys."

"Oh, Tommy Lee, I'm so sorry."

He half-turned, stubbing out his cigarette. "Yeah, well don't be. It was Roz's and my fault, not yours. Maybe if we'd have loved each other more we would have been the kind of parents to raise better kids. I don't know."

"And they live with her?"

He nodded. "In Mobile."

"Do you ever see them?"

"As little as possible. When we're in the same room you can see the sparks in the air."

"Do they write to you?"

He lifted sad eyes to hers. "When they need money. Then good ole dad gets a letter."

Her heart melted with pity. He looked lonely and defeated, and she wondered if losing a child the way he had wasn't more devastating than giving one up for adoption.

"And what about...Beth?" The name was difficult for Rachel to say.

He smiled ruefully, shook his head, then crossed to take the chair opposite Rachel, dropped an ankle over a knee and drew circles on the white Formica with the bottom of his glass. "Beth is hovering on the balance. I'm not sure yet which way she'll go. She and her mother don't get along and I'm out of the picture."

"You had her with your second wife."

It struck Tommy Lee that Rachel had kept close tabs, indeed, but for the moment he answered her non-question by going on, "Yes, my second wife, Nancy. Do you know why I married Nancy?" His glass made dull murmurs on the tabletop. When she looked from it to his face, she found his eyes on the giraffe at her throat. They moved up and locked with hers as he admitted quietly, "Because the first time I saw her, she reminded me of you. Her hair was the same color as yours, and her mouth was a lot the same. And when she laughed, there was always that little half-hiccup at the end, just like you do."

The pause that followed was anything but comfortable for Rachel. She was embarrassed, yet flattered, and her heart seemed to thump in double time while she couldn't think of a single sensible thing to say. Thankfully, he went on. "But before we were married a year I realized she was nothing at all like you. She's a vicious bitch. I married her because I was lonely, and on the rebound from another marriage. That—granted— wasn't so hot, but at least it was company. I needed the sound of another human voice at the end of the day, and somebody across the supper table. So I married Nancy."

She could well imagine his loneliness at the time, for by then he'd cut himself off from his family.

"And your third wife, Sue Ann?" she prompted.

He flexed his shoulders against the back of the chair, glanced out at the night, chuckled ruefully and shook his head. "What a joke. The whole damn town knows why I married Sue Ann Higgenbotham.'' He swallowed the last of his drink, set the glass down and crossed his forearms on the table, meeting her eyes directly. "I think most people refer to it as male menopause.''

She smiled at his candor but recalled her mortification upon reading of his third marriage to a woman fifteen years his junior, and one known for her licentious relationships with countless older men around town. She recalled the snickers and raised eyebrows, and the way she'd always reacted to them with a quick defensive anger. How many times had she bitten back a quick rebuttal on Tommy Lee's behalf? She experienced again the quick flash of anger she'd felt toward him then for making himself vulnerable to speculation and gossip.

"But did you have to choose someone that much younger than yourself? And a girl like *that*?''

"Why, Rachel,'' he noted, grinning, "do I detect a spot of temper?''

She colored slightly, but unloaded her convoluted feelings at last. "I used to get so angry with you for... for cheapening yourself that way. There were times when I wanted to smack you in the head and ask you just what in the world you were trying to prove! And you realize, don't you, that you left *me* open to questioning, with all your antics. People remembered that we were practically born and raised together, and they'd come up to me and ask the most embarrassing questions, as if *I* still kept tabs on you.''

"Apparently you did."

"Don't get smug, and stop trying to evade the issue. I asked you why in the world you got tangled up with somebody like Sue Ann Higgenbotham."

"Chasing after my own youth, I guess. Trying to find it with somebody who was as young as I wished I was."

"But you *were* young." She leaned forward earnestly. "You were only thirty-five, Tommy Lee."

Again her record-keeping struck him, but he made no issue of it. "Rachel, I've felt old since I was twenty-one, fresh out of college, marrying some woman because it was the acceptable thing to do."

"That was different. She was your own age, and you were starting out together. With Sue Ann I always had the feeling you were throwing her into your parents' faces."

"How could I throw her in their faces when we weren't even talking to each other?"

"You know what I mean. Flaunting her, choosing the worst woman the town had to offer. They were just as aware of what a mess you were making of your life as everyone else in Russellville. Through the years I've often felt you came back to do it under their noses just to humiliate them."

He pondered, studying her steady eyes. "Maybe I did. God, I don't know. You as much as admitted there were times when you had the urge to get even with your parents, too."

"Yes. Times. But I wasn't raised that way, Tommy Lee, and neither were you. I realize they were as fallible as anybody else. The decision they made was made because they loved me and thought it was best for me."

There was a stern edge to his voice and his brows drew downward. "But it wasn't, Rachel, was it?"

Her heart thundered heavily as she met Tommy Lee's eyes and wondered if her own disillusionment showed as openly as his. "My life with Owen was very good," she argued, perhaps a little too quickly.

Tommy Lee's eyes swept around the room, returned to her before he asked very simply, "But where are the children, Rachel?"

Her polished lips fell open and a pained expression etched her eyes. Beneath the draping silk blouse he saw her breasts heave up once, as if she were struggling for control. He was terribly sorry to do this to her, but what she'd suffered—if she had—was important to him.

She dropped her eyes to her empty glass and admitted quietly, "We were never able to have any."

"Why?"

Their eyes met, delved deeply, and he saw fissures of vulnerability within the woman who always appeared so carefully in control. She pondered the advisability of revealing the truth to the man who'd fathered the only child she'd ever been able to have, but somehow it seemed right that he should know. Her lips trembled, paused in shaping the first word, but finally she got it out. "I . . . I was allergic to Owen's sperm."

He couldn't have looked more surprised if she'd slugged him. His jaw fell open and he tried to speak, but nothing came out. Though she was hidden by the table from the waist down, his eyes dropped to the point where her stomach must be, then as he realized where he was gazing, they flew back to her face again. But his own face was a mask of regret.

"Ironic, isn't it?" Rachel added. "But it's true."

"I've never heard of such a thing," he blurted out.

Her face was slightly pale, his growing increasingly pink as she went on, chafing her crossed arms as they rested on the table edge. "It's not all that uncommon. It seems my body had an excessive sensitivity to his semen, and put up what they called an immunologic reaction to it. I actually created antibodies that prevented the sperm from reaching the egg to fertilize it."

He was stunned by the queer twist of fate that had made her pregnant at a time in her life when she didn't want to be, but had prevented pregnancy during the years when it was what she must have most desired. Yet she stated it all with apparent clinical coolness while he sat before her, greatly discomfited by the personal revelation. Still, something forced him to go on.

"Couldn't anything be done about it?"

"Believe me, we tried. I visited gynecologists as far away as Rush Medical Center in Chicago. Different doctors said it could be treated in a number of ways, but none of them had a history of success. I took drugs, but some of them had unpleasant side effects. We even tried artificial insemination—something to do with bypassing the cervix and going directly to the womb—but that didn't work, either. In some women the antibodies disappear by themselves after a while, but I wasn't so lucky. More than one doctor felt that reducing my exposure to the sperm would reduce the sensitivity and the antibodies would disappear, or at least decrease enough so that I could conceive. We tried long periods of no contact, but when we resumed, there still was no pregnancy."

He drew a hand down his face, covering his mouth for a moment while studying her solemnly. Then he took one of her hands in both of his. "Rachel, I'm so sorry."

She met his empathetic eyes and saw how uneasy he was with the intimate subject, after all. She was disquieted, too, but forced herself to maintain a poised exterior. "It's all right. I've learned to live with it."

"But, Rachel, our ba—"

"Don't say it!" she warned, raising both palms, closing her eyelids momentarily.

But he didn't need to say it for the awful truth to be scintillating between them as their gazes met again. Together they had conceived the only child she was likely to have, and their parents had decreed that it be taken from her and given to strangers in Flint, Michigan. He felt devastated for her and curiously guilty, as if he'd unwittingly slighted her in some way.

At last he said shakily, "It should have been me you were allergic to."

She reached across the table and pressed her fingertips to his lips. "Shh." She'd thought the same thing countless times. *What if . . . what if. . . .* But it was shattering to hear him put her thoughts into words.

He grasped her hand and lowered it to the table. "God, Rachel, I feel so guilty. Me with three kids and my life so loused up not one of them is with me. It makes me realize I should have worked harder at being a better father, tried to make them shape up and make something of themselves." The expression about his lips grew soft and his eyes roved her face lovingly. "You'd have been so good at that. You'd have been a good mother, the kind who turns out successes."

"Maybe so. But it's too late to think about it, isn't it?"

Yes, he thought sadly, *it's probably too late.* The room grew quiet. She picked up their glasses and took them to the sink and he knew he should leave. But there were so many more questions he wanted to ask, and their time together had been too short. Walking away from her would be more difficult than ever, especially after the intimate discussion that had him feeling closer to her than he had in years. But he picked up his glasses from the table, slipped them on and crossed to stand behind her.

She felt his presence at her shoulder, but forced herself to remain as she was, staring out a black window over the sink. The words she forced herself to say were more difficult than she'd ever imagined they could be.

"I'm very tired, Tommy Lee. I think it's time—"

"You don't have to say any more, Rachel. I'm on my way out. Thank you for the drinks."

"You're welcome."

Neither of them moved. He studied the back of her neat black hair and a diagonal wrinkle on her violet blouse where it had been pressed against the chair. She smelled so good, so feminine.

"Rachel," came his strained voice, "I'd like to see you again."

She gripped the edge of the sink. "No," she replied shakily, "I don't think so."

"Why?"

"Because it's too painful."

"We could work on that, couldn't we?"

"Could we?"

"Once all the skeletons are out of the attic, we'll feel better."

"If tonight is any indication, I don't think so."

"I didn't mean to hurt you by coming here, you know that, don't you?" He turned her by an elbow, but she stared at his collar button instead of his appealing eyes. "Rachel, I'm sorry. I wish I could make it all up to you. You're the one who deserved three more babies, not me."

Her throat constricted suddenly. "Shh... don't. In spite of what I've told you tonight, Owen and I were happy. We really were. We were compatible, we had money, success. That was enough. Children aren't everything, you know."

Beneath his fingers her elbow trembled, but she wisely drew it from his grasp. He gazed down at the top of her head, but she refused to look up. "Could I take you to dinner some night and we'll talk about more pleasant things?"

And start all over again? she thought. But there was no starting over, only picking up from where they were. The load they had to carry was too heavy, and they had changed so much. Too much for things to work out between them.

"I'm sorry, the answer is no."

"Just dinner—"

But she knew he wanted more than dinner. "No. I'm not in the market for dinner, or dates, or...or...."

"All right. I won't push it." He turned and she followed him through the dining and living rooms to the entry. She opened the door and stood back, but he made no move to exit, standing instead with both hands buried in his trouser pockets, staring at his shoes. When at last he lifted his

head, the question in his eyes could not be disguised by concealing lenses. What he wanted
tingled in the air between them. One hand came
out of his pocket and he reached to lift the tiny
gold giraffe on a single fingertip. He leaned
closer...but the scent of Scotch came with him,
reminding her of the changes that could not be
denied.

She pressed her hands to his chest and turned
aside. "Don't, Tommy Lee," she whispered.

His head was half bent toward the kiss. It remained that way while his eyes swam over her and
he absently fingered the giraffe. Then he dropped
it against her skin. "You're right. It was a stupid
idea."

Her heart was thrumming crazily. Beneath his
shirt she felt his doing the same. For a moment she
was tempted, for old time's sake, but common
sense prevailed and she withdrew to take up her
pose as doorkeeper, outwardly poised, unruffled,
one hundred percent a lady. He backed off politely, leaving her feeling vaguely disappointed and
oddly guilty—it had been years since she'd had occasion to deny a man a kiss, and it was no less embarrassing now than it had been as a teenager. But
she forced her eyes to meet his, and knew beyond
a doubt that saying no was best for both of them.

"Goodnight, Rachel," he said, stepping out.

"Goodbye, Tommy Lee."

At her choice of farewell words he turned, gave
her a last lingering look, then spun away. She

watched him until he was halfway down the sidewalk, heading for his Cadillac. Then she closed the door, leaned her forehead against it and fought the tears.

CHAPTER FOUR

DURING THE DAYS that followed, Rachel tried to put Tommy Lee out of her mind. Her father and Marshall helped tremendously. Everett had taken to popping in unexpectedly in the evenings, and Marshall, whose two daughters were already grown and married, found it easy to do the same. On her three days a week at Rachel's house, Callie Mae always stayed until Rachel got home in the late afternoon. She would cast a droll eye on Rachel's slim profile, remind her there was a chocolate pie—or some such calorie-filled delight—in the refrigerator, then chastise, "If you don't put some meat on them bones, you gonna quit castin' a shadow, Miss Rachel."

Rachel would smile and tease, "You won't rest until I'm wearing a size sixteen, will you, Callie Mae?"

But Rachel's appetite remained paltry, and eating alone seemed to decrease it even more. But if Rachel often passed up Callie Mae's offerings, Marshall never did. He came often, to share a meal, check on Rachel, or to "get her out of the house," as he put it. Having shared many of the same friends for years, it seemed quite natural that together they'd round out a table at bridge, attend backyard barbecues or an occasional movie, and even go shopping for the new furnishings for the master bedroom, which Rachel had decided to have redecorated.

Owen's life insurance had come through, and Marshall solemnly delivered the check shortly after Rachel's return from St. Thomas, then, together with Everett, mapped out an investment plan they deemed most prudent.

The three of them fell into the habit of driving up to one of the nicer clubs in Florence for dinner each Friday night, and though Rachel was most often grateful for their company, there were times when she felt smothered by them. Marshall was very much like Owen in many ways—quiet, steady, sensible, but, to her dismay, a bore. She grew tired of listening to him talk about his chief pastime—taking meticulous care of his yard. And of her father talking about his chief pastime— money and its management. Often when she was with them she found herself withholding sighs: Bermuda grass, investments, azalea bushes, interest rates, annuities, pruning, I.R.A. accounts.... The two of them droned on about the same dull subjects while Rachel grew listless.

But whenever they were not there Rachel found herself wishing she had children. How different these days would be if she could return home each day to the sound of their voices in the house, perhaps the blare of a stereo from one of the bedrooms, the clatter of a tennis racket being dropped in the middle of the kitchen floor, even the sound of adolescent bickering. She could imagine one of them coming to her, complaining, "Mother, will you tell him—" Or *her.* . . .

Don't think about Beth. Don't think about her father.

But every time she walked into the newly decorated bedroom, she thought of Tommy Lee. The room had been repapered with an airy yellow and white bamboo design, and the furniture was pristine white wicker—fresh, bright, a breath of springtime brought inside. Colorful silk flowers adorned a miniature dressing table, above which hung a wicker-framed mirror. The bed was strewn with the whitest, ruffliest spread she could buy, and piled high with yellow and white throw pillows. She'd dappled the room with potted palms and pothos, and changed the scents in the closet and drawers to a brisk herbal that complemented the new look. It was the bedroom of a fifteen-year-old girl now, as bright and different as Rachel could make it. But when she viewed it, she often thought with silent chagrin, "Is this my 'Sue Ann Higgenbotham'?"

And at night, when she lay with the new woven-wood shades lifted clear of the sliding glass door, she studied the reflection of the moon on the surface of the pool and took stock of her life, the void, the boredom that was becoming oppressive.

She wondered if she would simply drift into her fifties, then her sixties, accepting Marshall's and her father's company as her social mainstay, because the town was small and offered little more.

But it offered one other whom she could not erase from her mind.

She pictured him as he'd looked the night he'd come to the house, wearing the new glasses that made him seem half stranger, knowing in her heart that he was scarcely a stranger. She remembered the pain in his eyes as he'd told of his failed marriages and his everlasting feelings for her. She recalled his lips, as familiar as they'd been years ago, and found herself wishing she had kissed him again, then felt guilty for making such a wish when Owen had been gone such a short time. But Owen's illness had depleted him so rapidly during the last half year that their sexual relationship had been nonexistent. While he was alive, she'd been too preoccupied with concern for him to rue the lack, but now, alone in bed at night, memories of Tommy Lee and the past came crowding back, leaving her restless and unsatisfied.

Thank heavens she had the store to fill her days. She loved it and was tremendously proud of its success. It had taken ten years to bring the business to its current éclat—a Dun & Bradstreet rating of over $100,000 a year—and almost as long to acquire the eclectic fittings that made the setting at once genteel and warmly welcoming. Oddly enough, Panache was the antithesis of

Rachel's house, where each item had its place and
neatness reigned.

The front door boasted a stained-glass window
she had found at an auction. Apple-green carpeting created a soothing backdrop for well-chosen
touches of pink in the accoutrements.

An elegant French provincial sofa of shell-pink
velvet sat before the front bay window, surrounded by hanging ferns. At the rear of the store
a tall French armoire spread mirrored doors wide,
its illuminated interior highlighting the current
display of Giorgio Sant'Angelos and Gloria
Betkers draped artistically over the gaping doors
and tilting from willow hangers.

At one rear corner was the fitting room: nothing
more than a length of fringed French moiré, again
in pink, shirred upon a circular brass rod. Inside
was a delicate wicker chair, which matched the
chest just outside, where a mountainous burst of
spruce-green eucalyptus exploded from a fat-
bellied pot in bleeding shades of rose. The spicy
fragrance blended with that of herbal soaps, bath
salts and sachets displayed in an open curved-glass
curio cabinet and the central display of Flora
Danica fragrances.

The opposite rear corner housed Rachel's prized
Louis XIV kneehole desk and matching chair with
its gilded legs and rose damask seat. There was
only one rectangular showcase in sight, and that
housed jewelry and scarves in the center of the
store. Otherwise, clothing was displayed hither

and thither: upon an antique butterfly table, hanging from the doe-foot supports of an oval shaving mirror, strewn with an artful eye upon the graduated shelves of a what-not and slipping from the drawers of a provincial lowboy with graceful acanthus-leaf pulls. Around the walls, dresses hung on charming brass extenders, alternating with the array of wall decor that brought the green-and-white trellised paper to life: miniature Renoir prints, framed cross-stitch embroidery, sprigs of feathergrass bound with green and pink ribbons, toadstools and unicorns on nick-nack shelves, decoupage fancies and gold-beaded neck ropes. The hand-made crafts interspersed with couturier labels lent Panache that look of classic clutter only the most talented can successfully achieve. And the store managed to reflect its owner: cool, elegant, tasteful, and always, always fragrant.

Rachel's workdays followed a routine: up at seven, open at nine, paperwork at her corner desk in between helping customers, post office at eleven, lunch at twelve-thirty—usually a piece of fruit or a carton of yogurt at her desk while perusing the latest issue of *Women's Wear Daily*. The afternoons were slightly more varied: dust the furniture, water the ferns, steam the wrinkles from any newly arrived garments, tag incoming merchandise, straighten the stacks, rehang the tried-ons, then, at exactly quarter to four, walk down to the bank with the day's deposit before returning to the shop to help Verda close up for the day.

Given this regimentation, the biyearly clothing markets presented an inviting change of routine for Rachel. It was on a Wednesday in early April, when she and Verda were discussing the upcoming market in Dallas, that the phone rang on Rachel's desk. Verda, who happened to be standing right beside the desk, automatically picked it up. A moment later, wide-eyed, she covered the mouthpiece with her palm and announced in a stage whisper, "It's for you! It's him!"

Rachel's head snapped up. "Who?"

Verda's eyebrows nearly touched her hairline. "It's the one who kept calling you while you were gone to St. Thomas. The one who'd never give his name."

Rachel's stomach did a somersault, but she gave away none of the trepidation she felt as Verda handed over the phone, then stood listening, making no effort to appear as if she weren't.

"Hello?"

He needn't have given his name; this time she recognized the voice. There followed a long pause, then Tommy Lee's voice came again. "I've been thinking about you."

With Verda right there, Rachel measured her reply carefully. "Is there something you wanted?"

"Yes. I wanted to know if you'd like to come out and see the lake rise. The dam's been opened for two months, and the water level's finally coming up at my end of the lake."

"I'm really sorry, but I won't have time."

"How do you know? I haven't told you when yet."

Verda now had her ear cocked like a robin listening for a worm. Unable to dream up an evasive reply, Rachel was forced to ask, "When?"

"Friday afternoon. I thought we could drive out together after we're both finished with work."

It sounded so much more appealing than dinner with her father and Marshall, but she quelled the urge to accept. "I'm sorry. I have plans for that night."

"I don't believe you, but that's okay. I'll try another time."

"That won't be necessary, T—" She caught herself just short of pronouncing his name.

"I know. But I'll try just the same." Then he ended softly, " 'Bye, Rachel."

"Goodbye."

Verda followed every motion as Rachel hung up the phone and slipped her large, squarish reading glasses back on her nose.

"Well, who was it?" the clerk asked, point-blank.

Rachel managed to exude an air of total indifference as she relaxed against the chair with one slim wrist draped over its rim. "Oh, just someone I knew years ago who heard of Owen's death and wanted to express his sympathies."

"That's not what it sounded like to me. It sounded like somebody asking you out on a date."

"A date?" Rachel pushed her glasses low and peered at Verda over their rims, hoping she didn't look as shaken as she was by the sound of his voice. "A date? With a widow of less than two months? Don't be silly, Verda." Then she returned to her study of the calendar and the market announcement. "I'll make my flight reservations this afternoon." The subject of the phone call was successfully diverted while they discussed the upcoming trip.

But that afternoon when Rachel made her three forty-five walk to the bank, Tommy Lee was standing in the doorway of his office building as she passed on the opposite side of the street. When she saw him, her navy-blue high heels came to an abrupt halt and she clutched the zippered bank pouch more tightly against her ribs. She'd been passing his office for ten years, and the few times he'd happened to come out while she was directly across the street he'd moved to his car with no indication of having seen her.

He raised a palm now, silently. While she acknowledged it with a silent nod, she mentally calculated how many people up and down Jackson Avenue might have witnessed the exchange. Then she hurried on, breathing freely only when she reached the comparative safety of the bank lobby. From inside, she turned to see if he was still there. He was, studying the bank steps, his expression unreadable from this distance. He found a cigarette, lit it, tossed his head back in that masculine way she sometimes pictured when she thought of him—late at night when she couldn't sleep—and turned then disappeared into his office.

Rachel spun around, her eyes zeroing in on her father's glass-walled office. He was sitting behind his desk, watching her with a disapproving look on his face. Had he seen Tommy Lee? A disquieting memory came back to her at that moment. She'd heard it said that when Tommy Lee graduated from college and returned to Russellville to set up his business, he had come to the bank to apply for a small business loan, and her father had personally seen to it that Tommy Lee was thwarted. Odd that the recollection had come back after all these years.

Her father watched her like an eagle as she turned toward the teller's window to make her daily deposit. She felt his eyes augering into her shoulder blades and became angry that he should still have a modicum of control over her where Tommy Lee was concerned.

But when her business was completed, she squared her shoulders, put on a false bright smile and clicked into his glass office, seeking to reaffirm their Friday night date so she wouldn't feel tempted to take Tommy Lee up on his invitation after all.

"Hi, daddy. Are we still on for Friday night?"

"Of course. Just as usual."

But Friday night sounded more lackluster than ever. Stepping back onto the sidewalk to make her return walk to Panache, Rachel glanced immediately to the red-brick building half a block away. But Tommy Lee had not come back. His car was parked out front though, and she had the disturbing feeling he was watching her through the window.

The following day Rachel happened to be folding some silk scarves at the jewelry display case when she absently glanced up to see the tail end of a white Cadillac cruising by at a sloth's speed. Her heart seemed to slam into her throat and she snapped a glance at Verda. But Verda was busy with a customer and hadn't noticed.

Tommy Lee Gentry, don't you dare!

If only he drove some mundane mid-sized car in everybody's blue! But everyone in town could count the times he cruised past in that Cadillac. And if he started making a habit of it, what would she do?

Before two days were up she understood. . .he'd started to make a habit of it. How many times had she glanced up to see the car easing along the street at far less than the thirty-miles-per-hour speed limit? Adolescent tactics! Yet each time she saw it her heart fluttered and she felt hot and weak.

On Friday when she stepped out of the bank with the empty zipper pouch in her hand, she again came up short. There he was, on her side of the street, visiting casually with three other businessmen as if they'd just *happened* to meet on the sidewalk. The quartet broke up just as Rachel stepped abreast of them, and Tommy Lee turned, quite naturally, falling into step beside her.

"Well, hello, Mrs. Hollis."

"Hello, Tommy Lee."

"You're looking exceptionally pretty today."

She walked a little faster and kept her voice low. "Tommy Lee, what on earth are you trying to prove, waiting to ambush me on the street? And who do you think you're fooling, calling me Mrs. Hollis when everyone in town knows we grew up on Cotako Street side by side!"

He grinned down charmingly. "Sorry then. Hello, *Rachel*, you're looking exceptionally pretty today."

Good Lord, how long had it been since she'd blushed? But it was impossible to be unaffected by his nearness, his compliments. "Tommy Lee, stop it! And stop driving past my store at five miles an hour ten times a day!"

"Today I only drove past six times. Could I see you sometime this weekend?"

"No, I have plans."

"I don't believe you, Rachel. And if you don't want me to grab your elbow and drag you to a stop you'd better do it yourself and act as if you're giving me a civil time-of-day." They were directly across the street from his office now, and Rachel obediently halted, then lifted her flustered eyes to his. "Who are you going to see tonight?" Tommy Lee demanded, standing before her with both hands in his trouser pockets, shirt sleeves rolled to mid-forearm and tie loosened over a freed collar button. Looking up at him gave her that strange familiar feeling in the pit of her stomach, just like years ago when he'd stop her this way in the halls at school. It struck her that he was handsomer than either Owen or Marshall, though the thought appeared out of nowhere to rankle her.

"My daddy. He's taking me to dinner in Florence."

"Oh." He scowled, glanced toward the bank and thrust his lips out in a peculiarly attractive fashion.

"Yes. Oh. I can hardly tell him I'm sorry but I'm breaking our date to go out with Tommy Lee Gentry, can I?"

"What about tomorrow? The water's up enough that we could go out on the boat."

It sounded absolutely wonderful. "Tomorrow I'm working. I gave Verda the day off."

"Sunday then."

"Sunday I'm going to church. You remember church, don't you, Tommy Lee? That big red-brick building down there on the corner where you used to go?" It was as close to snide as Rachel had ever come as she pointed to the First Baptist, several blocks away. But the more she was exposed to him, the harder she had to fight to remind herself that he wasn't exactly parlor fare anymore.

"Sunday afternoon?"

She sighed heavily and her face looked slightly

crestfallen. "I'm sorry, Tommy Lee. I can't see you. Please don't ask me again."

Their eyes locked for several electric seconds, then Rachel resolutely turned and continued down the street.

That night over supper she was distracted and forlorn. Everett and Marshall carried on a dull conversation about how investment institutions were slowly usurping the bank's role as chief money-holder for many private individuals. While Everett expounded upon the droll subject, Rachel tried to keep her mind off Tommy Lee, but he slipped into her thoughts time and again. *I could have been with him at this very moment.* She wondered what his house was like, and if he'd invited someone else to go boating, and if so, who she was. She recalled the sun sparkling off the dark hair on his arms below his rolled up sleeves, and the inviting shadow cast upon his throat by the loosened collar and tie. She imagined another woman enjoying his company and shivered with a sudden inexplicable wave of jealousy.

Later that evening when Marshall saw her home he seemed worried about her.

"You seem rather blue tonight, Rachel," he noted as they stood in the entry, preparatory to his leaving.

"Blue?" She tried to put on a gayer expression, but failed. "No, just tired. It's been a long week."

There came into Marshall's eyes a look she'd never seen there before, and as he took her gently into his arms she sensed a difference in the pressure of his hands upon her back.

No, not Marshall, she thought in a panic.

But as he leaned back to look into her face, she saw a flicker of emotion that went beyond fraternal care. "You've been doing great. Pushing ahead, getting on with life. I'm very proud of you, you know." He touched her cheek and she wanted to shrink back, wary of allowing him to think for a moment that she wanted any kind of relationship with him other than the one she had. He leaned to touch his lips to her cheek. She was already searching for the proper words to fend him off when he straightened, gave her arms a platonic squeeze and said good-night.

For some reason the experience with Marshall made her wonder how she would have reacted had it been Tommy Lee who'd given her such ardent glances and pulled her into his arms that way.

Dangerous thought! She promised herself she'd stop dwelling on Tommy Lee this way, and the next time she saw him, she'd walk straight on by with nothing more than a polite hello.

But the next time she saw him she *couldn't* walk away. It was the following Friday at four-thirty. Verda was running the vacuum cleaner over the carpet prior to closing and Rachel was seated at her desk, putting away the empty bank pouch.

The door opened, Rachel looked up and froze.

He was dressed in an open-collared black sport shirt topped by a gray sports coat a shade lighter than his trousers. His hair was tousled by the wind, and as he closed the door his eyes were already seeking her out.

Her stomach went fluttery and she felt fifteen again. *This time I'll end up saying yes.*

The vacuum cleaner wheezed into silence and Verda greeted, "Well, howdy, Tommy Lee. Now what in the world are you doin' in a place like this?"

He carefully avoided glancing Rachel's way and sauntered farther into the store with a charming smile for Verda. "I need to buy a present for someone."

"Well now, I'm sure's eternity not goin' t' ask who it's for. I might not like the answer."

He laughed and looked down at the rectangular glass showcase in the center of the store, studying the accessories arranged there, fingering silk scarves, poring over a basket of earrings. Rachel sat watching him, the pulses hammering out a warning in her throat, but he scarcely gave her a glance. Momentarily, Verda spoke up again. "Y'all just take your time lookin' while I finish up this floor. If there's anything you like, maybe Rachel can help you."

He looked up as if only now realizing Rachel was there. "Oh, hello, Mrs. Hollis. Never been in your store before." He glanced around, drummed four fingertips on top of the glass cabinet. "It's very nice. Classy." His eyes returned to her and he flashed a quick smile. "Smells good, too."

It smelled of Rachel. It was no particular scent, and all scents, lingering together in a potent mixture that spoke of things delicate and feminine. Her eyes dropped to the desk top and she busied herself writing something, sitting at a chair almost as delicate as she, her legs crossed and the hem of a melon-colored skirt riding just above the knee. In the cleft of her white embroidered collar lay a collection of chunky coral and brown beads that looked as though they belonged on a Zulu native; on Rachel they looked chic.

Her eyes met his again as the vacuum cleaner cut off the possibility of further talk, but he noted the quick rise and fall of her breasts and the tendons of her right wrist standing out boldly as she clutched the fountain pen. Who but Rachel still used a fountain pen, he wondered. Then he dropped his eyes again to the jewelry counter and she turned away. Covertly he glanced up from time to time to see if the pen moved over the paper, but it was held poised while Rachel's back remained stiff, her head dropped forward.

It struck Verda then who belonged to the voice on the phone, and the vacuum stopped moving, though the brushes still whirred against the carpet. She glanced up sharply at Tommy Lee Gentry, then at Rachel. But Tommy Lee was flicking through the earrings, and Rachel wasn't paying him the least attention.

Rachel wasn't paying him the least attention?

Since when did Rachel ignore a customer? But

Verda turned back to her task, deciding to stretch it out as long as possible, to see what Rachel would do.

After some minutes he signaled and she rose to help him. Verda turned off the machine, fussed around putting away things left in the fitting room and listened.

"Those little red ones," he was saying.

"These?"

"Yes, ma'am."

"These are for pierced ears. Does she have pierced ears?"

"Well now, I'm not sure I ever noticed," he drawled.

"Most women do these days."

"If she doesn't, could I bring them back?"

"I'm sorry, pierced aren't returnable. State law."

"Oh. Well, it's only nine dollars. If hers aren't pierced, maybe she'll have a friend."

Rachel was incensed, and having a hard time hiding it. How dare he come in here and buy baubles for his tootsies! The shop had grown incredibly quiet. Rachel was aware of it, and of Verda wrapping up the vacuum cord and of Tommy Lee studying her own trembling hands as they removed the red button earrings from the case and began scraping the gummed label from the back of the card with a perfect long peach-painted nail.

"Did you want them wrapped?" Rachel asked, braving a glance at his face to throw Verda off balance. *See how unaffected I am by him?* But the moment she raised her eyes, she realized her mistake. Once their gazes met she felt heated and uncomfortable and angry all over again.

"You do that here?"

"Yes. It's a customer service. No charge." The words were difficult for Rachel to say, given the fact that she wanted to sling the red earrings in his face. It angered her further to realize that she couldn't help wondering who they were for. But then, according to the gossips, he had innumerable female friends to whom he might offer such a gift. Rachel's fingers were still shaking as she placed the jewelry into a small apple-green box, wrapped it in identical paper, and placed a pink lace bow upon the cover.

Tommy Lee had wandered to the armoire and stood studying a midnight-blue slip displayed there with matching bikinis and a scanty brassiere. He reached out to finger the lace edging at the hem of the slip and, as he moved, his face became visible in the mirror. He looked up, caught Rachel studying him and had the audacity to smile! She waggled the box in the air.

Immediately he turned. "All wrapped?"

"Yes. That'll be nine dollars and sixty-three cents."

"Do you take Visa cards?"

"Yes, Visa will be fine."

The two of them moved toward the end of the glass case, where an enormous brass cash register reared its curlicued head. Tommy Lee extracted a card from his wallet and she dropped her eyes; there was something masculinely attractive about a man pushing back his jacket to reach for a wallet. Throughout the exchanging of the card and while she ran it through the imprinter and he signed it, Rachel searched her mind for the countless inanities she usually exchanged with a customer at a time like this but came up with none. She watched his dark hand scrawl a signature while the expensive diamond ring flashed, and again she wondered who the woman was, and damned him for coming here and putting her through this.

"There you go." Smiling, he handed her the pen.

Verda pushed the vacuum cleaner off into the back room just then, and the moment she disappeared through the doorway, Tommy Lee bent across the counter and whispered, "Do you work tomorrow?"

"No...." Then, realizing her mistake, Rachel amended, "Yes."

"Want to go water ski—" The ping of the ancient cash register bell cut off the rest of his question and the drawer sprang out at the same moment Tommy Lee reached across the counter and grabbed Rachel's wrist.

"Rachel, come out to the house, please." His mouth looked intense and sincere.

How dare he come here and do this to her!

Verify the fact that there were other women while inviting her to become one of them!

"No!" Her eyes veered toward the back room. "Please, Tommy Lee...."

From the rear of the building came the scrape and thump of Verda putting away the machine. Rachel's wrist strained against his hold.

"Sunday?" he asked quickly, his fingers tightening.

Her startled eyes held both anger and an undeniably tempted look, so he hurried on. "Beth will be there, so we wouldn't be alone. I want you to meet her."

Verda's footsteps were coming back and he was forced to drop Rachel's wrist. When the clerk emerged from the doorway Tommy Lee was putting his credit card away and Rachel was dropping the gift into a tiny floral paper sack.

"Thank you for stopping in," she said cheerfully, handing him his purchase. "And have a nice weekend."

Tommy Lee carefully wiped his feelings from his face and brought forth a lazy smile. "Y'all do the same, Mrs. Hollis, and you too, Verda."

He nodded to the clerk, who called out the customary, "Y'all come back." Then he strolled from the store without a backward glance.

The moment the door closed behind him, Verda propped a hand on her hip, raised one eyebrow and repeated, "Mrs. Hollis?" Her shrewd eyes homed in on Rachel. "What's going on?"

"Going on?" Rachel busied herself arranging the scarves on top of the showcase. "Nothing's going on, Verda. What ever in the world do you mean?"

"I suddenly put a name with the voice on the phone. It's his. Tommy Lee Gentry." She peered closely at Rachel. "He been pesterin' you?"

"Oh, for heaven's sake, Verda, don't be silly. What would Tommy Lee Gentry be doing pestering me?"

"What does Tommy Lee Gentry do pesterin' half the women of this town?" She glanced toward the door. "Which one of his doxies d'you reckon those earrin's were for?"

The question shot a flash of cold through Rachel. She wanted to cringe and defend him simultaneously. Why should she care about his indiscretions or what the town thought of him because of them? Yet the fact remained, she did. She always had.

"Do you want to stand there wondering about it all weekend, or would you rather lock up and go home?" Rachel forced an amused smile to her lips, as if she, too, were curious about the woman whose ears would be decorated with the red beads.

"You sure it wasn't him?" Verda couldn't resist asking one more time, scrunching up her eyes and studying Rachel closely.

"Tommy Lee Gentry?" Rachel turned away casually, heading for the light switch in the armoire. "I swear, Verda, if I have to put up with any more ridiculous questions from you I'll begin

to wonder if I've given you enough time off lately."
Rachel's low laugh followed, and Verda gave up.

"Oh, all right, but I could've sworn it was him
when he walked in here and started talkin'."

Duplicity was not Rachel's long suit. When she'd
locked up and was on her way home, safely away
from Verda's inquisitive eyes, she pulled over to the
curb along a tree-shaded street, crossed her wrists
on the steering wheel and dropped her forehead on
them.

*Rachel Hollis, get the man out of your mind. See
what people think of him? And just what do you
think they'd be saying about you if you were seen
with Tommy Lee Gentry when Owen is scarcely
cold in his grave?*

But it hurt, having to lie about Tommy Lee. She
felt as if she were injuring him more, yet what else
could she have done with Verda all ears and eyes?
But she remembered his wind-whipped hair, his
fingers on her arm, the soft invitation in his voice as
he leaned across the counter. And his lips . . . those
lips that hadn't changed a bit in all these years. And
she thought of the empty house, contraposed
against images of herself in a boat, or on water skis,
or riding off somewhere beside him in the white
Cadillac to have dinner.

But then, remembering how many countless
others would have done those same things—and
more—with Tommy Lee, she shook his image from
her mind and continued home to the waiting, silent
house.

CHAPTER FIVE

BUT BY SUNDAY AFTERNOON the house had grown too silent, too oppressive. It was spring, and Alabama had embarked upon that time of color and rebirth. Blossoms were exploding everywhere: azaleas in shades of red and pink, dogwoods in white, wysteria in violet and redbuds like a purple haze limning the countryside. Was there a time of year that tugged at the heartstrings more than this? That drew memories out of hiding and made them even more poignant in recollection than they'd been in reality?

Rachel lay in the back yard while bees buzzed in the blossoming pyracantha bushes bordering the high brick wall. She moved restlessly on the chaise lounge, closing her eyes against the sun and the loneliness, but seeing dancing pictures upon her closed eyelids. Pictures of Tommy Lee, past, and Tommy Lee, present. She rolled to her stomach, trying to shut them out, but they persisted even as she searched for a distracting sound to take away the memory of his voice, inviting, "Come out to the house...please." But there is nothing so silent as a small-town Sunday afternoon.

When she could tolerate it no longer she flung herself up and marched into the house, driving her fingers through her twenty-five-dollar hairdo, realizing that stubbornness was a poor substitute for company. *Don't think about whether it's wise or not—for once, just go with your heart.*

She bathed, applied fresh makeup, dabbed scent behind her ears and dressed in a sporty knit pink-and-gray striped top with matching skirt, both of which snapped up the front. She slipped her bare feet into white thong sandals, debated about what bathing-suit to take and decided to stop at the store and pick out a new one.

The store was different on Sundays—empty and shadowed. The display lights were off, the silence oddly disquieting, and Rachel had the strange feeling she was being given this pause as a last chance to come to her senses. But today spring controlled her senses. Almost defiantly, she stepped to the bathing suit rack. She flipped past the array of bikinis, which were for the most part too revealing, but cast a disdainful eye on the one-piecers, which seemed sexless and dull. In the end she chose a modest two-piece design of shimmering gold with a diagonal bar of red slicing from left hip to right breast, interrupted by a band of naked skin. Assessing herself in the full-length mirror, she tugged the waist up securely and checked to make sure it fully covered the scar on her stomach, then turned to view her back. *Lord, Callie Mae is right. If I don't gain some weight this thing will fall right off me.*

She turned full front to the mirror again, and her dark eyes appeared uncertain. Standing with her fingertips resting on her stomach, she thought she could feel nerves jumping inside.

He said his daughter will be there, so what can happen when you'll be chaperoned by a fourteen-year-old?

The suit had a matching cover-up of luxurious velour that reversed the design and colors, sporting a diagonal bar of gold on red. Its elasticized waist closed with a single gold catch, leaving provocative glimpses of the bathing suit and her bare midriff showing above and below the closure. But, considering her shape, Rachel hardly felt provocative, and decided the outfit would do. She stripped it off, packed it in her straw bag and dressed in her street clothes again, then locked the store and bounded to her car before she could change her mind.

The drive out to Cedar Creek Lake was beautiful. She took old Belgreen Road as it wound through the hills west of town, curving through pine forest and past areas where orange peaks of overburden from long ago strip-mining created a stunning contrast against the lush greenery surrounding it. The old limestone quarries gave over to glimpses of the TVA transmission towers, which were responsible for changing the area so much. Nestled in the foothills of the Appalachian Mountains, Franklin County rolled and undulated, presenting unexpected vistas: blue-hazed hills and endless rolling forests abounding with wildlife. Even the hated kudzu vine was beautiful now, carpet-thick in the ditches, blossoming in purple. Beneath the hickories and turkey oaks flashed an occasional cloud of white dogwood. The road straightened, then doglegged, angled uphill and down, but she knew the route as if she'd driven it every day. Somehow she'd never forgotten where his house was, once it was pointed out to her.

His driveway twisted through a stretch of some five acres of untainted wildwood before arching around in a loop that brought her to his front door. She turned off the car, then peered up at the house, feeling a knot tighten her stomach. Slowly she opened her door and stood for a long time in its lee while staring over the roof of the car at the sheer cliff-like stretch of diagonal cedar siding, the irregular roofline, the ebony doors and railed ramp. She removed her sunglasses and studied further. How odd—the place seemed familiar. Yet this was the closest to it she'd ever been. The smell of the woods was rich and fecund. Her gaze lifted to the heavens—cedars and sassafrass trees and one venerable magnolia at least 150 years old.

Drawing a deep, shaky breath, Rachel slammed the car door, slipped her glasses on and made her feet move toward the wooden ramp.

She came up into a deep ensconsing entry, holding two redwood tubs of boxwood that were badly in need of watering and glanced up at the only window facing this side, the large hexagon above the doors. A faint memory shivered through her. *Don't be silly,* she thought. *How can you remember something you've never seen?* Then she quickly rang the bell before she could lose her courage.

Two minutes passed and nothing happened—except Rachel became aware of a tiny pain at the back of her head—tension. *He's probably out on the lake with his daughter.* She rang again and felt a trickle of sweat drizzle down the center of her back while the seconds ticked past and a woodpecker thwacked away someplace in the trees behind her.

Suddenly the door was jerked open and there stood Tommy Lee, looking as if he was recovering from a four-day drunk and wishing he'd died instead. His hair was smashed, face grizzled by an unkempt beard, shirt dangling limp and wrinkled and unbuttoned. The knees of his jeans were buckled and his feet were bare. He stood staring at her as if she were a reincarnation.

"Rachel, my God, you came!"

"Yes. You invited me, remember?"

"But I never thought you would." Unconsciously, he closed a single button at the waist of the shirt, which only pronounced its hapless condition.

"The house was driving me crazy, it was so quiet. And the lake sounded good."

He remained in the open doorway as if too surprised to orient himself. She felt the rush of con-

ditioned air cooling the fronts of her legs and wondered how long he intended to stand gaping at her.
"Am I intruding?" she asked, tilting her head
slightly.

Abruptly he jerked awake. "Oh...no. No!"
He stepped back. "Not at all. I was asleep. Come
in." He finger-combed his hair while she cautiously entered. When the door closed she found herself
in an enormous entry and peered up at a contemporary brass and smoked-glass fixture hanging before the hex window from a height of eighteen
feet. She removed her sunglasses and glanced at
what she could see of the rest of the place from
here: a lot of wood, windows and staggered levels.
The house was silent as a tomb as Rachel's gaze
made a circle and came back to him. Their eyes
met. Tommy Lee's hand still rested on the fancy
doorknob. He flashed her a self-conscious smile,
which she returned with a quavering one of her
own, then dropped her eyes to the floor only to en-
counter the bare feet she recognized from all those
carefree days of swimming at City Park. His second toes were longer than the big toes, and his feet
were shaded now with dark hair. Quickly she
glanced up at the living room, which overhung the
entry.

"Come in." He gestured her ahead of him, up
six steps into a room that looked worse than its
owner, if possible. Dirty glasses, full ashtrays and
worn clothes littered the furniture. The carpet,
though dense, hadn't been touched by a vacuum

cleaner in weeks, and the hundreds of dollars'
worth of potted plants along the glass wall were
drooping, drying up and dusty. Newspapers were
scattered upon the expanse of sofa, which turned
two corners and seemed to sprawl forever, its
mother lode of ottomans creating a veritable field
of cushions before a glorious fireplace. Glancing
at the array of flotsam, Rachel wondered how
Tommy Lee could possibly manage to look so neat
in public when his entire wardrobe seemed to be
flung around his living room.

She glanced back uncertainly and stopped in her
tracks.

"I wasn't expecting company," he explained,
and moved around her to scrape an armful of garments off the back of the davenport.

"You told me your daughter was coming for the
weekend."

"Yes, she was, but at the last minute her mother
decided not to let her." His eyes dropped to the
shirts in his hands, then wandered off with a dismal
expression to some distant point across the lake. "I
was going to come home Friday night and get everything in shape before Beth got here, but when she
called to say she wasn't coming it seemed pointless."

Somehow she believed him, that he hadn't in-
vented Beth's visit to lure her here with a false
sense of security. His eyes swung back to Rachel
and he seemed to make a conscious effort to put
away his troubled thoughts. "But even though
she's not here, I'd still like you to stay."

In this? she thought. The place smelled like an unaired saloon—stale smoke, used filters and alcoholic dregs, and even if she could find a spot to sit on that davenport, there wasn't a single place to do so without putting her feet up. Furthermore, she didn't want to be next after the woman with the red earrings.

Sensing that she was close to having a change of heart, he hurriedly moved around the room, leaning over the back of the sofa to sweep up newspapers, socks and neckties. "Just give me a few minutes and I'll run upstairs and grab a quick shower, okay?" He straightened with his arms full and appealed, "Now don't go away, okay?"

She shook her head and dredged up a faint smile while he gazed at her hopefully, backing away. Then he turned and with a flash of shirttail, bounded up a stairway and out of sight.

She looked around, reluctant to sit down on anything, though the room was luxurious at its core. She moved around the corners of the U-shaped sofa, studying the dirty glasses, the dried rings where others had been, the dust caught and held in gray overlapping circles, the empty matchbooks and full ashtrays. Coming to one glass that was still sweating, she reached down and touched it. It was still cold. She held it to her nose and sniffed. Gin, diluted by melted ice. She set it down distastefully and dropped her eyes to the sofa. The picture was clear: a depressed alcoholic, lying in an inert sprawl, sipping away his lonely weekend while the cobwebs collected around him, and his mind and body dissipated.

It had been a mistake to come here.

She turned her back on the living room and moved toward the end of the fireplace wall where the dining area was announced by caned chairs surrounding a fruitwood table. Empty containers from take-out food lay amid his unopened mail, a half-eaten bag of cheese curls and an open jar of peanuts. *He doesn't eat right,* she thought, and the realization saddened her as she gazed at two cold French fries and a blob of dried-up ketchup. A fingernail clipper lay beside them, and the sight of it rent her heart as she pictured him here at the table, clipping his nails in silence, then eating his suppers alone.

She turned to glance at the working end of the kitchen, but the cabinets held only dirty glasses and an array of booze bottles, all partially empty. Again she closed her eyes, wishing she had sensibly stayed away.

She sat on one of the cane and chrome chairs and turned her eyes to the lake, to something that was pleasant and clean and told no tales. From overhead came the sound of the shower, then in a few minutes the buzz of an electric razor, and in record time Tommy Lee's footsteps thumped down the stairs.

At first he thought she'd left, for the living room was empty, and as he raced through it his heart seemed to stop. But then he caught sight of

her at the kitchen table and his shoulders slumped
with relief. How many years had he pictured
Rachel here? The sight of her with her tanned legs
crossed, a white sandal hanging from her toes, a
delicate elbow resting on the table edge, seemed
too good to be true.

"I'm sorry I kept you waiting, Rachel."

"I've been enjoying the view."

He looked down his chest. "I dressed for the
water. I wasn't sure what you wanted to do."

He wore white swimming trunks and a matching
terrycloth coverup snapped at the waist, revealing
a V of skin with far more hair than he'd had on his
chest the last time she'd seen it—and some of it
glinting silver in the light from the long windows.
His hair was neatly combed and, from this angle,
as thick as it had been in high school. But as he approached she made out the wiry texture of the gray
at his temples and was surprised to find it not altogether unpleasing.

She forced her eyes away. "I brought a bathing
suit. It's in the car. But I . . . I expected Beth to be
coming along."

Her reluctance was so obvious that he felt obliged to give her a choice. "Do you want to put it
on?"

No, she thought, *not anymore. Not since walking in here and realizing your life-style is precisely
what it's purported to be, and nothing I want to
become involved with.*

"I'll run out and get it for you," he offered

with boyish eagerness. And seeing how much it meant to him to have her here, she relented.

"No, I'll go."

She felt his eyes follow her as she arose and crossed the living room, moved down the steps and outside. When the door closed behind her, she tipped her head back against it and sucked in a long breath. Tears stung her eyes. *Oh, Tommy Lee... Tommy Lee. We can never go back.* Her nostrils flared and she opened her eyes to see the tips of the trees blurred as she contemplated the loneliness she had just witnessed. *What am I doing?* she wondered as she made her way to the car and reached inside for a wide-mouthed straw tote-bag. But something made her retrace her steps up the ramp to the shiny black doors.

He had put away the pile of newspapers while she was gone, and she caught him carrying dirty ashtrays and glasses to the kitchen. Their eyes met, then swerved apart.

"You can use the guest bedroom upstairs at the first landing."

Her footsteps were muffled by the deep pile of the indigo carpeting. Against the white walls and natural wood, it was stunning. At the first landing an unexpected window cranny looked out over a steeply canting roof, and a potted fig tree drooped before it. She peered around a doorway into a beautifully decorated bedroom of eggshell, muted blue and brown, its double bed covered with a geometric quilted spread whose design continued

in a mountain of throw pillows, then up the wall
between two long, narrow windows decorated
with nothing but a pair of mobiles.

The tiny metal sailfish circled slowly as she
stepped inside the room and surveyed a bare-
topped Danish dresser and chest of drawers with
natural waxed wood finish, costly lamps and a
large glass-fronted photo of a pair of well-used toe
shoes with their ribbons worn and sides mis-
shapen.

Beth's room—she must be a dancer.

For a moment his Beth and their Beth melded
into one, and she had the awesome feeling that she
was stepping into her own daughter's room, and
again that feeling that she'd been here before. But
she shook herself and crossed to a far doorway
that led into a lovely bathroom with blue fixtures
and a shower curtain of the same design as that of
the bedspread. Lush blue towels hung from the
towel bars, but as she moved closer she saw that
their folds bore a line of dust. At the foot of the
tub another window looked out over the roof and
the shimmering lake beyond. Over the tub hung a
dead ivy.

What a beautiful house, she thought, glancing
once more around the bedroom and bath. But
their stark, unused look contained a message as
poignant as that of the abject disorder downstairs.

It was a house that cried out for life.

She tried to put the thought from her mind as
she changed into her swimsuit. But when she was

slipping on her bottoms she confronted the cesarean-section scar on her stomach, realizing afresh what an irony it was that the birth of her and Tommy Lee's baby had left a permanent mark as a reminder that their baby was the only one she'd ever have. She tugged the waistband into place and told herself to stop thinking senseless things about the past. But again, when the halter was tied behind her neck, Rachel studied her reflection in the mirror, then cupped both breasts, pushing them high, dismayed to see that even doing this, she could create no cleavage. It was impossible not to remember that at sixteen she had been fuller-breasted than now, or to imagine that Tommy Lee would not notice.

Her distraught eyes scolded those in the mirror. You foolish, middle-aged woman, what are you doing? You shouldn't even be here in the first place, and you're looking for cleavage? She dropped her hands and covered herself with the beach jacket, glanced disparagingly at the glimpse of skin still revealed above and below, sighed, grabbed her towel, slipped on her thongs again and left the room.

In the hall she paused and glanced at the carpeted stairs that continued up two more levels with windows and potted plants announcing each floor. Steps, handrailings and white walls rose to the heights of the house, which had appeared so tall from outside. Tommy Lee's bedroom must be up there. And it must have as stunning a view as that from an aerie.

It struck her then, why she'd sensed a feeling of déjà vu about the house, and her head snapped back as she stared up the steps, trying to calculate where the chimney flue rose up through the walls, if the master bedroom had a fireplace...a deck overlooking the lake. It struck her like lightning. *My God, it's our house! The one we planned together when we were starry-eyed teenagers!* For a moment she felt dizzy, and her stomach seemed to tilt. *No, you must be wrong, Rachel.* But a quick mental assessment of the rooms below confirmed it. This was their dream house. It had just taken her some time to recognize it beneath the clutter and loneliness. She returned to the lower level feeling shaken, and though she thought she'd approached soundlessly, Tommy Lee's voice called, "I'm out here, Rachel."

She found him in the kitchen, a black towel slung over his shoulder as he hunkered before the open refrigerator while packing a cooler. When she rounded the corner he lifted his eyes to her, dropped them slowly down her tanned legs, swallowed in a way that made his Adam's apple thrust, then returned his attention to the interior of the refrigerator. "What would you like to drink? I've got beer, rum, vod—"

"Do you have limes?"

He looked up again. "Sure. Gin and tonic with a twist of lime?"

"Just plain tap water with a twist of lime will be fine."

Again he went on piling cold beer into the red-

and-white cooler, and as she counted the cans, she wondered how many he intended to take. From the crisper he took two limes, dropped them into the cooler and asked, "Perrier water okay?"

She nodded and several small bottles joined the cans, then he snapped the cooler shut and stood up.

"Ready?"

She forced a smile and he gestured toward the door, following her to slide the heavy glass panel aside and allow her to step through before him. They crossed a slatted redwood deck, moved down steps to a grassy stretch of lawn and on toward a dock where a black-and-white speedboat waited beneath a yellow canopy. He tossed his towel down onto a seat, then presented a palm to help her board. To ignore it would have made more of an issue than to touch him. His fingers clamped hers tightly as she stepped down and the boat rocked. Though the contact was brief, it left a residue of awareness that Rachel tried to put from her mind.

"Sit there." He pointed to the front passenger seat, then busied himself freeing both bow and stern lines before leaping down to join her. She was extremely conscious of his long bare legs and feet, peppered with dark hair, and of the casual way his glance washed over her as he squeezed through the small opening between the seats, his thigh nearly brushing her shoulder, before he settled himself behind the wheel with the cooler close at hand and inserted the key into the ignition.

The touch of a button brought the soft buzz of the motor lowering, then the inboard growled to life, followed by the swish of water purling against the hull. The lake was as calm as a glass of water, and as the boat got under way it skimmed the surface with scarcely a vibration. He eased the throttle forward and Rachel's hair lifted, then flurried back. Instinctively she brought her nose into the air, sniffing, feeling life flowing back into her veins as she dangled an arm above the water.

Tommy Lee turned to watch her as her eyes closed and she nosed the wind. Lord a'mighty, had there ever been a woman as perfect? She'd been a knockout in high school, but age had only refined her fragile beauty. She had weathered the years so much more gracefully than he had. And she'd achieved a reputation of highest regard in both her personal and business life, while he had become merely déclassé. It seemed quite unbelievable that she was here with him at last, for in spite of all his dreams, he'd never really believed it would happen.

Rachel hung her head back, felt the cool droplets spray her fingertips, heard the snick of a lighter, then caught the faint drift of cigarette smoke. Even with her eyes closed, she knew he was studying her.

The boat suddenly thrust forward with a jerk that lifted its nose above the water and snapped Rachel's head farther back. Her eyes flew open and she shot a look at Tommy Lee.

He had a cigarette clamped between china-white teeth while his broad teasing smile shone devil-ishly. Left hand on the wheel, right on the throt-tle, he studied her with a challenge in his glinting eyes.

"Let's cool off." The words were distorted around the filter as he spoke, but they gave him a rakish appeal much as he'd had in those days when they'd roared off, carefree, in his '57 Chev.

A tiny smirk appeared at the corners of Rachel's mouth. "You always did like speed."

"Always!" he shouted above the wind, while she herself became exhilarated by it as the boat gained momentum then leveled off with the flut-tering wind pressing against her ears, lifting and swirling her hair.

It was wonderful! Releasing! She turned to him and shouted to be heard above the motor and the thump of the hull bouncing on the water. "I can remember my daddy saying to you, 'Now drive carefully, and don't speed.' Then we'd get one block away from the houses and fly like the wind."

He laughed, throwing his head back while tak-ing the cigarette out of his mouth as an ash flew backward. "I still love it!" he shouted.

"So I've heard!"

His eyes returned to hers and they measured each other silently. Then he shouted, "Do you want me to slow down?"

By now the minute ripples on the surface of the

water had become nothing more than a blur, and the rumbling inboard a dynamo. She pushed the whipping hair back from her temple with the flat of one hand and yelled, "No, it feels wonderful. I think it's exactly what I needed."

But he couldn't hear her and leaned across the aisle, lowering his ear.

She leaned close enough to smell fresh after-shave. "I said, it feels wonderful! I think it's exactly what I needed!"

He straightened, smiled wider and warned, "Hang on!" Then he anchored the cigarette between his teeth, dropped his hand to the throttle and pushed it full forward. Their hair became flags, their jackets billowed sails. Their bodies jiggled as they rocketed toward a vanishing point on the far horizon, wrapped in the ebullient sensation of near-flight.

Tommy Lee cramped the wheel and suddenly Rachel was high above him, the water spuming wide from the hull, churning out a rabid wake behind them. She laughed and he tossed an appreciative glance her way, then spun the wheel in the opposite direction. She made an owl face at him and pressed a hand to her stomach while rolling her eyes. His answering laugh sounded faintly above the roar of the wind in her ears and the thrumming cylinders, then they were snaking right and left, right and left, lifting and falling until Rachel's stomach felt giddy. Again she laughed, gay and unfettered for the first time in months, letting the reckless ride take her deliciously off kilter. But finally she reached out and squeezed Tommy Lee's forearm, shaking her head, pressing a hand to her stomach once more. He straightened the wheel but left the speed where it was until Rachel finally reached out and covered his hand on the throttle with her own, drawing back both until the boat quieted and slowed and drifted in the abrupt lift of its own backwash.

In the sudden quiet their combined laughter drifted above the lake. As if directed by a baton, they stilled simultaneously and found themselves gazing at each other. At that moment Rachel realized her hand still rested on his, the pads of her fingers contouring his knuckles, and she withdrew it as casually as possible, but not before his eyes fell to the sight of their joined hands on the throttle, then came back to her face.

"It's nice to hear you laugh again," he said.

"It's been a long time since I have. It feels good."

She thought for a moment he was going to touch her; the look in his eyes said he was thinking about it. But then, abruptly, he twisted to fetch himself a beer from the cooler.

"Want one?" He popped the top and tossed it over his shoulder into the water.

"No, thank you." She bit back the reprimand about littering the lake with pop-tops and told herself it was none of her business. She was only spending one afternoon with him. "Just lime water."

He wedged the can between his legs, tight against his swim trunks, while twisting to reach for the cooler again. Realizing her gaze had followed the can of beer, she turned sharply to study the water beyond her side of the boat until a cold touch on her arm announced the lime water.

They cruised the lake, too aware of each other, yet maintaining a cautious distance at all times. She counted the cigarettes he smoked, the butts he threw into the lake, the beers he downed. When he'd begun his third, she moved restlessly and suggested, "Why don't we swim?" thinking that if he was swimming he couldn't be drinking.

"Anything you say," he complied. "Anyplace in particular?"

"You know the lake better than I do."

"All right. Hang on." His latest cigarette butt went the way of the others, and again the boat shot forward at hair-pulling speed until a few minutes later Tommy Lee throttled down and killed the engine completely.

Rachel glanced around quizzically. "Here?" she asked. They were in an inlet with trees all around, but it was a long swim to shore in any given direction, and there wasn't a soul in sight.

"You want to go somewhere else?"

"I thought we'd go to one of the beaches."

"With all those people? You really want to?"

She turned to find his shaded lenses facing her, but couldn't make out his eyes behind them. "No...no, this is fine."

"Okay, I'll drop anchor." At the touch of his finger, an electric buzz accompanied the soft "shrrr" of the anchor rope paying out. Silence followed, vast upon the sunny stretch of the blue water with its canopy of matching sky. The sun beat down and shimmered while Tommy Lee downed the last of his beer, fished a styrofoam floatboard from beneath the foredeck, tossed it over the side, leaned down again and came up with a portable ladder.

"You first." He waved Rachel aft, and she slipped between their two seats toward the rear of the boat, then turned to find him bending to hang the ladder on the side. Straightening, he was already yanking at the single snap at his waist, and a minute later the terrycloth jacket lay on the seat and Rachel found herself confronted with the entire stretch of his bare chest, mesmerized by the dense Y of pewter-gray while it struck her again how much more masculine a man is at forty than at sixteen.

Guiltily, she turned her back while releasing the hook at her waist and removing her cover-up. She found it difficult to confront the changes wrought upon them by the years, not only her thinness, but his heaviness.

"Last one in buys two bucks' worth of gas," he said quietly.

She looked back over her shoulder then turned to find him with a nostalgic look on his face. Years ago, when they'd crowded into somebody's car with a gang of kids and driven out to City Park to swim, it had always been the battle hue. Nobody had money then, and how happy they'd all been. Now they both had all the money they needed. . . .

She searched for something to say, anything that would lift the heavy weight of remembrance and bear her back to the present. But the past created a tremendous gravity between them, and she sensed him deliberately training his eyes above her shoulders. She knew what control it took to keep them there, because it was equally hard for her to keep her eyes above his waist.

Attempting to sever the skein of sexuality that seemed suddenly to bind them, she quipped, "If I were you I'd take my glasses off before you issue challenges." Then with a deft step she was over the side, diving neatly into the deep, cool sanctuary of Cedar Creek Lake. She heard the muffled surge of his body following, then opened her eyes to bubbles and blueness, kicking toward the surface while Tommy Lee was still on his way down. Emerging, she skinned her hands down her face, then saw his head pop up six feet away.

He swung around, throwing his head sharply, sending droplets flying in a glistening arc from his hair.

"Waugh! That's a shock!" he bellowed.

"But much better," she added. "Now I can see your eyes at last."

"I didn't know you wanted to or I'd have taken off my glasses an hour ago."

"They're very attractive, but it's hard to tell what a person's thinking when you can't see his eyes. Can you see without them?"

"Enough to know where I'm going. Come on."

He struck off at an energetic crawl while she followed at the carefully paced stroke of a well-tuned swimmer. In no time at all she met him coming back, puffing. She chuckled and continued on a leisurely turn around the boat, passing him once, twice, then three times while he floated on the miniature surfboard. His arms were crossed upon it, feet drifting idly as she came around for the fourth time and joined him.

"You're back." He smiled.

Rachel dipped below the surface, emerged nose first, her hair seal-slick, and crossed her arms on the opposite end of the four-foot board.

"Yes, I'm back." She propped her chin on her crossed wrists. "You didn't last very long."

"I'm all out of shape."

"You shouldn't be. Not with the lake right here. You should be swimming every day."

"It looks like you do."

"Just about."

"It shows. Rachel, you look great."

The water washed over the surfboard and she swished it lazily with one hand, her chin still propped on the other. "I told you. I'm too thin."

"Not to suit me." His eyes without glasses were extremely sparkly, almost beautiful with a wealth of deep-brown lashes shot with droplets of glittering water. With his chin on a fist, he reached his free hand to swish the water along the surface of the board too, missing her fingers by a mere inch. "Do you remember when I used to see if my hands could span your waist?"

She watched his hand brushing near hers. "Mmm...in those days I'd have been ecstatic if they had. But now, when they probably could, it would only point out that I'm shriveling up."

Tommy Lee laughed, his teeth white against his dark-skinned face. "Shriveling up? You're a long way from shriveled up, Rachel. I'd say you're in your prime."

"My prime," she said thoughtfully, "That's a palliative offered to people in their forties who don't want to be. I feel shriveled up after the last two years."

His hand stilled and his expression turned concerned.

"Was it bad, Rachel, going through all that with Owen?"

She shrugged and the motion brought a wave of cool water between her arms and the board. "At the time you don't stop to wonder if it's hard. You just do what you have to do, carry on from day to day. Toward the end, when his pain got worse...." She stopped, mesmerized by the stunning brown eyes studying her across the float board. "I didn't come out here to talk about that. I came to forget it."

His cool, wet fingers captured and held hers

loosely. "I'm sorry you had to go through that, Rachel. When I heard he had cancer and how bad it got, there were a hundred times I wanted to call you, just to say I was thinking of you, and ask if you needed anything—if I could help you in any way. But I figured your daddy was there with you, and what was there I could do for you anyway?"

Rachel blinked, focusing wide eyes on his. "You did? You really did? It's an odd feeling to think you were following the events of my life all those years."

"But you knew what was going on in mine, too."

"Only what I read in the papers and what people told me. I didn't go driving past your house."

His fingers were warm as he continued holding hers. His thumb moved along her knuckles then circled her diamond before he went on reflectively. "Funny how people who remember we used to date never missed a chance to tell me what was going on in your life. Sometimes I wanted to tell them to keep their damn mouths shut, keep all their social tidbits to themselves. I didn't want to know how happy and successful you were becoming with Owen. Other times I fed off it. And, naturally, I'd drive past your house and wonder."

Rachel's heart lilted. He was much more honest than she. There were times when she'd experienced some of the same feelings, only she was reluctant to admit it. "Wonder?" she prompted now.

"If he knew about us."

For a moment she didn't answer, thinking of the scar on her stomach that could hardly have been hidden from a husband.

"Did he, Rachel?" Tommy Lee asked softly.

"He knew I'd had the baby, but he didn't know whose it was."

"Wasn't he curious?"

"We made a pact early in our marriage that the issue would never come up again, once we'd talked it out."

"It says a lot about a man that he can live with a question like that unanswered and never let it come between you."

She wasn't about to tell him that it *had* been between them, always. They may not have talked about it, but there had been hundreds of times when she'd caught Owen studying her across a room, and she'd known instinctively what he was thinking.

Tommy Lee's eyes pierced her across the speckled blue surface dividing them. "If you had been my wife all that time, I'd have gone crazy wondering."

"From the things you told me the night you talked about your wives, I would have said you weren't a jealous man."

His fingers pulled her hand closer to his chin and he said raggedly, "They weren't you, Rachel."

"Don't," she breathed, trying to pull her hand away. But he held it fast.

"Don't? Don't for how long? Until you really are shriveled up? Until your debt to Owen is paid—whatever it might be? Until you decide to take off his rings?" His hand squeezed so hard the rings dug into her skin. "How long do you intend to wear them, Rachel?"

Her heart was racing faster than before. "I don't know. It's...it's too soon."

"Is it? Let's see." Without warning, Tommy Lee gave the float board a push that sent it sideways, and in one swift kick brought himself only inches from Rachel's nose. Her heart hadn't time to crack out a warning before one powerful hand circled her neck and scooped her close. He kissed her once, a hard, impromptu meeting of two water-slicked mouths while the wavelets lapped at their chins, accentuating how warm their lips were. During the brief contact their legs instinctively moved to keep them afloat, and the sleek texture of skin on skin brought shivery sensations.

The kiss ended and somehow they were each hanging onto the float board with one hand. Rachel's surprised lips dropped open as Tommy Lee pulled back, staring into her eyes. Her hair coiled around his fingers like a silken tether while he moved a thumb just behind her ear. Water beaded on his dark, spiky lashes and gleamed upon his cheeks. They stared at each other, breathing hard, for several stunned seconds, then Tommy Lee's hand drifted from her neck down one slick shoulder, and beneath the water his calf whisked between her knees, then was gone. "Come on. . . ." He smiled. "Let's play." And with a twisting, sideways dive, he disappeared beneath the surface.

It had been an elementary kiss. His tongue hadn't even touched her, yet she was trembling inside and felt hot and threatened and insidiously sexual. Needing to cool off, Rachel, too, did a surface dive, then took several enormous breast strokes underwater, hoping to come up a safe distance from him.

When she nosed into the daylight again he was trying to get to his feet on the surfboard—with little success. From behind, she watched him battle it, wondering how many women he'd kissed in all these years, and if his reputation had women chasing him, or if he did all the chasing. In particular, she wondered about the woman to whom he'd given the red earrings.

"What did you do that for?" she shouted, treading water.

"What'd I do?" The surfboard rocked and bucked him off. Immediately he began trying to master it again, giving it all his attention.

"You kissed me, Gentry, and you know it!"

"You call that a kiss? Hell, that was barely a nibble. I've learned a little more than that since we were teenagers."

"I'll just bet you have. And with how many different women?"

"I lost count years ago."

"And you have no compunction about admitting it, do you?"

"None whatsoever, because you could become my last if you wanted to."

He had one knee on the board, his backside pointing her way as he struggled to make it to his feet. With several deft strokes she swam up behind him, hollered, "Not on your life, you no-count Lothario!" and gaily tipped him over.

Instead of bobbing up, he caught her ankles and hauled her under. She grabbed enough air to survive, but felt as if her lungs would explode as they struggled. His teeth nibbled the arch of one foot and his chin tickled it while she writhed and fought, needing to laugh. Their antics stirred up a froth of bubbles in the silent blue depths until at last she coiled around and pinched his nipple hard. He released her and they shot to the surface like geysers, both of them gasping and laughing, hair hanging everywhere.

"Ouch, damn you!" he scolded, rubbing the wounded spot.

"Good enough for you! You nearly drowned me, pulling me under like that."

"I just wanted to find out if you were still ticklish."

"Now you know, so leave me alone," she spouted in mock indignation, striking out for the ladder on the boat with him right behind her.

"In all the same old spots?" he teased as she lunged up onto the first rung, streaming water into his face. He caught her around the waist and hauled her back down with an enormous splash. Again they became a tangle of arms and legs and slithery skin as his hands snaked along her ribs and his arms circled her playfully. But in the midst of the skirmish they suddenly fell still, staring at each other with a gripping sense of rediscovery while the only sound was that of water lapping against the boat. One of Tommy Lee's hands held a ladder rung, the other arm circled her waist, and her hands quite naturally had fallen against his chest where the wet hair felt as elusive as mercury. Their eyes remained fixed upon each other, taking in gleaming skin, tangled hair, dripping faces and rapt expressions. Their drifting thighs brushed. A streak of water slipped down Rachel's cheek and his eyes followed till it fell over her lip and the pink tip of her tongue curled up to sip it away. "Oh, Rachel," he breathed softly, spreading his palm wide and warm upon her cool, sleek back, drawing her infinitesimally closer...closer....

But she pressed a palm to his chest and turned aside. "Please," she begged breathlessly, "don't kiss me again, Tommy Lee. Please."

Beneath the water their limbs brushed again, washed by the current they'd stirred up. His thighs were silicon-sleek and distractingly inviting. His gaze covered her face and she knew it beseeched her for more than she'd come here to give. At the small of her back his hand caressed the bare skin, then slid up between her shoulder blades.

"Are you sure you mean that?"

"Be sensible, Tommy Lee."

"I've never been sensible in forty-one years, why should I start now?"

And though she, too, would have welcomed tossing sense aside for a brief time with him, she realized she had the power to wound him terribly. "Listen, I came out here today because I was very lonely and I...I needed someone. But I never meant for this to happen. Honestly I didn't, Tommy Lee."

His eyes traveled across her face, as if memorizing each feature. "If you needed me, only to make you laugh for one afternoon, that's a start."

A start of what, she wondered, but realized if she continued seeing him the answer was understood. Yet he *had* made her laugh, for the first time in months. And in the end, he'd made her forget Owen and the cares that had beseiged her for so long. And though his kiss had been startling, and not unwelcome, much of the excitement had been generated by nostalgia, and by the fact that he was socially off limits to a woman like her.

"I'm starved," he said, with an abrupt swing of mood and a crooked smile. "What do you say to some catfish and hush puppies?"

"You still go wild for catfish and hush puppies?"

He grinned, squeezed her waist once and answered in one of his favorite catch phrases from long ago, "You betchum, Red Rider." And once again Rachel was laughing, charmed by the Tommy Lee she'd known so long ago. And oh, he could be so charming. It was no wonder the ladies liked him.

CHAPTER SIX

THEY WENT TO CATFISH CORNER, a tin-roofed shanty out in the country at the intersection of two county roads off the Huntsville Highway. They took his car, and he drove it exactly like they all said he did—too fast, too carelessly, and always with that everlasting cigarette crooked through one finger. Yet Rachel felt safe with him.

At Catfish Corner the crowd was mostly black, friendly and vocal. "Hey Tommy Lee!" someone shouted as soon as they entered the smoky, low-ceilinged room. "Been wonderin' when we'd see y'all around these parts again. C'mon over, boy, and bring yer lady with ya!"

Tommy Lee waved at the gregarious black man whose backside was twice as wide as the red plastic seat of the barstool, but he took Rachel's elbow and guided her to a table instead. "If it's all the same to you, Eugene, I'm gonna keep my lady away from a sweet talker like you. No sense takin' chances."

A chorus of laughter went up from the group at the bar, while Tommy Lee directed Rachel to a vintage kitchen set with chrome legs and gray

marbled plastic seats amid a group of others much
like it. He pulled out her chair, then seated himself
across from her. At their elbow a crude window
opened outward, hinged at the top and braced
with a stick of wood. The trees pressed close to the
building and insects worried themselves against
the screen. A potted candle in a red glass snifter
sent flickering light up to join that from the neon
beer signs around the bar and the weak splashes of
color from bare gold bulbs overhead.

When they were seated, Tommy Lee grinned
teasingly. "Well, there's one thing you can't ac-
cuse me of, and that's trying to impress a lady
with atmosphere. I brought you here because Big
Sam fries the meanest catfish this side of the
Mason-Dixon Line. And I don't know about you,
but I worked up an appetite swimming."

Rachel studied the hand-written menu to cover
her disillusionment over his choice of restaurants.
"Mmm...me too." But she felt she needn't put
catfish in her mouth to taste it—the smell was
everywhere, mixed with a strong odor of onion-
flavored grease.

"Rachel?"

She met his eyes and found him still grinning,
one shoulder pitched lower than the other as he
leaned back against the chair. "Don't judge until
you've eaten, okay?"

Before she could answer, a buxom woman appeared, her breasts the size of cantaloupes, earrings
the size of handcuffs. She laid her hand familiarly

on Tommy Lee's shoulder. "Well, I declare, if it isn't the most handsome honky to put foot in Catfish Corner since the last time he was here. What you mean by stayin' scarce all this time?" And she shamelessly leaned over and kissed Tommy Lee full on the lips.

Rachel watched, shocked, as his hand rested on her hip while her breasts brushed his chest. She checked to see if others were watching, but just then the man behind the rectangular window dividing the main room from the kitchen, bellowed, "Hey, Daisy, you leave off kissin' the customers so's they can order catfish, you hear?"

Everyone at the bar laughed, and Daisy lingeringly raised her head, cocked a wrist on one hip and toyed with the hair above Tommy Lee's ear. Her eyes appeared hooded and sultry as she looked down into his smiling face and drawled, "We want him to come back now, don't we?"

Rachel was horrified. Never in her life had she seen a white man kiss a black woman, yet Tommy Lee did it with obvious relish. When Daisy finally disengaged herself, he belatedly reminded her, "I've got a lady with me tonight, Daisy. Meet Rachel."

Daisy turned laconically, still with one hand on her hip, the other cocked at the wrist. "Don't pay no never-mind to me, honey. I been kissin' your man since before there was catfish in that creek outside. He's like a son to me."

Tommy Lee gave her a nudge and ordered,

"Get out of here, Daisy, and bring us two orders of the usual, and a glass of lime water for the lady."

"Lime water! What you think we runnin' here, a fruit stand?"

"Just ice water then. Now scat."

She turned away with a chuckle and sauntered off while Rachel watched her bulging backside wriggle in tight cerise-colored pants. When her eyes returned to Tommy Lee, she found him smirking at her.

"Just like a son, huh?" she repeated dryly, cocking an eyebrow.

"That's right."

Rachel pulled a hard paper napkin from a metal dispenser, scissored it between two fingers and cocked her wrist while handing it to him. "I think you'd better wipe that shiny purple lipstick off... *son*. We wouldn't want it to get in your food and poison you."

Tommy Lee laughed while rubbing the garish lipstick off his mouth. "Don't think anything of Daisy. She's Big Sam's wife—that was him hollering through the porthole from the kitchen."

"His wife!" Rachel was shocked at the familiarity just displayed under a husband's nose.

"She kisses all the customers that way. And every time she does Big Sam hollers through the kitchen window, and everybody at the bar laughs on cue. That's how it is out here. We're all friends."

But Rachel couldn't help harboring reservations at his choice of friends.

During their wait for the meal, Tommy Lee had two drinks, then another while they ate. The food was exceptional, and served in such sumptuous portions that Rachel barely put a dent in hers. Tommy Lee eyed her plate and asked, "You all done?" At her nod he inquired, "Mind if I clean up the rest?"

While he did she thought about his eating habits, probably fasting all day, living on alcohol and ice, then feeding on fatty foods in periodic spurts of excess. It was no wonder his physique had suffered. After some consideration she asked, "When was the last time you ate a decent meal?"

He glanced from his plate to her and back again.

"Oh, I didn't mean including this one—it's delicious, really. I just have a feeling your diet is rather slapdash."

He only shrugged, wiped his mouth and lifted his eyes to find her studying him contemplatively. "You don't like it here, do you?"

"Oh, the food was wonderful!" she replied brightly, but coloring.

"You don't have to say it. I know what you're thinking. But I wanted you to know where I've been, who my friends are. . .no secrets."

"Why?"

"Just so you'll know. I find people like these far more genuine than the bigots in town." He tossed his napkin onto his plate. "The country-club set—you can have 'em."

Just then a small black boy bounded to the table and flung himself across Tommy Lee's lap. He looked to be no more than seven years old, had a front tooth missing and wore a stretched-out T-shirt with Darth Vader on the back.

"Hey, Tommy Lee, Tommy Lee, where you been, huh? Been savin' them rocks like you said to, so you'n me can show Darla she ain't so hot! Gots *a-a-a-ll* these." He dumped a double fistful of rocks on the tabletop. "See? They just as flat as pee on a plate."

Tommy Lee's face lit up with laughter, ending with a grin as he indulgently scolded the precocious youngster, "Hey, hey, mustn't talk like that around a lady." He roughed the child's hair and asked, "Where have you been hiding?"

"Mama, she wouldn't let me come out till you was done eatin'." The boy reached up to loop an elbow around Tommy Lee's neck. "You reckon we can make eleven?" He beamed into the man's face with excitement and obvious hero worship.

With one arm coiled around the little boy's waist, Tommy Lee looked across at Rachel and explained, "Darrel and I are trying to find the perfect rock that'll skip eleven times. So far the best we've done is nine. But his sister, Darla, claims she's done ten."

"She ain' done no ten—I know she ain't! She lyin'!" spouted Darrel. "And besides, lookit these what I found."

Tommy Lee sifted through the collection of prize rocks, nudging them around the table while his dark wavy head bent near the much smaller one of black close-cropped curls. "Whoa! This one looks like a prize!" Tommy Lee held it aloft.

"Can we go out and try it now?"

Tommy Lee smiled down at the boy. "Reckon it's too dark to see tonight."

"You come back on Sunday? Then we c'n show Darla? Please Tommy Lee?"

"Today's Sunday," he reminded the child.

"But I mean *next* Sunday, like we used to. And you can stay for dinner after church and we can all play ball and—"

"Come to think of it, I do have next Sunday free. You tell Darla she'd better be ready to put her money where her mouth is." He affectionately swatted the boy's backside and watched him barrel off toward the kitchen. "He's Sam and Daisy's boy. A bundle of dynamite." At last he dragged his eyes back to Rachel, who wore a slightly amazed expression. "Something wrong, Rachel?"

"No. . . ." Rachel sat up straighter. "No." But after adding it all up she queried, "You come out here and go to church with them on Sundays?"

He deliberated silently for some time and finally answered, "Sometimes. They've got a nice little white clapboard church out in the pines about a mile from here. Well, you know what those little Baptist country churches are like. Peaceful. I prefer it to the brick one downtown."

She studied him silently for a while, then it all came clear.

"Your surrogate family, Tommy Lee?" she questioned softly.

He reached for a cigarette, took some time to light it and blow out a cloud of smoke, then studied her thoughtfully before answering, "I guess you might say that."

Rachel's heart wrenched with pity. He had children of his own, yet he came out here to play ball and skip pebbles. He had a church of his own, yet he came out here to attend theirs. He had parents of his own, yet he shunned them, though it obviously cost him much to do so. She pictured Gaines and Lily Gentry— Did they long for their son while he gave his affection to a black family who ran a catfish house by Bear Creek? How terribly much they all must be hurting. Suddenly she wanted that hurt mended, for all their sakes.

"Tommy Lee, why don't you go see your mama and daddy?"

He carefully ironed all expression from his face and snorted through his nose.

"But they're getting old, and if I can forgive, why can't you?"

But again they were interrupted. "Beg pardon, ma'am." It was Big Sam, standing beside their table with four green bills in his hand. "Tommy Lee, got the next installment for you on that loan." He proudly peeled off and laid down four five-dollar bills, counting carefully. "Five, ten, fifteen, twenty dollars." He raised a beaming smile to Tommy Lee. "You write that in your book like always?"

"You bet, Sam. And how's the dishwasher running?"

"Runnin' slick as a skinned eel, Tommy Lee. And Daisy, she comes around snugglin' the end of a hot day like this, just thankin' me for not havin' to wash them dishes by hand like she used to."

Tommy Lee laughed, reached for a napkin and wrote something on it, then handed it back to Big Sam. Sam glanced at it, then looked up. "It say the same like it always say?"

"Yessir. Received of Samuel Davis twenty dollars on dishwasher loan. And I put the date there."

"Good." Big Sam pocketed the napkin carefully in the breast patch of his sweat-soaked shirt, then patted it. "See you next week. Darrel say you comin' to dinner. You bring the lady if you want to."

"Thank you, Sam. That's up to her. This is Rachel, a girl I used to go to high school with."

Sam nodded from the waist, three times. "Miss Rachel, how was the catfish and pups?"

"The best I've ever eaten," she replied truthfully, warming to the big man who hovered self-consciously beside the table.

"Got to get back to the kitchen. Y'all come back. Tommy Lee, you bring Miss Rachel back, you hear?"

"I'll do that, Sam. And would you fix me one for the road?"

"I sure will. Comin' right up."

When they were alone again Tommy Lee reached for the check as if to leave, but she covered his hand on the tabletop. "You lent him money to buy a dishwasher for this place?"

His eyes remained carefully noncommittal as they met hers. "He tried to get it in town, but the bank took one look at this tin heap and decided he didn't have either enough collateral or enough education to merit approval of the loan."

Neither of them had to say it to know that as president of the bank, her father was its chief loan officer. Their eyes held while the knowledge flashed between them.

"But how much money can a simple dishwasher cost?"

"Six hundred dollars," he answered, rising from his chair, dropping enough bills on the table that Rachel didn't have to count them to realize they included a more than generous tip.

"Six hundred dollars? And he pays you back twenty dollars at a time?"

"When he can. Sometimes it's five, sometimes ten. He must've had a good week. Should we go?"

She was still trying to digest what she had just learned about her father and about Tommy Lee, as the latter stepped politely behind her chair. On his way out, he picked up a drink from the bar. It had been mixed in a plastic tumbler, which he lifted in a goodbye salute as he opened the door for Rachel.

Outside it was black. Their soles crackled on the gravel as they made their way to the car, which was parked beneath the thick overhanging branches of a catalpa tree, nosing aginst the high bank of Bear Creek, which snuffled along through the darkness. The sound of hundreds of crickets undulated through the night while the scent of the damp creek bank rose up to meet the dust of the dry gravel lot.

After Tommy Lee had politely seen her to her side of the car she watched him in the glow of the overhead light as he slipped behind the wheel, his face introspective now and grim. She found herself evaluating this side of him, which nobody around Russellville saw. The interior of the car went black and she heard the keys touch the ignition. She reached out to touch his warm, bare arm—and immediately felt the muscles tense.

"I'm sorry, Tommy Lee," she said softly. "You were right. I was judging them. I had no right."

"I suppose it's inevitable that you and I do that occasionally—judge people. We are, after all, our parents' children. But I try my damnedest not to anymore."

"Meaning I'm like my father in a lot of ways, is that what you're saying?"

"It's been so many years, Rachel, I really have no way of knowing that. But I hope not."

"He's not altogether bad, Tommy Lee, no matter what you think."

"Probably not. But he'd never take the time to make a run out here and order a platter of catfish to see what the place staked its future on, and to see how damn hard Sam and Daisy work, and that they're the most honest people on the face of the earth."

"Tell me something," she said, curious, yet at the same time sure of what the answer would be even before she asked. "Do you even charge them interest?"

But Tommy Lee mistook her reason for asking. She was every bit Everett Talmadge's daughter, he thought, and it rankled that he couldn't help himself from loving her.

With a flick of his wrist he started the engine. "Rachel, do you have to be told what it does to me when you lay your hand on my arm that way?" She jerked her hand away and clasped it in her lap. He gave one humorless chuckle and said coldly, "That's what I thought," then threw the car into reverse and peeled out of the lot, spraying gravel twenty feet behind. When he straightened the wheel the car fishtailed, and Rachel released a quiet sound of fright. By the faint dash lights she saw him glance her way, then he let up on the gas until they'd slowed to a nearly reasonable speed. But as he studied the headlights, which cut a golden cone through the narrow opening between the close-pressing trees, he added offhandedly,

"Don't worry. If there's one thing in this world I'd never want to hurt, it's you."

Her head snapped around and her heart lifted. All day long he'd been doing that to her, making her emotions vacillate until she was utterly confused about her feelings for him. He had two distinctly different sides, and she was attracted to the one and repelled by the other. Back at Catfish Corner she'd found herself drawn to a Tommy Lee both virtuous and vulnerable. But here she was, another in a long string of women, riding along with the Tommy Lee who'd had more than his share to drink, who was even now sipping something that smelled of pine needles while he wheeled nervelessly down a dark country road, brooding. A man who hadn't the emotional wherewithal to bind the frayed edges of his life and make something more than a financial success of it. A man who was a three-time loser and had rightfully gained one of the most unsavory reputations in the county.

Rachel dropped her head back against the seat, letting her eyes sink shut, while wondering for the hundredth time that day what she was doing here. She heard him light a cigarette, then they rode in silence, locked in their own thoughts.

Just before they reached the turnoff into his place, he lowered the window and slung his empty glass out into the weeds. Rachel sighed and straightened in her seat, looking away. His car negotiated the twists and turns of his driveway, and when he pulled up behind Rachel's car and killed the engine, all was silent.

He propped an elbow on the open window, gripped the edge of the roof and stared straight ahead while Rachel sat hugging herself. Outside the night sounds buzzed and chucked and the smell of cedar was thick. Tommy Lee took a last drag from his cigarette, then set it spiraling in a red-tailed whorl before expelling a last breath of smoke that clearly told of emotional exhaustion. Almost angrily he reached for his door handle and lurched out. She followed suit, and they met near her car, both apprehensive and wary.

"Thank you for everything, Tommy Lee."

Though it was very dark she sensed how tense he was, standing with feet spraddled, hands buried in his back pockets, keeping a safe distance from her.

"Will you come again, Rachel?" he asked tightly.

"I...I don't know. It probably isn't such a good idea."

He released a rush of breath and ran an exasperated hand through his hair. "So you're going to put me through it all again, is that what you're saying?"

"I never meant to *put you through* anything. You say it as if I'm guilty of some gross social misdemeanor, Tommy Lee!"

"I don't know about social misdemeanors, but I do know about feelings." Suddenly he captured her upper arms and brought her to her toes. "God-dammit, Rachel, I love you. I've never stopped lov-ing you, don't you know that by now? Did you think you could sashay into my life for one after-noon, then sashay out again as if you'd done no damage?"

Her heart raced at his touch, but she was fright-ened by the mere fact that it did.

"I didn't know I was under any obligation when I came out here."

"Oh, didn't you?" he bit out, almost nose to nose with her. "So you thought you'd just toy around with good old Tommy Lee for a few hours, see how far you could push him. Do I count so little to you?"

"You're not being fair, Tommy Lee. That's not why I came out here and you know it."

"I don't know anything, least of all why I can't get you out from under my skin." His fingers tightened, and her heart clamored harder.

"Let me go. There's too much in our past to. . . to. . . ." But she stammered to a halt and his voice turned a shade softer, silkier.

"To what, Rachel? To start it again. . .? That thing that's been on both of our minds all day long?" Already he was drawing her close. "This. . . ."

His open lips came down on hers with a soft, firm pressure, and immediately his tongue came seeking.

"Don't!" She jerked her head aside and pushed on his chest.

"Why?"

"Because everything is different now. I'm different, you're different, our life-styles are totally incompatible."

His mouth followed her jaw as she arched fiercely away from him. "I can change. I will... for you if—"

"I said, don't! It won't work and all we'll end up doing is hurting each other." She tried to twist free, but his hold was too sure and his fingers dug into her arms.

"I would be anything you wanted me to be, don't you know that, Rachel? If it meant having you back again...Rachel, please...." His hands spanned her head and drew her once again nearly onto tiptoe for a deep, thorough kiss. But as his questing tongue entered her mouth, it brought the aftertaste of gin. Angrily she pushed him away and stepped back.

"Don't you dare kiss me with your sixth drink of the night still foul on your lips! Or maybe it was the seventh or eighth. I don't know. I've lost count!"

"Oh, so you've been counting?"

"Yes, I've been counting. All across the lake in the boat and tonight through supper *and* on the ride home!"

He loomed before her but made no further move to touch her while she stood with fists clenched, angry that he couldn't see what he was doing with his life.

"I can stop drinking any day I want," he stated belligerently. "Just give me a reason to!"

She ran a hand through her hair and twisted aside. "Oh, Tommy Lee, you fool. Don't you see, nobody can give you that reason but yourself? And it isn't just the drinking. It's the way you live. In that...." She flapped a palm toward the house. "That beautiful, sad, unkempt mansion where you sleep on your dirty laundry!"

His shoulders wilted slightly. "Rachel, I didn't know you were coming or—"

"It shouldn't have made a difference. For God's sake, Tommy Lee, you weren't raised in squalor. How can you live that way? And don't blame it on our parents! It's not our parents who ruined your life, it's you! You've become content to just...just drink yourself into oblivion and... and *atrophy*! But it's not too late to do something about it if you really wanted to. You could start by going in there and cleaning up that place, or if you don't want to clean it up yourself, at least hire some help to do it for you. And while you're at it, make it somebody who'll cook you something besides greasy, fattening foods!"

He stiffened and pulled back while she felt heartless for striking at his most vulnerable spot. But if she didn't try to make him see the light, who would?

His voice was tight with suppressed anger as he invited caustically, "Well, don't quit now, you're on a roll."

At his words she felt a rich, roiling rage that he had so blithely profaned both the body and spirit of the Tommy Lee she had once loved and been so proud of.

"All right, you asked for it," she shouted, and pointed into the woods. "Go walk back a mile down that road and pick up the litter you threw out the car window, and stop throwing your trash in the lake and...." Her hand fell to her side and her fists bunched. "And stop driving by my dress shop fifteen times a day and coming in to buy red earrings for your women!" She was nearly in tears as she finished.

"Anything else?" he snapped.

Her lips were trembling and she knew in a moment she'd be crying. It was terrible, finding herself falling in love with him again while admitting a thousand reasons not to be.

"Yes! And water your plants!"

He did a silent doubletake. "Wha*ttt?*" His head jutted forward and his face scrunched up.

She felt foolish for having brought up such a picayune grievance, which had nothing whatever to do with anything, and to make matters worse, the tears were beginning to flood her throat and eyes. She spun from him and began to pace while appealing, "Oh, don't you see, Tommy Lee, we've grown into two such different people than we used to be. All the time I'm with you I find myself wondering what people's reaction would be if they knew." She faced him and spread her palms helplessly. "All right, so I'm a snob, but I can't help it. I'm...you've changed so much... you...you're...." She pressed her lips tightly against her teeth and turned away, not wanting to hurt him any further.

"I'm what?" He stalked her, his voice coming from just behind her shoulder. "That whoring, drinking, fast-driving no good sonofabitch our parents made me into when they forced you and me apart and made us give up our baby? Do you think that's what I want to be, Rachel?" She was suddenly whirled around and found him bending above her, gripping her arms again. "Do you think I don't know what the whole town calls me? That *hellion*, Tommy Lee Gentry." She tried to escape his hands but he jerked her erect before him. "But you know something, Rachel? I don't give a damn about what they think or say. All I care about is you. Why do you think I didn't take you to some classy restaurant in Florence tonight? Why do you think I asked you out on my boat instead of someplace in town where we could be seen? Do you think I don't know how shocked the residents of Russellville would be if they saw the prim and proper Widow Hollis in the company of that hell raiser Tommy Lee Gentry? But I can change, Rachel. You just watch me. Because no matter how you try to hide it, there's still something between us. I could see it in your eyes today when you didn't think I was looking. I could see you wondering if it would be as good as it used to be, and if we could make it over the hundred and one hurdles we'd have to face if we decided to go public and announce to the world that we were going to pick up where we never should have left off twenty-four years—"

"You're wrong. You—"

"Shut up, Rachel, and get it into your head that you're not done with me yet. Not by a long shot. We *will* pick up again, only it won't be where we left off because we've both learned a lot since then, both about life and what to do in the back seat of a car...."

"Let me go, Tommy Lee! I don't want—"

"I said shut up, Rachel, because you're going to be kissed whether you like it or not, and I'll be back to get the rest later—daddies or no daddies!"

He hauled her up against him, took a handful of her hair to tip her head back, and crushed his mouth to hers while his tongue writhed against her tightly sealed lips, trying to force them open. Her heart thrust mightily against his chest as she wedged an elbow between them, gripping his shirt while the heel of one hand bored into his chest. But he was powerful in his anger and she was as defenseless as a doll in his arms. He felt her muscles strain and quiver while she fought him, but his arms and tongue were relentless until the ferocity of his kiss gradually mellowed. And only then did she slowly, cautiously begin to relax against him, allowing herself to feel what might be possible for them to have again. The silken circles he drew over her lips at last unlocked them, and her body rose up slightly to accommodate his, while the hand clasping his shirt rested easy, just short of caressing. Somewhere in the depths of her mind it registered again that he'd grown taller, for her head tilted sharply back. His chest was fuller beneath her palm. And he'd learned a thorough and sensual technique of kissing that soon raised responses, as his tongue explored the interior of her mouth while one hand prowled beneath her elbow to boldly caress her breast.

But the contact had scarcely begun before Tommy Lee abruptly pushed Rachel away, spun around and stalked to his car. He yanked the door open and threw himself into the driver's seat, then slammed the door with uncontrolled vehemence. The engine was already gunning before Tommy Lee realized he wasn't going anywhere.

Rachel stood where he'd left her—trembling, angry, aroused. Suddenly the engine died and the car door was flung open again. It slammed into the night stillness and he faced her with that same hulking stance he'd presented earlier.

"Well, what're you still doing here?" He took a single ominous step her way. "Git! If you know what's good for you, Rachel, you git!"

She turned and ran for her car, her heart raising a furor in her body. And this time it was Rachel who tore all the way back to town.

CHAPTER SEVEN

THE REFORM OF TOMMY LEE GENTRY began in earnest the very next day. He arose earlier than usual, put on a pair of shorts that were too tight around the waist and went for a jog down his curving driveway as the sun sent splinters of pure morning through the leaves. But he scarcely noticed. He was absolutely miserable—sweating, side-aching, leg-cramping miserable. He hadn't gone fifty yards before he had to stop, brace against a tree and pant. *Fifty yards! Lord a'mighty, in high school the coach sent us ten times around the track!* He made it to the end of the driveway with six stops, then had to walk back to the house, clutching his left side. The waistband of the shorts was nearly slicing through his skin by now, and he kicked them off with a foul curse and ran down to the lake buck naked, dove off the end of the dock and found out why they call it a belly flop.

Cursing again, he determinedly trudged through the water in a formless crawl, the muscles of his arms and legs aching from yesterday's unaccustomed workout. *With the lake right here, you*

should swim every day, Tommy Lee. Remembering Rachel's words he dragged his arms through
the water and thought, *I'll show you, Rachel!*

Damn it, he loved that woman, and if it took a
full year of this misery, he'd prove he could do it!
But as he slogged from the water after a torturous
four-minute swim, panting so hard his throat
hurt, checking his bright-red stinging belly, he
wasn't too sure he didn't dislike her intensely.

Back in the house he dressed in faded blue jeans
and called Liz Scroggins to say he wouldn't be in
till later, then faced the horrendous job of housecleaning. Standing at the edge of the living room,
he grimaced, cursed again, and attacked the job
like a belligerent child whose allowance has been
withheld pending an improvement in cooperation
and attitude.

All through that wretched morning, while he
forced his sore muscles to do tasks they abhorred,
while he suffered a hunger such as he hadn't
known in years, while he returned time and again
to his empty refrigerator searching for nourish-
ment that wasn't there, Gentry ranted. He worked
for hours, then took a break to search again for
something to give him sustenance, but all he could
find was beer, hard liquor and limes. He drank a
glass of despicably bitter lime water, picturing
Rachel's skinny little ribs, and puckered up his
face, then cursed again while vowing, *damn you,
Rachel Hollis, you'll kiss me next time without a
fight.*

But the housecleaning was scarcely half done. Thinking of all there was yet to do he slammed several cupboard doors hard enough to break the filaments in the lightbulbs, then gave up, strode out to the car and drove to Catfish Corner.

"Daisy!" he bellowed, slamming through the deserted bar area toward the living quarters in the rear. "Where the hell are you?"

Daisy's smiling face appeared around a corner. "Uh-oh, what I done now?" she teased.

"Daisy, I need two things, and I need 'em fast. A maid who can cook and something to eat that hasn't got any calories in it!"

Daisy fed him some summer squash that nearly gagged him, then called her sister-in-law, who called her married daughter, who called her first cousin by marriage, who said, sure thing, she'd be happy to work for Mr. Gentry, but taking a job for a holy terror like him was kind of risky, so she wanted two hundred a week, the first week in advance, and a room of her own—after all she wasn't made of money and didn't have no car, so how was she supposed to get back and forth to that no-man's-land of his? She'd live *in* or she wouldn't do it at all. And she wanted Saturdays and Sundays off, and a ride back to town so she could spend them with her family and could attend her own Baptist Church, then she'd need a ride back out to the country no earlier than 9:00 P.M. on Sunday night to give her plenty of visiting time.

Daisy stood with one hand on her hip, dangling the receiver over her shoulder, smirking across the kitchen at Tommy Lee while on the other side of the room Sam smiled behind his hand. "What should I tell her?"

"If she can cook better than you, tell her yes, I'll meet her outrageous demands, but if she ever puts summer squash in front of me she's fired on the spot!" He glared at Daisy and added for good measure, "And ask her what the hell ever happened to slavery!"

Daisy moved her shoulders saucily but her face was all innocence while she replaced the receiver on her ear and spoke to Georgine in an exaggerated Uncle Remus accent. "Mr. Gentry, he say yes, two hunnerd a week is nuttin', and if he too busy entertainin' his ladies to carry you home, you jiss plan on fetchin' yoself in one o' his big fancy cars. He say he *know* how all us black folk like big fancy Cadillac cars."

Tommy Lee came half out of his chair. "Daisy!" he roared. "A simple yes will do!"

Before the day was out Georgine was installed in Tommy Lee's house. She was given a pretty little guest bedroom and the keys to the Blazer so she could drive into town and stock the cupboard shelves properly. That night when Tommy Lee sat down to supper he demanded to know what the hell she'd spent a hundred and twenty dollars on when all he found on his plate was turnip greens and a piece of broiled, butterless fish that'd leave a mediocre-sized cat howling for seconds!

Georgine replied with a wordless pursing of her lips as she whipped her apron off and headed determinedly for the front door. Tommy Lee was forced to plead with her to stay, though when he bit into the tasteless fish he had no idea why he'd bothered.

Later that evening he wanted a martini so badly he went up to his bedroom, where Georgine couldn't see him, and tried to do pushups to take his mind off the drink—only to find out he couldn't do pushups anymore. When in the hell had *that* happened? He sat in a dejected heap on the floor, staring at his traitorous biceps and hating them. He'd been intending to call Rachel that night and apologize for jerking her around so roughly and for telling her to shut up, but after the failure of his body to perform, he was too angry with both himself and her to pick up the phone.

He ended the night starved, thirsty, and suffering through twelve of the most painful situps he'd ever performed in his life.

ON TUESDAY he called Panache, but Verda claimed Rachel wasn't in. "Humph!" he snorted, and slammed down the receiver with typical dieter's temper.

On Wednesday he managed the downward stroke of a pushup, but after quivering in the suspended state for thirty seconds, still could not push himself back up. He called Panache again, and this time when he was told she wasn't in barked, "Well, how the hell can she run a business when she's never there!" Then he hung up again.

On Thursday he made it to the end of the drive-way without stopping. But when he got there he threw up. None of his calls to Rachel's house turned up an answer and Tommy Lee raged inwardly. How dare she ignore him when he was suffering like a blue bitch—and all for her!

On Friday his arms ached from the pair of six-pound "executive dumbbells" he'd bought the day before and had overused in an effort to strengthen his traitorous biceps, which would only push him up once. His stomach growled constantly, and every time it did, he pictured a plate of Big Sam's catfish and hush puppies. And tried phoning Rachel again. And got angrier. And finally stalked into Panache to confront her personally only to find her out, and himself forced to buy another pair of earrings as an excuse for having come in.

MEANWHILE, RACHEL was spending a long tiring week in Dallas at the Trade Mart, meeting with the representatives of the various clothing manufacturers at appointed times, trying to determine what would sell and what wouldn't next fall. "Going to market" was always harrowing. A poor decision was costly, and since her merchandise turnover was limited, it was imperative her choices be prudent. Nor could she buy in quantity. In a small town no woman wanted to confront her newest designer dress walking toward her on another woman.

Discounts were discussed, haggling done, the autumn line of garments viewed.

Dallas was hot and dry and very lonely. At night she returned to her hotel room to lie and think about Tommy Lee and try not to cry. She remembered the evidence of his abject loneliness and her heart broke for him. That house—oh, Lord, that house. It was a monument to what they'd once had, and thinking of it again stirred her in a heart-wrenching way. What kind of devotion drove a man to build a house for a woman who was married to someone else? And what woman could see it, recognize it, and not be moved by it?

She thought of him living in that beautiful place, dreaming his dreams while years rolled on and made him older, more lax about the direction his life was taking. . . and the tears gathered in her throat. Had he really been waiting for her to be free again? Unbelievably, it seemed to be true.

The house itself evidenced the fact.

She remembered them returning to it after their swim, and he'd paused on the flight of stairs above her on his way to his room to change. He'd looked back down and said, "You can't imagine how many times I've dreamed of you being here in my house, looking exactly like you do right now." She had clasped the door frame and stood gazing up at him, feeling again the magnetic appeal he still had for her. It was one of the rare uncomplicated moments she'd experienced that day. She'd held all extraneous circumstances in abeyance and had allowed herself to admit that she still had—probably would always have—deep feelings for him.

It had been on the tip of her tongue to tell him she recognized "their house," but if she had, she wasn't sure she could have kept from asking to see the bedroom. And that would have been a mistake.

For the longer she was with him, the more her thoughts wandered in that direction. How odd that in spite of his flaws, in spite of all the others he'd known, at times she still looked upon him as her Tommy Lee. And when she thought that way she felt prickly and decidedly female.

Lying sleepless, huddled in a lonely bed in a Texas hotel room, thinking of Tommy Lee, she again felt the sensations creep along her skin. It did little good to remind herself of his bad reputation, for it held an odd attraction all its own. He was forbidden, thus tempting. She supposed with all the practice he'd had, he was a superb lover by now.

Shouldn't that repel rather than entice?

She tossed restlessly, trying to put him from her mind. But her body was exerting demands of its own that had gone unsatisfied for months and months. She thought of his kiss, of their bare limbs brushing silkily beneath the water, and knew again the sweet yearning of arousal.

But in the end she was forced to ask herself the question that was weighing heavier and heavier on her mind as the days passed. Was she attracted to Tommy Lee as he was today or as he was remembered by a lonely, childless middle-aged woman who'd been spending altogether too much time lately dwelling on the past?

RACHEL RETURNED to Russellville on Saturday, exhausted and in a bad mood, only to learn that *he* had called more than once during the week, and that Tommy Lee Gentry had been in yesterday to buy another pair of earrings. Hot pink ones this time.

And once again her anger flared. How dare he tread a second time onto the hallowed ground of her business world. And to buy hot-pink earrings yet! The look in Verda's eyes stated very clearly that she knew Tommy Lee and the caller were one and the same man. In an effort to escape those speculative looks, and to cool her own anger, Rachel went for a shampoo and styling by her own Selma. It felt marvelous to have the Texas dust washed away by competent hands that knew her hair better than the strange beautician in the Dallas hotel.

In the late afternoon she carefully arranged herself on an inflated plastic raft, making certain her meticulous hairdo stayed dry, trailing only one foot in the water as she closed her eyes and drifted lazily, shutting out all thought.

She was dozing peacefully when an angry voice brought her head up sharply off the raft.

"You don't believe in answering bells, do you!"

The buyer of hot-pink earrings! She pushed her sunglasses down on her nose and scowled over the frames at the last person in the world she wanted to see. He stood with his hands on his hips, pushing back the jacket of a tailored suit, while above his white shirt and tie his chin wore a bulldoggish expression.

"How did you get in here?"

"I walked through the damn hedge, that's how. After standing at your front door ringing the bell for five minutes."

She lowered the glasses and lay back as if he weren't there. "The air conditioning is on. I didn't hear it through the sliding glass doors."

"And what about the thirty-seven phone calls you didn't answer? Were you out here floating on your air mattress *all week*?" Let him think what he would. She didn't reply. "Rachel, damn it, how do you get off ignoring a person who's trying to get in touch with you?"

She dipped a hand into the water and spread it on her chest while he watched and felt his stomach begin to hurt harder than any hunger pains had caused it to in the past week.

"Rachel, talk to me, damn it!"

"I didn't invite you here. Please leave."

"Go to hell, Rachel," he said with the coolest tone he displayed since arriving. "Are you going to Catfish Corner with me tomorrow?" But the invitation was issued with all the warmth of a general ordering his troops to open fire.

She peered at him over her glasses for a moment and found him standing as before, like an angry samurai. "Catfish Corner?"

"They invited you, too, you may recall." She fell back, eyes closed behind the sunglasses, not a hair out of place and every rib showing while Tommy Lee glared at her and recalled the past week of aching muscles and abstinence, all for her. And now she refused to open her eyes and glance at the results. He'd lost five pounds, and was as proud as if it were fifty! He wanted her to notice, damn it!

When she calmly went on ignoring him, his anger freshened. "Rachel, I was trying to call you all week to tell you I was sorry for acting like a caveman last Sunday, and for all the things I said."

She didn't flinch.

"Damn it, Rachel, will you come out of that pool and talk to me?"

"I just got here."

"Rachel, you smug, supercilious...socialite! I'm trying to apologize to you, damn it!"

"Do you know how many times you've said damn since you got here?" This time she scooped the water onto her midriff. The lazy movement was like the wave of a matador's cape before a bull. Tommy Lee glared at her for a long minute, then the expression on his face turned foxy while he methodically began slipping off one loafer, then the other, calmly removed his billfold from his pocket and descended the steps into the pool.

As he struck out in a crawl he noticed that it didn't even hurt him to swim anymore. He was already experiencing a jubilant feeling of accomplishment as he reached the raft and unceremoniously tipped it over.

Rachel went sprawling onto her belly while she let out a surprised squawk, accompanied by an ungainly thrashing of arms and legs. The shriek was severed as her head went under, sending up a series of bubbly glugs. She emerged coughing, hair straggling into her eyes, water streaming into her mouth, while she blindly reached for the raft and began swearing a blue streak.

Some of the more choice words that fell from her tongue made Tommy Lee's eyebrows shoot up in gleeful surprise as he struggled toward the shallow end followed by the doused Widow Hollis. Finally she pushed her hair back, snorted the water from her nose and glared at him. "You... you damn crazy no-count redneck jackass! I could kill you!" Tommy Lee reared back and laughed uproariously. She slammed her fists into the water and yelled, "Go on, laugh, you damn hyena!" Then she rolled her eyes upward and wailed, "Ohhh, my hair!" and clasped her head in despair. "I just paid twenty-five dollars to have it done and look at it now!"

But he was still roaring with laughter, standing in water up to his armpits, his tie floating on the surface and a two-hundred-and-fifty-dollar suit puffing out around his body.

"Get out of here!" she screamed. "Get out of my swimming pool!"

When he could talk again he perused her with an insufferable grin on his face. "The last time I made you that mad was when we were about thirteen years old and I asked you if you'd started your period yet and you slapped my face and told me to grow up, then went off bawling and said you hated me and would hate me to my dying day. And it wasn't a year later I was kissing you crazy, and you loved every minute of it."

Rachel stood outraged, watching him turn and slog toward the steps, blissfully unconcerned about his expensive clothes.

"You're a despicable, crude...yokel!" she shouted at his back, ramming her hands onto her hips, shaking with anger.

He only tipped his head back and laughed again while mounting the steps, then turned and pointed at her cheeks. "Your mascara's running, Rachel."

Angrier than ever, she shouted, "You're exactly what they call you, you hellion! And I can't for the life of me see what all those stupid women find to chase after!"

He took one warning step back into the pool, grinning wickedly. "You want me to show you, Rachel?"

"You just stay away from me, you egotistical maniac!"

He gave her an assessing glance and shrugged disinterestedly. "No, I guess I won't. But maybe if you'd put a little meat on those bones I might give it some thought.''

"And maybe if you took a little meat off yours, I'd let you!" she retaliated.

His expression soured. He crossed the patio, then leaned sideways from the waist with practiced nonchalance, plucked up his billfold, extracted some bills and dropped them on the patio table. "Twenty-five dollars, you say? Here, have it fixed again on me. It was worth every cent."

Then Tommy Lee calmly picked up his shoes and disappeared, leaving a sputtering Rachel behind to pound the surface of the water and promise herself she'd never speak to him again.

Rachel was so incensed, tears of frustration stung her eyes. She stormed into the house mopping her ruined hair and vehemently denying all the tender thoughts she'd had in Dallas.

Of all the nerve! Were there actually women who put up with treatment like that and came back for more? And he hadn't been content to tip her into the pool, he'd inferred that she was skinny...*skinny!* She stepped before a mirror, analyzed her reflection...and burst into tears. Lord, she was so mixed up about him. He *had* been trying to apologize, and the least she could have done was accept his apology gracefully. She thought about his anger, the names he had flung at her. All right, so she was a...a smug supercilious socialite. But she couldn't help it. She'd been raised to believe that one's public image was important.

Did he think she should blithely open her door to him one day, then ring up his hot-pink earrings the next?

On Monday a package arrived for her at Panache. She opened it to find an electric hair blower and a note: "Learn to fix it yourself so you can be prepared for the unexpected."

She raged inwardly and swore she'd have him put under lock and key if he kept pestering her this way. Then she wrapped the hair blower and mailed it back to him with a note saying, "You'll need this to dry your suits when you stumble into the next woman's pool."

The following week Rachel got home one day to find an enormous bouquet of white roses and leather-leaf fern on the dining-room table. The card read, "I'm sorry, Rachel. I found out you were in Dallas. And you're not too skinny. Please have dinner with me Friday night at my house. We'll be well chaperoned this time."

So what was he doing now, going around town asking people questions about her comings and goings?

Callie Mae watched Rachel's face closely as she read the message. She noted the scowl, then the dismissing look Rachel gave the flowers before tossing the card down and never looking at it again.

"Mighty pretty flowers," Callie Mae remarked. "Expensive, too." But her curiosity was not to be satisfied. Neither Rachel nor the card gave any clue as to who they were from.

TOMMY LEE WAITED EACH DAY for her to answer his invitation but soon realized she wasn't going to.

He tried to run the disappointment out of his system. By now he could jog to the end of the driveway and back with no trouble at all, and as the days passed he worked himself up to four miles a day. He ran to the beat of her name—Rachel, Rachel, Rachel. Every day he swam, too, and worked with the weights and did situps. His muscles tautened, his stomach began to flatten, and even his chin grew firmer. The exercise, coupled with Georgine's parsimonious cooking, soon gave his skin a healthy elasticity that seemed to dissolve the webs from about his eyes.

But it mattered little, for Rachel had neither answered his invitation nor thanked him for the flowers. Weeks passed and he stopped driving past Panache, hoping it would help evict her from his thoughts. But nothing helped. Nothing.

There were times when he grew righteously angry, thinking, *The world is full of women, why do I waste my time mooning over one who keeps saying no? There are plenty of nice women in the world, and how do I know one of them wouldn't please me just as much as Rachel? Hell, I haven't been with a really decent woman in years!*

He was in precisely such a mood one day as he

stepped to the doorway between his office and
Liz's, glancing up to ask her about an invoice he
was holding. But she was on the phone so he stood
for a moment, waiting for her to finish the conversation.

She had a pleasant way about her when doing
business on the phone. She never got upset or impatient, and laughed readily, as she did now, at
something being said on the other end of the line.
She lifted her eyes to Tommy Lee and gave him an
I'll-be-done-in-a-minute signal.

He stood listening and watching while she con-
cluded the conversation, realizing once again how
attractive she was. Her blond hair was shorter now
for the summer and she wore a fresh butter-yellow
suit as tasteful and attractive as anything Rachel
might wear. Come to think of it, she was a lot like
Rachel. She was nice, decent, and infinitely re-
spectable. She dressed and acted like a lady at all
times, was poised, efficient and friendly. No matter what his own mood, hers remained cheerful—
and he realized he'd been grouchy more often than
not lately.

Liz hung up the phone and said, "Sorry. What
can I do for you?"

And out of the clear blue sky, Tommy Lee answered, "You can go out to dinner with me
tonight."

Liz's eyebrows lifted in surprise. "To dinner!"

"Well, it's about time, isn't it? You've worked
for me for six years and I've never even treated

you to a night out. And you deserve it. I've been a regular bear lately. I don't know how you put up with me."

She laughed and replied, "Come to think of it, you have."

"Does that mean yes?"

"I'm sorry. The boys will be home and I probably can't find a baby-sitter on such short notice."

"How about your parents?" He saw her waver momentarily and pushed his advantage. "Come on. Help me celebrate—I've lost over half the weight I've set out to lose."

"And you want to celebrate by putting some of it back on? A real friend would say absolutely not."

"I'll pick you up at seven—what do you say?"

She chuckled and was already turning toward her typewriter as she gave in. "Oh, all right, but if you don't let me get back to work I'll still be here at seven."

They had a delightful meal at a Mexican restaurant in Florence, and afterward talked all the way back to Russellville. Their years of working closely with each other put them very much at ease, and they found themselves readily able to converse on a variety of subjects, laughing at amusing anecdotes she shared about her boys, discussing the personalities of various people Tommy Lee did business with, and reaching back into their ample store of high school and college stories to come up with the most outrageous pranks each had pulled in their youth.

When they reached Liz's house he walked her to the door, their spirits still bright, both of them feeling relaxed and easy with each other.

"Thank you so much, Mr. Gentry. The dinner was delicious and I've had a wonderful time."

"That goes double for me, but you could drop the formalities and call me Tommy Lee."

"But it wouldn't seem right to call my boss Tommy Lee."

"But tonight I'm not your boss...just a friend, okay?"

"Well, in any case, good night, and thank you again." She was already turning away toward the door when he captured her arm and swung her back to face him.

"Hey, not so fast there."

"Tomorrow's a work day and I wouldn't want to be late," she replied perkily. "The boss might get upset."

"I guarantee he won't."

Though she gave the expected chuckle, he sensed a change in her the moment he touched her. The smile fell away and she dropped her eyes. Her arm was soft and bare and she wore a familiar cologne whose scent he readily associated with her after smelling it all these years around the office. He realized again that much of her attraction stemmed from the fact that she was every inch a lady, the kind who very naturally commanded a man's respect, the kind who probably didn't do this kind of thing either often or lightly.

We've both wondered for a long time, he thought. *So let's find out.*

Her blue eyes closed and her pink lips opened as he dropped his mouth over hers in a soft, undemanding kiss. She was honest enough to allow herself to sample him—just as he sampled her—before pressing a hand to his chest and backing away.

"No, I don't think so," she answered quietly, as if he'd asked her a question.

His head lifted in surprise. "No, you don't think what?"

"This isn't really what you want."

"It isn't?" He was baffled by her unusual response to the kiss—very different from what he'd expected.

She shook her head. "Uh-uh. I know you've wondered, and I'll admit I have, too. But what you really want is someone else, I think."

He was still smitten by surprise as he asked, out of curiosity, "Who?"

"Rachel Hollis."

Oddly enough, he didn't even think of denying it. "How did you know?"

"How did I know? I've worked for you for six years. I've had more than one occasion to watch your eyes follow her when she walked along the street to the bank. There's a certain way a man looks at a woman that tells it all, and you can't even watch her pass by without giving yourself away."

He'd never realized it showed. He felt rather like a schoolboy caught cheating on a test.

"I've also seen you talking to her on the street lately. When you come back into the office afterward, you're a bundle of frustration." Tommy Lee hung his head and tried to think of something to reply. "Oh, don't look so guilty, all right? I think it was high time you and I did what we just did, just to get it out of our systems and clear the air. But I'm only a substitute, and I'd just as soon be a good secretary as a poor substitute."

"I never realized before how perceptive you are, Liz."

She crossed her arms, leaned back against the wall and invited, "Do you want to talk about it? I've got a willing ear."

So, to his surprise, he ended up telling her nearly the whole saga about himself and Rachel Talmadge/Hollis. It felt wonderful to discuss it with someone impartial, who neither made demands of him, nor judged.

When the story ended, she asked him matter of factly, "Well, you aren't going to give up now, are you?"

He was slightly taken aback by the question. "I don't want to, but she seems dead set against seeing me."

"Do you think she loves you?"

Why should it be so difficult to answer the simple question? He'd asked it of himself countless times and had always come up with the same answer, the one that made him wonder at Rachel's stubbornness. Answering Liz now, he felt rather timid.

"Yes. Sometimes. . . yes."

"Well, then. . . she's scared, don't you see? And she's got a perfect right to be. Why, look at your record! What woman would willingly want to take on a man with a record like that? You've got to assure her you mean it when you say you've changed. But whatever you do, don't give up on her. If she loves you, believe me, it's the last thing she wants."

"It is?" The idea was stunning. Women were strange birds—why would they do one thing when they meant to do another?

"Take my word for it."

He carried the idea away with him, and it stayed on his mind throughout that sleepless night. The following day he thought about it again, and wondered how he could show her he had changed and was so much happier with the new Tommy Lee that he wouldn't dream of backsliding. That afternoon he was jogging past the end of his driveway when he stopped and eyed the kudzu vine tangled across the ditch. He pondered for some time before finally picking up three rocks and flinging them in, to dissuade snakes. Then he forced his way through the thick vines to the place where he always used to toss his empties.

As he moved through the ditch, he grew amazed. *Lord o' mercy, did I drink all this?*

He picked up a can, tossed it up absently and caught it. Then his eyes narrowed and he stared off into the distance. *All right, Rachel, we'll try one more time.*

The following day Rachel came home from work to find a huge black plastic trash bag on her front step, bound at the top by an outsized red satin bow. She approached it cautiously, surveyed its lumpy-looking exterior, touched it with a toe and heard a metallic chink. Gingerly she untied the bow, peered inside and found it filled with aluminum beer cans. And a note. "All right, Rachel, you win. I'm cleaning up my act. What else do I have to do to get you to say yes?"

What the hair blower and flowers had failed to do, the sack of beer cans accomplished. Rachel pressed four fingertips to her lips and burst into tears. *Oh, Tommy Lee, you crazy, off-beat, irresistible hellion, can't you see it would never work?*

Callie Mae was immediately concerned to find a tearful Rachel dragging a huge black bag into the house.

"Why Miss Rachel, what's wrong?"

"Everything!" The bag sent out a mysterious sound as Rachel dropped it and dissolved in tears on Callie Mae's shoulder.

A sympathetic hand patted the back of Rachel's head. "Now you just tell Callie Mae everything."

"I c-can't."

"Course you can. You want to start with what's in that bag that set you off?"

"Oh, C-Callie Mae," she wailed, "it's a g-gift from Tommy Lee."

Over Rachel's shoulder Callie Mae gave the bag a second look. "So that's it."

Rachel drew back and mopped her eyes, still sniffling. "He won't stop. . . p-pestering me, and I . . . we. . . ." Her words trailed off and ended with a woeful look of misery and renewed weeping.

"You don't have to explain nothin' to Callie Mae. I see how it is with you two. I always seen."

"How it is between us two is impossible." Rachel threw her hands out and began pacing agitatedly.

Callie Mae pursed her mouth and grunted, "Hmph." Then she asked, "You mind if I take a look at what he brung you?" Rachel shook her head and Callie Mae opened the sack to peer inside. "Well now, what do you know about that!" she exclaimed softly, then asked, "He the one sent you them flowers, too?" Rachel nodded while Callie Mae noted her crestfallen expression. "Jus' *when* he call you skinny?"

"Don't you go getting that. . .that *look* in your eye, because it isn't going to work. He isn't going to sweet talk me into making a fool of myself. Not with a philanderer like him."

Callie Mae crossed her hands against her stomach and affected a sober, judgmental expression. "Yup, he's a wild one, that Tommy Lee."

Rachel paced. "And he couldn't make a single one of his marriages work."

"Nope. He sure couldn't."

"And he hasn't gone to church in years." It wasn't exactly true, but it felt reassuring to heap blame on him.

"At least ten, fifteen."

"And he still drives like a maniac."

"He's one crazy white boy, for sure."

"And you should see the way he lives." Rachel threw up her hands. "Why, his house looks like a pigpen!" Suddenly she came to a halt, looked up and felt herself color.

Callie Mae cocked an eyebrow and said, "Oh?" But she wiped all expression off her face and busied herself unnecessarily dusting a table with her apron while advising softly, "And you mustn't forget, there's the fact that Mister Owen, he's only been gone a few months. And your daddy would have a conniption fit if he was to find out Tommy Lee been nosin' around his daughter again. And, o' course, we all know what the Good Book says about honorin' fathers, no matter if they're right or wrong. But there couldn't be no question about your daddy bein' right. After all, he's got one o' the best heads in this county. Why, he runs that bank over there like them Yankees run the war—merciless. You know he always gonna end up winnin', and though he don't always smile a lot, people got respect for him, and there's them that say he's a mite cold and calculatin' at times, but he seems to get along just fine without a lot o' friends since your mama died.

Yes, ma'am, your daddy, he's one smart man, got the respect of everybody in this county. And folks say you're turnin' out just like him. You want I should put this sack of junk out for the garbage man to pick up tomorrow?'' Callie Mae looked up innocently, holding the sack of beer cans now.

Rachel glanced from the sack to Callie Mae's face, then back again, trying to think of something to say. But she was too shaken to know what to say, and finally Callie Mae trudged off through the house, dragging Tommy Lee's offering with her while mumbling something about it being worthless and wondering what that crazy white boy was thinking to drop such trash on people's front steps!

Rachel remained where Callie Mae had left her, round-eyed and stunned, digesting what the woman had just said, quite horrified at the thought that she might be turning out just like her father. Was she really all those things? Merciless? Cold? A person who'd rather have the town's respect than smile a lot? She swallowed convulsively, closed her eyes and bit her trembling lip, wanting to deny it.

But that made two people now who'd told her the same thing, for hadn't Tommy Lee called her a smug, supercilious socialite?

And if it wasn't true, why was she crying?

CHAPTER EIGHT

TO RACHEL'S UTTER SURPRISE, Tommy Lee showed up at church the following Sunday morning. He was standing on the steps when she arrived, and she realized her mistake the moment her feet stopped moving. Their eyes met, and her first thought was that he had new glasses, styled like the old ones, except these had clear lenses through which she could clearly see him taking in her white-and-brown linen dress and matching spectator pumps.

She felt herself blush but could not tear her eyes away from him. He looked magnificent! His skin was brown and healthy looking, and somehow he appeared thinner, dressed in a pale-blue suit with a rich navy shirt. The mid-morning sun caught the black and silver strands of his hair and threw chips of gold off his tie clasp and the rims of his glasses while a light breeze lifted the end of his tie and gently turned it back, then settled it into place again.

She wasn't certain how long she stood staring before becoming aware of the girl at his side. She was tall and lanky with dark shoulder-length hair, and from the way she took his arm and gazed up at him, there was no question she adored him. Just then the breeze furled the girl's hair and blew it back from her temple, and as Rachel caught sight of the red button earrings, her heart sank.

Oh no, she thought, *not again. This one's young enough to be his daughter.*

Just then the girl turned, revealing the same cupid's-bow mouth as Lily's and a pair of brown eyes that might easily have belonged to Tommy Lee himself at age fourteen. Rachel stared, transfixed, feeling her composure slip as she confronted the girl who, had circumstances been different, might have been her own daughter. Her eyes were helplessly drawn to Tommy Lee's again and they stood like a pair of marble statues. *Move!* she told her feet. *Half the town is watching you gape at him, including his daughter and your own father!* For in that horrifying moment Rachel realized Everett had joined her, after parking the car, and stood watching the silent tableau with growing disapproval.

Beth's eyes flashed from her father to the pretty dark-haired woman and back again, then, to Rachel's relief, Tommy Lee gave a silent nod and moved away with her.

Beside her Everett said stiffly, "Rachel, for God's sake, people are staring."

To her horror, she glanced around to find it was true. Several pairs of curious eyes had taken in the scenario, but as Rachel looked up, they all quickly glanced away.

The church service seemed interminable. It took a great deal of self-restraint for Rachel to face front for a full ten minutes before checking behind her under the guise of picking up a hymnal from the seat. Just as she'd suspected, Tommy Lee and Beth were only a few pews back. Surreptitiously she glanced at her father, but he faced front with a stern, forbidding expression on his face. Though she opened the hymnal, the printing seemed to blur, and she was terribly conscious of Tommy Lee's eyes boring into her back. In a panic, she wondered where Gaines and Lily Gentry were sitting. Were they watching him watch her? Undoubtedly they were as shocked as she was to see him here this morning. After countless years of absence, he couldn't possibly resume attendance without being conspicuous.

When the service ended and everyone flooded the center aisle, she picked him out from behind by the thinning hair at the crown of his head. Odd how the sight of it lent him a certain vulnerability; she felt guilty to be studying it. And a little sad.

Outside, she witnessed the stunned reactions parade across the faces of Tommy Lee's parents as they paused to watch their son and granddaughter leaving the church behind them. Gaines Gentry's hand went to Lily's elbow, and her free hand covered her lips while their eyes followed Tommy Lee's progress until he became aware of them and halted in mid stride, pulling Beth up short, too. Rachel sensed the girl's momentary confusion, and the yearning among the other three. But then Tommy Lee nodded brusquely and headed toward his car with long-legged steps, already lighting a cigarette as Beth trailed along beside him.

Everett drove Rachel home in stony silence, but the moment they were inside he confronted her directly, his face rigid and darkened by a scowl. "What's going on between you and Gentry?"

She spun to face him angrily. "Nothing!"

"Nothing?" He snorted. "I wasn't born yesterday, Rachel. If nothing's going on, then tell me what was all that about on the church steps?"

"All what? I didn't even speak to the man!"

"You didn't have to, to set the whole town talking."

Suddenly Callie Mae's words came back, and Rachel stiffened her spine. "The town, the town! That's always your first concern, isn't it, daddy—what the town might be saying! What business is it of theirs anyway?"

"Rachel, are you forgetting what you have made of yourself? You're one of Russellville's leading citizens. You're a businesswoman whose reputation must—"

"Oh, for heaven's sake, daddy, stop." She pressed her forehead and turned away. "I don't want to hear it."

He whirled her around by an arm. "Well, you're going to! I will *not* have you seeing Tommy Lee Gentry. Is that understood?"

For a moment she was a girl again, hearing

those same words, experiencing the same eruption of anger she'd felt then. It swirled up in a red haze, bringing with it the rage and fight she'd been unable to display then, when she could do nothing but bend to his will. But she no longer had to buckle under to a father's demands. Her jaw clamped in defiance, her face took on a belligerent expression, and there came a sweeping sense of release in rebelling against him at last.

"I'm not seventeen anymore. By what right do you tell me who I can and cannot see?"

"You're still my daughter, and when you start acting irresponsibly, what else is a father supposed to do?"

"You could try letting me make my own choices," she returned brittlely. "I'm forty-one. Wouldn't you say it's time?"

His face took on an apoplectic hue as he shouted and pointed toward the church. "And *that's* the kind of choice you propose to make?"

"Suppose I did, would that be so terrible?"

"For God's sake, Rachel, Owen is scarcely dead in his grave and you're taking up with a . . . a hellion like Gentry?"

"Tell me," she said, narrowing her eyes. "Exactly what do you think made him that way?"

"That's not the point!"

"Oh, and what is?"

"The point is, I will not have you spoiling your reputation by being seen with the most notorious skirt chaser this county's ever seen!"

She was every bit her father's daughter as she returned coolly, "And if I choose to?"

"So you *are* seeing him!"

She studied him levelly for some time before asking quietly, "What are you so scared of, daddy?"

He let his shoulders wilt, blew out an exasperated breath and gestured appealingly. "Rachel, for heaven's sake, he's been married three times, he drinks like a fish and he—"

"No, daddy," she interrupted, shaking her head slowly. "That's not it at all and we both know it. You're afraid that if I should start seeing Tommy Lee again you may be forced to come face to face with your own guilt."

"*My* guilt!" He was enraged now, gesturing angrily. "You disgraced us with him once. Wasn't that enough?"

She again shook her head, saddened by his inability to bend, to recognize his own fault in creating some of the scars that had gone unhealed all these years.

"No, daddy, we didn't disgrace you. You disgraced us. By sending me away and treating me as if what we'd done was unforgivable. To us it wasn't. To us it wasn't sordid or...or immoral. We loved each other!"

Again he gestured with an upturned palm. "Rachel, we did what we thought best for all."

"Did you?" she asked softly, sadly. "Then tell me why you and the Gentrys never talked to each other again."

The room grew hushed and neither of them moved a muscle. Everett's face slowly grayed while Rachel stood firm, facing him squarely. Then suddenly he lurched around her, heading for the door. She grabbed his arm, begging, "Daddy, could we talk about it? Please?"

But Everett jerked free and proclaimed angrily, "There is nothing to talk about!" then slammed out the door leaving her feeling hopelessly depressed and wondering if it would ever be possible to untangle the webs of the past.

Why did I goad him? Why didn't I just come right out and say that there really is nothing between Tommy Lee and myself?

The answer was simple. There would always be something between them, no matter how hard she fought it. And it seemed only a matter of time before it would all come to a head.

RACHEL WAS STILL BLUE later that day when Marshall stopped by after his usual Sunday afternoon visit to his daughter's. She answered the bell to find him standing on her step with slumped shoulders and a dejected face.

"Why, Marshall, what's wrong?"

"Carolyn and I had a fight."

"A fight!"

Rachel might have chuckled; in a way it was amusing to think of the mild-mannered Marshall fighting with anybody. But she could see he was truly down in the dumps even before he added,

"And furthermore, I hate the idea of facing the empty house. Want to take a ride?"

It was so rare to find Marshall in low spirits that Rachel wouldn't have dreamed of refusing. Especially not after all the times *he'd* cheered *her*.

"I haven't been exactly on top of the world myself today. Why not?"

He drove as if not caring where he was going, and they ended up near the small town of Phil Campbell about ten miles south of Russellville. When he turned in at the entrance of the Dismal Gardens, Rachel teased, "The Dismals? On an evening when I'm supposed to be cheering you up?"

Marshall smiled distractedly. "Apropos, isn't it?" Then he glanced out the window. "I haven't been out here in years. Have you?"

"No, not since I was a child."

"Care to take a walk through?"

"Why not."

They parked, and Marshall paid their admission as they entered the gardens through a little country-museum house, then stepped down into a rocky depression surrounded by house-size boulders that created the gateway to the park. They wandered through the waning afternoon, companionably silent, letting the surroundings ease their troubles.

Unlike their name, the Dismal Gardens were stunningly beautiful, a refreshing breath of untainted nature in a setting left untouched by man since the canyon and its surrounding woods and caves had been inhabited by the Paleo Indians 10,000 years before. The gardens took their name from the "dismalites," tiny incandescent worms that lived in the moss on the rock cliffs and shone like stars at night.

As Rachel and Marshall entered the park, the sun was still above the cliffs, and they followed a clear tumbling river into shaded coolness where the air was thick with the fecund smell of moss and leaf mold. They explored stunning rock formations with such names as Pulpit Rock, The Grotto, and Fat Man's Misery.

It was peaceful here, restorative. A pileated woodpecker flashed through the forest in a wink of red. Wild hydrangea vines clung to the high walls where trailing arbutus sprouted magically from the face of sheer rock. Farther along they came to Phantom Falls, a tiny opening no more than ten feet in diameter. Inside, they stopped and lifted their faces toward the small circle of sky overhead, listening to the roar of water echoing mysteriously through the depression, though the falls themselves were some 250 feet downstream.

When Rachel dropped her eyes, Marshall was studying her with an odd look on his face. She laughed nervously and moved along the trail, calling back, "Well, come on, slow poke, get a move on!"

The expression changed to a sheepish grin as he followed at her heels. But when they reached

Rainbow Falls, she again sensed his gaze on her as if he were puzzling something out. She lifted her eyes to the twin rainbows high overhead, which were caught by the sunlight that couldn't reach into the shady depths where they stood. She feared he hadn't invited her here for anything as simple as a breath of fresh air. In a moment her suspicions were verified as he spoke in a serious tone.

"Rachel, I heard something today that's rather disturbing."

"Oh?" She dropped her eyes to find he'd been studying her intently, but immediately he glanced at his feet.

"It...well, it could be a rumor. You know how small towns are."

"Gossip, you mean?"

His eyes met hers again. "I hope so." He suddenly captured her hand and tugged her toward a large boulder. "Let's sit down." When they were seated side by side he dropped her hand, seemed to struggle for the right words and finally lifted his gaze to hers, asking, "Rachel, have you been seeing Tommy Lee Gentry?"

With unexpected swiftness her blood came to life and her heart started banging. "What do you mean, have I been *seeing* him?"

"His car has been seen at your house."

Frantically she searched for an answer. "Tommy Lee and I are old friends," she answered vaguely.

"That doesn't answer my question." He swallowed and continued. "Friends or no friends, you know what kind of man he is."

She suddenly grew incensed with everyone pointing fingers at Tommy Lee when they knew so little about what drove him. "Oh? And what kind of man is he, Marshall?" Rachel surprised even herself with her brusque tone.

He jumped off the rock, presenting his back while jamming his hands into his pockets. "Oh, come on, Rachel. He's got women from one end of this county to the other, and nobody would put it past him to try to move in fast on a new widow."

Growing angrier by the moment, Rachel questioned, "Did my father put you up to this?"

Marshall swung around to face her again. "Your father? Why, no! I heard the rumor, that's all, and I wanted an answer straight from you."

It suddenly dawned on Rachel that this was what Marshall and his daughter had argued about, and for the first time ever she grew more angry with them for gossiping than with Tommy Lee for making himself vulnerable to their gossip. But just then Marshall came close and reached for her hand again. "Rachel, don't get angry with me. Please. That's the last thing I wanted."

At his apologetic look she softened. "You don't have to worry about me, Marshall. I have a very level head on my shoulders."

"Yes, I know you do. But even so...." His words trailed off and she saw how disconcerted he was, which was terribly unlike Marshall, who was always very low key and unruffled. "Rachel, may I speak frankly with you?"

Though something warned her she might not like what he had to say, she could only respond, "Why, of course, Marshall. What else are friends for?"

He solemnly studied their joined hands. "I wasn't going to say anything for some months yet, but after what I heard today, I realize I can't put this off." He swallowed nervously and his eyes flicked briefly to hers, then away again. "Rachel, I know that for the last half year or more you and Owen had no ah....." Marshall nervously cleared his throat. "No...sexual relationship. He talked to me about it because he was very depressed over it. He was...well, worried about you." She felt her face grow hot and resisted the urge to yank her hand from his. "You're normal and healthy...and at this point in your life, extremely vulnerable."

Though her face was now fully flooded with crimson, she said pointedly, "To a man like Tommy Lee, you mean?"

Now it was Marshall's turn to color. "Yes." He cleared his throat and swallowed again. "Rachel, at the risk of sounding calculating, I'll admit to you that I've been thinking for weeks about taking care of you since Owen died, of marrying you as soon as a decent length of time had passed."

"Marrying me!" Rachel tried to retract her hands, but he held them firmly, meeting her brown eyes squarely at last.

"Does it come as such as surprise, Rachel? Surely you've guessed that I began loving you long before I had the right to say so."

"But, Marshall, I—"

"I know. I know. I'm not the debonair type, not the kind with flash and style like Gentry. But I love you, Rachel, and I'd be good to you."

Oh, there was no doubt in her mind about that. But...Marshall? Marshall with his sober sensibilities, his nondescript brown hair and wing-tip shoes? She looked at him and tried to imagine spending the rest of her life watching him putter and prune his yard on Saturdays, then on Sundays going off to visit his married children. And in between, she could listen to him and her father discuss interest rates and twenty-pay-life plans. He was gazing at her pleadingly now, and she had to think of something fast.

"But, Marshall, Owen's been gone such a short time, and I...I...." It had always been embarrassing for Rachel to turn down even so much as a kiss. This was devastating. Marshall was gazing at her as if he wanted to gift wrap those two rainbows and lay them at her feet!

"I had no intention of asking you so soon," he went on nervously. "I told you that. But when I heard the rumors, I got scared.'

"Oh, Marshall...." she said softly, moved in spite of herself because he was so sincere and flustered.

"I guess I took you by surprise, didn't I?" He

hung his head quite boyishly while idling with her hands. "I thought you knew all along how I felt about you. There have been times when I've felt rather disloyal to Owen because of my premature feelings for you. Times when I'd leave your house and go home alone and think about...." He lifted his eyes to hers and drew her gently to her feet. His Adam's apple lurched and his face looked pained as he took her into his arms, gazing adoringly into her face. "Oh, Rachel, I've never even kissed you."

His warm, open lips were something of a shock, simply because they belonged to Marshall—old, reliable Marshall. His tongue parted her lips, and when it touched hers she struggled not to recoil. But kissing Marshall seemed unholy and about as exciting as kissing a brother.

To Rachel's dismay, his hands dropped lower upon her back and he pulled her flush against him, revealing the fact that he was fully aroused. Rachel's heart hammered in shock while the kiss grew more ardent and she wondered how to get out of this without hurting him more than he deserved. She wedged her hands between them and turned her face aside. "No...please."

He was breathing laboriously when the kiss ended, then he transferred his lips to her jaw and ran his hands more demandingly along her hips and spine. "Rachel, darling, I love you. I have for so long."

"But I...." Why should it be so impossibly

hard to come right out and say she didn't love him? Instead she softened it by saying, "No, Marshall, it's too soon."

He was surprisingly strong as he forced her head around and held it immobile while covering her mouth with his once again. Rachel began to stiffen and was about to rear back and stop him before he went any farther. But she found his protestations of love flattering. Some devilish gremlin tempted her to find out just how far he'd go, and whether her reactions would be as quick and fiery as they'd been to Tommy Lee, so she relaxed in his arms and let his tongue stroke the inside of her mouth.

When he felt her acquiesce, his hand swept up her ribs and captured a breast, caressing it while his tongue delved between her lips with growing fervor. She waited for that magical surge of sexual reaction, but when her nipple puckered and hardened she felt mildly repulsed. Marshall's tongue felt alien within her mouth. His body seemed too long and bony. His hands only made her wish they belonged to another man. All that came were thoughts of Tommy Lee, and how his kisses and touches had set off a series of involuntary responses that had left her shaken and wanting more when he'd turned her loose. Marshall made a soft throaty sound, feeling the distended nipple through her thin summer dress. But when his hips began thrusting against her she realized she was only leading him on fruitlessly, and gently pushed him away.

"Stop, Marshall!" His breathing was agitated and his eyes bright with desire while hers remained as calm as if she'd just awakened from a nap. He cupped her jaws and she had to force herself not to recoil.

"Please, Rachel, I realize you're alone as much as I am, that you have needs, just like I do. If you aren't ready for marriage yet but you need a man in your life, for God's sake, don't turn to one like Gentry."

Good heavens, he was suggesting an affair! Horrified, she stepped back and gaped at him. "I...I'm sorry, Marshall, but I...I just don't feel that way about you. We've been friends too long to become lovers."

"I thought you needed—"

"Well, you thought wrong." She turned away, growing angrier by the minute that he should point fingers at Tommy Lee, then propose a liaison to serve his own purposes. At least Tommy Lee was no hypocrite.

"Rachel, I'm sorry. I didn't mean to insult you."

She turned to confront a very pink-cheeked Marshall. "Should I be honored, Marshall, that you've suggested having an affair with me right after lecturing me on the inadvisability of having one with Tommy Lee Gentry? Right after practically accusing me of having one with him! What makes you that much better than him?"

Red to the roots of his hair now, Marshall stammered, "Rachel, I didn't mean...please don't misunderstand."

"Oh, I understand perfectly, and frankly, I'm rather dismayed."

"Please, dear, d-don't let this c-come between us. We can still be friends."

But Rachel was reasonably certain the last five minutes had put a strain upon their friendship that would never ease. She was also sure that half the town already had her paired up with Tommy Lee Gentry, so why was she fighting it?

The ride home seemed endless. The few attempts at conversation dwindled into a silence that became more and more uncomfortable as the minutes passed. Sometimes Rachel sensed Marshall's eyes on her, but she found it difficult to confront them now.

When he pulled up in her driveway she quickly said, "Thank you for the ride, Marshall," then jumped out before he could turn off the engine. She leaned down to look at him through the open window. "I've changed my mind about Wednesday night. All things considered, I think it's best if you find someone else to be your fourth at bridge."

"Rachel, wait!"

But she was already heading for the house at a half run.

Inside, she leaned her back against the door and breathed a sigh of relief, waiting for her stomach to stop quivering. How acutely embarrassing.

And, in a way, how sad. Dear friends were treasures not to be valued lightly, but how could she ever face Marshall again?

She wandered through the quiet house, pausing in the kitchen to stare out at the pool, recalling Tommy Lee sitting here at the table, confessing that he'd never stopped caring while she gave him no encouragement whatsoever. She meditated on Callie Mae's caustic assessment of the direction her life was taking. Was she really cold, merciless? She didn't want to be. She wanted warmth in her life just like any woman. But in Marshall's arms she'd felt nothing. Only with Tommy Lee did she come alive. Even when she was angry with him she felt exhilarated. And wasn't she the one who had so recently admitted to herself that what she'd wanted in her life was occasional tumult? Like being overturned in a swimming pool by a crazy fool who waded in, in a full dress suit? Then having him send her a blow dryer with a note intimating any woman worth her salt should fix her own hair? And why hadn't he told her the earrings were for Beth?

Rachel glanced at the phone and her heart accelerated at the very thought of hearing his voice. She recalled her father's stern orders that she not see Tommy Lee again and asked herself if the reason she wanted to was simply to demonstrate her own headstrong independence. But it was something more, something deeper, a compulsion that simply could not be denied any longer.

She picked up the receiver with a trembling hand, wondering while she listened to the electronic beeps and rings if he might possibly have another woman with him, and how to open this conversation, which had her heart pounding even before it began.

He answered in a disinterested grunt, "Yeah, Gentry here."

The breath seemed to catch in her throat, then she closed her eyes and replied quietly, "Hollis, here."

"Rachel?" The way he said it made her imagine him slowly rolling his back away from a chair in disbelief.

"Yes."

A long silence passed before he said again, "Rachel...." More softly this time, as if his world had suddenly come aright.

It took great effort to keep her voice steady. "I've received three curious gifts in the past several weeks. You wouldn't know anything about them, would you?"

"Me? Nuh-uh." But in spite of his levity there was an unmistakable quaver in his voice.

She smiled, picturing his dark teasing eyes. "None of the cards were signed."

"What kind of guy would send a card without signing it?"

She heard the snick of the lighter, then the soft rush of breath as he exhaled, and she pictured him stretching across a davenport or bed to reach for an ashtray.

"That's what I'd like to find out."

"So, what'd he send you?"

"A blow dryer, and a dozen roses and a sack of beer cans." But suddenly she dropped the game and her voice turned gentle as she held the receiver in both hands. "Thank you for the roses, Tommy Lee. They were lovely." She sensed once more how pleasantly shocked he was by her phone call and how careful he was being about what he said. She herself felt shaken as she tried to think of a proper comment regarding the beer cans, but being unsure if their cryptic message meant what she thought it did, she safely avoided the subject.

"Listen, Rachel, I acted like a damned idiot, tipping you over in the pool that way and carrying on like a Neanderthal. It'd be my own damn fault if you really meant it when you said you wanted to kill me."

"I do," she replied wistfully, suddenly feeling like crying. Then she added softly, "Sometimes."

Neither of them spoke for several electrified seconds, and she wondered again what his bedroom looked like, and if that's where he was, and if he'd been asleep when she called.

"You invited me to dinner on Friday night, but you didn't say which Friday. Am I too late to accept the invitation?"

His voice sounded forced and slightly breathless. "Oh Lord, do you mean it, Rachel?"

"If you still want me to come."

"Want you to come!" He laughed ruefully.

"God, it's all I've thought about for weeks and weeks. This Friday?"

Something in the question sounded tentative. "Oh, are. . . are you busy?"

"No. . . no!" She relaxed her shoulders, not realizing how much she'd tightened up at the thought that he might have other plans. "And this time we *will* be chaperoned. That's a guarantee."

She wasn't sure whether to be disappointed or not.

"Your daughter?" she asked.

"No."

"But that *was* Beth with you at church, wasn't it?"

"Yes, things went sour between her and her mother so she's living with me now."

Rachel's heart felt a surge of joy for him, but he went on quickly, "We'll talk more about it when I see you. Now, about Friday night."

"But if it's not Beth who'll be chaperoning us, who is it?"

He chuckled and replied indignantly, "A dragon named Georgine that I hired to keep house for me. But I've been tempted at least three times a day to tell her to ride her broom out of here back to where she came from."

"You hired a housekeeper?" Rachel's lips fell open in surprise.

"That's right. Isn't that what you told me to do? One who could cook me low-calorie foods?"

"But I. . . ." She felt slightly chagrined at having been so outspoken, then having her criticism acted upon so spontaneously.

"Tommy Lee, I'm sorry too, for the things I said to you that day in the pool. I called you some terrible names and—"

"But you were right!" he interrupted. "There've been a lot of changes around here. You'll be surprised when you see them. And Georgine will be cooking for us Friday night."

She thought about his trimmer profile when she'd seen him at church, and about the message in the beer cans, and felt her heart lift with hope.

"What time should I come out?"

"Rachel, I...." She heard him pull in a deep breath and sensed a boyish hesitation that seemed totally out of character for a man with a reputation such as his. "Listen, I'd like to pick you up at your house, all proper this time." He chuckled nervously, then added, "I promise I won't dunk you or manhandle you or do anything that's not thoroughly polite. I'd be there at six-thirty."

She remembered the other time she'd opened the door to find him on her step, and what a shock it had been. What a thrilling shock. But to get dressed and wait for him as it had been years ago—Rachel closed her eyes for a second and felt a thrill of girlish anticipation at the thought.

"All right. Six-thirty."

"Six-thirty..." he repeated.

Then a full ten seconds passed while neither of them said anything more.

Finally Rachel put in a wistful, "Well. . . ."

He cleared his throat and repeated in a more businesslike voice. "Six-thirty."

She laughed nervously and reiterated for the fourth time, "Six-thirty. Well, goodbye then."

" 'Bye, Rachel."

When Rachel hung up the phone her face lit with an ear-to-ear smile, then she clasped her hands to the top of her head and spun in a circle.

When Tommy Lee hung up the phone he sat on the edge of the bed with his elbows on his shaky knees, covering his face with both hands. He sat for a long time with his pulse racing, listening to his breath beat against his palms. *My God, she said yes! Incredible! She really said yes!* Then Tommy Lee frowned at the floor.

No kissing, no touching, no cussing, Gentry, you hear? Show her you can be the gentleman she deserves.

He fell back, arms thrown wide, eyes closed, imagining. After ten minutes of pure bliss, he leapt to the floor and did thirty pushups in record time—and all with a smile on his face.

CHAPTER NINE

IT WAS A GOLDEN AUGUST EVENING with scarcely a wisp of breeze stirring. The week seemed to have crawled by with sloth-like slowness while Rachel agonized over what to wear, what to say, how to act. Just like on that first date with Tommy Lee after he'd kissed her in the break of the boxwoods years ago.

It was a strange sensation to be feeling girlish at her age when she'd thought she'd given up giddiness years ago. But she actually had butterflies in her stomach, doubts about whether the gold earrings might have been better than the silver, and misgivings about the dress she'd chosen.

But it was too late now. The white Cadillac was already pulling up beneath the magnolia and she drew back from the window, feeling pulses beating through her body in the places they had no business beating, as she watched Tommy Lee slowly get out of the car then pause to look up at the house a moment before finally slamming the door. He buttoned his suit jacket, glanced down at his stomach, then unbuttoned the jacket again and slipped a hand down his carefully knotted tie like a schoolboy at his first recital.

Rachel touched her lips, smiling. *Why, he's as nervous as I am!* Her smile grew wider. Imagine that, The Hellion of Franklin County, getting all unstrung over walking to a woman's door!

She watched him come up the walk, assessing his new honed profile, and the hand dropped from her lips to her skittering heart. The bell rang. Her eyes closed for a moment while she savored the wild anticipation. Then she smoothed her skirt unnecessarily and moved to open the door.

And couldn't think of a single word to say.

They stared at each other with a breathless hush of appreciation, standing as still as the long shadows across the yard, feeling the awesome tug of nostalgia and the even greater one of reality. She had caught him smoothing his tie again, and his hand remained half-hidden inside the suit jacket at waist level, unmoving now. At closer range she saw things she'd only glimpsed on the church steps. The puff of skin was gone from above his tight, crisp collar. The bulldog jowls had disappeared, leaving the skin about his jaws looking healthy and resilient. His eyes seemed clearer, the pockets of loose flesh gone from beneath them. And his coloring had changed from drinker's pink to runner's bronze.

After what seemed eons, he finally dropped his hand to his side and breathed, "Hi."

"Hi," she managed, though the word seemed to stick in her throat and came out in a queer falsetto. Her eyes swept him from shoulders to toes and she blurted out, "You look wonderful!" Then she felt herself blush abominably.

With a lift of his chin he laughed, and the sound relieved some of the tension. "Thank you, but I think you stole my line. You look—" his appreciative gaze scanned her, missing nothing "—absolutely perfect. Prettier than when you were sixteen."

"Well...." She flapped her hands stupidly and stepped back. "Come in. I'll get my purse." *Rachel Hollis, act your age! You're gawking and blushing like an adolescent in the throes of hormone change!*

He watched her walk away—slim hips moving with scarcely a sway, narrow shoulders bare beneath delicate spaghetti straps that emphasized her fragility. Her shoes were very high heeled and backless and made a soft slapping sound upon her heels as she went. Her muted-blue floral dress was elasticized at the waist and just above her breasts, and appeared to have no foundation except her body. Tommy Lee's bones seemed to turn to jelly as he watched her bare shoulders disappear. She was—plainly and simply—the most desirable woman he'd ever known. How ever would he make it through the evening without touching her?

In no time at all she was back, holding a tiny white purse, a shawl caught in the crook of a wrist. Several feet before him she stopped, glanced up uncertainly and gave a fluttery half smile, then dropped her eyes to study the clasp of her purse as she toyed with it. "After being married all these years I'm afraid I'm out of practice at the art of dating. I feel rather inept and awkward."

He studied her for a moment, then a grin lifted one side of his lips. "Awkward? You, Rachel?" He chuckled and moved toward the entry. "You haven't been awkward since you lost your baby fat at...let's see, when was it? About thirteen?" He cocked his head as he opened the door. "Fourteen?"

She swept past him with mock imperiousness, scolding, "Thomas Gentry, I never had baby fat!"

He couldn't resist slipping a hand to her waist as they moved toward the car. "Oh, yes you did. I've got pictures to prove it."

"What pictures?" His hand sent shivers along her arms and raised the fine hairs of her spine, as did the sight of his car, freshly washed and waxed for the occasion. As he leaned to open the car door for her, she caught the scent of sandalwood and spice in his aftershave.

"I've got pictures of us as far back as when we used to go bathing together in a plastic pool. Remind me to show 'em to you sometime."

She knew to which pictures he referred, and felt uncharacteristically ruffled and shy at the thought of the snapshots of their two plump naked baby bodies, side by side. But the subject was cut off as he slammed the door and rounded the hood of the car. She watched him pause to light a cigarette before getting in beside her, bringing the sharply pleasant tang of freshly-lit tobacco with him.

The interior of the car was immaculate, and the

man at its wheel the essence of companionability as they drove out to his place without once exceeding the speed limit. When they approached the spot where he'd flung out his plastic glass the last time she was riding with him, she leaned to peer around him at the woods and ditch. Then she gave him an impish grin.

"Mmm . . . not tossing your glasses out into the weeds anymore?"

He only swung his eyes her way, gave a lazy smile then carefully tamped out his cigarette, dropped the butt into the ashtray and closed it. She noted each improvement in manners with an uplift of the heart.

"Do you know you're the first man who ever gave me a bag of beer cans?"

"And you're the first woman who ever chewed me out and gave me a lecture on demon rum." They smiled at each other, remembering that night.

The car swayed through the curving woodsy drive, and when they pulled to a stop, he ordered, "Wait here," then got out with a bounding movement and appeared at her door to open it. They took the wooden ramp side by side, untouching, then he solicitously opened an ebony entry door to let Rachel precede him into the house. Music was playing softly and a delicious aroma wafted through the air. He touched her elbow lightly and gestured toward the stairs leading up to the living room, calling, "Georgine?"

In the next moment Rachel was standing in the spotlessly clean room and his new maid came around the corner from the kitchen.

"Georgine, this is Rachel Hollis, a girl I used to go to school with. Rachel, Georgine, who's been given the task of keeping me from perdition."

Georgine tipped a small bow. "I know Mrs. Hollis.... You run the dress store in town." Then she turned to Tommy Lee, informing him he'd had a call from someone named Bitsy who said she wanted him to call back. Finally, she asked, "Are you ready for your drinks now?"

"Drinks" proved to be a delicious concoction of pineapple juice and coconut cream, served in narrow stem glasses with garnishes of fresh pineapple and cherries on long skewers. Rachel sipped hers, tasted no alcohol, and raised her eyebrows. "Mmm...delicious." She wondered if his drink was plain or spiked, but didn't ask, only glanced around the living room to find the plants had been trimmed of drying leaves, washed, and sprayed with leaf polish. The tables gleamed and the carpet hadn't one dot of lint or ash upon it. Under Georgine's care the lavish room had truly come to life.

"How about taking our drinks on the deck?" he suggested, and pulled the door aside, then followed her out. The sun was hovering an hour's ride above the western rim of the lake, sending a highway of shimmering gold straight at them across the water. Overhead a pair of gulls caught the sun on their wings and squawked their tuneless call. It was warm, peaceful and private. Rachel rested her glass on the railing, then leaned her hips against it, squinting into the bright reflection. "This place is really beautiful."

She watched him find and light a cigarette. Odd how the simple motions held a new attraction for her as he tilted his jaw, flicked a thumb on the wheel of the lighter and scowled through the cloud of smoke. He threw his head back, exhaling, turned abruptly and caught her watching him intently.

Immediately she looked at the lake.

"You like it?"

"Yes, very much. Who could help but like it?"

He turned his back to the view and perched a buttock on the rail, one knee riding wide and the suit jacket gaping open as he swiveled toward her. "I built it for you," he said matter-of-factly.

Her eyes flew to his and they stared at each other for an endless moment. His new untinted glasses left the expression in his brown eyes open for study, and she saw there a grave sincerity that rocked her senses. Gone were the days when she wanted to turn away from his probing gaze. Now she wanted to immerse herself in it. He looked so different. Younger. Less worry lined. Head-turningly handsome. She stood riveted before him while he made no move whatever to touch her, yet she felt touched in a wholly wonderful way. She became acutely conscious of his masculine, widespread pose, and the tailored beige jacket fallen aside to reveal expertly cut brown trousers stretched between his cocked hips.

At last she found her voice. "Yes, I know. I recognized it the moment I walked into it."

"Did you?" His voice was gently gruff.

"It was unmistakable."

"And what did you think?"

Again she gazed out over the lake. "That I was married to Owen when you built it."

"So you were." He lifted his glass, watched her over the rim as he took a drink, then dropped the hand to his knee.

"Oh, Tommy Lee, whatever were you thinking, to do a thing like that?" Her eyes were troubled, and the corners of her mouth tipped down as she turned toward him.

He remained silent for a long time, studying the contents of his glass while swirling it distractedly, bumping it against his kneecap. Then he captured her brown eyes with his own and spoke softly. "Remember how we used to dream about it?"

"Yes, I remember. But that was. . .years ago."

He went on as if she hadn't spoken, glancing lazily over his left shoulder at the lake. "It's right where we always said we'd like to live." She felt his eyes move back to study her profile. "And it has all the windows you said you wanted, and all the natural wood I said I wanted." He drew deeply on the cigarette. "And the master bedroom with enormous walk-in closets made of cedar, and the view of the lake, and the fireplace for winter, and the sliding doors and deck for summer.'' He pointed above their heads with the tip of the cigarette. ''That set of steps leads directly down from there, right to the lake for midnight swims.''

Rachel's heart was thundering and her lips dropped open as she resisted the urge to look up at the deck cantilevered over their heads. My God, he remembered everything. She recalled walking in here the first time, noting his choices, adding them up and wondering what the bedroom looked like. Why should it come as such a shock to know it, too, was designed from secrets whispered in the dark more than two decades ago?

The sliding door rolled back and Georgine asked, ''Would you like your salads out here?'' At the far end of the deck was an umbrella table and four cushioned chairs.

''No thank you, Georgine, we'll come inside.'' Tommy Lee eased his leg off the rail. ''Rachel?'' He swept a hand toward the door, and she let her eyes meet his. But they skittered away again from the impact.

The table was simply but elegantly set with thick slubbed placemats and matching blue napkins in ivory napkin rings, a centerpiece of blue and brown, and a pair of ink-blue candles, already lit. When Tommy Lee had solicitously settled Rachel into her chair, he took one directly opposite, reached for his napkin and glanced up to find their view interrupted by the tall tapers. Without a word, he leaned over to push the centerpiece and candles aside, smiled and settled back into his chair, saying, "There...that's better."

She busied herself removing her napkin from its ring, but felt tingly in the ensuing silence, and even more unnerved when she looked up to find him relaxedly lounging in his chair, studying her bemusement with a look of total appreciation.

The salad was made of crabmeat, endive and waterchestnuts and was served without wine. Scrambling about in her mind for a subject of conversation, Rachel finally asked, "So...did you and Darrel make ten?"

His head went back as he laughed, and the movement gave him a look of renewed youth that caught at Rachel's heart.

"Yes, we made ten, and tied Darla. Now the fight is on for eleven."

Their eyes met. Rachel felt a rich closeness to him in that moment as they spoke of things linking them to more than this night. But when the subject died, she sensed him in little hurry to pick up the strings of another. He seemed content to sit there in silence, studying her while the fork trembled in her hand.

When she could stand it no longer she finally insisted, "What are you *looking* at?"

A grin tugged at his cheek. "You. Trying to get my fill."

"Well, you're embarrassing me."

"Sorry, I didn't mean to." But still he didn't

look away. "I'm trying to grasp the fact that you're really here at last, sitting at my table across from me. Incredible...."

She didn't know what to say, so she fiddled with the hem of her napkin.

"You know, Rachel, through the years I watched you maturing, and sometimes I'd grow angry with you. I'd want to call you on the phone and say, why don't you wither up or get gray or haggard! But instead you just grew more and more beautiful as the years passed."

She braced an elbow on the table, dropped a forehead onto her knuckles and shook her head. "Keep that up and I'll have to leave."

"Is that a blush I see?" he teased, cocking his head as if to see behind her hand.

She braced her chin on the hand and presented him with a tight-lipped grin. "What do you think? I told you, I'm out of practice."

He laughed, sending a flash of white teeth through the growing shadows. "Ah, I love it."

"Could we please change the subject, Mr. Gentry?"

"As you please. Pick one."

She clasped her hands in her lap and said softly, "Beth."

"Which one?" he asked.

She felt herself color again as she answered quietly, "Your Beth. You said she's living with you."

He cleared his throat and sat up straighter in his

chair. "Yes, for two weeks now, but she's gone off with some kids to the movies. She met a bunch down at the beach the first week, and already she's saying she wants to register for school here."

"Well, you must be ecstatic."

"I am." His expression sobered slightly. "But it takes some adjusting."

"I imagine it does. What...how...?" Rachel became discomfited and waved an apologetic palm. "Oh, I guess it's none of my business."

"Of course it is." He leaned his elbows on the table edge and met her eyes directly. "Nancy and Beth haven't gotten along well at all for a couple of years now. Nancy is what you might call an overprotective mother, unwilling to let her birdling out of the nest for the first time. They have terrible fights, and the result of the last one was that Beth ran away from home. She was gone for three days, and when we found her it was decided it'd be best if she tried living with me for a while. And so, it seems I've been granted a second chance to be a father."

"You mean she might stay? Indefinitely?"

"If things work out right. If she's happier here. If I can keep on the straight and narrow."

Her dark eyes lifted to his. "And can you?" she asked in a near whisper.

He studied her with a loving expression in his eyes. "At this moment, Rachel, I feel like there's nothing in this world I can't do."

The elation caused by his words lasted through

the main course, which was beef Stroganoff. He ate his without any rice, and uncomplainingly drank lime water without so much as a grimace. The wine or champagne she'd expected was nowhere in evidence.

He talked some more about Beth, asked Rachel's advice on buying school clothes, which led to a discussion about her own store. She entertained him with humorous tales of the idiosyncrasies of her various customers, then asked him about his development corporation.

They ran out of things to talk about and found themselves staring at each other. Out of the blue Rachel blurted, "I like your new glasses much better than the old ones."

He grinned, but remained as before, bracing a jaw on one hand. "Oh, do you?" And she knew without being told, he'd changed them because of her.

She felt color washing upward and knew a sense of expanding sexual awareness between them. She dropped her eyes to the banana-cream pie on her plate, but they wandered from it to his coffee cup and the cigarette crooked in dark tapered fingers that toyed with the cup handle while his unwavering gaze rested on her.

"Aren't you having any dessert?" she asked, letting her eyes skip up to his.

He answered simply, "No, not tonight."

And suddenly she admitted how serious he was about his reform, and that it had not been under-

taken solely because of Beth coming back to live
with him. She, Rachel, had laid down parameters
and he was striving to fit himself to them. And it
was working. A rush of blood thrummed through
her body, bringing again that sensual pounding
deep in her vitals. As untamed as their longing for
each other had been when they were teen-agers, it
seemed insipid compared to this mature reaction
she was feeling for him. Yet he lounged in his
chair with all the indolence of a sated maharaja,
studying her closely while she fidgeted with the
cloth of her skirt and grew hotter beneath his
scrutiny.

Then Georgine took away their dessert plates
and said if there wasn't anything more she was going to bed, and the gentle bump of her footsteps
sounded up the carpeted stairs before all was still.

"She lives here, too?" Rachel asked, wide-eyed.

Tommy Lee fingered the rim of his coffee cup
while studying her through the smoke that lifted
between them. "Yes, in one of the guest rooms."

"Oh." So, he could no longer bring his women
to that sprawling sofa.

"Weekdays," he added, then snuffed out his
cigarette.

"Oh," she said again inanely, and wondered if
he would ever try to get her onto that sofa with
him. She thanked her lucky stars it couldn't possibly happen tonight with Georgine asleep upstairs
and Beth probably due back any minute.

"Would you like to take your coffee into the

living room?'' he asked, as if reading her mind and deciding to foil her.

Rachel twitched and her eyes grew rounder. "Oh. . . ." She glanced skittishly at a corner of the sofa visible beyond the fireplace. "All right," she added belatedly, but missed the grin on Tommy Lee's face as he watched her peruse the field of ottomans fit for a harem.

But he pushed the ottomans back, and they took separate places with a decorous space between them, and he was everything he'd promised to be: the perfect gentleman.

And Rachel was the slightest bit disappointed.

THEY HEADED BACK TO TOWN before Beth returned home, and all the way Tommy Lee smoked continuously, the only indication that he might be as tense as she. He had kept his promise all evening, never saying or doing anything untoward. By now it was driving her crazy. She turned to study his face, illuminated by the pale dash lights, which reflected from his lenses and lit his knuckles on the wheel. He glanced her way. Her eyes veered out the side window then closed upon the thought that it had been years and years since she had become this aroused by merely looking at a man.

There could be no question that the most sensible way to end the evening would be with a graceful, polite parting. But being sensible was far from her mind, as she was sure it was from Tommy Lee's. There was no denying he was tempting, so tempting that these hours with him had been a study in control.

They were wheeling slowly through the city streets when Rachel drew a deep breath to ask, "Tommy Lee, who is Bitsy?"

His eyes measured her for some time before he answered, "Bitsy is a woman I was seeing."

"Was?" Afraid to look at him, she trained her eyes on the headlights.

"Yes, *was*. She keeps calling and suggesting that we get together again, but I seem to have lost my taste for other women lately." He drew deeply on his cigarette before going on. "There's no use denying it, Rachel—there've been a lot of them. I suppose that bothers you."

It did. It made her mentally step back a pace when she wanted to move nearer. But beneath her reservation a disturbing tingle of jealousy made her reply defensively, "Should it?"

"Does it?" he rifled back.

The moment sizzled with their acute absorption in each other as their eyes met and clashed, then she forced hers toward the windshield again. "Yes, it does. But it's more a disappointment than anything else."

"I didn't know I had the power to disappoint you."

"Well, you do."

"Why?"

"Because." She searched for a way to express it. "Because we were children together, good friends even before we became lovers, and I wanted you to remain that...that hero you'd always been for me. When rumors spread about you and yet another woman, I used to get so...so *angry* with you, I'd want to rap you on the skull and knock some sense into your head!" He laughed and immediately she scolded, "Don't you dare laugh. You don't know what you put me through. Somehow I always ended up in a position of having to either defend or blame, and I didn't want to have to do either."

He grinned her way beguilingly. "And which did you do?"

She turned a snooty nose in the air. "None of your business."

"All right. Fair enough. So, what about Marshall True?"

Her head snapped around. "M-Marshall?" Her face burned at the memory of her last confrontation with Marshall.

"The town has the two of you linked together. Surely you know that."

"I'm not seeing Marshall anymore."

"Oh?" His eyes flashed over her, but she looked straight ahead.

"Marshall made a pass at me that I didn't like at all."

"You don't like it when a man makes a pass at you?" he questioned quietly.

She picked at her purse catch with a thumbnail. "I didn't like it when *Marshall* made a pass at me."

Just at that moment they reached Rachel's house and he drew up at the curb beneath the deep, shielding branches of the magnolia, eased the car into neutral and turned on the parking lights, then sat back smoking. "I take that to mean you never had an affair while you were married to Owen."

She was shocked by his words, appalled that he might even think her capable of it. "No, never!"

"Not even in the end?" Again she flushed at the realization that he, too, had guessed the extent to which Owen's illness had incapacitated him.

"No, I could never have handled the guilt."

"And what about now?" he asked.

"Now?" Her eyes flew to his dimly lit profile, the crisp knot of his tie, the crisper outline of his lips, chin and nose. "Are you one of those widows who would feel disloyal to her husband's memory if she had sex with another man?"

The warning rockets went off in Rachel's body. How many times had she asked herself the same question and come up with no answer? Twenty years with the same man had left her feeling shaky and doubtful about considering another. Yet she knew when Tommy Lee made his move, she would not turn him away. And there was no doubt, he was about to make it. She held her breath, waiting for him to turn off the engine and draw her into his arms, but instead he strung an arm along the back of the seat, half turning to her to say, "Rachel, I can't thank you enough for tonight."

Disappointment made her stomach go hollow as she realized he'd been sitting there waiting for his cue, which she had not given. Maybe it was best this way. Her common sense knew a thousand reasons why she should hurry to the house and let him drive away, but her heart knew as many more for wanting him to stay. His company was pleasurable...and he'd changed. So much. But would the changes last? At that moment it ceased to matter, and she groped for a means to keep him a while longer.

"But I should be thanking you."

"No...no," he said quietly. But still he sat politely on his side of the seat while her heart hammered crazily.

"Tommy Lee, I...." Did he really intend to say goodnight without even kissing her?

"You what?"

She didn't know what she was going to say next until the words fell from her mouth. "Why didn't you tell me the earrings were for Beth?"

"You wanted to believe the worst about me."

"I did?"

"Of course. That would make it so much easier to deny what you were feeling."

"A-and what am I feeling?"

"You tell me."

But she really didn't know. There was this powerful attraction, but at the same time she feared his wildness, his reputation, the very real possibility of his backsliding.

So she asked, "Did you get the new glasses because you knew I didn't like the old ones?"

His hand rested very near her shoulder. "Absolutely," he answered in a voice as soft as the fall
of a dogwood petal.

Her eyes dropped to his lapel. "And your suit is
new, isn't it?"

He, too, glanced down at his chest. "I'm afraid
it is. I had to buy it to replace a perfectly good one
I ruined in your pool." They laughed quietly, then
fell still again, feeling the tension grow.

"And you've been...." She was suddenly
afraid to broach the delicate issue.

"I've been what?"

"You've been dieting."

"High time, wouldn't you say?"

She had saved the most delicate issue for last.
"And how long has it been since you've stopped
drinking?"

His hand left the back of the seat and fished for
a cigarette. "Six weeks," he answered, leaning
forward to push in the dash lighter, leaving his
arm extended while waiting for it.

She added it all up, as she'd been adding it up
all evening, and her heart melted. She laid her
hand on his crisp jacket sleeve. "Oh, Tommy Lee,
that's wonderful."

His eyes flashed to the spot where she touched
him, then quickly away. "You made me see I was
on a fast train to nowhere. I decided it was time to
change tracks."

The lighter popped out and she dropped her hand from his arm while the tip of the cigarette took fire. The idling engine was making her more nervous by the second and she sensed his impatience to get away if the evening were going to end here with a simple goodnight.

Suddenly his face took on a hard expression as he studied the glowing coal of his cigarette and asked, "Rachel, why did you come tonight?"

She was so surprised at his change of mood she didn't know what to answer. She only stared at him, big-eyed.

"You wanted to check me out, find out if I really meant it when I said I could change. But what does it mean to you that I have?"

"Mean. . .? I-I'm not sure what you—"

"Let me put it this way, then. Just because you asked me to change, don't expect that even though I have I'll stand a chance with you. That's how it is, right, Rachel?"

"No! No that's not it!" But it was. In spite of the sexual awareness she felt, she was afraid of people finding out she was spending time with him, afraid of the way he played romantic leap-frog, afraid that they were attracted to each other more by the tug of yesteryear than of today.

"Oh, isn't it? You've already told me you're not a woman who has affairs, and it would be stretching the imagination to believe you wanted anything permanent. So if I kiss you, if I start something, where does that leave me except hurt?"

He studied her intensely now, waiting for some response. She felt like a hypocrite, wanting him sexually, yet unable to deny that she wouldn't want the town to find out. He turned to face her, crooking a knee on the seat and draping an elbow between the headrests. She was reminded of his similar pose on the deck railing earlier and pictured his trousers drawn tight, his jacket fallen open. With the hand that held the cigarette, he lifted a strand of her hair and let it fall. "It's all right, Rachel. You don't have to say it."

She closed her eyes and let the sensation of his touch thread down through her limbs and bring goose pimples as the hair dropped from his fingertips time and again. A thought filtered through—something about too much water over the dam—but it felt so good to be touched again, even in so casual a fashion. From above her head the smoke curled, filling her nostrils, while he played with her hair and made her shiver. At last she opened her eyes and found him watching her carefully.

"But still I can't resist you," he said throatily. "You know that."

All was still. Their eyes clung and questioned while intensity spun between them. *He's right*, she thought sadly, *you could hurt him so badly*.

"We have so much working against us," she said, in a soft pained voice.

"Do we?"

She was hazily aware of his arm lifting over her

head, and of the way he reached toward the ashtray to tamp out the cigarette while studying her over his shoulder. Then he turned to her again, and one strong hand closed about the back of her neck.

"Come here, Rachel," came his thick-throated appeal.

He drew her halfway across the seat, meeting her there with the kiss she'd been afraid would happen, afraid wouldn't. His lips were open, soft and suckling, covering hers in a first exploratory hello-again that made her heart carom. The tip of his tongue drew persuasive lines along the seam of her lips, and she could no more have kept them closed against him than she could have stilled the wild thrum of her heart. Their tongues met—a sleek, hesitant greeting filled with uncertainty.

When they drew apart, their eyes shone like flinders of glass as they studied each other in the faint greenish-white light. He tucked a strand of hair behind her ear. "Now tell me," he ordered softly. "What do we have working against us?"

It was difficult for Rachel to reason with her pulses racing this way. She forced herself to ease back to her own side of the seat, but the moment she did he took up the sensual fingering of her hair again. She shivered, came to her senses and shrugged away. "Don't do that, Tommy Lee," she demanded sensibly, forcing herself to evaluate the situation rationally. He was justified in asking her exactly why she was here and what she wanted from him.

"Sorry," he said, dropping the hair. "A minute ago I thought you were enjoying it."

"A minute ago I was, but I shouldn't have been."

"What are you afraid of, Rachel?"

"The same things you are. You...me...the past...the future."

"Broad answers. Could you narrow them down?"

She sighed and looked away from him in hopes she could think more clearly. "Oh, Tommy Lee, you're so...so practiced!" She made an irritated gesture with her hands.

"Practiced!"

"Yes, practiced. I have the distinct feeling you've done it all, said it all a thousand times before. Do you blame me for being put off by the thought of all those others?"

"All right," he snapped, "so I'm not a fumbling schoolboy anymore. Is that what you want?"

"I don't know," she said miserably, propping her forehead with her knuckles. "I'm so mixed up."

"I told you before, Rachel. They were only substitutes."

"And when you say things like that it only makes me wonder if you give this standard line to every one of us."

He tensed, then the lines of his face hardened, and he removed his arm from the back of the seat. "I don't have a *standard line*," he stated angrily.

"You wanted me to tell you what we had working against us, so there it is—part of it—and I'm not sure I can ever get past it."

He studied her profile for a full minute, then went on with stern reproof in every word. "Let me tell you something, Rachel. When you first came home from college, you wore your hair down to the middle of your shoulder blades, and had a saucy little red shiny-looking coat that barely reached past your butt, and the day you were married it was only sixty-seven degrees and raining. You honeymooned in Greece, came back and lived in a rented house at 1400 Oak Street, and your phone number was 370-6891. You went to work for the Chamber of Commerce during the time when your hair was screwed up in Afro ringlets, and you wore a more sedate gray cloth coat that fall—that was when you had the maroon colored Chevy Nova, the one that kid sideswiped that time when you hit your head on the windshield and had to have stitches in your scalp—let's see...." With seemingly clinical detachment he clasped her head in both hands and explored her hairline with his thumbs. "I forget which side it's on, but I know it's right here someplace...."

She chuckled and pulled away. "Oh, Tommy Lee, you're impossible."

"Do you want me to tell you about the cinnamon-colored suede suit that really knocked my socks off when I first saw you walking by in it? Or the grand opening of your store, held on September fif—"

She cut him off with four fingers on his lips. "No, you don't have to tell me any more," she answered meekly.

He kissed her fingertips then pressed them to his lapel before declaring in a soft sincere tone, "I don't have a line where you're concerned, Rachel."

"I'm sorry I said that. I really am."

"But I don't know what you want from me. What is it, Rachel?" His hand gripped hers harder. His eyes, so close now, held a vulnerability he made no effort to hide.

"I don't know. Sometimes the thought of you scares me. You're so...so...."

"When I kissed you, you weren't scared."

"When you kissed me you caught me with my guard down."

His eyes dropped to her lips. He smoothed the back of her hand, and even through his stiff lapel she could feel the strong, fast thud of his heart. "You're afraid I'll use you and move on, is that it?"

"That's part of it."

"And the other part?"

She looked into his eyes with a sad realization that there were no guarantees in this world. "That I'll use you and move on," she admitted, then continued softly. "There are still feelings between us, I won't deny it. But why? Simply because we were denied the right to each other once a long time ago? And if and when we've explored those feelings, what then? Please understand, Tommy Lee, I don't want to hurt you, but it's becoming more clear all the time how easily that could happen.''

"But suppose I'm willing to take the risk?"

The longer she sat with her hand over his clamoring heart, the more willing she herself was becoming. She withdrew her hand and searched for more reasons to stop this folly.

"There's something else." Her lips dropped open and the tip of her tongue came out to wet them. "People say things about widows...unkind things." She swallowed and felt herself beginning to blush, recalling Marshall's readiness to become her lover, and his reasons for believing she needed one. And though she'd be the first to admit he'd been right, Rachel was chagrined when she faced the fact. Finally she blurted out, "I don't want to be thought of as a...a sex-starved widow. But I...I...." She stammered to a halt, feeling tears sting her eyes, hating this confusion, which was so foreign to her.

"You what? Say it. Don't be afraid," he prompted.

I suddenly find you more than I bargained for. I want to feel your arms around me, your mouth on mine, your hands on my body. I want to feel alive again, desired, loved. But I'm so afraid to let it happen with you.

"I'm afraid to," she said shakily.

He reached to touch her cheek, reading in her

eyes the unmistakable tug of carnality against which she fought. "Poor Rachel, so mixed up, wanting one thing, telling herself she wants another."

He studied her thoroughly, puzzling out this new, uncertain Rachel. Then he smiled, leaned close and grazed his lips along her jaw. "So, what'll it be?" he murmured teasingly. "Wanna neck a little bit and see how it feels?"

She laughed unexpectedly, feeling the tension ease. And he kissed her neck with a fleeting touch that could scarcely be felt. But his scent was in her nostrils, smoky, mixed with the remnants of his shaving lotion and the starchy smell of new fabric from his suit. Her eyelids drifted closed and his nearness sent the blood roaring to her ears.

"Mmm...." She murmured softly while he worked his way toward her earlobe and worried it gently with his teeth.

"Nice?" he murmured in return.

"Mmm...." It was more than nice. It was heady, enticing. "Tommy Lee," she whispered, "why did you leave the car running?"

He drew back to study her eyes, his arms forming an open harbor for her to sail into if she chose, resting on the wheel and the seat, but not touching her. "If you want it off, turn it off yourself."

And so here it was—the choice. If she shut the car off there would be no turning back. If she didn't, she had the feeling she'd regret it forever.

Her hand trembled as it reached toward the keys

that dangled from the ignition on a silver chain. They chinked softly, then the car fell silent. Neither of them moved for a long, tense moment. At last, with his eyes rapt upon her, he reached through the steering wheel and shifted the car into park, felt for the light switch and brought darkness descending about their heads. His hand lifted slowly to his temple, and with a twist of his head the glasses came off, then he laid them on the dash. In slow motion, his hands closed about her neck, urging her near until she tilted toward him. For the space of several thundering heartbeats they hovered with their lips an inch apart.

"I don't want an affair," she claimed in a shaken whisper, but she needed very much **to** be kissed and caressed again.

"I know." His lips brushed hers in a kiss as tentative as the first one shared years ago in the break of a boxwood hedge. Her right hand came up to rest shyly against his chest, while his shifted to her hair, his long fingers threading through it.

They backed apart slightly, gauging each other's reactions and the dangers of carrying this to its limits. Those dangers were many and very, very real. But the great force of sexuality pressed down upon them, lying in their vitals with a heavy anguish of longing while their heartbeats scudded like thunder before a summer storm.

"Tommy Lee . . . we're crazy," she whispered.

"No," came his whispered reply. "We deserve this. We paid for it long ago."

CHAPTER TEN

THEY MOVED WITH ONE ACCORD, tipping their
heads until their lips met again in tremulous reunion, sweeping them back in memory to the time
of sweet innocence, when only bright dreams lay
ahead.

Rachel's fingertips moved from his lapel to his
shirtfront, and felt the skin warm through the cotton as his breath came with a celerity that matched
her own. Their heads swayed in a lovers' choreography, seeking a firmer fit of mouth upon mouth.
His hand flattened upon her warm, bare back,
drawing her nearer as his tongue slipped between
her silken lips, bringing the taste of tobacco and
some long-remembered essence as individual as a
fingerprint. A sound rose in his throat—the end of
the bitter, rebirth of the sweet—and came a second time while his tongue scribed ever-widening
circles over her eager mouth.

Ardor flared. Intimacy beckoned.

"Rachel...Rachel," he murmured, the words
slurred between their hungering mouths. And as
the kiss grew more greedy he reached between
their paired chins to loosen the knot of his tie,

then settled more firmly against her, slipping a hand to her ribs as he pressed her shoulders against the resilient leather seat.

The kiss swept them with the realization of how easily sensuality had been revived between them, and the pleasure they still found in each other. They experimented, recalling how it had been in the past—a scrape of teeth against a soft inner lip, a gentle bite, an interchange of tongues in the most secret recesses of their open, willing mouths, a suckling that seemed to tug deep within. Rachel's body shimmered in response. It had been so long...so long. His body pressing hers was vital, resilient, healthy. Her breasts peaked and yearned for the warmth of his hands.

But the kiss ended and he backed away to look down into her face. "Rachel," he whispered in wonder. "I can't believe it. After all these years." He wrapped her in two tight arms, her chin catching on his shoulder as he rocked her in jubilant celebration. "God, I can't believe it."

She smiled against his jaw and hugged him back. "I can't, either."

Abruptly he backed away, but his eyes held embers as he ordered gruffly, "Turn around." Deftly he manipulated her, twisting her about until she was cradled in his lap, and in the same sweeping motion he returned his mouth to hers. Sealed beneath his lips she felt herself settled against his chest while a hand swept down to draw her knees up onto the seat. Then he stretched backward into his corner and angled his legs toward the opposite door.

And it felt like coming home—birdling to nest, cub to den, Rachel to Tommy Lee. How warm and secure and familiar was this spot she'd known uncountable times before. And, ah, how their bodies fit. So natural with her arms twined about him until their joined breasts left space for nothing more than the paired heartbeats between them. He shifted a hip, raised one knee to buttress her spine and buttock while kissing her in a remembered way that brought welcome sensations sizzling through her body.

She had thought the years would have created obstacles that would interfere, present warnings. But instead of warning, she felt only impatience. This was right. This was where she belonged.

She reveled in the feeling, exploring the back of his neck, sliding her long nails into his midnight hair while his hands played over her back and his tongue blandished, coaxed, and sent shivers scattering along her skin.

When he finally lifted his head their hearts were beating crazily. Rachel's limbs felt weighted. Her eyes drifted open to find his mouth still close, his palm lazily stirring the fabric on the side of her breast.

"How many times do you think we laid like this in my car?"

But she couldn't even guess. She could only recall the grand and terrible temptation of those days when they'd gone only so far but restrained themselves at the last moment. It had been heaven. It had been hell.

"Too many to remember. A hundred...two hundred...more."

"Do you remember the last time?" His hand made patterns that threatened to cup her breast but never did, bringing back the sharp thrill of the forbidden.

"No, I don't remember."

"It was the night when we'd driven up to Muscle Shoals to go to a dance, and you were wearing a flared skirt with green squares on it, and you could hardly get it buttoned anymore because you were pregnant."

She lay back comfortably in the crook of his arm, feeling again the seductive sense of security—how painless it was to talk about the past, wrapped in his arms this way. She touched his lower lip tenderly. It was puffed and moist from kissing. "You remember everything."

"Yes," he confirmed softly. "Where you're concerned, I remember everything. The smell of your skin, the exact brown of your eyes, the texture of your hair...."

In that moment it was incredibly easy to love him, and she wondered how she would find the resistance to turn the tide of their desire. His head dropped and he crushed her close while lowering open lips over hers. The past melded with the present to bring a desire more potent than any they'd known in their youth. Their tongues imitated the act they'd shared in the days when they were raring and insatiable, and they felt again the supreme urgency they'd thought themselves able to curb.

His hand slipped to cover one tiny breast at last, working the sleek cloth over her aroused nipple. She writhed in complementary circles, lifting toward his touch, making a faint mewling sound in her throat. Beneath her side she felt his tumescence, sheathed tightly but straining warmly through his trousers as she moved restlessly upon it. His hips began thrusting, and she instinctively drew common sense back into its rightful place, pressing a restraining hand against his chest.

Immediately his body stilled. He drew a tortured breath and buried his face in the fragrant curve of her neck. "I swore I wouldn't rush you... but it's damn hard."

She was breathless, floating, realizing how naive she'd been to think she could tread such a tightrope again without falling. Had she thought being forty-one instead of sixteen was adequate insurance against desire? Her voice shook as she answered, "And I swore I'd be sensible and settle for a few kisses...." She laughed tightly, ending with the familiar little hiccup he had never forgotten. Then she surged up, holding him tightly, pressing her forehead to the inviting hollow below his jaw. "But you guessed right. It's been a long time since I've done anything like this, and the last time was with a man who was ill and unable to dredge up the fire I needed.'' She held him possessively and said through clenched teeth, "But you feel so good, so healthy. It's terribly hard to stop.''

His hand caressed her breast, then slipped down one buttock and stroked it deftly before moving to the warm hollow behind her knee.

"Why should we?''

"Because it's the most sensible thing to do. Because I've only been a widow for a few months. Because our motives may be strictly carnal. Because if we start something it could get to be a habit,'' she recited in a rush against his neck, willing herself to believe it.

"I believe, Rachel—'' he kissed her eyelid "—it's already started—'' and her nose "—and out of our hands.''

When his mouth opened hotly over hers she found herself clinging, kissing him back with nothing held in reserve. His hand caressed her hip, then sought her flat stomach before moving in one unerring swipe to cup the yearning warmth between her legs, pressing her skirt against the damp curve of femininity, tracing arousing circles on her flesh until she murmured inarticulately into his mouth.

"We have to stop...'' she tried to say, but the words were muffled beneath his lips.

"You feel so good...so tiny...just like I remember....''

"It's too tempting."

"Just like the old days."

His hands moved over her freely while she lay across his lap, her heart pounding so hard it seemed it must certainly have been making the leaves of the magnolia tree tremble above them. His fingers curved—contouring, pressing, stirring, kindling while she lifted and drifted, thinking, *just a little more, just a little. . . .*

Then her dress rustled up and his hand sent fire-flashes dancing up her thighs and stomach as he sought naked skin.

At her waist she stopped it.

His head lifted. His eyes questioned.

"Don't, Tommy Lee. . . please," she whispered stridently. To her surprise, he immediately complied, but took up the idle rhythm through her clothing again.

"Rachel, remember the first time?" he whispered.

"Yes. It was out by the quarries, and I was very scared."

"So was I."

"You were? I never knew that before. You seemed so confident, as if you knew everything about it."

"I didn't know any more than you did." He bit her lower lip, adding persuasively, "but I've learned some new things since then."

She chuckled throatily. "So have I. Like how disastrous it would be to get caught like this if a prowl car came by and shined his spotlight on us.''

He laughed softly, caressing her stomach. ''It wouldn't be the first time, would it?''

''No, but it would be a lot more embarrassing at our age. Why don't we take a walk and cool off?''

''So you're teasing again, Rachel?'' he questioned, but without rancor.

''Again?''

''Yes, again.''

''When have I ever teased you?''

''You teased me plenty back then before you finally let me.''

''Oh, back then. Well...I was scared I'd get pregnant. And besides, it was forbidden.''

''And what about now? Is that what's holding you back?''

She considered for a moment, then ran the tip of an index finger along his lips. The nail skimmed his teeth until they opened and suckled the fingertip, then clamped down lightly upon it. ''Will you understand if I say maybe that's partly true? You're that...that naughty Tommy Lee Gentry,'' she whispered. ''And there's something inside every woman that's drawn to a bad boy. I'll admit I'm shamelessly attracted to the forbidden side of you. But no matter how many times I analyze it, there's still a part of you that's *my* Tommy Lee, the one who gave me my first kiss in the break of the boxwood hedges. That's the Tommy Lee who keeps crowding my mind when I try to sleep at night and can't.''

"You mean I've kept you awake, too?"

"Ceaselessly. Thinking about what we're doing now. Which is why one of us needs to be sensible and get us out of this car so we can cool off."

He sighed as if put upon, but obediently released her and pushed her up. "All right. A walk it is," he obliged, then opened the door and got out, watching her slide beneath the wheel, hair tousled, lips swollen, dress twisted at the waist. When the door slammed he dropped his hands to her hips and adjusted the disheveled dress until it hung properly again. "What an untidy little mess you are," he teased. Automatically she reached to smooth her messed-up hair. "No, don't. Leave it." He pulled her hands down. "I love it that way. You look like you used to after we'd been out parking. Not a glimmer of lipstick left on your mouth, and your lips all red and puffy." He caressed them lightly with a thumb, weakening her resolve again. And when his hips pressed her back against the car, she looped her arms around his neck, unable to stop herself from inviting his warm kiss or the capture of her breasts in his two wide palms.

After several tempting minutes, she drew away and reminded him shakily, "I thought we were going to take a walk and cool off."

"Yes, damn it, we were." He draped a wrist over her shoulder and she entwined her fingers with his, their joined hands bumping her collarbone with each step. They ambled aimlessly along the darkened street, talking of their pasts. He told of the dreams he'd had of coming back to Russellville after college and succeeding in business, of achieving that success but finding it hollow as relationship after relationship failed and he had no one to share it with. She confessed how badly she'd wanted a child to replace the one they'd lost, and of the slow death of that dream, and how devastated she was upon learning she could not conceive again. They walked then in silence, nothing but the night chorus of crickets and peepers accompanying their lazy footsteps along the somnolent avenue where shadows were deep. They returned at last to her familiar magnolia, crossed the night-damp grass, which wet her nylons through her open-toed shoes, then passed beneath a hickory tree, blacker than black, and wandered thoughtlessly toward her backyard. They moved beyond the soft hum of the filtering equipment, then all was silent but for the burble of water circulating somewhere in the pool, and their own matched, lazy footsteps clicking on concrete.

It was very late, and they were both tired, but unwilling to call an end to the night as they stopped, Rachel with her back to Tommy Lee and his hands resting upon her shoulders. They looked up at the myriad lights burning across the night sky. The moon was at its apex, a lopsided blue-white smile amid the winking eyes of the stars. From the dew-laden juniper bushes along the brick wall came the thick scent of evergreen, and somewhere crickets sang in tandem.

Tommy Lee turned Rachel to face him, leaving his palms in an undemanding parenthesis about her neck. He drew a shaky breath but spoke with uncommon steadiness.

"I told you once in anger, but that's no way to say it—I love you, Rachel. There. I've wanted to tell you for so many, many years."

"Oh, Tommy Lee...."

She found herself near tears. *What am I going to do with this man? How long can I fight him?* Her arms circled his neck and she kissed his left cheek, then his right, wondering if she loved him too, in the same way he'd meant he loved her. But to say so without being sure would be cheating them both. She meant her kisses to express affection without commitment, but when she would have backed away he suddenly pulled her flush against him, lifting her onto tiptoe, matching her curves to his. Tongues, hips and hands soon began taking an active part in the kiss, and by the time it ended, both Rachel and Tommy Lee were breathing as if winded.

"Rachel, this is silly. You want it too. Let me come in with you."

She managed to shake her head and back away.

He studied her for a moment, wondering just what it would take to make her break down. "All right, have it your way. We'll cool off again." Then, calm as you please, he began removing his suit jacket. Her first impression was to giggle, but when she realized his intent, she grabbed his lapels.

"Oh no you don't, not in the pool!"

"Why not in the pool?"

"Because that's the oldest ploy in the history of seduction, and I'm not about to fall for it."

He nuzzled her ear. "Come on, Rachel, it could be fun."

"And dangerous."

"Have you ever done it before? Shucked down in the dark and gone in with nothing on?"

"No, and I'm not going to start now."

Suddenly there came a snap as he whipped off his tie. "Mind if I do?"

"And what do you expect me to do? Stand here and watch?"

"Mmm...it could be interesting." He leaned close and bit her earlobe.

"You haven't changed a bit!"

He chuckled and moved away toward the pale shadow of the patio table, and before her astonished eyes he went on undressing, slipping off his shoes, then hanging his jacket neatly on the back of one chair before reaching for his belt.

"Tommy Lee, don't you dare!"

"Ain't no damn way I'm ruining another suit." She watched in utter helplessness as his trousers came off and were laid across the table, followed by his socks. Panic and excitement turned her skin hot.

"If you take off one more stitch, I swear I'll go in the house and lock the door and call the police to tell them there's a naked man using my pool without permission."

Her threats bounced off him like the moon's reflection from the surface of the pool. His fingers lazily worked their way down his shirt buttons and she sensed him grinning at her out of the deep shadows. She had a flashing thought about occasional tumult, but if Tommy Lee continued what he was doing, it would be more tumult than advisable. He'd already half-shrugged out of the shirt when she appealed in a desperate voice, "Please. . . please, don't."

He stopped in mid-motion and flipped his palms up. "Okay, you win. I'll leave the rest on." But he casually removed the cigarettes from his shirt pocket and set them aside, then strode leisurely toward her. As he advanced she sensed the feral gleam in his eye and retreated.

"Tommy Lee. . ." she warned.

But he kept coming, deliberately, unrelentingly. "You're the one who said you wanted to cool off."

"Tommy Lee, you wouldn't."

"Oh, wouldn't I?" He was a mere foot in front of her when she reached out a hand to fend him off. In the blue-white smile of the moon she saw his devilish grin a second before he lunged.

"Tommy Lee Gentry, don't you dare!" she squealed, but his arms were dauntless, clasped beneath her knees and armpits as he headed for the steps of the pool.

"Kick your shoes off, Rachel, if you don't want them to get wet."

"Gentry, you hellion, put me down!" She was still squirming as his feet splashed into the water.

"The choice was yours—with our clothes on, you insisted." The water touched Rachel's derriere. Her hips bucked, and she squealed and grabbed his neck. "Mmm...nice. Do that again," he teased, lowering her again until the water soaked six more inches of underwear and her toes went under.

"My shoes!" Her knees straightened like a switchblade, sending a spray of droplets scintillating across the surface of the pool.

"Too late now. You should have taken them off when you had a chance."

Down she went again, deeper this time, until the water's cold fingers slipped between her thighs. A shudder pelted across her skin, bringing a chuckle from Tommy Lee as he nuzzled her neck. Then he licked her skin with his warm tongue while bobbing her lower and lower and lower into the water.

"The chlorine's going to ruin my dress," she insisted, but with waning urgency.

Against her neck he mumbled, "Send me a bill."

She stopped fighting him then, hanging suspended and helpless in his tight grip, feeling the water lick up and down her thighs with a faint suction and slap each time she was drawn free, then plunged beneath the surface. The shivers were steady now. Goose bumps sprouted up and down her arms and across her bare shoulders. Her breasts—dry though they were—had puckered up like a pair of gum drops.

"Tommy Lee, you're crazy...crazy." But the words came out in a breathless murmur as her knees relaxed and her shoes trailed in the water.

"I know—crazy white boy who builds crazy houses, and dreams crazy dreams, doing crazy things because he's got his woman in his arms at last and he doesn't want to let her go."

He kissed her fiercely, the contact so warm when contrasted against the cool seeking water swashing between her thighs. Her arms twined about his neck as she went pliant and welcomed his probing tongue, which sent a new, different set of shivers up her spine. He started nipping her— sharp, enticing tugs between teeth that knew exactly how hard to bite, and where.

"Crazy..." she whispered, letting her head loll back.

Her eyelids slid closed and the water seemed to grow warmer as Tommy Lee turned them both in a circle. One of her shoes drifted free and sank somewhere in the water. But she no longer cared. Riding weightlessly in his arms, she felt the cool caress of the night water slithering along her skin. It pressed the wet nylon tight against her calves, then shimmied along her thighs to make the dress cling then furl as he reversed directions.

The scents of her—both woman and perfume— drifted through the night, released from garments and skin by the intruding water. She opened her hands on his tensile shoulder blades, then drew back to meet his eyes, which reflected the moon and a wealth of desire. He came to a halt, his shirt-tails drifting in a pinwheel on the surface of the water.

His voice was gravelly, intense. "I want to make love to you. I want to do all the things we were too ignorant to know how to do back then. For twenty-four years I've wanted it."

His head blotted out the moon and his lips were summerwarm as they opened over hers. She kissed him back with delight, which swiftly changed to impatience, seeking out each changing texture and mood of his mouth as it demanded more, then less, then more again. The wrist beneath her knees slipped away and the water bore her weight for a moment before she was drifting down, down, until her toes settled upon something stationary and she found herself standing waist-deep in water, fully dressed, kissing Tommy Lee Gentry, their bodies coalescing, half-dry, half-wet, but all aroused.

He gripped her hips, drew circles upon them with his own, swaying, kissing, losing balance and righting again as the water nudged them. His hands slipped deeper, cupping her buttocks, holding her securely as he rocked against her. The next moment she flinched and gasped as he brought both palms up, dripping, and clamped them upon her breasts. Her nipples cinched tighter as the wet fabric clung, but soon the warmth of his palms eased through as he teased, caressed, heated. His hands lifted to skim the straps from her shoulders, drawing the flimsy dress to her waist.

Then his open mouth possessed her breasts one by one and her head fell back, eyelids closing, blanking out the moon. He dipped lower, and the shocking sensation of heat and cold sent renewed shivers through her limbs as the water lapped near his lips. She drove her fingers through his hair and clasped his head tightly against her stomach.

"Oh, Tommy Lee...it was inevitable, wasn't it?"

He straightened, and their eyes met in a moment of surrender. She slipped her hands inside his shirt, spreading it wide to kiss his chest, his collarbone, his neck, his chin. His mouth. Ah, his warm, long-denied mouth. Her hands rode his shoulders, divesting him of the garment, which soon lay adrift upon the water. Moments later it was joined by her dress and a brief scrap of white they had together shinnied from his loins. Her hosiery came next, followed by an even tinier scrap of white as he grasped her beneath the arms and held her buoyant while she kicked free of her panties. Before the garments drifted to the surface, Rachel's legs were clamped tightly around Tommy Lee's waist.

He waded toward the steps, his mouth communing with hers, then laid her down on the concrete, warm yet from the day's sun, her feet trailing into the water, while he fell to one hip beside her. The moon shimmered along her wet limbs like a rich silver garment while his hand followed its path, relearning the curves of breast, stomach, thigh and mons.

"Rachel," he managed throatily, "I've loved you since we were fourteen years old—maybe even before that. There were times when I thought I'd die without getting the chance to tell you again."

She raised her arms in welcome and he came to her, pressing his length to hers as she caressed his back and buttocks, whispering, "Oh, Tommy Lee, none of us can ever quite get over our first love, can we? And you were that for me. I loved you so much...so much. And some of that love has always stayed with me, no matter who either of us was married to or what was going on in our lives." She felt him shudder and gently pushed him back to delve the dark mystery of his eyes. "I feel it yet, and it grows stronger each time I see you." This was the supreme surprise, that she should at last recognize the love lying fallow within her heart, untouched, untarnished all these years, and be so eager for it to be nurtured and brought to bloom again.

A piercing stab of wonder pressed up beneath his heart, and she saw it in his eyes, realizing fully what this moment meant to him. And she was suddenly filled with the need to give him back a thousandfold all the happiness he had missed in life.

She kissed his eyelids, held his face in both hands. "When I saw you tonight, walking to the door... this started then. You looked so devastatingly wonderful to me as if the past twenty-four years had never happened." She praised his sleek shape with the brush of her hands and felt him shudder.

He kissed her eyelids, uttered her name in a pained murmur and returned to her mouth with an impatience he found reflected there. "Ah, sweet woman, the things I want to do to you... things I was too green to know about then. Do you realize that I've given you a baby but never a climax?"

"Mmm...." Yes, she realized it only too well, had thought of it often, especially during these last months alone. "Please feel free...."

Their exchange sent a fresh current of sensuality rippling through Rachel's limbs. As his hands reacquainted themselves with her body, time spiraled in reverse, taking her back to that first nubile exploration, when he'd initiated her into the rites of sexuality. Once again he brought her the thrill of anticipation, then the even greater thrill of sensation as he touched the inner Rachel, whose secrets could no longer be withheld.

Her palm gathered the moisture from his back, transferred it to his belly, and closed about his flesh, still chill from the water, but quickly warming beneath her touch. He groaned, and the wasted years fell away. He twisted low, following the moonbeams down her wet breasts, sipping the dampness from them with his warm tongue, dipping into the shallow navel where more water pooled, like dew in the chalice of a flower. He kissed the glistening hair at the juncture of her legs, where droplets still clung, bringing again to her lips the mewling sound. And only the heaven-borne stars and the guardian moon stood witness as he moved lower, inundating her with rapture.

And when they hovered at their pinnacles, bodies taut and trembling, he turned again to place his length upon hers, poising on the brink of entering to vow, "I love you, Rachel Talmadge," unconsciously slipping back to the name he'd planned to change to his own when first they'd loved this way, eons ago.

She touched his face with great tenderness while savoring this wondrous exchange about to happen.

"And I love you, Tommy Lee Gentry," she whispered with tears in her eyes.

Then the hurts of the past were lifted away as he thrust deep and fell into the rhythmic appulsion that made their bodies leap and flow. Soon the cry that shuddered from her throat was joined by his deep growl of release.

And in this world of false starts and misgivings, they knew at last where they belonged.

CHAPTER ELEVEN

THEY HAD DIPPED INTO THE POOL and rinsed each other off, to emerge dripping and shivering. "Show me your bedroom. I'm tired of concrete."

She laughed and reached for his hand. "This way." And so simply was it decided he would stay the night.

The air had chilled their skins, bringing goose bumps and puckers as they ran for the house, two laughing spectres with slapping feet. Inside, all was midnight shadow as they groped down a hall and found a linen closet, exchanging intermittent kisses, then swipes of thirsty towels. They paused for a heartier kiss, damp skins sealed by the residue of water warming between them, sending out a sharp smack as they drew apart.

He touched her face lovingly. "The bedroom," he reminded her, and again she led the way.

She stopped in the center of a darkened room where the only thing visible was the moon's silver reflection lilting across the surface of the pool beyond a set of sliding glass doors.

"Is this the room you shared with Owen?"

"Yes, but everything in it is brand new."

He glanced at the shadowy bed. "Everything?"

"Yes." She turned into his arms. "Even me."

Their kiss was brief, but welling with rebirth. "So turn on the light and let me see." Immediately he sensed her reluctance, even before she spoke.

"But it's nothing special, just yellow carpet and wicker and bamb—"

He covered her lips with an index finger. "Turn on the light, Rachel," he commanded quietly.

She thought of her thinness, and the breasts that were so minuscule they hardly showed when she was dressed, and of course the scar on her stomach.

"B...but why?"

"Because we're not children anymore." His palms bracketed her neck, thumbs lightly pushing on her underjaw. His voice became even softer. "Because I've made love to you more times than I can remember, but have never seen you naked." Timidity intruded and she tried to drop her chin, only to have his thumbs press it upward unrelentingly. He kissed the corner of her mouth, whispering, "Please, Rachel. I'm forty-one, too, and I have my insecurities just like you do. But turn it on anyway...for me."

She crossed the room with the faint brushing of bare soles upon carpet and clicked on a low bedside light, pausing with her hand beneath the shade to glance back over her shoulder, her eyes wide, dark and exquisitely beautiful. At last she turned to face him.

The two of them studied each other. Tommy Lee's towel was draped about his neck. Rachel's was clutched against her stomach. His eyes traveled a slow path from her brown pupils to her pink toenails, then back up. Hers moved lingeringly from parted lips to strong brown feet, then returned to rest within the rich, waiting depths of his gaze. How amazing that they should never before have seen each other this way. In her eyes he was unutterably perfect. The marks of age became only testimony she cherished.

"You have much more hair on your chest than you used to," she noted shakily.

"And most of it's gray."

"Gilding," she praised softly. Her heart lifted expectantly as he slowly moved toward her, sliding the towel from about his neck with singular lack of haste. He ran it down the shallow ravine between her breasts, where beads of moisture caught the light and sent it radiating like polished chips of amber. Their eyes clung while the towel skimmed her naked back. "You're beautiful, Rachel. Perfect. Too perfect for this world." Then Tommy Lee dropped to one knee and meticulously dried her legs. When he arose, his eyes locked with hers as he drew the towel from her fingers and tossed it aside with his own.

He stepped back. His eyes slid down her exposed body, but when they reached her stomach, the dark brows curled and he flashed her a questioning look.

"Rachel, what's this?" Automatically he reached.

Automatically she shielded. "Nothing...nothing."

He clasped her wrists and drew them to her hips, searching first her stomach, then her eyes again. "You had the baby cesarean?"

"It doesn't matter," she reassured.

"Doesn't matter?" He made a throaty sound as with one swipe he lifted Rachel and placed her diagonally across the bed, bending above her. Gingerly he touched the pale scar. "Everything about you matters. That's what this is from, isn't it?"

Tears shimmered on her eyelids and her heart eased with the blessed relief of sharing it with him at last, after all these years. "They said I was too small to deliver it naturally."

His eyes seemed unable to pull away from the telltale line running from just below her navel into the black pubic hair. He traced it with four curious fingertips, then his eyes darkened, glittered, and filled with the past as he opened a hand wide upon her stomach and uttered thickly, "Our baby...God, she was our baby. Think of the waste...."

His voice broke, and suddenly he bent to caress Rachel's stomach with his face, placing warm lips at the spot where the scar disappeared into the dark triangle, breathing upon her while wondering at all she'd gone through because of the seed he'd planted within her, letting the hurt rush back and take him one last time.

He felt a sting behind his eyelids and slipped both arms around her hips, cradling his cheek against her warm stomach. "Rachel, I wanted to marry you so badly, and keep her. I wanted to take care of you and have other babies with you, and watch them grow, and get old with you."

It had taken Rachel years to get beyond self-pity and regret, but at the sound of Tommy Lee's emotional outpouring, sensing how close he was to tears, her own eyes blurred. "I know, darling, I know." She rolled to her side, coiling about his head and shoulders, caressing his warm skull while they let the anguished past in to cleanse.

"What did she look like?"

She closed her eyes, remembering.

"She had a perfect cap of dark, dark hair, just like yours...." Her fingers knew again that hair, finding it crisp now at his temples, while she rued each wasted year that had grayed him and thinned her and kept them from knowing these changes daily. "And gray eyes in a face with the tiniest, most perfect mouth I'd ever seen. I only got to hold her once."

"Rachel...Rachel...." His tortured words were muffled against her and she saw again the rosebud mouth of the child they had created together, while the pain billowed within them both. "Our baby..." he murmured—a prayer now, "I wanted her...took you both away from me...my Rachel...all these years...."

They had only one solace to offer each other, and as his mouth, hands and body moved over her in recompense, her heart cried and sang at once. Their lovemaking was fierce this time, an attempt to dissolve a past that could never be dissolved, for when they came together in cataclysm, that past bound them more surely than vows.

THE BEDSIDE CLOCK READ 3:18. The lamp glowed softly on two dark heads and across the yellow and white bamboo-designed sheets that covered Rachel's breasts as she lay tucked in the shelter of Tommy Lee's arm. He was propped against a cache of ruffled pillows, smoking, while her temple pressed his slow-thudding heart.

"And what happens now, Rachel?" he asked, staring at the surface of the pool beyond the open shades.

"I don't know."

He took a deep, thoughtful drag and she heard the air enter his lungs beneath her ear. "Then I'll tell you. You marry me, like you should have twenty-four years ago."

Her fingers stopped combing the coarse hair on his chest. How simple things became in the throes of passion; how complex upon reconsideration.

"Oh, Tommy Lee, how can I marry you?"

"Do you mean, what would people say?" His voice held a honed edge as he rested a wrist across an updrawn knee.

What *would* people say? She had pushed the

question aside all night, but now it pressed for an answer. "Owen's only been dead for five months."

"And the fact still remains that I've had three wives and a stable of lovers the whole county knows about, and I've spent a hell of a lot of years drinking like there was no tomorrow, and you're scared it set a precedent I can't break, is that right?"

She tried to sit up, but he held her fast. "Rachel, don't run away. Did you think I kept after you for nothing more than a roll in the hay, and now that I've had it I'll let you walk out of my life again?"

"I didn't think that, I just—" *Just what? Needed my sexual thirst slaked? Wanted to see if I could still bring Tommy Lee Gentry to heel? Am I so shallow that I'd use him, then toss him aside, knowing all along how vulnerable he is where I'm concerned?* Slowly she pushed herself up. He let her go this time, watching her naked back curl and the side of one breast slip into view as she doubled her arms across her updrawn knees.

"You just what, Rachel?" His voice sounded brittle, hurt already. Miserably she dropped her forehead onto her arms and shrugged. "You don't have much faith in my reformation, do you?" She felt small and guilty while silently admitting the truth. "Well, you would if you could crawl inside my body and know what I've felt for you all these years. Without you nothing and nobody mattered.

Now, everything is possible. Don't you understand, Rachel? Even *I* matter now.''

She lifted her head and stared at the wall, torn by his words. ''We have to be honest with ourselves. Are you sure we aren't just. . .just searching for our lost youth in each other?''

He studied her naked rump, the delicate shadow disappearing down its center, the sheet caught in the fold of her hip. He drew deeply on his cigarette, forced his eyes away from her so he could think more clearly. ''I can't answer for you, but I know how it is for me. If it had happened overnight I might suspect that was true. But I told you before, it's been going on for twenty-four years, every time I'd see you on the street, or in your car, or going into your daddy's bank.''

At the mention of her daddy, Rachel's head swung around and their eyes clashed momentarily before she turned away again. He worked the edges of his teeth together, then studied the glowing tip of the cigarette while drawing circles with it on the bottom of the ashtray. ''You're still scared of him, aren't you, Rachel?'' he asked quietly.

Was she? She didn't want to think so, but she couldn't deny how much she hated the thought of all the strife there was bound to be if her father found out about tonight. And there was a facet of her misgivings that Rachel had been afraid to examine too closely up until now, because she didn't want to believe it might be true. But she could hold it inside no longer.

"By marrying me, you'd show them all, wouldn't you, Tommy Lee? You'd have your revenge for what they forced us to do all those years ago?" It was a thorn that had pricked each time he'd called, each time she'd seen him over the past several months. No, she didn't want to believe it, but wasn't it possible?

"Is that what you think, Rachel? That I'm only using you to get back at them?"

She covered her face with both hands and shook her head until her hair fluttered. "Oh God, I don't know what to think. All of this would be so much simpler if you'd made your peace with your parents, and if they'd made their peace with mine. But everything's so...so complicated!"

His warm palm caressed her back, sending shivers around her ribs to the tips of her breasts. "There are some things I can't change. But those that I can, I have. I love you, Rachel...for yourself, and for no other reason. And that's why I want to marry you. You've got to believe that. You're the only thing I ever wanted...not other women, not...not liquor and fast cars and shiny boats and—" He broke off and dropped his head back wearily, letting his eyes slip closed and swallowing noisily. "Oh God, Rachel, I'm so tired of being that way. I need you in my life to give me some peace at last."

A sob escaped her throat as she whirled and flung herself into his arms. He caressed her head, embracing her with a strength close to fury, closing his eyes against the thought of facing more Rachel-less years, now that he'd come this close.

"Oh, Tommy Lee, I'm so mixed up. Sometimes I don't think *I* deserve *you*. You've been more faithful to me than a husband in a lot of ways, no matter how many women you've known."

"There haven't been any others since the day of Owen's funeral. Nobody but you, Rachel. I love you so much...do you really think I'd blow it all now that I stand a chance of having both you and Beth in my life again?"

There came a time when trust had to take its rightful place in a relationship. He *had* changed. Dramatically. And if he thought the changes were permanent, her belief in him could be all he'd need to make it true. She thought about all he'd said that first night he'd come to her house, the years of misery he'd suffered. She thought about the house he'd built, the hope that had spawned such a task—and there wasn't a doubt in her mind that he loved her. So wasn't it time she began believing in the wonders love could work?

His voice rumbled quietly beneath her ear again. "You said you love me. Is that true, Rachel?"

"Yes..." She squeezed him mightily. "Oh God, yes. I'm falling in love with you harder than the first time, and it's the scariest thing I've ever gone through in my life."

"Then we'll have to face some things...some people. But it'll work out, you'll see," he promised, then stretched to set the ashtray on the bedside table and settled back against the pillows, cradling her again, catching his chin on top of her head. She let his confidence imbue her, and lay in his protective embrace while peace settled over them like a soothing palm.

The minutes slipped by, and his hand moved absently in her hair. "You know," he murmured, "she's old enough to have kids of her own already. Do you realize that? Somewhere in Michigan we might have grandchildren."

She chuckled tiredly against him. "Oh, Tommy Lee, I don't think I'm ready to be a grandma yet. I surely don't feel like one tonight."

He jiggled her a time or two and grinned down lovingly. "You sure's hell didn't act like one. Grandmas are supposed to bake gingerbread cookies and go to sewing circle."

"Remind me to join when I grow tired of this."

She felt his chest lift with silent chuckles. Again his fingers sifted idly through her hair. "Have you ever thought about trying to find our Beth?"

"Yes, I've thought about it. But never for long. It would be too hard to see her, possibly even talk to her, then walk away. And what good would it do? She has parents to love. If she learned about us it could be devastating for her, too. Does it bother you?"

He shrugged. "No, not like it used to. Especially since my other Beth has come to live with me."

They lay silently for some minutes, then Tommy Lee said the most startling thing.

"Rachel, supposing you're pregnant right now."

She snapped back and gaped into his dark, amused eyes. "B...but I can't be pregnant now!"

"Why not? You're only forty-one, and you're not on any kind of birth control—" his brow wrinkled "—are you?"

"But I'm allergic to sperm!"

"You were allergic to Owen's sperm, not mine. If we had one baby, why isn't it possible for us to have another?"

Suddenly Rachel burst out laughing. "Tommy Lee, you're crazy!"

He smiled crookedly. "Maybe. But it's fun thinking about it...cause then we'd have to get married." He settled her back where she'd been before. "Imagine the expressions on our parents' faces when we walked up those church steps together, and you pregnant out to here." His hand caressed her abdomen, and they laughed together, imagining it. Then Rachel fell serious.

"Forty-one is too old to become parents."

"Who says?"

"I do, for one." But her heart lurched at the thought, gave a little kick of independence, and left her feeling slightly giddy.

"I know I wasn't much of a father, but I always thought, if it had been you and me together I'd have been so much better at it, loving you like I did. They say a child's security stems from the love of its parents for one another, so think about it, okay?" He reached to snap off the light and knocked a few pillows onto the floor, then curled her tightly against his body. "With or without a pregnancy, we're both getting a second chance with Beth."

What a stunning and beautiful thought. Mulling it over, Rachel fell asleep.

THEY AWAKENED to a butterscotch sun streaming through the bedroom. Tommy Lee stretched and quivered magnificently, then opened his eyes to find Rachel braced beside him, watching.

"Hi." He grinned with half his mouth.

"Hi." She thought he looked wonderful with his hair tousled and whiskers beginning to show.

"What're you grinning at?"

"What're *you* grinning at?"

"Rachel Talmadge, all messed up."

"Yeah, well, look who messed her."

"Tell me, Miss Talmadge, what do you think about morners?"

"I always kinda liked them myself. Tell me, Mister Gentry, what do you think about morners?"

"They rate right up there with nooners and afternooners."

"In that case I don't suppose you'd care to indulge with a messed-up woman who just *may* be a grandma."

He reached out lazily and ran a knuckle across her lips. "Ohh, grandma, what nice lips you have."

"The better to kiss you, my dear." And she made a pretense of gnawing his knuckle.

His hand moved down to cup one small breast. "Ohh, grandma, what nice breasts you have."

She gyrated the breast against his palm. "The better to entice you, my dear."

He came up slowly and turned her to her back while running a hand down to explore her sweet mysteries. "Ohh, grandma, you ain't like no other grandma I ever come across in the woods."

She smiled and indulged in some sensuous writhing that felt positively wonderful. She nuzzled the silver hair on the side of his head, then bit his ear and asked seductively, "Isn't this the story where somebody's always eating up somebody else?"

"Oh, nasty, nasty grandma," he said against her lips, then lowered his open mouth to her breast as they set about ushering in the morning properly.

A HALF HOUR LATER Rachel was dressed in a floor-length robe of pink satin and the coffee was perking as she wrung out Tommy Lee's shirt in the laundry basin.

"Rachel, can I use your brush?" he called from the bathroom.

"Sure. It's in the top left drawer of the vanity."

She heard the drawer open, tossed the shirt into the dryer and turned it on, then stepped into the kitchen.

When the rush of running water stopped at the far end of the house, she called, "Help yourself to towels." Then she cocked her head and asked, "Do you like bacon?"

"I love it, but it's fattening!" he called back.

She smiled as she lay several thick strips on the hot griddle. The bacon was sizzling and the buttons of the shirt were ticking noisily against the tumbling dryer so she didn't hear the sound of the front door opening.

She wasn't aware of Everett's presence in the house until she turned the corner into the family room with a glass of juice in her hand.

At the sight of her father she came up short and her stomach seemed to tilt. He was standing in the middle of the family room, staring at the surface of the pool, where miscellaneous pieces of clothing were caught in the skimmer. Her eyes darted outside to find even her shoes visible, lying in the aquamarine depths of the shallow end. Everett's stormy gaze moved from the pool to scan her pink wrapper, pausing for the briefest second on the fabric shimmering unmistakably over bare nipples.

"Daddy," she gulped.

"I came to have coffee with you before you left for the store," he said acidly. But just at that moment Tommy Lee stepped out of the bathroom and entered the room from the opposite direction, dressed in nothing but trousers, toweling his wet hair. When his face emerged from beneath the towel he stopped dead in his tracks.

The suffocating moment seemed to stretch forever while Everett fired angry glances from one to the other and nobody said a word. His face turned stony while Rachel's began to redden.

"Well, well..." he drawled after several interminable seconds. "What have we here?" Tommy Lee glanced helplessly at Rachel while Everett went on silkily. "But I guess it's obvious what we have here. The county's most notorious whoremonger, preying on one of its most vulnerable widows."

Tommy Lee and Rachel both spoke at once.

"Now just a minute!"

"Daddy, it's not that way!"

But he pierced his daughter with malevolent eyes and pointed an outraged finger. "You shut up, girlie, I'll get to you later!" Then he spun on Gentry. "How dare you set foot in my daughter's house!"

"I didn't realize I had to ask permission to see a forty-one-year-old woman."

"See?" Talmadge hissed. "It appears you did more than see her! It isn't enough that you have every two-bit whore between here and Montgomery, you have to drag my daughter down with you!"

Tommy Lee's hands tightened into fists on the ends of the towel. "Your daughter is a lady, and my being here doesn't change that."

"Oh, doesn't it? I wonder if her neighbors agree with you!"

Suddenly Rachel came to life. "Daddy, stop it."

But he whirled on her again. "Have you no respect for yourself, or for Owen? He hasn't been gone fo—"

"Don't keep throwing Owen up in my face. I married him and gave you the kind of son-in-law you wanted, and I stuck with the marriage, no matter how dull and disastrous it was. But I will not keep revering a dead man at the cost of my own happiness!"

"No, instead you cheapen yourself with trash like him!" Everett thumbed over his shoulder, and Tommy Lee had all he could take. He stalked across the room and whirled Talmadge around by an elbow.

"I'm getting mighty damn sick of you thinking you can control our lives, so get this through your head—" He nudged Talmadge in the chest with two strong fingers that set him back a step. "You're all through interfering!"

"Not when she's about to make the same mistake twice, I'm not!"

Tommy Lee's face was grim, his fists clenched at his sides while blue veins bulged up the lengths of his bare arms. "The mistake wasn't hers, it was yours! But you just can't admit it, can you, Talmadge? You took something away from her that you had no right taking away, and the disaster was doubled when you found out it could never be replaced. And now here I am, back in her life, bringing it all back for you to face. That's what you're fighting against!''

Talmadge's face was mottled and his jowls shook. ''I love my daughter, but I won't st—''

''Love her! Hah!'' Tommy Lee glared, jamming his fists onto his hips. ''If you love her you've got a damned strange way of showing it. You don't give a damn what she's feeling. All you care about is protecting yourself from having to admit that the decision you made twenty-four years ago made more people miserable than you'd care to count!''

''Don't go laying the blame on me, Gentry. You screwed up your life all by yourself. You didn't need any help from me!''

Exasperated, Tommy Lee rammed four fingers through his damp hair and shook his head. ''How blind can you be, man? How long are you going to keep fighting what's right before your eyes? Rachel and I never should have been forced apart—never! We tried to tell you that twenty-four years ago, but you and my mama and daddy knew so much better than Rachel and me what was good for us, didn't you?''

''And if I hadn't, where would she have ended up? Married to a drunkard who couldn't be satisfied with one woman.''

"She was the only one I ever wanted, and you know it," Tommy Lee growled dangerously.

"Well, you finally got her, didn't you? And you made sure the whole town knew it by leaving your car in her driveway all night long!"

Suddenly Rachel intervened. "What about me? You talk as if I had no choice in the matter. Daddy, I asked him here. I did *not* ask you. I should think since you saw the car you would have had the common decency to respect my privacy."

"Don't you go preaching to me about common decency, missy! Not when I walk in here and find your clothes floating on the top of the pool and him half-naked at eight o'clock in the morning!"

"That's exactly what you did! You walked right in as if it were your God-given right. Well, it's not. I'm all grown up now, daddy, and this is my house, and you have no right to walk into it unannounced and give me a lecture on how to live my life!"

Her fists were clenched and the tendons in her neck stood out. Everett raised a hand in appeal. "Rachel, for God's sake, don't you care what people think?"

"No, not anymore. I've lived my whole life according to some nebulous code that you pushed down my throat. But there's no room in that code for mitigating circumstances, is there? Tommy Lee has changed. I've changed." She pressed her hands against her chest and leaned toward him supplicatingly. "Why can't you see that?"

"All I see is a daughter I have to be ashamed of. Lord, girl, I protected you from gossip all these years. What do you suppose it does to me to see you take up with him again?"

"Daddy, please, for once, could you think about my feelings instead of your own? Would you ask yourself *why* I'm with him again?"

His face grew hard and he pierced Tommy Lee with a venomous gaze that passed from his naked chest to his bare toes. "I believe that's altogether too obvious."

Rachel moved a step nearer Tommy Lee until her shoulder blades touched his chest. "No. You're seeing only what you want to see. It's your own stubbornness that's making you blind, though. Daddy, I love him. Can't you accept that and let us all try to forget the past?"

Everett's face turned scornful. "Love him! For God's sake, girl, don't delude yourself just because I caught you redhanded."

Tommy Lee's hands came up to rest on Rachel's shoulders as he stated, "It's you who are deluding yourself, Talmadge. I have a feeling it's the only way you could have lived with the decision you made all those years ago."

The sight of Tommy Lee's hands resting possessively on Rachel's shoulders made Everett cringe. "Marshall would have—"

"No, daddy." Rachel's eyes closed for a long moment, as if in finality. "You've chosen all the men for me you're ever going to. Marshall is a carbon copy of Owen, and though it's taken me some soul-searching to admit it, Owen was not the kind of man I needed to make me happy. This time I'm doing the picking,'' she ended prophetically.

Her voice softened to an appealing note. "Daddy, Tommy Lee has asked me to marry him, and if I did, would we have to fight you every step of the way, just like before? Would you do that to us... again?"

Everett's shock was complete. He gaped from Rachel to the man behind her, and to his daughter again. "You can't mean it. Rachel, you've never had a vindictive bone in your body, but if you're doing this just to get back at me for—"

"No, daddy. I told you, I love him." On her shoulders, Tommy Lee's hands tightened reassuringly.

Everett sensed himself losing ground and blustered, "You love some...some teenage fantasies. But we're talking about real life here. We're talking about a man with three ex-wives!"

To Tommy Lee's surprise, she smiled and squeezed his fingers, which still rested on her collarbone. "Then I'd better watch my P's and Q's, hadn't I?"

Everett was stupefied. "Rachel, for the love of God—"

But she calmly stepped forward and cut him off. "Daddy, as I said earlier, I didn't invite you here." She led the way toward the foyer without turning to see if he followed, but when she reached it, he was right on her heels, hoping to talk some sense into her. However, he didn't get the chance. She opened the door and stood waiting for him to walk through it. "In the future when you come to see me, I'd appreciate your knocking before you come in."

When she had closed the door upon his angrily stalking form she turned to find Tommy Lee waiting in the archway. He opened his arms and she walked into them and clung, her cheek pressed against the silky hair on his chest, and his arms circling her shoulder tenaciously. "Darling, I'm so sorry," he said gruffly.

She was trembling uncontrollably as she shook her head against his chest. "No, it's not your fault. Oh, Tommy Lee, how could he just... just come in here like that and start shouting at you."

He rubbed her shoulder and kissed the top of her hair. "He's desperate, Rachel. He's clung to his self-righteousness for a long time. Imagine how frightening it is to a man like him to have to admit he was wrong."

"But he's so bullheaded! Would it hurt him for once to say, okay, Rachel, go ahead and love Tommy Lee, and be happy?"

Tommy Lee's warm palm rubbed her spine. "Did you ever stop to think that maybe he's a little jealous, too? He's had you to himself for quite a while."

She pulled back and gaped up at him in surprise. "Jealous? But he was never jealous of Owen or . . . or Marshall."

"He didn't need to be. He could control them."

She sighed wearily and fell against him again. "Oh, I'm so tired of it all. All I want is for everyone to see how foolish all this hostility has been, and settle it once and for all so we can get on with our lives." He folded her against him again, and rocked her gently. After several minutes she murmured plaintively, "Oh, Tommy Lee, remember how it used to be? When we were young and our mothers would be having iced tea on the lawn and you and I would come charging out of the house with our tennis rackets? They'd smile and wave, and tell us to have a good time. I've often wondered, if my mother had lived, would it have made a difference? She was so different from daddy."

She heard Tommy Lee swallow against her temple. "They were like second parents to me."

She rubbed her hands along his back, feeling his steady heartbeat against her breast, wondering again if love was powerful enough to overcome such longstanding enmities. Loving him, even marrying him, would never be enough. Until the hostilities were over, the two of them could never know complete serenity.

"Tommy Lee?"

"Hm?"

"I want to make a bargain with you."

He drew back, tilting his head to see her face. "A bargain?"

She looked up with eloquent brown eyes, hoping what she was doing was right.

"A bargain."

"What kind of bargain?"

"You . . . you still want to marry me?"

He released a breathy, rueful laugh that said it all, and she went on, fixing him with her steady eyes. "I'll promise to marry you if you'll promise to go see your mama and daddy and make peace with them."

She felt him begin to stiffen and quickly framed his jaws with both hands, holding him where he was. "Please, hear me out. When you pull away and get that look on your face you remind me of daddy. In your own way you're as stubborn as he is, don't you see?"

But Tommy Lee didn't appreciate being compared to Everett. He gave an ironic sniff, but she forced him to listen to reason.

"The only way it'll work for us is if we make every attempt at forgiving. You've just said my daddy is frightened of admitting he's been wrong all these years. Well, aren't you, too? So where do we start putting an end to it all?" When he tried to pull away again she held him, continuing persuasively, "Oh, Tommy Lee, I've seen the look on your mama's face—and your daddy's, too—when they saw you walk up those church steps. They love you and they miss you terribly, and whether you want to admit it or not, you miss them, too. You're their only son, and Beth is their granddaughter. Isn't it time you became a family again?''

Beneath her palms she felt his tense muscles and quivering nerves, and made small soothing circles with her thumbs on his cheeks. ''I want to tell you something that I've never told you before,'' she said in an equally soothing voice, studying his deep, dark eyes. ''Your mother and father were against sending me away. My mother told me before she died. She was never happy with the estrangement between the two couples, but there was little she could do, given my father's stubbornness. He's very strong willed, and he talked your parents and my mother into agreeing with him about giving the baby up for adoption. I spent years blaming all of them equally, but it's really my father who forced the issue. And if I can forgive him, can't you forgive your parents, too?''

She could see his defenses weakening and rushed on. ''I'll help you. I'll go with you if you want. You and I together have a chance to show them how to forgive. Maybe...just maybe, if we take the first step they'll follow suit.'' She smiled at the idea. ''Imagine it—we could set off a whole chain reaction.''

But Tommy Lee still remained unconvinced. ''So idealistic. And what if they throw me out?''

But behind his words she sensed a vulnerability that touched her heart. ''They won't. You know they won't. All it'll take is for one of you to make the first move.''

"And you really think if we can patch things up with them they'll suddenly soften toward Everett?"

"It's worth a chance, isn't it?"

"And what about this newest fracas? Are you forgetting you just threw your daddy out of your house? I'd say that leaves you and him with some patching up of your own to do."

She dropped her hands from his face, but captured the two ends of the towel that hung around his neck. "We've fought before. But in the end we always seem to realize that we're the only family left. You leave him up to me for the time being. When he sees me happily married to you, he's bound to soften." She smiled up at him. "There's something you have to realize about my daddy. Underneath all that bluster he has a grudging respect for anybody who'll stand up to him." She tugged on the towel and drew him down for a short kiss. "So what do you say?"

"You drive a hard bargain, Rachel."

Suddenly she saw through the idealist's eyes he accused her of having and slipped her hands beneath the towel, locking her fingers behind his neck while meeting his brown eyes intensely. "I want it to be like it used to be."

"It'll never be like it used to be."

"It could be better," she averred, squeezing the sides of his neck for emphasis. "It *could* be... you know it. You, me, your parents, my father... and Beth. What about her? You're cheating her out of her own grandparents by carrying this grudge."

"I know," he breathed wearily and drew her into his arms, resting his chin on top of her head. "I know."

"Grandparents can be a wonderful influence on young people, and vice versa. And besides..." She kissed his Adam's apple. "I thought I was the woman you'd do anything in the world for."

Somewhere in the house, bacon was burning and the buttons of a shirt sang out against the metal tumbler of a dryer. Tommy Lee folded Rachel against his heart and buried his face in the flower-scented skin of her neck, realizing that if things went right he had within his grasp the chance of gaining back everything he'd once had taken from him.

Rachel was very wise, knowing even better than he himself how badly he needed old wounds cauterized. "You'll really do it, Rachel? You'll marry me?" he asked hoarsely.

"Don't you think it's time?" came her trembling reply.

He drew back to look into her dark eyes, and his own traversed her face, cataloging it feature by feature while his thumbs brushed the crests of her cheekbones. Her lips were slightly parted, her hair in disarray, and the expression in her eyes was one he'd dreamed of seeing there during the endless years when nothing and no one else could quite fill the empty spot in his heart.

"Oh, Rachel...my Rachel." He dropped his forehead against hers, letting his eyes sink shut, capturing the essence of the moment to carry within as a talisman during the days ahead. "How I love you."

She swallowed back the tears in her throat. "I love you, too...so much."

Then their mouths were joined and emotions billowed. They clung together sharing an ardent kiss, pressing their bodies close, hands wandering impatiently now that the decision was made.

Abruptly Tommy Lee drew back, holding her head with both hands. "When?" Without giving her time to answer, he rushed on, "Right away, as soon as we can get a licence and find somebody to do it. I want us to have a honeymoon so you'll have to make arrangements at the store, and afterward...which house do you want to live at? I'd live here if you asked me to, but...oh, Rachel, say you'll move into my house on the lake. God, it'll be like a dr—"

"Hold on." She couldn't resist chuckling at his impetuousness. "Aren't you forgetting something?"

He frowned in puzzlement. "What?"

"Beth. Shouldn't I meet her first? Don't you think we should get her approval, since she's going to be part of the family, too?"

"Oh, Beth." He wrapped Rachel loosely in his arms and rocked her. "Beth is going to love you."

He said it with such thoughtless conviction there seemed no other way it could be.

CHAPTER TWELVE

THE EXPRESSION on his daughter's face when Tommy Lee walked into his house less than an hour later warned him trouble lay ahead.

"Where *were* you all night?" She stood with both hands stuffed into the tight pockets of her blue jeans, a scowl on her face.

"Oh!" He came up short, searching for a reply. "Did you wait up for me?"

"Hardly. That's what *parents* usually do. Georgine wanted to leave for home and when you weren't getting up and weren't getting up she sent me in to wake you but your bed wasn't even slept in."

Tommy Lee was saved from replying when Georgine came around the corner with her purse in her hand, her lips drawn up tight and a disapproving tilt to her chin.

"We already had breakfast *and* cleaned up the dishes *and* called town to say I'd be gettin' there late!"

"I'm sorry, Georgine. If you're ready I'll take you now."

"If I'm ready...hmph." She snorted past him

on her way to the door, and Tommy Lee asked himself for the hundredth time why he put up with her insubordination. He truly disliked the woman, but now that Beth was here, he needed her more than ever.

"You wanna ride along, honey?" he invited Beth.

"No," she pouted, crossing her arms stubbornly.

"You sure? We could talk."

"I'm sure."

But he could see the hurt in her eyes. "Back in half an hour and we'll spend the day doing whatever you want to, okay, sugar?"

For a minute the stubborn expression remained on her chin, but at last she nodded.

In the car Georgine sat as if she had spine trouble, her mouth as sour looking as if she'd just bitten into a kumquat.

"Georgine, I'm sorry I wasn't here to get you into town right away this morning."

"Ain't me you should be sayin' you're sorry to, it's your daughter. Impressionable young girl like that—what she gonna think?"

Tommy Lee imagined she'd think exactly what she was thinking, but he wasn't going to admit it to Georgine. He hadn't given a thought to Beth last night and realized too late the import of his having been out all night, especially given Beth's age. He was not accustomed to having restrictions put on his freedom, but Georgine was right. He certainly hadn't been a good example.

When he got back home he found Beth in the kitchen stirring something at the stove. Her hair fell down the center of her back in a single French braid, and even from behind he could see the first curves of maturity already beginning to sculpt her body. She had a waist now, and gently swelling hips tapering into long legs. She had fought with her mother over a boy after Nancy caught the two of them kissing, which had started the whole fiasco that finally led to Beth's running away and ending up here.

The eternal tabu of sex, he thought ruefully, going back for a moment to when he and Rachel had been the same age Beth was now. He stood for a long minute with his hands draped in his trouser pockets, studying her, wondering how to handle the delicate situation. He could tell from the way her head was drooped that she was upset with him and maybe a little shy about facing him.

"Still mad at me, huh?" he asked quietly.

She shrugged, but still didn't turn around.

"You don't even want to talk to me?"

Again came the sheepish shrug. He couldn't help smiling—so young, so idealistic. He moved up behind her and cupped a hand around the side of her neck.

"I'm sorry, baby. I've got no excuses."

She stared into the kettle and kept stirring. "After the show I brought the kids back here to meet you, and you weren't even home."

"I said I'm sorry. It won't happen again, and that's a promise."

"Where *were* you?"

This time it was his turn to withhold an answer. In spite of the fact that he'd planned to tell Beth about Rachel immediately, he was reluctant now, for fear it might cast a shadow over his daughter's impression of the woman he loved.

"You were with a woman, weren't you?"

"Beth, I'm forty-one years old."

At last she turned and lifted accusing eyes to his. "I know who it was. It was that one on the church steps, wasn't it?"

For a moment their eyes clashed, then Tommy Lee sighed and held her by both shoulders. "What makes you say that?"

"I could *see* how you were looking at her, daddy. I'm not exactly a *child*."

"Her name is Rachel, and the first thing I want you to understand is that I love her."

"Mother always said you liked other women too much and that's why she got divorced from you."

"Beth, I'm not going to argue with you about your mother. It's pointless."

Suddenly tears brimmed on Beth's eyelids. "But I don't understand...she got mad at me when all I did was kiss a boy. But you...well, you...you stayed out all night. You mean it's not okay when you're fourteen, but it's perfectly all right when you're forty-one?"

Tommy Lee didn't know how to answer. There could be no double standard, and to claim there was would be hypocritical. He had wanted a second chance at being a father, now here it was, and he was finding out exactly how difficult it could be.

"No, sweetheart," he admitted, "I'm not saying that. I'm saying that at forty-one a person is better equipped to handle the consequences of his actions. But your mother is wrong about one thing. There's no reason to feel guilty for kissing boys when you're fourteen years old. As a matter of fact, that's exactly how old I was when I started kissing girls, and you know who the first one was?"

She shook her head, mesmerized by the sudden turn of the conversation.

He smiled, looking down into her pretty brown eyes, the freckles on her cheeks, her generous bowed lips, which were very much like his. "It was Rachel Talmadge—that was her name then."

"Y. . . you've known her that long?"

"Uh-huh. Since we were kids."

But instead of impressing Beth, the fact made her stiffen and pull away. Puzzled, Tommy Lee watched her turn toward the stove again, and the momentary rapport between them was broken.

"I made you grits and sausage while you were gone, since Georgine didn't hold breakfast for you."

He watched her get a plate and begin to spoon

grits onto it, then move to the sink to fill the kettle with water, and he was suddenly weary, wondering how to deal with her jealousy. She stabbed three sausage links and added them to the plate, switched off the burners and turned expectantly with her offering in her hands, and Tommy Lee thought, *Lord, will the way ever be smooth for Rachel and me?*

"You don't like talking about Rachel, do you?"

Her tone was defensive as she blurted out, "I wish mother had been your first girlfriend, then maybe you'd still be married to her."

And after that it seemed best to drop the subject of Rachel for the time being until things smoothed over a little bit.

But during the weekend Beth displayed an increasing possessiveness about her father. Though he admitted he was again being manipulated by a female smart enough to realize he felt guilty and to use that guilt to get what she wanted, he went along readily with her plan for him to take her shopping for school clothes in Muscle Shoals. The following morning when they glimpsed Rachel on the church steps, Beth commandeered Tommy Lee's arm and maneuvered him inside before he got a chance to talk to her. The remainder of that day was devoted to taking Beth's new friends waterskiing, and when the afternoon finally ended, Tommy Lee wanted nothing so badly as to see Rachel for a couple of hours, having thought of nothing but her for two solid days. But when he casually mentioned that he thought he'd drive into town to pick up some things from his office to glance through at home, Beth immediately said she'd ride along with him.

Finally, late Sunday night, Tommy Lee escaped to his room so he could call Rachel. At the sound of her hello a sharp upthrusting stab of love pressed beneath his heart and suddenly everything seemed right again.

"I've missed you," he breathed, closing his eyes, lying flat on his back across the bed.

"And I've missed you. I looked for you all day today."

"I'm sorry I couldn't make it, but it appears we have one problem I hadn't counted on."

"It's Beth, isn't it?"

He rubbed the corners of his eyes. "God, is it ever. She acts like she doesn't want me out of her sight for a minute. She wasn't exactly happy to see me getting home in the middle of Saturday morning and wanted to know where I'd been."

"Did you tell her?"

"She guessed." He scowled at the ceiling.

"She guessed? . . . But how?"

"She called you the woman on the church steps."

"Ahh . . . of course."

"Was I that obvious when I looked at you?"

Rachel's soft laugh came over the wire. "Was I?" He pictured her as she'd been Friday night, soft, pliant, smelling sweeter than anything nature had ever conjured up. He felt his body nudging toward arousal at the mental images.

"All I've thought about since walking out of your house is you. While I was chauffeuring Beth all over Muscle Shoals, and driving a speedboat full of shrieking teenagers, I wanted to be only one place."

"Where?" she murmured in a soft, seductive voice. But it was not the words that mattered, rather the subtle nuances of two lovers infatuated with the mere act of listening to each other breathe.

"In your bed. In you."

Her breath again seemed to brush his ear. "Tommy Lee, I want to see you tonight. Can't you come over?"

"I'm tempted, darlin', but if I did I'd never come back home, and I promised Beth I'd be spending nights here from now on."

She sighed in disappointment, and he pictured her curling into a ball in the middle of her bed. "When will I see you again?"

"Tomorrow afternoon. I'll pick you up as soon as you close the store."

"I'll have my own car there. Meet me at the house instead."

"Do you think we can hang in there till then?"

"I don't know. We have a lot of lost time to make up for, don't we?"

His voice held a tremor as he declared, "But we will, babe, we will."

"I can't wait. Can you stay for supper?"

No matter how much he wanted to, he answered, "I'm afraid not. Beth's got something special planned for the two of us. She's doing the cooking."

"Well, next time then."

"Next time for sure." Tommy Lee stifled a yawn—he hadn't had much sleep all weekend. "Rachel, I'm exhausted. I've been on the water all day."

But she wasn't ready to give him up yet. "Are you in the bedroom?" she asked.

"Yes, staring at the ceiling and picturing you as you were Friday night."

"*Our* bedroom?" she inquired softly.

"Yes...*our* bedroom."

"What's it like?"

"It's carpeted in blue to match the lake. The whole west wall is glass and it's the only room in the house with draperies—they're the color of the sand on the beach. There's a king-size bed with a bedspread that's kind of stripy and soft."

"What's it made of?"

"Made of?" He rolled his head to check it out, smiling at the questions women came up with. "Hell, I don't know, it's got stitches all over it."

"It's quilted, you mean?"

"I guess so."

"Well, if I'm going to sleep there I have to know these things. Go on. Tell me more."

As teenagers, late at night after curfew, they

used to talk on the phone like this—lazy inanities, unimportant gibberish meant to do nothing more than delay the inevitable goodbye. Tommy Lee smiled, assessed the room and imagined her entering it for the first time. "Across from the foot of the bed is a fireplace smaller than the one downstairs and with an arched opening. And do you remember once years and years ago when you told me you liked rocking chairs?"

"No, did I?"

"Well, there are two of them, big fat things covered with some kind of fuzzy blue stuff, one on each side of the fireplace. There's a walk-in closet big enough to put your whole store into." She chuckled appreciatively and he went on. "And beside the closet door is a valet chair with nothing on it at all right now. Everything's neatly put away."

There wasn't even a hint of laughter as she sighed. "Oh, Tommy Lee, I love you. I can't wait to live there with you."

At her confession his heart cracked like a flag in high wind and he experienced the renewed wonder of dreams coming true.

"Tell me again, Rachel—I still have trouble believing it."

"I love you," she whispered.

He closed his eyes, absently running his free hand over the quilted spread as if it were her skin. "I want us to get married as soon as possible."

"I do, too. Did you tell Beth we want to?"

His eyes opened to study the ceiling again, and

the hand that had been stroking the spread rested with its wrist against his forehead. "No, not yet."

"So she really is upset about the other night?"

"I'm afraid so."

"I should have thought of her. How selfish of me to keep you here overnight."

"You'd have played hell trying to get me to leave—don't you know that?" She laughed, but the sound was slightly strained. He drew a deep breath and went on, "Don't worry about Beth. I'll tell her soon, then I want the two of you to meet. Properly. Out here at the house where we're all going to make it as a family. We are, Rachel, I swear it," he pledged intensely. Then, as if sealing a vow, he added prophetically, "Tommy Lee and Rachel and Beth."

"I'll hang on to that thought," she promised. "And I'll see you tomorrow at five."

THE CLOCK SEEMED TO CRAWL as the following afternoon waned. Just before closing, Rachel stepped into the washroom to check her hair, dust her cheeks with blush, touch a wisp of scent to her throat and apply fresh rosy gloss to her lips.

In fifteen minutes I'll be with him again.

Her heart felt borne aloft by a bevy of butterflies. Life was a constant surprise. Who ever would have said, one week ago, that she would be experiencing this resurgent zest that lit her eyes, put a lilt in her step and made her press a hand to her heart, as if to hold it captive within her body?

And all this at the mere thought of Tommy Lee Gentry.

It was uncanny how one could revert to self-indulgent daydreaming when smitten by love, no matter what one's age. All day long she'd been wondering what he'd be wearing, what he'd say when he first saw her, fantasizing about their first kiss, making love, and following it up with an intimate talk, snuggled close in a nest of pillows.

His Blazer was in the driveway when she pulled around the corner and depressed the activator for the automatic garage door. He got out and stood with his hands on his hips, watching her drive past him into the garage. He was dressed in tight tan jeans, white leather tennis shoes and a sporty baby-blue pullover with a V-neck. The first thing he said was, "Come here." He had opened her car door and was waiting to haul her into his arms even before she captured her purse from the seat. They stood in the wedge of the open car door, her arms clinging to his neck, her breasts buried against his hard chest, kissing recklessly, murmuring in the wordless, insatiable way of lovers who'd thought this moment would never come.

His tongue was hot and insistent as it roved the contours of her mouth, and hers brought an answering urgency as it tasted and tantalized. His hands spread wide, covering her back with demanding caresses before dropping low to ride her hips, then the curve of her buttocks as their bodies pressed together in anticipation, then gyrated from side to side in an age-old message of accord.

Their heads slanted, changing directions as their mouths remained locked, open and impatient. His hand cupped her breast and hers found his naked back, slipping beneath the ribbed waistband of his shirt onto the warm flesh. His thumb rubbed her nipple and she shivered and thrust her tongue more forcefully into his mouth. She ran her hands over the back pockets of his jeans, drawing him as close as was possible, holding him as he'd held her a moment ago.

When at last the initial rush of possessiveness had been accommodated, they drew apart, found each other's eyes, then clung again, rapturously.

"My God, did you ever think it could be this way again?" he asked breathlessly.

"Never! I've felt like a teenager all day!"

Again he backed away to look into her radiant eyes. "You too?"

She smiled and nodded a little sheepishly. Then they were laughing and holding hands as he impatiently hauled her after him toward the back door. He flung it wide and tugged her inside behind him, both of them giddy, giggly and slightly flushed... and came up short at the sight of Callie Mae, spreading chocolate frosting on a pan of brownies.

The older woman swung around, her eyes flew wide, and she gave a chortle of amusement. "Well, I declare, if it ain't that nasty l'il Tommy

Lee Gentry, used to come snitchin' my cookies just before suppertime.''

Tommy Lee and Rachel gaped at the maid then at each other, then burst out laughing again before Tommy Lee lunged across the room to give the woman a bone-crushing hug. ''Callie Mae, you crusty old despot—damn, it's good to see you!''

She backed off to adore him with glistening eyes while his hands pressed her thick waist.

''Lord, Lord, but ain't you a sight for these tired old eyes—you and Miss Rachel, come a-laughin' in the way you used to.'' A tear plumped on her eyelid as she hugged him again, and Rachel looked on with a glowing expression in her eyes. Suddenly Callie Mae pulled back and her heavy pink lips took on a scolding pout. ''Been wonderin' when the two o' you would come to your senses.''

Tommy Lee cocked one eyebrow and suppressed a grin. ''Oh, you have, have you?''

She turned back to her brownies, giving an indignant sniff, while Tommy Lee's and Rachel's eyes met and shared an instant of powerful nostalgia. Memories tumbled back, of another time, another kitchen, two sun-drenched children scampering in to the ever-gruff but loving maid who, like they, never questioned their rightful place together. Washed now in Callie Mae's benediction—the first, after facing so much opposition—they felt hopeful and ebullient. It was like stepping into a scene in which the action had been frozen twenty-four years ago and had been waiting all that time for them to walk on stage and bring about a happy conclusion.

Tommy Lee looped an arm around Callie Mae's shoulders and turned his attention toward the counter. "What're you cookin' up there, darlin'?"

"Why, just one o' your favorites. My prize-winnin' chocolate brownies with plenty of pecans, just how you like 'em."

"Whoo-ee!" He licked his lips. "Them's mightly hard to resist." Tommy Lee pointedly checked his watch, then let a grin crawl up one corner of his mouth. "And besides, it's a whole hour before supper." He snatched the spatula from Callie Mae's fingers and dug a bar from the corner of the pan, lifting it to tongue an icicle of fresh frosting that oozed over the edge.

Callie Mae laughed, gave him a playful swat and nodded backward in Rachel's direction. "You wanna do something, you git *her* to eat brownies. She's the one needs 'em!"

Tommy Lee turned around, smiling.

Rachel chuckled and said to him, "See what I've been putting up with all these years?"

"Mmm...she's kind of mouthy all right. She might not work out after all."

"She might not. On the other hand, I *am* rather used to her outspokenness. And you'll have to admit, she *is* a pretty decent cook."

Tommy Lee swallowed his mouthful of brownie

and shrugged indifferently. "Yeah, these are all right, I guess."

"All right?" Callie Mae exploded, swinging around with her hands on her hips.

Tommy Lee took another nonchalant bite, grinned at Rachel and asked teasingly, "Think we should tell her?" He wandered over and held the brownie to her lips.

She took a nibble, grinned, and returned conspiratorially, "I don't know. What do you think? Should we?"

"Tell me what?" Callie Mae insisted.

Rachel took a bigger bite of brownie and the frosting fell in a string down her lip. She reached to swipe at it, but Tommy Lee waylaid her hand, then held the wrist while leaning to lick the frosting off. Without removing his eyes from Rachel's, he smiled and answered Callie Mae, "Might be a new job opening up for you."

"A new...." But Callie Mae's lips fell open and her eyes sparkled with speculation as she watched Tommy Lee lean down and place a lingering kiss on Rachel's uplifted mouth, the brownie all but forgotten in his fingertips.

He lifted his head lazily, and still gazing into Rachel's eyes, added, "Out at my place."

Callie Mae's beaming eyes rested on the two she'd loved for so long, as Rachel raised up to brush Tommy Lee's lips once more then added dreamily, "Working for both of us."

Callie Mae rolled her eyes heavenward, threw

her hands wide and exclaimed, "Lord o' mercy...at last!" She watched them kiss again, and when they drew apart, they seemed to have forgotten anyone else in the room. "Hmph!" Callie Mae snorted. "I can see there ain't no need for me to hang around here no longer. Act like I don't count for nothin'...." She grumbled on in mock reprimand while whipping off her apron. "Person ain't never done teachin' children their manners...fine thing, bein' ignored...." She threw open a pantry door, hung up the apron with a flourish and swept up her purse. She was still muttering as the door slammed behind her.

At the sound, the pair in the kitchen seemed to come awake. They glanced at the door, then at each other, and laughed while Rachel flung her arms about Tommy Lee's neck.

"Everyone will know now," she said.

"Do you care?" he asked against her hair.

"No. All I care about is you...us. I missed you so much."

"I missed you, too...every minute."

Their mouths met again eagerly as he reached blindly to set the brownie on the cupboard. His fingers were coated with chocolate and when he lifted his head to impatiently lick off a thumb she captured the hand and carried it from his pursed lips to her own, meticulously laving each finger, slipping it into her mouth with sensual slowness, aroused by the salt-sweet taste of him, by the heavy, hooded look that overtook his eyes as he

watched. When the fingers were clean she ran her
tongue down the palm of his hand and bit its heel,
while his relaxed fingertips rested upon her closed
eyes. She kissed his wrist, the metal band of his
watch warm beneath her lips, then moved beyond
it to the soft warm skin of his inner elbow.

Suddenly he pulled her head to his chest, groan-
ing softly, and beneath her ear she heard his
pounding heart as his fingers plowed through her
hair to contour her skull and cradle her head possessively.

She felt an outpouring of love, far too powerful
to be voiced. And as she raised her eyes to his, she
saw it returned a thousandfold. They stood close,
caught in the shaft of late-afternoon sun melting
through the window. It glinted off the golden rim
of his glasses, scintillated from her open lips,
gilded the gray above his ears. Had they loved this
fully at sixteen? Perhaps it had seemed so then.
But in this moment as they stood bound together
by feelings so profound as to be voiceless, their
lorn love of long ago seemed paltry by com-
parison.

She reached both hands up to slip the glasses
from his temples, and laid them beside the
brownie on the cabinet. His hands clasped her
jaws as his mouth descended—open, hungry, pur-
poseful. Her answering lunge and lift were all he
needed before his fingers trembled over buttons,
hooks and zippers, and they knew again the swift
swelling of sexual appetite, appeasing it with little

thought of time or place. In moments they stood upon scattered articles of clothing, pressing their naked bodies together, exulting. He lifted her to his waist and her legs twined about his hips, the vacant core of her femininity seeking only one restitution: to be filled by him. The contact was sleek, immediate and restorative as their bodies reunited and their arms clenched possessively.

He perched her on the edge of the kitchen counter and the sun burned warm on her shoulders as his lean hands parenthesized her hips. Dark eyes captured and held hers. Lips parted. Breaths mingled. The movement began.

And in moments Rachel and Tommy Lee shared that glorious outpouring of body and soul found only by the very lucky—by those who bring unquestionable love to the act. When their matched cries echoed through the kitchen, she held his head to her breast and sighed in repletion.

His shoulders were damp—she brushed the sheen from them.

His heartbeat was uneven—she pressed a palm to it.

His eyelids were closed—she kissed them.

And in the end he stayed for a late, late supper.

CHAPTER THIRTEEN

A WEEK PASSED, during which Rachel and Tommy Lee had only stolen hours together whenever possible, but "stealing" time left them dissatisfied and impatient. Only one thing happened that brought them smiles. Tommy Lee had to make an unexpected overnight trip, and before leaving town he stalked, unannounced, into Panache, crossed straight to Rachel and dropped a heedless kiss on her mouth. "Hello, darling. I've got to fly to Atlanta and I won't be back till tomorrow. Thought I'd better let you know before I left."

Verda stood taking it all in, her jaw hanging slack.

"Atlanta?"

"Uh-huh. I'm on my way to the airport now." Oddly enough, Rachel didn't even consider subterfuge. She merely removed her reading glasses, left her desk and followed his impatient figure to the door.

"Business?" she asked.

"Yes. Some land I've been thinking about buying that somebody else has suddenly taken an interest in. I'd rather not go right now, but it can't be helped. If anything comes up, you can reach me at the Sheraton. Okay?'' He was already reaching for the doorknob.

"Okay. Have a safe trip and see you when you get back."

Distractedly he dropped a parting kiss on her mouth while she held the door open, and then he left in a rush.

When he called her, late that night, she casually mentioned, "You threw Verda into major shock when you came sashaying into the shop that way and kissed me."

His laughter came across the wire, then he asked, "What'd she say?"

Now it was Rachel's turn to laugh. "Are you sure you want to know?"

"Of course. You've piqued my interest."

"She said, 'I thought he wasn't pesterin' you!'"

When his second round of laughter died, Tommy Lee asked teasingly, "Am I pesterin' you, Rachel?"

"You bet. Please hurry home so we can get on with it."

But their bit of mirth at Verda's expense was the only lighthearted escape they shared during those days when immediacy was denied them. He returned the following evening straight to her arms as if he'd been gone a fortnight. They shared a quick and frenzied reunion then he tore himself away, declaring he *had* to get home and spend some time with Beth, especially since he had missed the supper she'd painstakingly prepared for him several nights earlier plus several others, and had found little time to devote to her since.

"I'm sorry, Rachel. I'd like to stay longer, but I'd better go home and try to soothe the waters."

"You don't have to apologize, darling. I understand. But don't you think it would be better if you introduced the two of us so that she can see I'm not trying to snatch her father and lure him away from her?"

He smiled and squeezed her arms. "You're right."

But she could see he was apprehensive about it. "When?"

He drew a deep breath and seemed to pluck an answer from the air before he could change his mind. "This weekend. When the dragon isn't around."

But one day before the weekend, the shop door opened and Rachel glanced up to find three teenage girls entering. Since her merchandise was targeted chiefly at mature, middle-income women, girls of this age rarely shopped at Panache. She smiled a welcome, then her heart seemed to pause in trepidation as she recognized Beth to be one of the three, though Beth didn't give Rachel so much as a glance.

She had a pretty little face, and Tommy Lee's mouth, but her attractiveness was spoiled by a smug expression as she sauntered into the store

with her giddy friends. They were obviously in one
of those abhorrent adolescent moods that can
seize a band of normally polite teenage girls and
change them into rude little minxes who delight in
disdaining anything smacking of middle-aged
maturity.

They were a little too loud and disruptively
brash as they invaded the store, plucking at this
item and that, dropping them in distaste and making faces at each other that sent them into spasms
of amusement.

"Hello, girls, can I help you?"

One of the trio hooked her thumbs in the rear
pockets of her jeans, answering while she chewed
gum exaggeratedly, "Naw, just checkin' things
out. Gotta buy somethin' for my grandmaw."
Then she made some inside comment to the other
two that sent them into giggles as they sashayed
toward a rack of autumn dresses. More rude gig-
gling started as one of them plucked a hanger
down and held the dress against her.

"Well, look as long as you like, and let me
know if there's anything I can show you."

"Sure, lady," their spokesman said, then
turned away, adding something under her breath
that brought snickers to her friends and a flush of
anger to Rachel's cheeks.

It was Verda's day off, so Rachel was alone in
the store, sitting at her desk in the corner, working
on invoices. She slipped her reading glasses back
onto her nose, pretending to go back to what she

was doing, but stingingly aware that Beth Gentry
had still not even glanced her way.

The girls worked their way through the store
systematically, while Rachel carefully ignored
them, wondering whether to get up and politely in-
troduce herself to Beth. But before she could decide, the other two moved to the French armoire
where they began distractingly trying on a wide-
brimmed felt hat, leaving Beth to pore over the
jewelry at the center counter. Rachel wrote her
name on a check, inserted it into an envelope and
licked it shut. Finally she gave in to the urge and
raised her eyes, only to have the blood seem to
drop to her toes.

The deepset eyes of Beth Gentry were fixed upon
her in unconcealed dislike, issuing a hard, cold
challenge that said, "Hands off my father." And
while skewering Rachel with that unmistakable
message, Beth blatantly slipped a silver bangle
bracelet over her wrist. Rachel's eyes dropped to it,
and her lips opened to protest as she instinctively
began to leave her chair. But she froze, her hands
still braced on the edge of the desk, and glanced up
at Beth again to find the undisguised defiance still
sizzling at her. It was obvious Beth considered her a
rival for her father's attention.

Rachel remained poised, tense and shocked, her
mind racing with indecision, while she and Beth
faced off in a pivotal moment that would undoubtedly dictate the tone of their future relationship.

There was scarcely time to think. Rachel's reaction happened within seconds, though it seemed hours that she hovered with Beth's defiant eyes locked on her own. Then Rachel relaxed her shoulders, dropped her hands from the desk and sat back in her chair while Beth lowered her wrist, shook the bracelet into place and let a victorious grin slip to the corner of her mouth. Without removing her eyes from Rachel, she called, "Come on, you guys, there's nothing in this place even your grandma would want." Then, with an imperious toss of the shoulder, she swung around and led the way out the door.

Rachel sat stunned.

What should I do?

It's too late now, you've made your choice and she won.

She threw her glasses off, leaned her elbows on the desk and covered her face. The nerves in her stomach were trembling. She was angry and depressed and upset. Did the whole world have to defy her and Tommy Lee? Was there some unholy force working to thwart their happiness, no matter how hard they tried to achieve it? What had she done that was so terrible? *What?* She had fallen in love with a man and was willing to make room in her life for his daughter, share him with her and try to make a family. But how was that possible now?

She threw herself back in the chair and whammed a fist on the desktop—something totally out of character for Rachel.

Damn that girl.

Couldn't she see how little happiness her father had had in his life? Couldn't she understand how her jealousy was distressing him?

Rachel lurched from her chair, slipped her hands into the front slash pockets of her tailored skirt and stood at the front window, staring out unseeingly.

So what do I do now? Tell him? Add this to the burden he's already carrying? Give Beth Gentry the opportunity to deny stealing the bracelet and turn the situation to her advantage by declaring that *Rachel* was jealous of *her*? Could a girl of fourteen be that devious? Yet, given what she'd just done, the question seemed ludicrous. Tommy Lee had said she was hovering on the brink. Rachel's reaction to this incident could be the nudge that pushed her over or the tug that drew her back. Rachel dropped her chin to her chest, staring at her shoe as she pivoted the heel against the carpet, feeling inept and out of her league. Such a tender, malleable thing, the teenage psyche—and being childless, she didn't know the first thing about molding it. The wrong decision could be disastrous for all concerned.

Lord help me, what should I do?

She turned around and was staring dejectedly at the jewelry counter when the answer suddenly came.

RACHEL DRESSED WITH UTMOST CARE that Sunday morning for church. She chose a tasteful shirtwaist dress of periwinkle-blue voile, matching pumps and a delicately feminine straw hat with a floppy brim that cast dappled shadows over her forehead and made her appear younger. She added a single strand of pearls, a dash of scent, and sighed hopefully as she gave a last glance in the mirror.

She had called her father and asked him if she could ride with him to church, deciding that if he could be stubborn, so could she. He hadn't called or come over since the day of the confrontation with Tommy Lee, and she'd made up her mind if she had to do battle, she might as well take on all the opposing forces at once.

When Everett's car drew up, she grabbed her purse and hurried out, meeting him halfway up the walk. His hands were in his trouser pockets and he came to an abrupt halt as she slammed the front door and approached with a bounce in her step.

"Hi, daddy," she said brightly, tipping her head up to plunk a quick kiss on his cheek before airily continuing past him.

He scowled after her without returning her greeting, and after a brief hesitation she heard his footsteps follow. Without turning around, she said, "Thank you for picking me up. Tommy Lee would have, but he's running a little late this morning. His daughter is living with him now, and you know how poky us women can be. I'll be meeting her after church and riding back out to their house with them, so you won't have to haul me back home.''

As she opened the car door she heard Everett's footsteps come to a halt behind her, but she blithely climbed in and slammed the door.

In a moment he joined her, and she could see peripherally that he gave her a disapproving glance as he started the engine. But she had him stymied and she knew it. He might have been expecting her to maintain a stoical silence, as he had, or to vehemently argue her cause. But the one thing he hadn't been expecting was her gay mien and her openly filling him in on what was going on between herself and Tommy Lee. She hurried on while she had her father buffaloed.

"I'm terribly nervous...do I look all right?" She flipped her palms up and glanced down at her dress, then went on brightly. "Meeting a man's children is a bit unnerving, and of course I want to create a good impression, since we'll all be living together in the near future. She's already started school here and Tommy Lee says she's blending in beautifully. She's made some friends already and doesn't seem to want to go back to live with her mother.''

She saw her father's mouth drop open in surprise and rushed on before he could say anything. "You saw her with Tommy Lee on the church steps several weeks ago, the one with the long, dark hair and that unmistakable Gentry mouth. She's a pretty little thing, don't you think? But every time I look at her I want to teach her how to put on her makeup properly—you know how girls of that age tend to overdress, almost like playing grown up when they're first turned loose." She flipped the visor down, checked her lipstick in the mirror and smiled. "Ah, well, at least it'll give us some common ground to talk about. Lord, I hope so—I'll need something to break the ice with her." Up went the visor with a snap. "So tell me, daddy, how've you been?"

She felt positively winded after that mouthful, and her heart was pattering rather animatedly, but she turned to her father with a disarming smile, as if she greeted him this way every Sunday morning.

"Rachel, what in heaven's name has gotten into you?"

She leaned across the seat and pecked him on the cheek again, knocking her hat brim askew and giving a little laugh as she shot a hand up to hold it on. "I'm happy, that's all. Isn't everybody when they fall in love?"

He snorted and cast her a doubtful glance from the corner of his eye.

"Oh, daddy, don't be such a cynic."

"You're makin' the mistake of your life. A skunk doesn't change its stripes."

But again she threw him a curve by inviting, "Would you like to meet Beth since she's going to be your granddaughter?"

He gripped the wheel and blared, "I most certainly would not!"

She pulled away with a mock show of defense. "Okay, okay...maybe it is best if you wait until she's learned to accept me first."

By the time they reached church Rachel was weak from putting on her act all the way, but she crooked a hand through her father's elbow and kept her step spry as they moved directly inside and found their pew.

The moment she sat down she felt the tension between her shoulder blades and wilted slightly. The worst was yet to come, and she wondered if she was a good enough actress to pull it off when she faced Beth Gentry an hour from now. She had chosen the time and place for its very public aspect. What could Beth Gentry do with half the town milling about, witnessing their first meeting?

When the service ended she studied Tommy Lee's face as they converged in the middle of the crowd, and for a moment she forgot the young woman at his elbow and felt only the thrill of seeing him again.

"Hello, Rachel." His dark eyes adored her while he extended a hand.

"Hello, Tommy Lee." His palm was warm and large as it surrounded hers momentarily and she smiled up at him.

"I'd like you to meet my daughter Beth."

Rachel transferred her smile to the girl and offered her hand as benignly as if they'd never laid eyes on each other before.

"Hello, Beth. I've certainly heard a lot about you."

Color crept up Beth's cheeks and her mouth hung open in surprise as she let Rachel shake her hand.

"H-h'lo."

Still holding her hand, Rachel smiled up at Tommy Lee. "Why, she's a beauty, just like you said." Again she directed her comment to the girl. "You have your grandpa Gentry's eyes, but your grandma's mouth." And at last she dropped Beth's hand and tipped her head up to Tommy Lee again. "But then, so does your daddy."

He smiled and took her elbow, then did the same to Beth. "What do you say we stop somewhere for breakfast?"

"I'd love to. I'm famished." Rachel poked her head forward to peer around Tommy Lee. "How about you, Beth?"

From his far side came a grunt.

At the car Rachel slipped into the back seat, leaving Beth to share the front with her daddy, hoping Tommy Lee wouldn't make an issue of it. Thankfully, he didn't.

Throughout the meal Rachel tried by action and word to make it clear she had no intention of usurping Beth's place in Tommy Lee's life, but the girl remained sullen and untalkative, speaking only when asked a question.

Over coffee Rachel produced from her handbag a miniature apple-green box with a pink bow and offered it to Beth. "Here...a little something from my store, since your daddy told me how much you like them."

Beth shot a puzzled glance from Tommy Lee to Rachel to the box, then up at Rachel again. Obviously, she was as dumbfounded by Rachel's actions as Everett had been earlier. Rachel could read the question sizzling through Beth's mind as clearly as if it had been spoken—*you mean she didn't tell my daddy what I did?*

"Y-you brought a present for *me*?"

Rachel nodded, set the box on the tabletop and nudged it toward Beth. "Uh-huh. Just something little."

"B-but...." Again her eyes dropped to the gift, and Rachel saw how flustered Beth had become.

"Go ahead...open it."

Beside Beth, Tommy Lee braced a jaw on one palm and smiled, watching her. Her eyes darted up to his, then quickly away as she hesitantly reached for the box. When the bow was removed and the protective cotton drawn aside, a pair of tiny silver loop earrings were revealed, their florentine finish the perfect match for the bangle bracelet.

At the sight of them, Beth's face flushed brightly and she trained her eyes downward, refusing to lift them to Rachel again.

"Thank you," she mumbled.

"When I was your age girls weren't allowed to

wear earrings. How silly, huh? I remember fighting with my mother over every new thing I wanted to try—makeup, nylons, high heels.''

Tommy Lee shifted his gaze to Rachel across the table. "With good reason. I remember the first time you broke out in lipstick. It was the color of a matador's cape, and you had it uneven on the top, and painted too far down in the corners. I can remember thinking—yukk!''

Rachel laughed, her eyes sparkling up at him. "Yukk? You were thinking *yukk* when I thought I was stunning enough for the silver screen?''

"At the time I liked you better in grubby jeans, climbing the pecan tree with your hair all full of twigs.''

"Remember that time you fell out of it?'' She leaned forward and rested her elbows on the table.

"Do I ever. I wore the cast for the rest of the summer.''

"And we never did get that tin-can telephone strung between our bedrooms, did we?''

Tommy Lee chuckled. "Uh-uh. Instead we were forced to use the real one and drive our parents crazy.''

Rachel was conscious of Beth, looking on and listening with piqued interest. She gave her a quick glance. "Your daddy was a devil. Do you know what he used to do?'' She again fixed her grin up at the man across the table, and beneath it rubbed his trouser leg with her shoe. "He had this old purse and he stuffed it full of play money, tied a string to its handle and laid it out in the middle of the street in the dark of night. Then he'd hide in the bushes, hold onto the other end of the string and wait for some unsuspecting driver to come rolling along and spy the purse in his headlights. But, of course, by the time the car had jerked to a stop, or backed up, and the driver got out to investigate, the treasure had disappeared from sight!''

Tommy Lee laughed. ''God, I'd forgotten about that. The old purse-on-the-string trick. Remember the time we pulled it on old man Mullins? I thought that old dude was gonna admit himself by the time he finally gave up.''

''I was never with you when you duped old man Mullins. Once was enough for me, laying out in the weeds with the worms and snails and getting bitten up by insects, all for such nonsense.''

Though their reminiscing had intrigued Beth, she took no part in the conversation, nor did she show any enthusiasm during the remainder of the day. They spent it at Tommy Lee's house, and though time and again Rachel tried to draw Beth out, she was unsuccessful. Beth's reticence remained between them, intractable.

By the time Tommy Lee drove Rachel back into town, she had a pounding headache. She sighed and fell back against the car seat.

''I don't think it worked. She's totally belligerent.''

Tommy Lee drew on his cigarette, scowled and brooded.

"*Damn it*, she was a rude little snot!"

Rachel reached over and brushed his arm. "We have to give her time to get used to me."

"I'm sorry, Rachel."

"It's not your fault. And don't give up yet. We'll try again."

"I just don't understand her!" He thumped the steering wheel. "How could she sit there scowling at you all day long.... Didn't she realize how rude that was?"

"She was making her point, darling. I'm a threat to her—or haven't you heard? Women of all ages are infamous for being possessive about their men. She'll get over it, but we have to be patient."

But Tommy Lee had wasted too many years to wax patient when the woman he loved had agreed to marry him and the greatest stumbling block seemed to be his petulant teenaged daughter.

When he returned home and walked into his house it was as if a different personality had stepped into Beth's body. This one was smiling and gay and filled with chatter.

"Hi. Fixed us a snack—hot fudge sundaes with pecans. Should I scoop you out one now?"

He threw his car keys onto the table and swung to face her, suddenly upset with her constant attempts to win him over by playing the surrogate housewife. "I'm on a diet, I'll pass."

She stood in the middle of the room holding a dish of chocolate covered ice cream, licking the back of the spoon. At his curt reply she looked up innocently. "Oh. Well. . . should I slice you some fruit then?"

"Beth, I don't need mothering, all right? And I have a housekeeper, so you don't need to constantly try to please me with all this. . . this domestic subterfuge! What I want you for is to be my daughter."

"Well!" she huffed. "I thought I *was*."

"Then start acting like one and stop acting like a jealous brat!"

Her face soured. "I can see *she's* been working on you."

"*She* has a name!" Tommy Lee's face reddened with anger and he hooked his thumbs on his hips. "It's Rachel, and I'd appreciate it if you'd afford her the common courtesy of using it when she's here! And the last thing in the world she'd think of doing is *working on me*, as you put it. She was totally willing to excuse your unforgivable rudeness to her today." He tapped his chest. "But I'm not!"

"When she's with you, you forget that I'm even in the room!"

"That's not true and you know it."

"Oh, isn't it? All day long the two of you blabbed on and on about all that junk from when you were kids and left me out."

"And what did you do when she asked you about your dancing, and about school? You grunted a one-word answer and turned a cold shoulder on her. How do you think that made her feel when she was trying her best to be friendly?''

Beth's face was a mask of hatred. ''I will *never* be her friend. *Never!* Because she's the one...I know she's the one. I found that box of pictures and I know!''

Tommy Lee's brows curved into a frown. ''What pictures? What are you talking about?''

She pointed to a distant spot in the house. ''All those pictures of you and her, from the time you were babies, naked in a plastic wading pool, riding your tricycles together and all the way up through high school. You've got more pictures of her than you do of mother!''

''Beth, we grew up together. You knew that.''

''Yes, I knew that.'' There were tears on Beth's cheeks now. ''Mother has told me for years that there was someone in your past who made you go through three wives, but none of them could ever measure up to her. She didn't know who it was, but I do! And if it wasn't for your precious Rachel things would have turned out different for me. I'd have a...a mother *and* a father like other kids... and...and....''

But suddenly Beth threw her dish and spoon on the floor and spun from the room, sobbing.

''Beth, wait!''

''Go to your precious Rachel! Go!'' she screamed, slamming up the stairs.

Tommy Lee's heart thundered as he stood in indecision. Should he go to Beth and allay her fears, assure her he'd never leave her as he had her mother? For that was her greatest fear, it was plain. Years of living with a single parent—and a bitter one at that—had left Beth insecure and grasping.

Tommy Lee sighed and dropped to a chair, leaning forward and rubbing his eyes behind his glasses.

Complications. The need for love, that all-powerful drive experienced by all—must it work against him all his life?

He considered going upstairs and telling Beth the entire story about Rachel and himself, but she was only fourteen years old. She had her whole sexual life ahead of her. To tell a story like that might leave her with any number of false impressions—that he condoned sex at sixteen, that Rachel was a "bad girl" when she was young, that she was indeed responsible for Nancy's bitterness.

Lord, what went through the minds of fourteen-year-old girls? He didn't know. He'd never had one before. If he told her the whole truth, would it soften his daughter or add to the problem? And to tell it was to include, by necessity, his own estrangement from his parents. Surely she'd question him about that. He had promised Rachel he'd make an attempt at reconciliation, but stepping up to that house, then inside it, after all these years, was going to be even more difficult than dealing with Beth.

Gentry, how did you get into this emotional mess?

He held his head in both hands and stared at the floor between his feet. Then, with a weary sigh he unfolded himself to clean up the bowl of ice cream. It had left a stain on the carpet and he supposed he should have hauled Beth back to pick up the mess herself, instead of allowing her to throw a tantrum and get away with it.

How does a guy learn to be a father?

Hunkered on one knee in the middle of the living-room floor, a dishcloth dangling disconsolately from his fingers, he dropped his elbow and forehead onto the upraised knee and fought the urge to cry.

CHAPTER FOURTEEN

FALL MOVED ON with no perceptible changes in the attitudes of either Beth or Everett. In October Rachel listed her house with a realtor, believing the decisive move would force her father to accept the idea of her upcoming marriage, but he remained unyielding. The few times Rachel confronted Beth at Tommy Lee's house the girl was chilly and aloof, escaping to her room as soon as possible.

In November the realtor found a buyer for Rachel's house, and with that enormous obstacle overcome, she and Tommy Lee set the wedding date for the Saturday following Thanksgiving. But as the holiday approached, they still had not overcome the other even greater pair of obstacles that were casting shadows over their future together. And they both wanted very much to begin their married life without clouds hanging over their heads. They had done all they could to give the two time to accept the idea of their marriage, yet neither had.

And so, they agreed, it was time for ultimatums.

THE NOVEMBER WIND was chilly, catching at Tommy Lee's trouser legs as he strode purposefully from his office, crossed Jackson Avenue and covered the distance to the Russellville Bank. He flung the door open, marched inside and stopped before the receptionist, who looked up with a cheery smile.

"I want to see Everett Talmadge."

"If you'll have a seat over there, I'll ring him."

But Tommy Lee was too agitated to have a seat. He stood spraddle-legged before the receptionist's desk, riveting his eyes on the glass cubicle that was clearly visible in the far corner of the bank. He saw Talmadge reach for his phone, then the receptionist spoke.

"There's someone here to see you." Talmadge appeared to be distractedly scanning something on his desk when the woman answered his unheard question. "It's Tommy Lee Gentry."

Talmadge's head came up with a jerk and his eyes met Gentry's across the width of the business floor. His lips moved again and the receptionist asked Tommy Lee, "What is this in regard to?"

Still staring at the bank president, Gentry replied, "Tell him I want to make a deposit."

The woman pivoted the mouthpiece below her chin. "But depos—"

"Just tell him!" Tommy Lee interrupted.

Obediently she brought the phone to her lips. "He says he'd like to make a deposit, sir."

Even from this distance, Tommy Lee could see

the belligerent expression overtake Talmadge's face before his mouth worked again.

"Deposits are made at the teller windows, Mr. Gentry," came the relayed message.

"I'll make this one personally with the president," Tommy Lee informed her, then added impatiently, "Never mind. I can see he's not busy. I'll just go right in."

"But, Mr. Gentry—"

Tommy Lee was halfway across the room before the woman could rise from her chair. He opened the door without knocking to find Talmadge already on his feet, then slammed it with a resolute thud that shook the glass walls. He dropped a portfolio in the middle of the desk with a slap, then confronted his foe head-on.

"It'll take more than a timid receptionist to keep me out this time, Talmadge."

"There's a whole row of tellers out there. Any one of them can open an account for you."

"You'd like that, wouldn't you? But you're not getting off that easy, not this time! We're going to have this thing out once and for all—you and me." Tommy Lee planted his hands on his hips while his face took on a stubborn look to match any Everett Talmadge had ever exuded.

"I don't want or need your money in my bank, Gentry."

"This isn't about money and you know it—but my money's going to be here whether you like it or not. I'm sick and tired of driving up to Florence to do my banking, just because you had a burr on your ass twenty years ago and decided you'd show me who was boss. Well, I've proven myself, financially—without your help. I ran a quarter of a million through that damn Florence bank last year, and I've just closed my accounts there, so get used to the fact that you'll have to face my success along with a few other things."

"Gentry, I can have you thrown out of here!"

Tommy Lee bent over the edge of the desk, demanding, "And exactly what would that settle? Throw me out—go ahead!" He straightened and flung a hand in the air. "But you can't throw me out of your daughter's life, so isn't it time we both tried to live with the fact and reach some kind of compromise...for her sake?"

Talmadge only glared, standing stiffly with his brow beetled and his hands knotted into fists.

"I love your daughter and she loves me, and all the feuding in the world isn't going to change that fact."

Talmadge emitted a disdainful sniff and eyed Gentry askance while moving with calculated laziness around his desk chair. He stood behind it rolling a pencil up and down between his palms. "Been seein' any of the local trollops lately, Gentry?" he asked unctuously.

Tommy Lee resisted the urge to settle his fist in the middle of the old man's face as he went on resolutely, "I've asked her to marry me and she's agreed. Now we'd like to do it with your blessing, but if not—so be it. We've been fighting the whole damn world it seems—you, my daughter, even each other at times—but we're done waiting. We're being married next Saturday.''

Talmadge's eyes remained cold. "For how long?''

Tommy Lee swallowed his pride and said stiffly, "I'll admit, my past is far from spotless, but I don't feel compelled to justify it to you as long as Rachel trusts me enough to marry me, and she does.''

Talmadge flung the pencil onto the desktop. ''Rachel's got a bad case of conscience because of this affair she's been carryin' on with you—it's badly colored her judgment.''

Tommy Lee ground his back teeth together and met the insolent eyes directly, softening his tone slightly. "Can we quit butting heads for just five minutes and talk about what really matters?''

"And what matters more than Rachel's happiness?''

Tommy Lee braced his hands on his hips and studied the man before him, wondering how a person came to be so pugnacious and bullheaded. ''All right, I'll say it straight out—so Rachel had our illegitimate baby, and we gave her away against our wishes. I'll admit, I've carried a grudge over it for years, but Rachel and I have both learned to live with it, and we're willing to put it in the past if you are.''

Talmadge's face took fire, and he turned away.

It was the first time Tommy Lee had ever seen the man come up short of words, but still there remained that damnable stony pride. The younger man gestured in appeal at the back that was turned against him. "Can't you see what you're doing to her? She doesn't want to have to choose between us, but if you keep fighting me, I can't guarantee she won't. And if she chooses, it'll be me—then what will you have gained?"

Talmadge said nothing, so Tommy Lee tried one last time. "What do you say we bury the hatchet and at least make an attempt to grin and bear each other?"

"And you'd have your revenge at last, wouldn't you?"

Tommy Lee bit back a sharp retort, sighed and dropped his chin to stare absently at a granite pen holder on top of Talmadge's desk—just like the stubborn old fool who owned it, cold, unfeeling granite.

He looked up at Talmadge's back. "I'm going to make your daughter happy, in spite of what you think. She wanted me to tell you she's found a buyer for her house. We'll be living out at my place on the lake, and Callie Mae has agreed to come to work for us, just as she has for Rachel. When and if you finally decide to—" Tommy Lee shook his head, realizing the man would probably never soften. "Well. . .you're welcome there any time." Tommy Lee sighed, slowly picked up his portfolio from the desk and added quietly, "I'll see one of the tellers on my way out."

Crossing the main floor of the bank to a teller's window, Tommy Lee did not see Talmadge draw the draperies, sealing himself into his cocoon of loneliness. Nor did he see Talmadge fall wearily into his desk chair, prop his elbows onto the desk and drop his face into shaking hands while guilt besieged him and he wondered how he could ever face Rachel and Tommy Lee as husband and wife after the years and years—not to mention the child—he'd stolen from them.

RACHEL DREW HER CAR UP before the Russellville High School only minutes before the bell signaled the end of the day. She slipped on a pair of warm gloves, stepped into the windy afternoon and, slamming the car door behind her, crossed the street to the row of school buses waiting with their engines running.

Three times she asked, "Does this bus go out old Belgreen Road?" before she found the right one.

When the students came pouring out of the building she studied their faces, waiting beside the door of the bus with her coat collar turned up, holding it together at the neck until finally catching sight of Beth approaching with one of the girls who'd come into the store with her. The girl spied Rachel first, came up short and poked Beth in the ribs.

"Hey, Beth. . . somebody waiting for ya."

Beth glanced up at her friend, then followed the direction of her eyes, and planted her feet.

Her companion immediately digressed. "Listen, Beth, I'll see ya around, okay?" and disappeared into the stream of moving bodies. Beth dropped her eyes to the ground and moved toward the door of the bus as if to pass Rachel without a word.

Rachel calmly stepped in her way. "You won't be riding the bus today."

Defiant brown eyes snapped up. "Oh yeah?"

Rachel raised one sardonic eyebrow and replied coolly, "Oh yeah. Unless you want me to make a scene in front of all your new friends by attempting to drag you off bodily to my car. I imagine they'd find it quite amusing, don't you?"

Beth considered a moment, gave a one-shouldered shrug and trudged around the hood of the bus, leaving Rachel to follow. They crossed the street, climbed into the car and drove off with Beth slumped down in the seat in a typical pose of adolescent rebellion.

But Rachel's opening question straightened Beth's spine perceptibly and brought her halfway out of her slouch.

"Have you ever been in love, Beth?" There came no answer, but Rachel didn't need one to see she had captured Beth's attention fully. Nor did Rachel forget for one moment that she was speaking to a girl whose mother had been outraged by what Rachel gathered had been an innocent teenage kiss. "What's the matter?" She gave Beth a half glance, then returned her eyes to the windshield. "Somebody give you the idea that you couldn't possibly feel such an adult emotion at fourteen?" Rachel let a ghost of a smile tip up one corner of her mouth, knowing her passenger eyed her keenly. "Well, don't let 'em fool you. I fell in love at fourteen—well, let's be honest and make it fifteen, after all it's been a long time ago and I could be off by a year or so."

Rachel flicked on the left-turn signal, looked over her shoulder and changed lanes, then kept her eyes on her driving. "I fell in love with your daddy, and—wonder of wonders—he fell right back. It came as something of a surprise after all the years we'd known each other. Of course, we've told you a little about those years, but I wanted to show you something. You don't mind going for a little ride before I take you home, do you?"

Rachel glanced at Beth to find herself being covertly studied, but immediately the dark eyes darted toward the front—obviously the girl was trying to decide what to make of all this. The car turned onto Cotako Street, and Rachel drew up at the curb in front of the two familiar houses. She let the engine idle, rested an arm along the back of the seat and pointed. "This is the house where your daddy grew up, and where your grandpa and grandma Gentry still live. And that...is where I grew up, and where my daddy still lives. See that window up there?" Beth's head swerved. "That was my bedroom window, and this one was your daddy's. Remember when we told you the story about the tin-can telephone we tried to rig up between our rooms? Well, I just wanted you to see how close we really lived.

"We were just children when our daddies planted this row of boxwoods here, but about halfway down they left one bush out, and that's where we all used to cut through between the two houses. If you look really close you can still see the spot."

Rachel put the car in gear, pulled away and headed up the hill while Beth craned around for a last glimpse of the houses. "I remember the day we started first grade, your daddy and me walking bravely up this hill to school, holding hands. I don't know who was more scared—him or me." She chuckled softly, remembering. They arrived at the top of the hill and she glanced across to the red-brick building and the adjacent playground, noting that Beth did the same. "Once he got himself into big trouble and ended up in the principal's office for punching Dorsey Atwater during recess because Dorsey said something nasty about me—funny, I don't even remember now what it was."

The reminiscing went on as Rachel drove next to City Park and circled the small lake surrounded by pole fences, scattered hardwoods and yuccas. A trio of geese drifted on the water, but otherwise the area was deserted. She passed a small building housing a snack bar and canoe rental, and a swimming pool, closed for the season. "Ah, the hours we spent out here. There was no pool, in those days, but we lived in the lake. Whole summers, with all the friends we'd grown up with."

As she drove on down Waterloo Road, which led through the park, Rachel recalled the many nights she and Tommy Lee had parked out here, and had a moment's pause to hope telling Beth was the right thing to do. So far she hadn't said a word, and it was difficult to gauge the impact—if any—her words were having on the girl.

"I guess you might say this is where we fell in love." They left the park behind and headed for the country. "As I told you, we weren't much older than you when we discovered it. We used to park down by the lake and talk about getting married." Rachel let a smile linger on her lips. "We'd pick out names for our future children, and make up stories about the house we wanted to have— it'd have lots of windows and natural wood and it would face a lake and have fireplaces and be carpeted in blue—oh, you know how it is when you're making up fairy tales."

Rachel adjusted her hands on the wheel and went on. "Anyway, our parents always seemed happy that we were dating each other, but then when I was sixteen...I found out I was pregnant." She saw Beth's head snap around to stare at her, but carefully kept her eyes on the road. "Tommy Lee and I were scared at first, but after talking it over we decided there was nothing to be scared about. After all, we were in love, and by the time the baby was born we'd be seventeen and there'd be just a little of our senior year left in high school, and somehow he'd manage to finish, and so would I. So we decided to get married.

"But when we told our parents the news they had other ideas." Rachel drew a deep breath, but kept carefully unemotional in her recital. "They talked it over and decided that the best thing to do would be to send me away to have the baby, and so I ended up in Michigan."

Rachel didn't need to turn her head to know she had captivated Beth's full attention now. She added quietly, "But they wouldn't tell your daddy where I was.

"Things were much different then, and when the baby was born I had little to say about it. The decision had been made by all four parents that she would be given up for adoption, and she was.

"But I did have a say about one thing. They let me name her, and I quite naturally chose the name your daddy and I had dreamed about for a girl... I named her Beth."

There was a sharp indrawn breath, but Rachel trained her eyes straight forward and resisted turning to Beth as she continued with her story.

"The decision about giving up the baby caused a tremendous backlash of guilt and remorse. Our parents could never quite face each other again, and it's been years and years since they've talked to each other. And Tommy Lee...he blamed his mama and daddy, and though he's been married to several women, he could never seem to find happiness with any of them. I had a...a good marriage, but my husband and I could never have any children, and that complicated matters between myself and my parents, though it wasn't their fault—they had no way of knowing how things would turn out at the time they made the decision about the adoption.

"Well, it's been a muddle for years, with your daddy and I avoiding each other as much as possible until...well, until my husband died. It had been twenty-four years, but when we saw each other again...." Rachel spread her hands and let them fall back to the steering wheel, giving a short helpless smile. "It might have been easier for all concerned if we hadn't gotten together again, but what we felt for each other was too strong. We could no more have fought it than...." She chanced a peek at Beth and found her sober, listening attentively. "Well, love is a strange thing. It always seems to have its own way."

They approached the turn onto Tommy Lee's property, and Rachel added plaintively, "It can hurt a lot. But it can heal, too."

The car came to a halt in the curved drive before the cedar house with its glossy black doors. When the engine stilled, it left an immense silence be-

tween the two passengers. The November wind
tilted the tips of the trees, and beyond the house
the lake was gone again, drained away until spring
dictated its return. The oaks now bore rusty
leaves, and the hickories had gone to husk.
Autumn...with Thanksgiving imminent. If
things went right there could be so very, very
much to be thankful for.

Rachel looked across at Beth to find her staring
at her thumbnails, which were locked together.
Beth blinked hard, then looked out her far window. When she spoke her voice was barely above a
whisper.

"This was the house you planned, wasn't it?"

Softly Rachel answered, "Yes, Beth, it was."

"And he named me Beth, too."

Rachel wisely remained silent.

"Did you ever see her again—that other Beth?"

"No, but it doesn't matter anymore."

"Except that she's my half sister." She turned
tear-filled eyes to Rachel, adding, "And they're
my grandparents."

"I know," Rachel replied sadly. "And I'm
working on that. I believe, in time, everything will
come out right. Your daddy is as stubborn as all
the rest of them in his own way. But he's promised
to do his best to set things right before our wedding." Rachel could see she had given Beth a lot to
digest in such a brief time. "Your daddy and I
thought you were old enough to know, but he
asked me to tell you because...well, he was a little

self-conscious about parts of it.'' Rachel touched
Beth's shoulder. "Oh, Beth, dear, please try to
understand him. He's been through so much pain
and he loves you so very, very much.''

The huge, brimming tears spilled onto Beth's
cheeks as she tried valiantly not to cry.

"I don't want to take him away from you, don't
you see? I want to share him with you, just as he
wants to share you with me. You're not the same
Beth we lost, and I would never substitute you for
her in my mind, but...but doesn't it seem pro-
phetic that you both have the same name...as if
you were given to us as our last chance to have a
daughter to love?'' Beth's lower lip trembled and
she clamped it between her teeth while Rachel appealed tenderly, "And I would very much like the
chance to get to love you, Beth.''

In a sweeping motion Beth threw herself into
Rachel's arms. "Oh, Rachel, I'm...s-so sorry,''
she sobbed. "I didn't know.''

Rachel felt tears sting her own nose and eyes.
"Of course you didn't.''

"M-my mother used to...to say terrible things
about how daddy couldn't forget his 'precious
teenage lover,' and I t-took her side. I hated you
because I thought if it w-wasn't for you...well,
you know.''

Beth retreated from Rachel's arms, hung her
head and self-consciously wiped her eyes.

"Yes, I know. You've been very mixed up
about where I would fit into your affections, but

please believe me—I would never try to take your mother's place. She'll always be your true mother." Rachel reached to tip up Beth's chin and meet her tear-filled gaze. "But you and I could be friends, couldn't we?" Beth swallowed, and her lips quivered as Rachel went on in a softly appealing voice. "Your daddy made a lot of mistakes along the way, Beth, but all he was really trying to do was be happy. It hurt him terribly to lose his children. He felt guilty and inadequate as a father and as a husband. But now you've brought him the chance to try again."

Beth swallowed hard and admitted, "I was such a b-brat."

Rachel laughed shakily and touched the silky bangs that had gotten messed. "I wish I could disagree with you, but I'm afraid you had me thinking the same thing for a while."

"Do you think he'll ever forgive me?"

Rachel smiled and hugged Beth hard, then pushed her back to look into her eyes. "Believe me, there'll be nothing to forgive if you'll only give us your blessing for our wedding Saturday."

"I'll do more than that. Maybe—" But suddenly she stopped.

Rachel ducked her head as if to peer up into Beth's downturned face. "Maybe...?" she encouraged.

Beth looked up hopefully. "Well, I was thinking, maybe I could be your maid of honor, or whatever you call it."

"My attendant?" Rachel returned, surprised. "You'd really want to?"

Again Beth shrugged sheepishly. "I think you deserve it after the hard time I've given you." Then she dropped her eyes self-consciously. "You never even told him what I did in your store, did you?"

"What good would it have done? That was something between you and me and I wanted to try to work it out without having him worry about it."

Beth looked up, and suddenly a light seemed to brighten her eyes. "Wait here!" she ordered, and jumped out of the car, then slammed the door and ran toward the house. Puzzled, Rachel did as ordered.

When Beth returned, she stuffed the silver bangle bracelet into Rachel's hands. "Here. Put it back in the showcase where it belongs."

"Oh, Beth, it's only worth—"

"No! Take it back and sell it!" Then in a more subdued tone she added, "I've never been able to make myself wear the dumb thing anyway."

Rachel tucked the bracelet into her purse. "Okay, back to the store it goes. And in the future, if you want to argue about your father, what do you say we do it honorably, straight to each other's faces?"

"Argue? B-but...."

"You don't think we're going to live together in one house, three adults—" Rachel considered

Beth before amending, "Well...*almost* three adults, and never disagree, do you? Your daddy and I have a lot to learn about being parents, but if there's one thing this family is going to do, it's talk things out. I've had all I can take of stubborn people who hold grudges for years and years and refuse to talk them out."

Beth smiled at Rachel for the first time ever. "All right. At the first thing you do that I don't like, I promise to get on your case."

Rachel laughed, too, and a tremendous weight seemed to have been lifted from her heart.

"Since we've agreed to talk things over there's something I should ask you. Would you be terribly disappointed if we let Georgine go? I'm afraid your daddy and she don't get along too well."

Beth made a face. "Georgine's a crab."

Rachel chortled, then put in, "I probably shouldn't say so, but your daddy agrees wholeheartedly. There's someone we have in mind to replace her. Callie Mae worked for my family when I was a girl. Your daddy and I were the light of her life, and we've promised her she can come and work for us as soon as we're married."

"You mean, she knows everything?"

"Everything. Including the fact that she'll have another teenager to coddle."

Beth's eyes lit up and another broken piece seemed to fall into place.

"Oh, Rachel, I think...well, it seems like...."

Beth seemed unable to voice all her newfound feelings, and finally blurted out, "Well, all of a sudden, I just can't wait!"

And as the two shared a last embrace, their newfound amity seemed a portent of peace ahead.

TOMMY LEE AND RACHEL had decided to go together to visit Gaines and Lily Gentry. Verda was already winding up the cord of the vacuum cleaner when Tommy Lee stepped through the door of Panache. He had come straight from work and wore a brown tweed sports coat and tie beneath a crisp oyster-colored trench coat, its collar turned up. The wind had messed his hair, and as he closed the door and turned, he combed it back with his fingers.

Watching, Rachel marveled again at the powerful swell of emotions his appearance never ceased to create in her breast. It was more than just the missed years—oh, they were part of it—but there was pride in how much he'd changed, exhilaration in the thought of their future and a vibrant sexuality that scintillated between them each time they encountered each other.

Seeing him, that first glimpse as he entered a room, rounded a corner, opened a door as he had just now, brought the most astounding response. Her heart accelerated as it had long ago, and she felt warm and knew her cheeks grew pink each time his eyes sought her out as they did now across the scented shop.

"All ready, darling?" he asked, crossing to her, touching his lips briefly to hers.

"Almost. We're just closing up." She moved to the armoire and switched off its light, then to her desk to tamp some papers into a neat pile and push the chair beneath the kneehole.

Verda looked on benevolently—by now she had grown used to Tommy Lee coming in this way. There was a new glow about Rachel since she'd been seeing him, and he was looking sexier than ever, though today he wore a distant, worried expression.

Verda offered, "You two go on. I'll lock up."

Rachel looked up and flashed a grateful smile.

"Thanks, Verda. See you tomorrow."

It was a matter of only minutes between the store and Cotako Street. As they pulled up before the Gentry house, Tommy Lee was silent and introspective. He smoked his cigarette voraciously, though Rachel was quite sure he didn't even realize he had it between his fingers. She reached over and brushed the back of his hand.

"Are you sure you want me to come in with you?"

The hand turned over and his fingers gripped hers. "Yes. Please. I need you."

"You're sure you wouldn't rather talk to them alone?"

But the pressure on her fingers told her how tense he was, how much he relied upon her for moral support. She leaned over to kiss his cheek and said, "All right, then let's get it over with."

It felt awkward, standing on the front step waiting for someone to answer the bell—after all, they'd scampered at will into and out of this house for years. Tommy Lee stood with his hands buried in his coat pockets, his collar still turned up, his expression grave as he stared at the black metal mailbox beside the door. The wind lifted his coattail and slapped it back across his thigh, and Rachel placed her hand on his sleeve to squeeze his arm reassuringly.

The door opened and there stood Lily, gaping as if they were ghosts, holding the edge of the door and not moving a muscle.

Finally Tommy Lee said, "Hello, mother."

His words seemed to shake her out of her trance. Her lips opened and her eyes skipped from Tommy Lee to Rachel and back, but though her throat worked, no sound came out. So Rachel added, "Hello, Lily."

At last Lily found her voice. "H-hello," she said, though it was no more than a weak, breathless squeak.

"We wondered if we could talk to you and daddy."

"Wh-why, of course. Come in. Come in." Suddenly she was all action and smiling solicitousness, stepping back and waving them in with fluttery, nervous gestures. "Well, my gracious, what a surprise this is. I was just...come, sit...where did he,...Gaines?" she finally called, glancing around as if she'd misplaced him.

"Lily, where are my slippers?" came his voice from upstairs.

Lily flapped her hands. "Oh, that man, forever losing something. Just...would it...excuse me just a minute...." She went to the bottom of the stairs and called up, "Gaines, we have company. Leave your shoes on."

"Company? Who?"

"Come see," she answered.

A moment later Gaines Gentry appeared at the foot of the stairs, and when he saw who stood across the room he stopped dead in his tracks. His eyes zeroed in on Tommy Lee, held for some time before shifting to Rachel momentarily, then settled on his son again. Disbelief registered on his face. His cheeks began turning an electric pink, and finally his feet started moving.

"Well, this is a surprise."

"Hello, daddy. I hope we're not interrupting your dinner," Tommy Lee began.

"No...no!" Gaines responded eagerly. "We hadn't started yet. Your mother was just setting the table." He stood near enough to touch, but both he and Tommy Lee refrained from reaching out to each other. Rachel sensed his breathlessness and noted a trembling in his hand as he patted his shirt-front and repeated, "Well, this is *quite* a surprise.

Tommy Lee." And as if just now remembering himself, Gaines turned to include his other visitor. "And Rachel, too."

"Hello, Gaines."

Tommy Lee cleared his throat. "We'd like to talk to both of you if you have a minute."

"Why, sure, sure. . . let's sit down. Lily, is there any coffee?" he rambled nervously.

"No," Tommy Lee interjected. "No coffee for us. We'll only be a minute."

"Well, sit down anyway. Can I take your coats?"

The whole thing was starting out just as Rachel suspected it would, with everyone walking on eggshells. Gaines' face was so bright by now he looked in danger of having a stroke, and Lily wore a porcelain smile that made it quite impossible to look her in the eye. Finally they were all perched, Gaines and Lily on overstuffed armchairs, Tommy Lee on a davenport beside Rachel, the only one to lean back with any semblance of composure.

Silence fell for several uncomfortable seconds, then Tommy Lee cleared his throat, rested his elbows on his knees and chafed his hands together, studying the floor between his feet, finally glancing up to ask, "So, how have you both been?"

"Fine!" they both replied together, then glanced at each other sheepishly while the room grew tingly with tension.

"Me, too. I ah. . . live out on the lake now."

"Yes, we heard."

"My daughter lives with me."

"Your daughter!" Lily said, as if surprised.

"Yes, the one you've seen with me at church."

"Oh, yes, of course. My, but she's pretty."

Tommy Lee allowed himself to smile, raising his eyes to Rachel as if for fortification. "Rachel says she looks like you." Lily grew fluttery again and Tommy Lee cleared his throat and lurched to his feet, then began pacing nervously.

"We, ah...Rachel and I have been seeing quite a bit of each other since her husband died."

"We were so sorry to hear the news, Rachel. Such a young man."

"Yes...well...." Rachel searched for something to say to cover the awkward moment. "Tommy Lee has helped me tremendously to get over Owen's death."

She lifted her face to Tommy Lee, and their eyes met and held as he added, "And Rachel has helped me, too. I've been managing, with her help, to get my life back on track." He drew a prolonged breath, and she offered a smile of reassurance to force him on. "I was running pretty wild there for quite a few years...thought I had the world by the tail, but actually I was on a self-destruction course. Rachel made me realize that." Still their eyes communicated as he added more softly, "Rachel's made me see a lot of things."

Gaines and Lily observed the tender expression passing between the two and dropped their eyes to the carpet, but their son suddenly seemed to draw himself back to the present, squaring his shoulders and facing the two seated on the matched chairs.

"You see, it's because of her that I'm here. She and I...we're...." Tommy Lee's troubled eyes wavered from his mother to his father, then he swung around, took two jerky steps toward the fireplace, shoved one hand through his hair and mumbled, "Oh, hell." Finally he spun to face them once more, and when at last he said what he'd come to say, it came out all in a rush. "Rachel and I are going to get married this Saturday, but before she'd agree to it she made me promise to come here and settle things with you, so here we are."

Not a sound adulterated the silence. From the kitchen came the smell of supper cooking, while in the living room four uncertain people faced each other and all waited for the next one to say something.

Lily was the first to respond. She pulled her surprised lips together long enough to breathe, "Married?" Her eyes were enormous as she looked up at her towering son, who stood with his hands buried in his coat pockets, a defensive scowl on his face.

"Yes, married. We thought you should know."

Lily's face was pale as parchment and she touched her heart and looked to her husband for a reply, but he stood as surprised as she. Though they had seen Rachel and Tommy Lee exchanging hellos on the church steps, they had no idea the two had been seeing so much of each other.

Tommy Lee crossed to his mother's chair and hunkered before it, taking her hand. "I love her more than I could ever begin to tell her. I've never stopped loving her. Having her in my life again has given me the strength to turn it around in the nick of time. But she's very wise, more so than any of us three...." His eyes moved to a stunned Gaines, then back to Lily. "She realized that a lot of what was wrong with my life stemmed from the bitterness I felt toward you two. And I want it over. Over and done with." Then he ended softly, "Don't you?"

The look they exchanged was poignant as Lily's eyes filled with tears. "Oh, Tommy Lee, I've prayed for years to hear you say that."

"Why didn't one of *you* say it?" he asked, a shadow of hurt in his tone.

Her eyes dropped to their joined hands. "Stubbornness, I guess. Pride." She looked up into her son's eyes and added quietly, "Guilt."

Still holding his mother's hand he turned his head to include his father as he said, "Rachel and I want an end to all that. It's over. She and I have a second chance and that's all that matters now. Beth will be living with us, and—don't you see? It's almost like providence decided in our favor after all these years. She's not the same Beth we lost, but that doesn't matter. Isn't it time we all put that incident behind us? God knows I'm as guilty of keeping old wounds from healing as anybody. But now there's going to be Rachel...and me... and Beth. I...I'm anxious for you to meet her."

"Our...our granddaughter." Lily's face had all but collapsed with emotion. She struggled to hold back the tears but they coursed down her cheeks.

Tommy Lee smiled crookedly and teased, "Well, it's nothing to cry about, mama."

And at last they could restrain themselves no longer. Lily threw her arms around Tommy Lee's neck and he fell to his knees beside her chair, hauling her roughly against him. Looking on, Gaines took a halting step toward them, and Rachel could tell by the expression on his face that he was having difficulty restraining his own tears.

When mother and son drew apart, Tommy Lee looked up to find his father hovering nearby. Slowly he straightened and the two confronted each other with a gravity that was palpable, while the eternal moment lengthened. Then they pitched roughly together and slapped each other's shoulders.

"Son...." Gaines choked.

Tommy Lee's eyes were closed, his throat working convulsively against his father's shoulder.

They backed apart, laughed self-consciously, then Tommy Lee was striding toward Rachel, reaching for her hand to pull her to her feet and include her in the celebration. She went from Lily's arms to Gaines's, accepting and giving embraces with a residue of self-consciousness still making the scene very strained.

"We all have a lot of time to make up for," Lily offered.

It seemed to Rachel that Lily had shrunken over the years, and it made her realize how old all their parents were getting. Yes, there was much to make up for. Lily began saying something several times before finally managing to complete the thought.

"Would you... Thursday is... well, I was just thinking, if you... hadn't made any other plans, Thursday is Thanksgiving, and it seems we have a lot to be thankful for this year. Would you care to join us for dinner? And bring Beth, too?"

The eagerness shone in her eyes. Tommy Lee and Rachel both saw it there before exchanging a silent glance. Actually, they'd made plans for Rachel to spend the day with Tommy Lee and Beth at the lake house. But now she answered for all three of them.

"We'd love to. Is that okay with you, Tommy Lee?"

"Uh... oh, of course!"

The look of delight that came over Lily Gentry's face was radiant while Gaines patted his shirtfront and rocked back on his heels, smiling and nodding.

Tommy Lee and Rachel left minutes later amid more stilted farewell pats and hugs. When they were walking to the car, Tommy Lee asked, "So what about that turkey we bought, and the plan to move your stuff out to my house after dinner Thursday?''

"We'll leave the turkey in the freezer and move my things at midnight if we have to. As your mother said, we have a lot to be thankful for this year, and I thought it rather auspicious to begin all together at a Thanksgiving table.''

As Tommy Lee opened the car door for her he added, "Just about all together.''

She glanced over her shoulder. The pecan tree was bare of nuts now, and beyond it the break in the boxwood hedge was merely a shadow. The sweetgum tree had dropped all its balls, too—everything looked wintry and cold. She lifted her eyes to the house beyond the hedge and thought of how wintry and cold its lone resident must be. Daddy, she thought, and her heart ached with pity for a man so steeped in pride he would remain in self-imposed exile rather than bend.

"We'd better go, Rachel,'' Tommy Lee said softly.

She looked up at him beseechingly. "Do you suppose he'll ever change?''

"It would take a miracle, I think.''

As they drove away, Rachel's eyes lingered sadly on the dim light in her father's living-room window.

CHAPTER FIFTEEN

THANKSGIVING DAWNED gray and misty, but Gaines had a cheery fire already ablaze in the hearth as Tommy Lee, Rachel and Beth arrived at the Gentry home. The aroma of roasting turkey filled the place and there was a sense of true welcome as the three stepped inside. Gaines and Lily were smiling and jovial, and though it was easy to see the excitement shining from their eyes, upon meeting Beth there was a first cautious reserve. To Rachel and Tommy Lee's delight, it was Beth who put it to rout.

With the offhand congeniality that can sprout from teenagers at the most unexpected yet opportune of times, Beth assessed the two eager faces, grinned over her shoulder at Tommy Lee, who stood behind her, and commented, "You're right, daddy, I do look like them."

The laughter that followed broke the ice, and within half an hour of their arrival they were all immersed in photo albums filled with pictures of Tommy Lee and Rachel, and for each picture there was a story. Beth listened raptly, laughing at the photographs of her father as a skinny teenager who appeared to be all bones and hair, and at Rachel in a pony tail and spit curls. Lily proved to have a marvelous talent for storytelling, relating tales even Rachel had forgotten.

Gaines served hot cranberry drinks and soon Lily excused herself to tend to things in the kitchen. Rachel offered her hand, and as they left the living room Lily turned back to suggest, "Tommy Lee, why don't you take Beth upstairs and show her your old room?"

"Oh, yes, daddy, please?" Beth pleaded.

And so it was that with everyone occupied, Gaines found himself alone. He sat before the fire, sipping his hot drink, staring at the flames and reliving the years, the happy memories revived by the photographs and stories.

Of course, there had been pictures of Everett and Eulice, and these, too, he admitted, had brought their share of nostalgia. A golden flame leaped and licked while he stared at it, unseeing.

Who was it that got stubborn first...me or Everett? he wondered. So long ago...it was hard to remember. The kids went away and all the happiness seemed to go out of our lives. We were ashamed of what we'd done and every time we faced each other we faced our own shame, and so it was easier to simply stop facing each other.

Gaines sighed, took an absent sip of his drink, listened to the sounds of the women getting things ready in the kitchen, an occasional spurt of laughter from overhead, and pictured Everett all alone in that empty house.

Everett, you and I have been a pair of mule-headed old fools and it's time one of us did something about it.

He set his glass on the coffee table, sighed weightily and went to the coat closet under the stairs to find his warm maroon sweater. Buttoning it from waist to hip, he slipped out the side door, closing it behind himself, and paused to look across the lifeless grass to the stone house beyond. He rolled the thick collar of the sweater up around his neck, stuck his hands into its pockets and studied his feet as he made his way toward the familiar break in the hedge. There he stopped and took a moment to survey the opening—so much narrower now but still not quite obliterated. It appeared to have been waiting all these years for one of them to breach it again and lay the past to rest. He ducked low, pushed a branch aside and crossed to the other side.

Front door or back? But a chill drizzle was falling, and the back door was closer. He climbed the steps, opened a squeaking screen and moved with echoing footsteps across the wooden floor of the porch to a closed door that led—he knew—into the back hall just beside the kitchen.

He knocked, stuffed his hands into his sweater pockets again and waited.

An interminable time seemed to pass while Gaines pondered the fact that nobody probably ever came to Everett's back door anymore. He had just raised his knuckles to rap harder when the latch clicked and the door wheezed open with a grating of old swollen wood.

When Everett saw who was on his back porch his face became a mask of concealed surprise. He seemed unable to move and didn't know what to say. The two men studied each other for several long, silent seconds while time spun backward to a day when they, like their children, had freely moved within the scope of each other's everyday lives. They had missed a lot of shared good times in the last twenty-four years, and as their eyes met and held, they both realized it. Then the wind blew in through the screen, sending a shiver up Gaines's spine, and he took the bit between his teeth to state, "I think it's high time you and I had a talk, Everett. Can I come in?"

THE TURKEY WAS ON A CARVING BOARD and the stuffing had been scooped into a serving bowl. Bustling trips were being made back and forth between the kitchen and the dining-room and Lily called again, "Gaines?" She scowled and fussed. "Now where is that man?"

Tommy Lee and Beth breezed into the kitchen. "Can we help?"

"Yes, carry that bird to the table and find your daddy. It's time he started carving it."

Board and bird disappeared through the doorway in the hands of Tommy Lee and were followed by vegetable bowls and gravy boats carried by the women. They were attempting to make room on the linen-covered table for the last of the dishes when the side door slammed and Gaines appeared in the dining room doorway.

"Set a place for one more, mother. Look who's here."

Rachel was leaning over the tabletop with a tureen of steaming sweet potatoes in her hands when Gaines stepped aside to reveal a slightly sheepish-looking Everett behind him. He hung back, his hands in his pockets, while Rachel stared, dumbfounded, then suddenly dropped the tureen and squealed, "Ouch!" as she pressed a burned palm to her thigh.

Somebody said, "Rachel, are you all right?" But she didn't hear. Her attention was riveted on the man in the doorway. His eyes found her and he gave a trembling smile that at last sent her moving around the table.

Even before she reached him, both hands were extended, and as he clasped them, she felt a tremor in his flesh.

"Daddy..." she said. Then she was in his arms.

"Baby..." he murmured against her ear, holding her as if she'd been lost and just now found.

Her heart felt as if it could not be contained within her breast; it threatened to swell and burst with its burden of joy.

"Oh, daddy, you're here."

She backed off and lost herself for a brief emotional moment in his uncertain eyes, then spun to bestow a hug of equal fervor on Gaines. "Thank you...oh, thank you," she whispered, kissing his florid cheek.

Then she returned to her father, taking his elbow to draw him into the room. She found tears in her eyes as she watched him pick out his hostess, nod, and murmur, "Lily."

"Welcome, Everett," Lily greeted, coming forward to offer her hands much as Rachel had a moment ago. And when she'd stepped back, Everett's eyes came to rest on Tommy Lee. Again he nodded stiffly, and though it was a stilted beginning, it was a beginning nevertheless.

"I don't believe you've met Tommy Lee's daughter, Beth," Rachel put in, to fill the awkward moment.

"Hello, Beth."

"Hi." Beth smiled.

Rachel's eyes met Tommy Lee's, and she didn't stop to question the awesome need that suddenly propelled her—she only knew she had to press herself against his chest, feel his arms around her shoulders, her heart beating vibrantly against his, while celebrating this moment for which they'd both waited so long.

He seemed to understand it, though, for when she came to him he held her tightly, his cheek against her hair, his chest solid and warm.

"I have everything I want now." Rachel whispered in his ear.

"So do I," came Tommy Lee's answer, while together they shared the overwhelming sense of true thanksgiving.

THEY WERE MARRIED two days later in the parsonage of the First Baptist Church. It would have been asking too much too soon to expect Everett to be present. And anyway, it was a celebration Tommy Lee and Rachel wanted as private as possible, so they decided the only witnesses they'd invite would be Beth, Sam and Daisy.

After the ceremony Sam drove Beth to her Grandpa and Grandma Gentry's, where she would be spending the remainder of the weekend, which was all the "honeymoon" Tommy Lee and Rachel were to have at present. It was the busiest season of the year in the retail business and impossible for Rachel to leave before Christmas. But as soon as the holiday rush ended, the Gentrys and their daughter were planning a family cruise together. Rachel didn't mind putting off the trip. There was really only one place she wanted to be on her wedding night....

THE CADILLAC PULLED TO A STOP near the venerable 150-year-old magnolia tree in Tommy Lee's front yard. The key was switched off, and the chain swung silently from the ignition. Tommy Lee slipped his arm around Rachel's shoulders and drew her against his hip.

"Mrs. Gentry...we're home."

"Yes...at last."

He kissed her ear, then left his lips pressed warmly against it while they both gazed at the house for a minute.

"It was a long road, getting here," he said quietly, the words stirring the hair at her temple.

"But we made it."

"Yes, we made it. Would you care to go inside and see what's in store for you for the rest of your life?"

She turned to brush a thistledown kiss on his lips. "I thought you'd never ask."

They smiled—brown eyes into brown eyes—with a look that spoke of unending love, then Tommy Lee got out of the car and waited while she slipped under the steering wheel and joined him. With their arms around each other's waists they strolled slowly across the gravel drive and up the wooden ramp to the twin doors leading to the home they'd planned when they were too young to realize all it would entail to build and take possession of it.

He pushed open one shining black door, swung her up into his arms and said against her lips, "This time we do everything according to the book—right?"

"Right," she agreed, looping her arms around his neck.

Inside, he did an aboutface, and Rachel kicked the door shut with a delicate mauve high heel. He mounted the stairs with her in his arms, all the way to the top level of the house, where he finally halted in the middle of a blue bedroom with a fire-place, balcony and view of the lake.

Setting her on her feet, he reached immediately for the single button at the waist of her mauve wool suit jacket. "Once upon a time," he began, "there was a little girl named Rachel who lived next door to a boy named Tommy Lee. Right from the beginning he had eyes for her—from the day they first sat together in their birthday suits in a little plastic swimming pool."

"In their birthday suits? Tsk, tsk, tsk." Rachel played along as he turned her around and took the jacket from her shoulders, then tossed it onto a chair before swinging her to face him again, pull-ing the waist of an ivory silk blouse out of her skirt.

"Uh-huh. That's when it all started, I believe. Then when they were about seven, eight years old, he had second thoughts—you see, the girl of his dreams lost *all* of her front teeth. Oh, she was quite a sight then! Nothing at all like the little doll he'd always known." The wrinkled tails of her blouse hung free and he raised his hands to the top button, working downward at a leisurely pace that matched his story.

"But things got even worse. She got freckles, and a shape like a bean pole, and he didn't know what in the world she was going to turn into. But along about this time he started thinking even though she wasn't much to look at, she wasn't so bad to have around. After all, she was just like one of the boys—liked to climb trees, punch, wrestle, build tree forts. Yup, he decided, this tomboy was for him!''

Rachel's face was bright with suppressed laughter while her husband grinned into her eyes and lazily reached for one ivory cuff, unbuttoning it without ever dropping his eyes.

"But you'll never guess what happened," Tommy Lee went on, while she docilely offered him the other cuff, her amused eyes locked with his. "One day, out of the clear blue sky, he looked at her and did a doubletake. Lord a'mighty—" the blouse flew toward the chair, missed and slithered to the floor, "—she'd grown up."

Rachel was growing warm and tingly at his leisurely seduction, but he took his own sweet time with the story. "Her tousled hair was all combed neatly and pulled into this cute little corkscrew of a ponytail. . . ." He drew her hair back from her temples and held it tightly somewhere behind her head. "And the freckles seemed to dissolve into peaches and cream—" he dropped her hair, brushed a knuckle over her cheek "—and she started wearing lipstick—" then over her lips "— and he began to be fascinated by it, and by her mouth. Until one day he decided to kiss her, just to see what it'd feel like." He leaned lazily and brushed his lips to hers, breathing warmly against her mouth after the kiss ended. "It felt absolutely wonderful. He decided he wanted more of that." And Tommy Lee took more, slipping his tongue into Rachel's mouth with a sinuous invitation she immediately answered. Her heart beat crazily, just as it had that first time. But all too soon he drew back and the story continued.

"It was about that time when she started getting curves." His hands clasped her shoulders, kneading them gently while she went loose and malleable and let his motions rock her on her feet. "A waist—" his hands slid down over her arms and clasped her waist "—and hips...." His hands dropped lower. "And pretty soon she gave up blue denims for skirts and sweaters, and that's when he realized she not only had a waist and hips, but breasts, too."

His hands rode up her silky slip to cup both lace-bound breasts, thrusting them sharply upward while finding their points with his thumbs, drawing circles that sent rippling sensations through Rachel's limbs. When her nipples were hard and erect, he drew back only far enough to bestow that lazy grin. "And the first time he touched them he knew it wasn't going to end there."

He released her breasts and freed the button at her waist. "They learned a lot together, these two...." The zipper snicked open and the skirt fell to the floor.

As Rachel stepped from it, she reached for his suit jacket, forcing it back over his shoulders. "It must have been scary," she said, "all those firsts." His jacket joined hers on the chair and she reached for the knot of his tie.

"Yes, it was. But by this time they realized

they'd fallen in love, and there was no way they could stop themselves.''

His tie slipped free and she went to work on his shirt buttons. "And?" she prompted.

"And so one day he got brave and undressed her in the back seat of his '57 Chev." Rachel's slip slid up her body, covered her face, and disappeared over her head as she raised her willing arms in the air.

Standing before him, half undressed, her heart doing a wild dance in her breast, she asked innocently, "And did she undress him?"

"No, she was too scared."

Rachel raised sultry eyes to his, letting her fingertips flutter over his shirtfront.

"Dumb girl...there's nothing to it," she murmured against his lips, before removing his glasses, setting them carefully aside, then turning her attention to his shirt, which she skillfully slipped off to caress his naked back.

She felt his hands at the catch of her bra. "Mmm, I see...nothing to it." And a moment later it, too, was gone.

Their warm skins touched, her breasts flattened against the silvered hair on his chest, and suddenly the game fell away.

"Oh, Rachel...remember how it was?" he uttered against her lips.

"Yes," she breathed. "Just like now...we couldn't hold back...and then we couldn't get enough."

"And I'll never get enough of you...never," he vowed, covering her face with kisses then stepping back, the better to see her eyes while clasping her head in his wide hands. He drew her up onto tip-toe, placed one hard kiss on her mouth, then deftly slipped the last of her clothing down her legs, stood and reached for his belt. But she brushed his hands aside and took over the welcome task, divesting him of trousers, briefs, stockings and shoes, dropping to one knee before him, then pausing on her way back up to kiss his hard thigh, his staff of masculinity, his stomach, his chest, the soft hollow of his throat. Joining her fingers behind his neck, she kissed his mouth last, lingering there longest while gently rolling from side to side, catching him high against her belly before stepping back to view him in his entirety.

"You are—" reaching to claim him, she searched for an adequate word "—resplendent."

He laughed indulgently, with a quick flash of even, white teeth, then stood back, running his palms from her armpits to her hips.

"Am I really?"

"Mmm-hmm."

"Funny thing...you are, too." They gazed the length of each other's bodies, experiencing a subtle difference this time—they were man and wife now, they belonged to each other. They touched...and trembled a little. Glanced up...and laughed softly. Glanced down...and fell silent.

They touched more freely. His bare foot covered

hers. His naked knee lifted to separate her silken thighs, then pressed high and hard against her eager flesh. She drew her hands up the backs of his thighs, clutching him close, holding him for a long, appreciative moment while contemplating the fact that she need never say goodbye to him again.

"Sometimes when I remember, I get greedy. I want the years we lost."

"Shh...don't," he whispered gruffly. "Only remember the good. Like the first time I kissed you here...." His hands again captured her breasts and he bent his head, rubbing soft closed lips back and forth across a turgid nipple while fondling the other. "You were exquisite...you still are."

In one swift motion he clipped his hand beneath her arms and fell backward onto the bed, taking her with him and lifting her high while his mouth opened and sought her flesh. When his lips surrounded and stroked her breast, she breathed a throaty moan, arching sharply, head tipped back and eyes closed while letting herself be overcome by sensation.

He took her other breast in his mouth, biting lightly, washing it with wet warmth, then suckling it in a way that started her body rocking upon his. His legs fell open, creating a lee where her body fit precisely while he took up a matching rhythm.

His arms trembled as he drew her higher, sliding her body along his until she straddled him, and he pressed his mouth to her flat stomach. And yet he forced her higher, murmuring unintelligible phrases while turning to brush his lips against the soft skin of her inner thigh, the warm secret hollow above it, then the core of her femininity. With his mouth still claiming intimate possession he rolled them onto their sides, nuzzling, stroking, bringing wordless replies to her lips.

Her body moved in lissome accommodation while heat radiated through her limbs and the blood quickened in her veins. Then with a sudden call, she forced his head back and withdrew.

"Stop." Her voice trembled as she looked down at him, her fingers threaded through the hair at his temple. "Together...the first time should be together."

"The first time," he repeated. His eyes closed as if in benediction and he kissed her stomach one last time before drawing himself up until he was gazing into her lambent eyes. "The first time as Mr. and Mrs. Gentry."

Her eager hands sought his flesh, coddled it, inciting his hips to seek hers as she rolled to her back, drawing him atop her.

"Come into me, Tommy Lee...where you belong."

She lifted...he lunged...and nature's choreography took over.

"Where I've always belonged."

Marriage...the blending of souls that lent meaning to the blending of bodies. Though each time had had a magic all its own, none other had matched the poignancy of this. Holding nothing in reserve they shared themselves freely. He was powerful and tensile as he drove within; she limber and lithe while lifting to receive. His arms quaked and his head hung low while the thrusts grew mightier. She gasped at the brink of climax, driving her head back sharply, lifting her shoulders in the timeless gesture of appeal.

Together they hovered on that awesome brink while savoring the coming cataclysm, and when it shuddered through them, they called out aloud, pressing together until the final ease.

THE AFTERNOON SUN splashed through the wide glass doors, throwing dappled patterns on the blue carpet beneath a leafy schefflera plant. The fireplace awaited its first fire. Beside it, two cozy chairs invited years and years of contentment, while beside Rachel rested a man who promised occasional tumult.

She chuckled and he lifted his head to find her eyes closed as the sound rippled from her throat.

"What's so funny?"

She opened her eyes, smiled a very satisfied smile and twisted a strand of his hair around her finger. "Nothing. I'm just so incredibly happy. I really do have everything I want."

He tucked her head beneath his chin, sighing with equal satisfaction.

"I love you, Tommy Lee."

He kissed her forehead and nestled her close once more. "And I love you, Rachel."

She snuggled against him, toying with the hair on his chest while dreaming of their future. Suddenly she pulled back, reminding him, "You never did finish telling me that story. So what ever became of the girl and boy?"

"Oh, let's see...." He pondered silently, absently caressing her naked spine. "She turned into a successful businesswoman, selling ladies' wear and showing all the women in town what *panache* means, and he became a thin, dashing, handsome, irresist—"

"You can skip the unimportant stuff," she teased. "The love story—how did it turn out?"

"Why, he married her, of course."

"Mmm..." she mused. "He married her after all."

"And carried her off to his beautiful castle on the shores of Cedar Creek Lake, and when she saw it, she knew it was where she'd always wanted to spend her life."

"And did she?" Rachel smiled up at Tommy Lee.

He kissed the tip of her nose. "Forever and ever. You see...they somehow managed to live happily ever after."

She closed her eyes, feeling his steady heartbeat against her temple, the soft brush of his palm on her back. Then Rachel Gentry tucked herself close to Tommy Lee, and together they sighed with satisfaction over the final chapter of a love story begun many years before.

ABOUT THE AUTHOR

With more than a million of her books in print, LaVyrle Spencer is a renowned, critically acclaimed author of romance fiction. This month she makes her debut in Superromances with *The Hellion*. LaVyrle is no newcomer to Harlequin. Her novel *Spring Fancy* launched the Temptation line earlier this year, and *Sweet Memories* starred as a Worldwide Bestseller in May. Besides contemporary romances, LaVyrle has several historicals among her writing credits, including *The Endearment*, for which she won the Romance Writers of America Golden Medallion Award for best historical novel.

LaVyrle chose Alabama as the setting for *The Hellion*. She and her husband, Dan, have relatives there, and, says LaVyrle, "We've had more vacations in Alabama than anywhere else except our home state of Minnesota. We fell in love with Alabama when our daughters were three and five. They're eighteen and twenty now, so that tells you how long we've been going.'' LaVyrle's writing sparkles, and she delights readers by having fun with her characters. *The Hellion* is no exception.

Introducing
Harlequin
Intrigue
Because
romance
can be quite
an adventure.
Available wherever paperbacks are sold.
INT-5
Watch for the Harlequin Intrigue Sweepstakes.
You could win a romantic Cunard Cruise for two!
No purchase necessary. Void where prohibited by law.

RIDE A PAINTED PONY

by BEVERLY SOMMERS
The third
HARLEQUIN AMERICAN ROMANCE
PREMIER EDITION

A prestigious New York City publishing company decides to launch a new historical romance line, led by a woman who must first define what love means.

Yours **FREE**, with a home subscription to

HARLEQUIN SUPERROMANCE ™

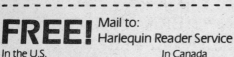

Complete and mail
the coupon below today!

- -